WOMAN

of

ill

fame

WOMAN

of Ill Fame

a novel

Erika Mailman

Heyday Books, Berkeley, California

© 2006 by Erika Mailman

Library of Congress Cataloging-in-Publication Data

Mailman, Erika.
  Woman of ill fame / Erika Mailman.
    p. cm.
  ISBN 1-59714-051-1 (pbk. : alk. paper)
  1. Prostitutes--California--San Francisco--Fiction. 2. Serial murderers--California--San Francisco--Fiction. 3. California--Gold discoveries--Fiction. I. Title.
  PS3613.A349345W66 2007
  813'.6--dc22
                    2006029659

Cover image: "Timberline: portrait of a young Dodge City, Kansas, prostitute." Courtesy of the Kansas State Historical Society
Book/Cover Design: Lorraine Rath
Printing and Binding: McNaughton & Gunn, Saline, MI

Orders, inquiries, and correspondence should be addressed to:
    Heyday Books
    P. O. Box 9145, Berkeley, CA 94709
    (510) 549-3564, Fax (510) 549-1889
    www.heydaybooks.com

Printed in the United States of America

10 9 8 7 6 5 4 3 2 1

To Debi Echlin and Stephanie Strand,
two of the strongest, most kick-ass women I ever knew

and

to Timberline and the other girls of the line:
I hope the world was kind to you

Chapter 1

While the other passengers disembarked, I was in the galley lying on a rice bag with my toes pointed toward the upper deck. The galley mate was young and full of vigor most ways, so I couldn't exactly account for why this was taking so long. Fortunately, my nausea was subsiding since we were tucked into harbor, far from the roiling waves.

I had agreed to this last-minute tryst as he said he'd not only pay but also lug my trunk to the dock, saving me the porter's fee. So while my heart was tugging toward the city our ship was now tied to, I attended to Sir Slow-to-Close, nipping at his earlobes and running my hands to the sweaty aspects of him that made him male—the parts that weren't already plunging and bucking.

"Ah, but you're built well," I said to spur him further.

It was a common stretch of truth the women of ill fame often used. He was skinny yet, but beginning to develop the muscles that would bring him into manhood. With his trousers around his ankles afore he dipped his ladle in, he looked like he should be at home still running chores for his father, not half-way around the world in a new port.

"Built as well as a pup his age would be," said the cook, who had to keep stepping around us. "Must you ruin the young ones as well, miss?"

"Keep your tongue in your head," I said crossly. "Ain't he got the working mechanisms?"

"Mayhap that would explain this torturous flailing," said the cook, gathering his stirring spoons together in a clatter.

I looked up at my lad's face, searching for signs of facial hair or aught to indicate his age. Just then, as our eyes locked, he gave a tiny cry, his face crinkled, and I felt the coursing of his natural fluids.

"That's done," he said, and immediately pulled out and stood. He made no gaspy blows of gratitude or amaze like I'd expected, but simply buttoned up his trousers. His cheeks were red with effort but his eyes didn't shine.

"You're welcome," I said. "The pleasure rests entirely with me. Would this have been your first time then, lad?" I smiled up, my skirts still at my waist, and reached between my legs to pull out the now damp cook's towel. There was no use to this variety of talk after all the doings were done, but I liked to leave my fellas with smiles on their mugs.

He nodded sullenly and accepted the towel from my hands.

"Here's proof of your being a man, then!" I said. "You certainly gave me a merry time and will be known for your pleasing of womenkind for the rest of your days. Congratulations on the carriage of your act!"

"Yes, it certainly seemed merry," said the cook.

"'Twas!" I said. "This boy is skilled!" I couldn't get sunshine from his visage, so I kissed his brooding lips and accepted his coins.

We left that close space and the unpleasant cook, and retrieved my belongings. Up on deck with the wind mocking my chignon I was shocked by the hundreds of ships rotting at the wharf, their masts tilted. I crossed myself, hoping it wasn't a sinister omen. Certainly didn't look a happy sight to welcome the newcomers to California. It reminded me of the cant and skew of stones in an old graveyard. I overheard the boatswain saying the forty-niners had all dashed off ship, hands and captains included, leaving the boats to fester in the salty bay.

I looked up at the hillsides, smoke puffing from chimneys on this dim day. Tents were as plentiful as houses, and I heard the far-off canvas flap against the wind as loud as the water grappling with the ship.

"This here's the place to assay my future," I muttered to myself. I was tired of being penniless and struggling for the least bit of crust. Booked my passage soon's I heard about that big chunk of gold some fella squatted down and plucked out of a millrace, and I didn't mind spending my last bit of coin to get here. Plying my trade aboard ship meant I could arrive with a *little* in my trunk: pure dowry money, ha ha.

And now today was a famous day in Nora history—November 3 in the Year of our Gold, 1849. I was sick as a pirate's mother from all the dashing of the boat against the water, but the long voyage and the leaning over the ship's side to donate all my dinners to the sea was worth it. Soon I'd be dipping my hands into the cold stream to pick up gold, without even getting out of bed: I'd let the men collect the shiny stuff, then I'd dig into their pockets and help myself. Call me a prospector of a different variety.

Following my escort, I walked down the gangplank, earning the shouts of men gathered at the dock. Women were scarce in San Francisco, and reports were that we could draw a crowd simply by being female. Sounded good to me back East. On the two ships it took to get here, there were few women. There had been five aboard this vessel, *The Lady's Peril*, two of us of ill repute. The other gal couldn't get through the sick and had lost all her business to me.

The men on the dock watching everyone debark could tell what kind of woman each of us was. On the gangplank, the wives and the one daughter, a shrubby girl of twelve, all kept their eyes on their boots and practically fainted under the regard, but I opened up my gaze like a lighthouse—one beaming a red light, I guess.

"Hey, Sal!" one of the men yelled to me. "I got a spot you can park that trunk!"

"Don't listen to him," another yelled. "He sleeps under the wharf pilings. You come with me, sweetheart; I've got four-tenths of a room at Randall's boardinghouse."

"Fellas, you don't have to take me home" were my first words spoken in California. "Just give me a few moments and we can all smile after."

One of the wives turned and narrowed her eyes at me. She pressed her skirts down against the weather—a heavy wind bedding down with light rain—but it almost looked like her flattened hands were pressuring that part of her she tried to pretend didn't exist. I could see her thoughts a-whirling through her tightly braided head. Now that she knew what I was, she likely recollected how her husband had stayed up late several nights to play cards with the gentlemen...or had he?

So the men at the dock graced me into San Francisco, smoothed my way like lard in a pan. They knew where I belonged and said they'd take me there: a cowyard on Jackson Street. Turned out they were hired men at that fine establishment, sent out especially to meet the boats. I immediately liked this city's brisk way of doing business.

"Off you go, miss," said the boy, slapping my trunk to signal he'd fulfilled his end of the bargain.

"Godspeed to you, lad," I said, and couldn't resist adding, "especially the speed part."

He gave me a strangely defiant look and I saw for the first time that behind the youthful clay of his face lurked a more adult anger.

"What, can't take a tease?" I asked lightly.

He looked at me sideways like a fish-stealing cat and ambled back up the gangplank.

"Don't think of him, miss," said one of the cowyard's hired men. "Too much of a snip to be on a boat so long; he's forgotten his manners. Come with us and we'll set you up nicely."

Who came up with that ugly name "cowyard" I don't know, but he sure don't put a twinkle in these eyes. We ain't cows and we sure as sin don't graze. But the fact is, those little cribs *do* feel like stalls, so maybe they should call it a stable. Make us whores into horses, not cows.

There were about thirty cribs in the row they took me to, facing a dusty street. Each had a door and window for the girls to display themselves in. The proprietress showed me my crib and stood outside while I made my inspection. She was short, coming only to my shoulder, and was extremely wrinkled in the face, despite appearing to be only in her forties.

The cribs here weren't any bigger than in Boston, and that broke my heart just a little. With all that gold, couldn't they make the rooms bigger? Float a bond past the rich voters of this newly famous city? I knew some ignorant folks even believed the streets here were paved with gold, with gold lighting standards and golden hitching posts for the gold-shod horses.

But standing with my back against one wall and taking a giant step, I found myself nose to board with the other wall. A tiny cot, a chair, a woodstove, and a washbasin. All that for fifteen dollars a month.

"It's highway robbery," I told the woman when I went back outside. "I rode a canoe up the Chagres River and put a mule between my legs to get to Panama City, and not once did anyone twist my purse like you're doing now."

"I came overland," she smirked. "My china closet's being admired by Injuns right now. Or buffalo. Left everything I had along the way as the oxen got skinnier and skinnier, and today look at what's mine. If you want to pay less, build your own yard."

"All the cribs filled?"

"A couple are empty right now; two girls got sick."

"Sick how?"

"Yellow fever. But they was down on the other end. You'll be fine."

"What's the trick price around here?"

She laughed and started walking back to her cottage, across the street from the line. "You'll have to work that out with God and the other girls. I wouldn't recommend going below what they ask; they're pretty unhappy with fresh fillies. And a couple of them keep stilettos under their mattresses. Rent's due end of the month in gold. Paper money here's not worth burning."

The girls eyed me as I walked down the line. I nodded at each of them, but they were for the most part doleful creatures who simply looked me over. A couple did say hello, though, and appeared curious.

"Just in!" I said if anyone seemed halfway slanted to listen. "Still have salt spray on my boots."

"Same as me," said one girl grudgingly. "Clock ain't even spun around once since I got here."

"You'll reckon yourself glad you come when you see the caliber of men we practice on," said another.

Most girls weren't visible, were inside making men puff and grunt. Just as well. Friendships with us kind ain't worth cultivating—girls come and go like mayflies, so why learn their names? Look at me, I was in three different yards in Boston, and I'm not even nineteen.

Nobody I saw was as fair in the face as me. That doesn't count for much anyway, though. Some of the ugliest girls have the most men return to them— it's all in what you do once the door closes. But I'm glad to be bonny anyway; makes it easier on me when I catch a sight of myself in a saloon's mirror. Fair but frail—that's what they call girls of my profession. Not meaning the frailness is physical—I myself have buxom bones and plenty of flesh to drag around—but that the weakness is instead in our morals.

But I had to revise my opinion of the girls' collective beauty when I saw the girl back at the top of the row. She was astonishing. That's why she got the prime placement, the first crib the men come across. Her shimmy had elaborate embroidered pansies all over it, and her skirt was so sheer I could almost see her walkers poking through. Her hair was deep, deep black, like a rock shined away until its roughness is gone.

I nodded at her, hoping she had the skills to match her visage. What a shame for the men if she didn't.

"*Bonjour*," she said quietly as I passed. Well, that explains a lot. French girls dominate this trade like bankers run that Wall Street. They can ask a lot more than a plain old American girl like me, and double what the Mexicans or Peruvians can. Don't even ask me about the Chinese girls; they've got it worse than any of us. Their nickname is a man's delusion: Daughters of Joy.

Even as I said "*bonjour*" back, I was shaking my head. If they let me do some of the naming, we'd be "Women of the Loud Bed" or "Lasses with Asses." And I'd do away with "cowyard"—we'd be housed in an "Emporium of Voluptuousness."

With the same dockman still hauling my trunk, I secured a place to live in a boardinghouse a few blocks away, on a short street called Stark. It was a risk financially—most girls lived in their cribs—but I planned to be rich in San Francisco. Funnily enough, the room wasn't much bigger than a crib, but there was a carpet and an oil lamp with a pretty rose-colored globe. It was nine dollars a month.

The landlady, a Mrs. Mehitabel Ashe, insisted on payment in advance, so I reluctantly took it from my reticule and put it in her hot palm.

"Don't trust folks?" I asked. She wore the sober dark silk of a matron and had a severe hairdressing to match. Her face, which was handsome enough for an older woman, bore no enthusiasm for transacting with me, yet there was interest in her gaze.

"Great numbers of strange people are coming into San Francisco now. Some have motives of greed and would be cruel enough to trick me out of my rent. I don't count you among these but must be cautious nonetheless," said she, a right lofty woman with the posture of a municipal statue.

"Well, my motives ain't greedy. In fact, I'm here to give away my money," I said.

"Doubtless an excellent plan," she responded, and left me alone in my new tiny parcel of earth.

It might be I focus too much on money. But it's just something women like me think about. Even when a gent is plugged in deep, moaning and sighing away, we're working out in our heads how much the day's take will be, and if this one might be willing to throw in a little extra if we do a little extra ourselves.

I lay back on my new bed and, since it was late afternoon, wondered if I should start working right away. It felt so odd to be in a bed that didn't sway with the ocean, and it would be nice to smell only my skin for a night. I stripped to the waist and washed myself at the basin, then pulled the curtains at the window to wash the rest. I'm funny that way. Although lots of our business depends on luring men through the window, when I'm at home I get a sort of shyness. I think about my mother sewing double layers for me and my sisters' curtains, so's the light wouldn't shine through to the street.

Instead of airing out my dresses as I ought, I slid into the bed with my skin raw and tingling from the lye soap. I ate a small apple I had thrust in the bottom of my reticule and idly watched the juice run down my wrist. There was roses in the wallpaper and that made me feel right comfortable. I slowed myself down and listened to my breath. *It's been a long journey,* I told myself, *and now you're here. Pay attention.*

So I let my body feel it. Back in Boston as a young girl, I remember the teacher explaining how the senses work. She had us close our eyes and then she sprayed toilet water. Made us hold a pinecone. Things like that. So on that first night in San Francisco, I stretched myself full length in my bed and let my body meet its new home.

First my ears. They heard singing in the streets, a drunk Irishman pining for home, which was apparently in the environs of "the arms of sweet Fionula, who has a gal's way in Galway." I heard a bottle being broken and the loud call that went up in protest.

My nose caught the smell of something old in the room. Perhaps the girl who lived here afore me kept some food under the bed and forgot about it, or never opened her window to keep things fresh.

The sheets were rough to the touch, not the fine many-thread cotton that came out of the mill in Lowell, Massachusetts, where most of my girlhood friends were now working. This was more nubbly, more homespun.

I opened my eyes back up and saw my own shadow there amongst the roses on the wall. The room getting smaller as the light from the window faded.

And then I licked the sticky apple juice off my wrist and hands and looked round the room for what else I might press this ribald tongue against. Nothing looked exactly lickable—but the dresser and corncob mattress were a damn sight more handsome than some of the men I'd scraped the salt off.

So then I tried to sleep. But someone like me just done with a seven-months voyage don't find it easy to lie there like a good girl. Quick as clockwork, I was up to root through my trunk for evening clothes.

I took the key from the cord between my breasts and knelt on the floor in front of the large lockplate. I put the key in but it wouldn't turn.

Pulled the key out, blew on it, put it in again. Still wouldn't work.

Maybe the salty voyage had warped the wood? I pulled at the lockplate and hit it with my fist.

"What's ailing you, trunk?" I shouted. I put my fingers at the join and tried to hoist the top open. That didn't help, but I did notice something I'd not seen before—a tremendous scratch down the side. My trunk was newish and hadn't been treated injuriously today; it had been cradled in men's arms and set down carefully.

It wasn't my trunk.

In a fury I dashed downstairs and grabbed the poker from the fireplace in the front room. Upstairs I used it to wrench off the lockplate. It was hard work and I cursed at the trunk, to make it more pliable. Finally the plate broke off and sputtered across the room, making a racket like Satan's congregation.

I opened the lid and shrieked when I saw the scattered cheap garments of the young galley mate. I plucked the things around and found a packet of letters and a bag of tobacco. With strength I didn't know I possessed, I lifted the trunk to my waist and threw it. If only I'd been so strong all along! Then I would never have required someone to tote it for me, and this mix-up wouldn't have occurred.

"Quiet yourself!" came the roar from a fellow boarder, and I fell upon the bed, beating the pillow silently.

Of course, I wouldn't have been able to lift *my* trunk: mine had money in it. Heavy coins. Not so many of them, but some. Plus it had dresses and hats and boots, not this meager assortment of discarded shirts.

This had been no error. I clawed at the pillow, and feathers began popping out their wispy heads.

The boy knew I'd been making coinage off passengers during the voyage and must have calculated my trunk would certainly be more valuable than his. Oh, the rat! I remember the defiant look that had blistered in his face as we parted; he knew then the thing that I was just now finding out.

I was murderous. That trunk was all I had. Most of the money in my purse I'd just given over to the landlady. I pictured my hands on the lad's throat and burned to think I'd been cheated by someone who had been inside my body. I'd even coaxed him through to his finishing! Well, I'd finish him now, well and good. I clapped my hat back onto my head and barreled down the stairs.

Chapter 2

It was easy to find my way back to the dock—bristling practically a foot above the ground in all my rage—but determining which of the hundreds of ships was *The Lady's Peril* was a harder task. At least its mast would still be upright.

I walked up and down, annoyed, craning my head to read the ships' names. Many of the vessels had been robbed of their sails for tent-making, perhaps by their own crews, and they emitted a certain forlorn sound as their wood creaked. They seemed betrayed, those poor schooners—having made a fine, safe crossing to their port, they were abandoned without a second thought. I too was guilty: I left ship without a single glance backward. Even the captains, who should've been penning their logs proudly, had spurted off the boards to shore, trading a sextant for a shovel. These large ships towered over me in mute wooden sorrow.

It was becoming dark, and the somber mood made me wonder suddenly if it was safe for me to be there without an escort. Each city has its own ways, but generally the docks are not for women. My anger was subsiding in the vast expanse of the bay and I thought perhaps I ought to return in the daylight to continue my search.

No! He'll be long gone by then, I told myself. *All the ship's hands desert the ship for gold-seeking, and if there's one time I'll find him here, it's tonight. If he slips off for his gold-panning, why, I'll not see hair nor hide of my money again.*

So I stepped quietly, hoping none would see me. The water slapped against the boats, which in turn gave off ghastly wooden moans. It was a large moon rising tonight, thankfully, and I tried to calm myself with its pretty, bonelike gleam.

Then I saw *The Lady's Peril.* I studied the portholes, which showed no light or movement. It looked like I was too late; the boy was already off with my money.

But mayhap he had left the trunk aboard with all my girlish gowns—what purpose could they serve him? I looked down at what I wore: gray twill.

The gangplank was still in place, no one having remained on ship to pull it back. Looking behind me nervously, I boarded.

Oh, la, it was a ghost ship already. I scarce could believe there had been breathing bodies aboard so short a time ago. My heels clattered on the deck, but there was no one to hear me. I walked the ship's length, noticing all kinds of rope and gear the sailors must consider valuable yet had abandoned for anyone to take. A lantern and matches were near the stairs to the interior, so I lit a flame and forced myself to go inside. *You want your trunk, don't you?* I reminded myself. *You'll have a rough time of it in San Francisco without it, won't you?*

Inside it was dark and smelled so. I had forgotten the close odor that was the ship's fragrance. I trembled like Bluebeard's wife in that horror of an attic.

Creeping into the galley, I saw there were still sacks of food here, including the rice bag I could blame for all this, cutlery, plates, and long spoons for stirring masses of soup. A few rats scampered away from the lamp I carried, but they were the only things moving.

"Hello?" I called. I went down another level on the tiny, steep stairs, nearly ready to faint with all the stories my mother had told me about haunts and dissatisfied spirits. The boat leaned from side to side as I looked in at the bunks the men had slept in.

Such a scattering of belongings! They were so fierce in their gold-seeking that they had left behind the things they had brought around the world with them. I saw all manner of male clothing and appointments, yet not the small brown trunk that would fit my key. Under a blanket on one bunk, I did find a pretty lady's locket—some forgotten gift—and tucked it in my purse. I could sell it and maybe eat for a week off its value.

But why had the sailors brought daguerreotypes of loved ones so far across the water if they were only going to leave them on the floor? I picked one up; the woman wore a mournful expression, as if she knew in advance she'd be abandoned.

And then I sank to the floor in grief. How could I have forgotten? So concerned about the money and garments, I'd had nary a thought about my sole daguerreotype, a portrait of my sweet, departed mother. I closed my eyes and furiously tried to call up her image. I wouldn't need a paper one, wrought from science, if she still resided in my head.

I sat there until I started to feel the sea-given nausea again. I couldn't remember the visage, only that it was kind. I knew the eye color and the style of hair, but I couldn't fix on a precise picture.

And this is what I had come to, worse than penniless: a girl without her mother's memory. I almost threw the lantern, ready to help this rotten ship end its life in a riot of flame, but then I thought of the rats and how they'd suffer.

Since the wick was running low, I rose and said a prayer for my mother before moving on. I explored the ship cabin by cabin, many of which I'd been invited into for short, energetic visits. Here I had sat to play cards on the berth with a shy fellow, smiling at how confusedly he played until I took pity and schooled him; there had I pressed my hot face against the porthole while a gentleman pushed into me from behind; here and there men offered be-ribboned gifts or sent me off with gruff thanks. My own cabin was already strange to me although I'd only left it hours ago. I stared at the expanse of floor where my trunk had sat for seven months, and then remembered the short wick of my sputtering lantern and kept onward.

Now there was only one place on the ship I hadn't seen yet and that was the cargo hold.

Frightening and vast, built for stacks and rows of boxes, it was void as an unused tomb. The space was large enough to echo.

"He has my trunk," I whispered in that cavern. "I'll never see it again."

There was a shadow at the far end that looked to be a pile of garments. I pictured the galley mate tossing out my frocks and leaving them there. With my last hope, I strode across the floor.

I went so fast I almost stepped on her. It was no pile but a woman on the ground. Her eyes glinted in the lamplight. My shoes stuck somewhat to the wood, and with a scream I realized I was treading in her blood. Her neck gaped open like a clamshell cleaved, and I saw the gore spilling out of it.

And then the wick ended, and I was left in the dark hold with a dead woman.

I dropped the lantern and heard its glass shatter as I bolted away from that horror. I screamed and was dragging in breath for more when I banged my head into the opposite wall. I knocked to the ground and scratched my way back up. Where was the door? Like a blind woman, I felt the air in front of me and kept my ears listening behind me.

She was dead, but surely not at rest.

My hands and boots scrambled together, trying to find a break in the wall. "Oh, sweet Savior, lend me your aid," I muttered frantically.

Then I froze. I *did* hear something behind me, a light clambering. I turned my head and tried to see into the blackness. Was the corpse standing and trying out her stiff bones? Was she clamping a hand to her open throat? I couldn't move.

My skin lifted off my flesh and my heart fought a battle with my ribs, nearly breaking them asunder.

Her eyes had been open. In fact, she had stared at me in the one moment light fell upon her before the wick finished. It was with those glittering eyes that she was walking toward me, step by slow step. She would press against me with her sticky, sodden dress and crane her head toward me with the jerky clumsiness of the dead.

*Oh feck, oh feck, sweet Jesus...*My heart battered on and my eyes darted with manic speed, trying to see shapes within the darkness, yet my body held all that commotion in paralysis.

And when the rat finally ran across my foot, I screamed so my throat burned, dashing through the opening that thankfully was finally there. Through the sailors' quarters I tripped on the cast-aside articles, falling and lurching back up like a skeleton in the *danse macabre*. I sputtered and moved through the darkness of the ship, bruising myself and screaming the whole way until I was back on deck.

I ran to the gangplank and began scutting across. My left hand, which had my purse securely wrapped around its wrist, clawed at the rope railing. And then, as if the world hadn't treated me rough enough, the string broke and that purse plummeted straight into the water.

But in that moment I cared not a whit and ran all the length back to the streets where men were teeming and merry. I propped myself up against a carriage and closed my eyes, my breast heaving. 'Twas over. I had nothing except my life. My blood was still contained within my veins and not spilled and forsaken for only angels to weep over.

I thought of going back to the boardinghouse, but preferred a hard gulp of drink. A gent to buy me a whiskey and compliment me—that was the only thing that could calm me now. I'd have a drink and then another and the third one would mend me. With my stomach still empty of supper, the liquor would work even quicker. I made my hands into fists and pressed them against my closed eyes. Oblivion: the drinker's secret. The drinking wasn't for carousing; it was to bring the blankness that seeps into the brain. I began walking.

Men all around me were drunk, blurry-eyed, grinning and stumbling. Each fandango house door gave off a listen of fiddle music or fellas singing their pub songs. I saw only a few women in the streets, faces flushed and skirts all tufted.

At one dance hall I heard a song I recognized, "Lill, the Lass with a Wet Kerchief," and stepped inside. A roar went up when I entered because my arrival brought the hall's female population up to three. The two other girls twirled their skirts, giving glimpses of their legs. All the other dancing couples were men, miners clutching each other to do a quadrille.

There was all manner of men here, red-headed Irish, Chinese men at the faro tables on the sides, and even their homespun shirts were varied shades of blue and earth, colored by womenfolk back East in vats of dye and then given to the sun to mellow as it wished. The Mexicans, though, they wore red—handsome shirts with bone buttons. Somehow their senoritas knew how to make that color. I grabbed one of the many outstretched hands and let my heels speak for me: kicking and frolicking in that mix and beating out a rhythm on the packed dirt floor.

I danced and drank the drinks that came my way, without pausing. Soon I was drunk and could barely feel the paws that pressed upon me, or the lips that delivered kisses cock-eyed onto my mouth.

Later, I sat at a table and ate a meatpie a gent bought for me. I considered working, and the barman let me know there was a space in the back for fifty cents a throw, but after what I'd seen in the ship's belly I thought I'd better concentrate on the whiskey drams.

I heard many good stories there, as much as I could listen. One man told of getting drunk with Lewis Keseberg, the last man left at Starvation Lake from the Donner Party. Everyone else had died or struck off through the Sierra, but he was too ill to move. He spent that winter in a tiny cabin with five half-eaten corpses until he was rescued.

"He was crazed by the experience," said the miner. "He told me what 'twas like to eat of the human flesh, and miss, I'm not ashamed to tell you it nearly crazed *me* to hear of it. He was like to bragging about that and all the ways he'd eaten it, and what pieces taste best and how you get to preferring it..."

"Aw, shaddup with that, now, you. This here's a lady for dancing and good cheer. Don't be bringing her tales of woe. Wouldn't you like to hear about the lovely and easy ways of finding gold?"

"Indeed!" said I. "Leave the cannibalism to the cannibals! I'm sure Mr. Keseberg could have found some berries or mushrooms to eat."

But this other talk weren't much nicer, really: they spoke of men cheated of their gold, of assayers who juryrigged their scales and then hanged for it, of donkeys collapsing under the weight of so much wealth.

"'Tis cruel," I said of the last one. "The wee beasts make your fortune and break their backs for it." The whiskey had worked. I was thinking only of the donkeys, sore concerned for them.

The men, a rough lot, laughed, thinking me joking. But one man saw my downturned lips and said, "Best keep yerself away from the bull and bear fights then. Yer heart will like to break."

This of course settled it for the others. These men who cared not to shave nor wend a comb through their locks made a chair of their arms and carried me two doors down, myself protesting all the way. The site for this entertainment was a huge canvas tent, glowing from the outside like a Japanese lantern, and as soon as we entered, I could smell the blood: the mangled, fur-knotted wretch scent of animal death.

"Lads!" I said. "I'm after a quadrille. Back to the dance hall!"

But they set me down in a crude wooden chair that faltered crookedly on the uneven ground and began explaining the game to me.

"That there's Triumph. He's the second biggest we've seen, caught in the hills across the bay. When he stands up on his two back legs, he's taller than any man alive."

The bear bore stripes of exposed flesh from previous fights, and dust covered his pelt like he'd been sitting in a cellar for years.

"And that bull—I don't know 'im, does you, Joe?" A round of headshakes followed for this unknown bull, whose horns were already dripping blood, for we'd walked into the beginning of the fight. "Betting ends in five minutes," went up the call. The men put their money in their laps, gazing at what they had to gamble.

The blood on the bull's horns made me start thinking about the torn throat in the ship's hold again, so I leaned over the fella on my right and took a couple of hardy swallows from his whiskey. He cheered me on and took a kiss in payment.

"I always wager on the bear," confided one fella. "Each one of them claws is worth twenty of them useless horns."

And certainly the bear was more agile, rambling out of the bull's way despite his size, graceful in his thick body.

The two animals snarled and kicked dust into each other's eyes. They circled, the bear swiping with his claws and the bull lowering his head to dash in with his horns.

"These woulda never met natural-like, would they?" I asked.

"No," said one of them. "And bulls ain't likely to learn how to climb mountains anytime soon, neither."

"Kind of like *we* woulda never met," I said. "San Francisco's an outsized meetinghouse."

"Well," he said. "Place a bet. Here's a dollar with the winning already in it."

"I'm sick at this spectacle," I said. "No thank you."

He shrugged. "They fight anyway, whether you approve or not."

So when the bet man came around, I gave him the dollar for the bull, sorry for the creature's flatland limitations. I found myself leaning forward in that rickety chair, shouting his name—which I'd learned was Ricardo Oro—and hoping my chant would sharpen his horns. The beasts were exhausted. I could see the bear wanted to lie down and run his tongue over those streaming grooves of blood, but each time he looked tired, his owner yanked the rope to rile him up again.

The bull was limping and kept jerking his head to the side as if the bear had sunk a claw in his brain as well as his ripped flanks. Both animals' blood muddied the floor.

"Do they go to the death?" I asked.

"Naw, miss, they go until one of them brews a lovely pot of tea for t'other."

Just as I was thinking I could forfeit the bet and walk on out, the bull ran itself in a quick circle and then bounced across the ring. Its hooves shook the ground under me and I saw Triumph's face: he knew Ricardo was going to be his last experience on this green earth. The bear reared up on his back legs and roared, and across the arena I saw an entire audience of men clutch their hats.

Ricardo lunged, all legs in the air, and drove his horns into the bear's belly, bringing him tumbling to the ground. That's a thud I felt in my very bones. And then they were stuck together, the bull dancing backward, pulling the bear's heft with him. The bear bellowed his agony and so much blood flowed I couldn't see Ricardo's head.

The man who had Triumph on a rope pulled, helping them detach. Ricardo then wheeled around, blinded by gore. The bear lay there moving his legs gently in the dirt, groaning with all his thimble-sized teeth showing. It was horrible.

"Shoot him!" I yelled across the ring, and despite the din, I saw that Triumph's owner heard me. He caught my eye and shrugged.

"I told you you wouldn't want to see this thing," reminded a voice at my shoulder, and I turned, enraged.

"As if I had a choice with your hands all clamped on my legs!" I shouted.

I turned my head back in time to see the owner put his gun against the bear's massive forehead and shoot. The sound terrified the bull, who spurted around the ring as a man leaped around him with a bucket of water, ready to throw it as soon as his target stopped moving.

Well, I tell you, I was feeble in my heart thinking that this happened every night and many times over. Ricardo Oro, after a good night's sleep, might be put into this very ring again tomorrow. Or God knows, perhaps he had to fight again tonight.

I no longer felt the blaze of drunken joy I'd had at the fandango house. That is, until my hands were filled with chips of pure gold. The bull had been a long shot.

Chapter 3

Unlike a mill girl or a shop girl, I keep my own hours. If I feel like sleeping in until the sun changes the color of my counterpane, that's my affair. Out the small window I could hear the goings-on: the hawkers praising the merits of whatever vegetables they sold; the horses making their way up and down; the men greeting each other, singing out their halloos on the wooden sidewalk. I got up and poured out the last dribbles of water into the basin and splashed my face, wondering if anybody was sitting down to bear sausage this morning. I looked at myself in the mirror woefully. My good gray eyes were droopy with sadness and, worse, red-stained from the drink.

Then I thought past the frivolity and drunkenness and remembered the body sprawled in the ship's dark hold, left to stare at naught but blackness, and inevitably to be tested by rats.

I sank back onto the bed and clapped my hands to my eyes. The disastrous turn of events for her: to make such a journey and never set foot on land again.

I thought of her face and realized for the first time that without the shocking array of blood, it would have been a face I recognized. The woman was no stranger to me. She was the other prostitute aboard *The Lady's Peril*, the one who was too nauseated to work.

Put it aside. This was something my mother had always said to me when I came to her in tears for something a girl had said at school, or for ruining a sweetie I was baking. *You can't change it, Nora, so put it aside.*

The only thing I could do was tell the police and then forget her. She was in no condition to be helped. I had come to San Francisco to improve my lot, and I couldn't let her misfortune weigh on me.

At least that's what I tried to tell myself.

I went through the galley mate's trunk a second time, slower, hoping to find something valuable in the pockets. Not a thing. I read the letters, thinking I could get his identity from them, but the envelopes had been discarded and the letter writer only called him Thomas, the name of thousands of men. Downstairs, the woman who owns the boardinghouse was sewing away at a pair of men's trousers and I halfway smiled, thinking it's girls like me who cause those tears the wives have to mend.

"Up late," she observed. "Breakfast is at six sharp."

"I was wearied by the long voyage," I said.

"And the late night."

Hmmph. She kept flashing her little needle all prim.

"Ma'am, I realized I made a mistake. I ain't going to be able to stay. Can you deduct the money for last night's lodging and give me back my rent?"

She shook her head. "I'm afraid we made an agreement. You may leave at the end of the month as we previously agreed."

"But my situation has changed," I said.

"Regretfully, I must stick to our agreement."

"That ain't fair!" My hands started trembling. "I can't stay in this house. I...I..."

Pride goeth before a fall, they say, and I ain't fell yet.

"I need a quiet place to sleep," I continued, "and there was some unholy racket last night! I don't know the class of people you rent to, but ma'am, I swear furniture was being hurled about like confetti. Woke me from a sound repose. I want my rent back so I can hie myself somewhere restful."

"I too heard the tumult," she said. "Coming right from your chamber."

"What a suggestion! From *my* chamber?"

She raised her eyebrow. How I hate them women with control of their eyebrows.

"Well, that's just insulting," I said.

"I need to tend to other matters this morning. Shall we consider this conversation concluded?"

"No. No, ma'am. I...oh fiddle's skinny string, ma'am. I have to have that money back. I have to. You don't understand."

"I don't need to understand. We had an agreement."

I grasped at the spindle of her chair, right behind her ear. I bent my face to hers. "I have to have it back," I whispered. "Some scoundrel stole my trunk and I lost my purse. I've got nothing. And I can live where I—" For some reason, I stopped. I had no urge to impress this ninny, yet I couldn't admit what it was I did to earn my keep.

Her face changed and I saw she grasped my unfinished sentence.

"I'm sorry for your circumstance," she faltered. "Truly I am. But this morning as you slept I spent the money for meat and to pay off an old bill. I don't have it to return to you."

We gazed at each other. That is until her eyes fell, shamed to be trading looks with a prostitute.

"That was quick spending," I commented. "I'll take my breakfast now. I'll be fine with bread and jam."

She set down the trousers, stood up, and walked into the kitchen. "Take a seat at the table in there," she said, motioning to a room off the front. But I followed her instead.

"I could live where I work after this month is up," I said pointedly, "but I like to have a place to get away. A nice place. Do you think things is gonna be nice here or not?"

She was nonplussed and put an iron kettle on the stove while she got her thinking together.

"You'll find it nice so long as you creep quietly when the house is asleep," she said.

"Ain't a problem. But are you going to keep your mouth all sewed up like that when you talk to me?"

"I don't cotton to what you do," she said, cutting bread off a brown loaf like she wished it were a rime of evil she could slice off the world. "But so long as you don't cut up a ruckus or carry on your doings here, we can keep civil company with each other."

She dolloped mint jelly and piled bread generously onto a plate and handed it to me with what really looked to be a smile. "You're so pretty," she said. "You could find a husband and live honestly. You don't even talk that badly. Here, go sit down and I'll bring you some coffee."

I stumbled into the other room feeling like my thin and sickly heart was on that plate with the bread. *You don't even talk that badly.* Why, back in Boston I won the spelling bee and elocution contests each year. Maybe I picked up the word "ain't" here and there trying to sound like the other girls, but that was just to make everyone comfortable.

I remember that the first time I ever undertook harlotry the man laughed at my fine speech, displaying a high percentage of gray teeth.

"You're a whore," he told me. "Stop talking like ships will set sail because of your high-falutin' lip and tongue."

"This is the manner in which I customarily speak," I had answered him, which was truth back then.

"Aye, and I'm the grotty king of Spain. Madame, would'st thou allow me to insert my royal cock into your equally noble cunt?"

Gasp, shock, blushing. "Of course, yes, certainly," I stumbled.

Another sneer was launched at me. "You ain't better than nobody here, so quit your airs."

Having airs. An insult propelled at me by gent after gent until I learned that throwing some "ain't" into my talk eased everybody. And then because I spoke with no one else, abandoning sisters and correct acquaintances, I slipped into a form of speech I'd never be able to rid myself of. So, "isn't" (which some folks find vulgar already because it's a contraction) degraded itself further into "ain't," and I used "them" sometimes when I meant "they." I conjugated verbs like a foreigner, and lapsed and lapsed until I weren't sure I was even genteel in the back cornice of my soul.

And now this boardinghouse proprietress was making me wonder again over something I'd trained myself to not care about.

"What's your husband do?" I asked her when she came in with a mug of coffee. She took a deep inhale and I saw her ready herself to talk to me. I must have been the first woman of ill fame she'd conversed with.

"He lies down a lot," she said. "Under a wooden cross with his name on it."

"Sorry, ma'am. Was that recently?"

"When we arrived here—back when this town was still called Yerba Buena—he already had a little cough. It wasn't two weeks before he turned his head and said, 'Mehitabel, I hope you find a way to make it back to your people,' and spewed out a little extra blood to say good-bye with."

I kept quiet, staring into my coffee.

"We weren't the best coupling of husband and wife. We fought like cats. It's just as well," she added.

"Did he leave you comfortable?"

"No. But I never considered doing what you do. I take in sewing and sell that good bread you're heaping far too much jam on. Eventually I got enough to build this house and take in boarders."

"And you're not going back to your family?"

She laughed. "You may not know it to see me now, but I was high society once. Went through the debutante season in New York City and had five serious suitors. I don't think with my rough manners and what I've seen of the world that I can go back now and sit at the piano playing sonatas for young men who actually brush their mustaches. I'm a new woman now."

"I couldn't go back either." I hung my head, both of us knowing the likes of my situation.

"Well, my dear, California's a big smithy's fire. You go in one shape and come out pretty different." She actually lifted my chin so we could look into each other's eyes. "And the fire's still hot. You might think of how to reshape your own particulars."

I swallowed. Nobody had made me feel this ashamed in years, yet there was no hot rush where I could toss my head and damn her to hell. Somehow she and her molassesy bread had got to the quiet part of me.

"I best get underway," I said. "Thank you for the breakfast and I'm right sorry about the clomping and the throwing."

"Well, welcome to San Francisco, Miss Simms. You may call me Mehitabel if you wish, and we'll resume our relationship with better footing than we began."

"Nora, then, for me."

This lady's smile was the kind they use in them pictures of a good mother whose children wear angel floss for hair. I thought to myself right then, *I hope to keep earning it.*

Upstairs, I looked at the gold coins Ricardo Oro had earned me. It was almost all the money I had in the world, pushed drunkenly into my bosom last night and toppled onto the dressertop when I returned.

I had the money, but I was back to owning nothing but my skills: I had no undergarments to titillate the gents, not even a change of clothes. And glumly I realized I also had no tincture "to keep my waist slim," as the girls put it. In my trunk I'd had four or five bottles of birthwort, which harlots drink throughout the day to kill any chances that a man's glassy syrup might have of becoming a child. I'd need to seek out a midwife to get some birthwort, or take more primitive measures after each fella's spurting.

Less important, but still disagreeable, was the fact that I had also lost my sign.

The sign gets hung above a girl's bed and has her name on it. We all take pride in its appearance, something suggesting our personality. Mine was painted by a man who wrote Nora in beautiful cursive, with spirals and curlicues coming off the N, and then painted flowers and butterflies all along the border.

I wondered what use the galley mate had for it. He had probably thrown it overboard, my sweetly printed name bobbing on the waves.

"If I ever see him again," I muttered to myself, "I'll slap his face as flat as the sign!"

I would either have to pay out another dollar for a man to paint me a new one or go without. A person might wonder why it's important for these two-minute fellas to know our names. Maybe it don't make much sense but it sure makes us feel like more of a person.

I stepped out onto the streets of windy San Francisco, breathing the gusts off the ocean and eyeing my prospects. Jackson Street was a steep one and

I could see all the lay of the city as I stepped carefully in my heeled boots. Below, I saw the masts and rigging of ships that were just now coming into harbor. I wondered how large San Francisco would be by the end of the year. Would I cease being such an amazing sight in a dance hall, making the fiddler drop his bow?

Luckily, it wasn't long afore I saw the mortar and pestle sign of a doctor. I walked into the small glass-front establishment where the physician was sitting with a miner, dressing his gashed hand. Both of them turned and ogled me wordlessly.

"Hello," I said. "Shall I return when you're completed?"

"Lovely, lovely, ain't she?" murmured the miner.

"She's a sight to flutter the senses," said the doctor. The two of them set their eyeballs upon me again and the miner continued to bleed.

"Well, doctor, I'm only after a quick question," I said. "My husband and I just arrived yesterday, and I've found myself in a very…delicate situation."

Their jaws dropped at the same moment.

"Is there a woman you can recommend me, doctor? For my situation?"

The doctor lifted his hand, red with spilled blood, and rubbed his chin. It left him with a gory beard. "You won't require the services of a midwife," he said. "I myself provide a full-service practice. I'll be sending this gentleman on his way and give you your first examination, to be ensured that all is progressing properly."

"Oh, sir, no!" I said in what I hoped appeared to be horror. "Oh, I beg your pardon tremendously, but I…"

The miner guffawed. "You ain't gonna be seeing what she's got, doctor!"

For his impertinent remark, he received a slap from the physician and my own indignant steps toward the door.

"Madam, please…arrest yourself. This is a crude city yet, and I apologize for this man's buffoonery. But I wish to examine you and wouldn't you like the satisfaction of knowing you are *safely* embarking on this newest and most tender journey available to a woman?"

I made myself tremble. "I wish the address of a midwife, sir."

He sighed deeply, and the miner did also, looking woefully at his seeping wound. Then the doctor went to a small desk and scratched a quick missive.

"Here you are, then. But if you should require any other services, such as the curing of a cough that troubles you, or bleary eyesight, or any other malady, I hope anew that you will seek me out," he said.

"I will," I said. I followed the directions he wrote me and trod up one street, then left onto another, and knocked at the door that seemed only a residence.

A plump woman in a lace cap answered the door and looked me up and down quickly. "Newly in your condition?" she queried.

"Just so very new, madam! I'm laying up my stores in anticipation of my birthing day, and hope to get from you a few bottles of birthwort." I showed her several of my gold coins.

"But you wouldn't need but one bottle, dear! And if you wish my services for that happy event, I'll bring the bottle when I come."

"Oh, I'm such a nervous one!" I said. "This is my first child, and my sister said as to how the birthwort made everything easy, so surely I'm overasking, but I would like as many bottles as this coinage will secure."

She squinted at me and laughed low. "I know why you want it, so you can stop with the nervous-mother role. Birthwort eases birth, but for women who are preventing such a circumstance, it does that opposite work as well."

"Really!" I said, trying to look surprised.

"This is clearly news to you, I see. Pure as the driven snow, you are."

I looked at my feet, clad in my only boots, accepting the hang of my only skirts. Then I lifted my gaze and smiled at her. She was all right, I could tell. "How about snow that has been trod upon and muddied by the horses and shoveled to and fro? I won't lie to you, ma'am; I will need your assistance in the coming months and years," I said.

"Now, I approve of that," she said. "Don't be thinking you can deceive me that you're issuing forth a child several times a year! I'll give you three bottles today and make up more for your next stop here."

"I'm obliged," I said.

"And if you know of other girls in similar straits, perhaps we could form a bit of a financial relationship. You charge them five cents above what I do and deliver it."

"Most girls figure out their own for themselves," I said. "Not too many helping hands to clasp among my type, but if there's occasion I'll surely do it."

She wrapped the bottles for me and took all but a few of my coins. "Be cautious with the birthwort, *wife*," she said with a gum-baring grin. "It only works when you remember it."

"Oh, I daren't forget," I said. "I'll see you after a time."

One task accomplished, and not too ruggedly, either. I loved the clink of the bottles as I walked; they were saying, "Nora's all right; she always figures a path out of a mess."

Of course, there was someone else in the world—or rather, no longer in the world—who had not found such a path. Sick for the length of the voyage, and then rewarded for reaching land by getting her throat ripped. But I had to keep my own intact body moving through this mire of a world. 'Twould be no comfort to her now to see me bow down to distress.

After a while of her image flashing into my mind, and then me determinedly replacing it with the plain midwife's face, I saw a thing to thoroughly distract me: a signmaker's shop. I poked my head in.

"Can you make me a sign with my name on it while I wait?" I asked the man with paint all over his shirt. He nodded and took his time looking me up and down.

"Would you like to make a trade?" I asked, thinking quickly. "I can't give you a full 'encounter' for the small cost of a sign, but I'll let you touch me here and there." I pointed.

"Small cost? Painting a sign will run you five dollars."

"Five dollars? For a wee sign with a few flowers on it?"

"Flowers you didn't mention. That will be six dollars."

"Soot in the chimney! I had a sign made in Boston for a single note."

"Things cost a bit more out here, miss. If you hadn't noticed, we're far from civilization."

"All right then," I said. "Fair trade. Have you a back room?"

"I'm not sure you're worth all of six dollars. Plus there's the cost of the wood."

"Surely you're joking. The *cost* of the *wood?*"

"Another three."

It had penetrated, what he said about me not being worth six dollars. Rude but true.

"I'm sure I can find a more reasonable signmaker," I said. "I ain't paying your price. You better build me a two-story house and paint butterflies in every room for nine dollars."

"You're pretty and your form looks right under your dress. If you get the wood, I'll paint it for the trade you mentioned."

"And where am I supposed to find wood?"

"The lumberyard."

"Where no doubt they charge double what you charge."

"I can't say," he said.

I stomped out, furious again at the boy who stole my trunk. Who knew such a thin piece of wood could cost so much? I didn't have nine dollars to give even if I wanted to.

Maybe it's not important the gents know my name. I walked up the street, sneezing at the dust and not even minding my steps. I could take a bit of burnt coal from my fire and write my name on the wall, but that was humiliating.

Across the street I saw a police man and thought I could take care of one task and be free of the image still behind my eyelids: the woman's staring dead face. I crossed the street to speak with him.

"Sir," I said. "I need to report a murder."

He bent his head to mine and sniffed. "Drunk in the morning, are ye? Telling fables and stories?"

I breathed out a gusty exhale into his face and hoped it smelled of yesterday's shipboard onions. "I ain't had a drop. You needn't make any assumptions before hearing my story."

"With bottles in a brown bag, miss, what can I suppose?" He had apparently heard the musical tinkle of the birthwort. "You girls are after me night and day to investigate this and investigate that. Half the time you're stealing money from men's pockets and only trying to accuse *them* before they accuse *you*. And we're volunteers, you know; we wear our uniforms to help God-fearing citizens, not to be abused by girls whose pretty fingers do a crook's work."

"A murder I'm talking of, sir. Not a petty thievery. I saw a woman's body, throat slit, lying in the hold of one of the ships at Clark's Point, *The Lady's Peril*. I can direct you there."

"Jurisdiction ends at the shoreline, miss. If we had to deal with every instance of sailors' mishaps and misdeeds, we'd be sorely tried indeed. I'm a San Francisco constable, not an oceangoing one."

"But she needs a decent burial at the least. You can't just leave her there."

"My beat is this street here. You go to Clark's Point and tell the officer there."

"I'm telling *you*. You pass the message along."

"I'm starting to think maybe you're not an innocent party here, miss. How did you know exactly where to find this corpse?" He shifted one hand to touch his club.

So that was how it was to be.

"Oh, *I* didn't find it, sir. I'm only passing along a report I heard, trying to do my duty as a respectable citizen. For all I know, it was just an invented tale. I'm much obliged to you for your help and now I'll just be on my way. The stories people tell, sir, and me so gullible!"

As I spoke I edged away, which was just what he'd wanted. When he nodded, I broke into a trot and got myself a distance away. So *The Lady's Peril*, abandoned at Clark's Point, would be her coffin. Some have certainly had worse.

I walked a spell, troubling over my own particular situation. I might as well go drag myself into the ship next to her and wait for death if I didn't focus on getting some money. Which meant having a sign.

Finally I turned on my heel and went back the way I came. I'd bargain with the signmaker. Two throws instead of just one, which was actually an excellent deal for me. He could come see me at the cowyard and I'd give him the second. He'd have to trust me, though, to extend the credit.

"Sir?" I said, interrupting him at a job painting a sign for a saloon. "I know you find me pleasing now, but with a few minutes' time I can make you think so highly of me you won't sleep for a fortnight. So why don't you let me tarry with you today for the sign, and then come to my place of business on a later day to finish our bargain."

"I've never 'tarried' with any woman twice. And I don't think I'll start with you."

"Fussy, ain't you? Well, once you've learned all I can do, you'll be anxious to make a daily appointment."

"Provide the wood or pay the three dollars. That's the deal."

For a second time I left in a flounce of angry skirts. I stomped into the alley alongside his shop and kicked the dirt around. Down the alley was the back-yard of his shop. He had a smallish pig there enclosed by a fresh picket fence.

I smiled. The slats of the fence were just about the length and breadth of my Nora sign. And I could liberate the pig, who could find a kinder master or at least have an interesting outing. I pried and booted three of the slats out and then used one to gently paddle the pig out of the yard. Another I threw aside, and the third I brought back to the signmaker. He showed no recognition of the wood's previous incarnation and asked my name.

"Nora," I said. "I prefer the light blue and rose colors, if you don't mind. Flowers and butterflies."

I have to say, he did a fine job. First he fixed hooks and threaded twine through so I'd be able to hang it. Then he mixed the colors with much deliberation and changing of his mind. He repainted one posy bunch three times over, just to be sure it was right. The sign was lovely, truly lovely. The butterflies looked like they really were attracted to the flowers, and he even added a bumblebee just emerging from a rose's center.

"All right?" he asked.

"Better than I thought possible. You're an artisan."

"Let's see *your* talent now." He pushed me to the back, through an empty gunnysack hung from nails that provided a sort of door.

"Get rid of all your painty things," I said. "This is my only dress and I can't spoil it."

He took off everything—an oddity for me—and pressed me against the wall. He checked his hands carefully, looking for paint, before he bent and pulled up my skirts. I wore no dainties beneath for I'd had to wash my only ones in the basin that morning and I was still waiting for them to dry. He sucked in his breath quickly at the sight of my exposed self. One hand gathered the skirts at the side of my waist while the other moved over my hips and down my thighs. He touched me with the same look of intensity he'd worn while he painted my sign. I shifted my weight from foot to foot as he touched more intimately.

"This is no principled trade," I murmured. "A beautiful sign and this as well?"

He touched and touched until I nearly fell over, then he hoisted me onto him and tucked my legs about him. Then there was no sense of wonder, no slow fingers feeling like they were painting flowers on my skin…it was all rough and fast like the men I'm used to.

I rolled my eyes unseen, for his head was buried in my neck. So much for that. I'd ride him another half-minute and then he'd be sending me on my way. And sure enough, as soon as I thought that, he was driving me back against the wall so I felt the rough wood against my bum. He let me loosen my legs and slide down.

"I work on Jackson Street in case you'd ever like to break your tradition," I said. He made no reply but rolled himself a cigarette. I shrugged. We owed each other nothing now. I stepped through the gunnysack and picked up my sign, which pleased me even better after not seeing it for some moments.

"The paint's still wet, mind you," he called.

"I'll be careful," I said, and with the birthwort sack tucked under my arm, I picked the sign up by its edges and carried it flat, like a tray. It was into the afternoon, I had spent my last dollars, and it was time for me to start working.

My first fella was one that followed me down the line, calling, "Wait! You're a new 'un!"

I put my key in the lock and told him to let his ardor cool for a moment while I readied things. Inside the crib there was a nail above the bed and I carefully hung up the Nora board there.

I had noticed on the way in that some of the girls had their names on the door too, near the window where we stand to wink at the gents and show them our wares. I thought I'd better do that too, when money came my way.

There were sheets on the cot already and I sniffed them. Sometimes crib owners cut corners but these seemed fresh, not that I'd be in them anyway. I blew on kindling to get a fire going in the little woodstove. It all seemed in order. I unbuttoned myself, slapped my cheeks to make me flushed and wanton-looking, and smeared a little lamp oil in the female parts to make things go more smoothly. Then I opened the door.

"Come on in," I said. "Make me glad to be a whore."

He was, as I could have foretold, fast and grateful. I raised my heels for him and that seemed to be a nuance he hadn't encountered before. The bed creaked away like we was working in a factory.

"I ain't hurting you, am I?" he asked, but I could tell he didn't care.

"Hell no," I said amiably. "You're the biggest I ever had, but I can take it. I like them huge red cocks."

That finished him off. Then came my favorite part, the exchange of coins. I still hadn't figured what the going rate was, so I said my Boston rate and watched his face.

"Two dollars? Hoo boy, here you go. I'll be here every day!"

"That's the first-time price," I said quickly. "Just to introduce ourselves."

"So what's the regular?"

"What do you pay the girl over there?" I pointed to my right, where we could hear the cot squeaking through the wall.

"She ain't so pretty and she's got a long scar up her leg. She charges three."

"And over there?"

"Five."

"And the French girl at the top of the line?"

"Six."

"I charge five," I said. "Come back soon."

I couldn't believe it. I sat down on that loud bed and calculated. I'd be earning more than twice what I made in Boston. They were right about San Francisco and the chance to make a fortune! I'd make back the stolen trunk's contents in a month or so. I laughed out loud in surprised delight. And to think not two hours ago I was sitting at Mehitabel's table feeling sorrowful about my state of finances and my shameful profession!

And of course the thought wriggled into my mind that maybe I'd go back home as a rich woman, showing up in a coach and four, and nobody'd know how my pile was made. I'd invent a husband who had died. Already that man—who in my mind looked suspiciously like the image I'd conjured for Mehitabel's husband—was developing a little cough that made me worry.

Glory be, things were instantly different. With the ability to make five dollars for what comes natural, my heart started singing. I was eager to get my hands on more and more of that good stuff, so I sallied to the window and pulled my chemise down so I was bare to the waist. I lifted my leg, propped it on the sill, and pulled my skirts up so I was showing a good deal more than I wasn't.

And then I saw a sight that made my heart droop like clients after the deed. A fella of about twenty years was walking down the line and all the girls was hooting at him, turning his head and confusing him. Worse, there was a pack of men pushing him onward, as vigorous as the bettors at the bull and bear fight. They were joshing him and knocking off his hat, replacing it only to flick it off again.

There was something off about this fella and I knew what it was. His smile was a little overmuch, like this boy I'd gone to school with back East, and I thought, *Ah, God has shite yet again and sent a baby into the world without the brains to make a way.*

He was red and unhappy-looking, but kept testing out that simplish smile on the girls. Those hateful cats, I thought. I opened up the window and leaned out, catching his eye without saying a word. I crooked my finger at him and he came to me, the girls laughing at how his step hastened.

"Come on in," I said kindly to him. I closed the door firmly behind him and the window as well. Several girls were peeping there, but I just ignored 'em and brought him to the back. It wouldn't do to make a face at them; I was too new and I was well-acquainted with how hellish sporting girls were to each other.

"What's your name?" I asked him.

"Abe."

"Are you a miner? Looking for gold?"

"Was."

"And now you want to see a lady?"

"They said I ought to."

"Those men?"

"Ayup." He gaped at my bubs, transfixed and frightened.

It crossed my mind to offer that he could stay here a few moments and then go back out, as if the deal had been transacted, but I wasn't in a position to turn down money. Besides, some girl would have to break him in, and who better than me?

"What's yore name?" he asked, and I pointed to my new sign.

He took his time pronouncing each letter's sound, giving my name four syllables. But finally he had it.

"*Nora.* That's like you," he said. "Pretty."

"Well, Abe," I said. "Let's show you what everybody's talking about."

I lay down on the bed and lifted up my skirts. He sat down and scrutinized it so long I thought maybe I was blushing now too.

"Unbutton your pants," I said.

He stood up and took off his hat and I like near to cried. What man does that for a lowly girl of the line? He placed it on the chair and then started working on his shirt buttons, hands clumsy and thick.

"You can leave that on, Abe," I said. "Things is quick around here. Just unbutton your pants and that'll be enough."

"What about my shoes?"

"Looky here," I said. I pointed to the oilcloth spread over the bottom third of the bed. "That's what this here's for. Your boots can't hurt my bed."

He looked like he didn't think it was right, but came over and sat down again. I unbuttoned the trousers myself and reached in to pull out what was needed.

"Can you tell what's going to happen?" I asked him. "This part's going to go here. Is that okay?"

He nodded and clamped a hand on my breast. "That's right," I said. "That helps." I eased his body over mine and inhaled his clean odor. He wasn't rank with rum or whiskey like most men are, and his clothes weren't stiff with never washing.

"You smell good, Abe," I said. "I like you."

At that, he broke into a smile that rivaled Mehitabel's, and I helped him right inside me. "Now we got to move," I coached him. "You do this and I do this."

I liked how slow he took it. He wasn't racing off to the saloon or the wharf or a game of dice. He was letting his body explore mine, and the small sighs that escaped his mouth were genuine wonderment.

"Feels good, don't it?" I asked.

"Nora," he said. "Nora."

My name, folks, printed on a sign for all to know it and none to say it until this very day.

I'll tell you what, I looked into those gray eyes and regretted telling him not to take off his shirt. It would be nice to feel the warm hair on his chest. I clenched what skin I could through his rough clothing and made the ride better. He moved his mouth onto my nipples and I thought, "Those rowdies that sent him here never even once *thought* to pleasure a woman like this. He could teach them a couple right good lessons!"

And then I had to close my eyes because Abe had the rhythm right and for the first time in my life I wasn't thinking about the money or the tip or deducting the crib price to see what my real profit was. For once, I was swimming in the same sea the men always were, the floods of feeling that made my body rock like it had on *The Lady's Peril*, the rush and pull that made me sweat like Abe.

"What is this?" I murmured to him, because my body was doing something new. It was pulsing like my heart and there was an intensity where Abe and I joined that I had never felt before.

Right when he looked at me puzzled, the whole thing smashed and I was hanging on to him for dear life. It was like silversmiths were working on me with dazzling lights and heat, sending shivers of sparks and fire through my body. Relentlessly. Reshaping me like Mehitabel had said.

Then Abe gave a special buck and thrust and I knew he was in that smithy's furnace too.

Ah, god, it was a fair enough sensation as to repair anything you had ruined in your soul. Incredible! I had heard tell of women reaching these shores, but since I was so terribly accustomed to swimming and never reaching them, I thought 'twas a fairy story. Maybe that tremendous throb came half from the body doing the thing and half from the mind doing something to augment it. For I was convinced that my cessation of mentally counting the cash was what brought me to that exquisite and body-wracking feeling. I grinned at the man and paid attention to that particular pulse within me as it finally slowed.

Can you imagine me, the girl who fleetly sends a gent on his way so the next one can open his wallet, spending hours and hours with one man? And we didn't even do it again, neither, we just lay there and talked and learned each other's life story. Abe was slow, it's true, but he could still string along his words real good.

"Where are you from?" I asked him.

"New Hampshire. Me and my brother Caleb come out for gold."

"And I came out here for the men that found some!" I said. "You and Caleb give up?"

"He died."

"Ah, weasel's chamberpot. Feck, I'm sorry to hear that."

"He got the cholera. I didn't want to dig no more without'n him, so's I came here. They said I'd find a job."

"What do you want to do?" I asked him.

"Work with the horses," he said. "I went to a livery today and they told me to come back tomorrow. Them horses like my hands."

"Gentle," I said.

"Yeah."

"You'll do well," I said. "A gentleman like you with a heart and a soft way of talking to beasts, you'll be topside."

"What about you?"

"I'm from Boston and I just got here yesterday. Stepped off at Clark's Point."

"And this here's your job?"

"You know it is, Abe. Why be issuing foolish questions?"

"I don't know." He hung his head. "Lots of times I think I know how things sit, then I find out I had it crooked. I ain't sharp like I ought to be."

"Who needs sharp?" I asked softly, regretting my speedy tongue. "I'd prefer a good man without all the facts to someone hard and cruel and clever."

"I got half the brains a man is entitled to. Some congressman or professor got the extra part of what's mine."

"Anytime you start the reckoning of who got what and who *deserves* what, you're bound to be unhappy," I told him.

Later, Abe put another log in the stove and I shamefully asked him for the five dollars since he was already standing. He emptied his pockets and gave me everything there. It looked to be about twenty-five dollars.

"No, Abe," I said. "Just the five."

"Take it," he said. "I wisht it was more."

Twenty-five dollars! Twenty-five dollars! Twenty-five dollars! But—he had not the wits to decide this. With an interior groan, I pushed the money back into his pants pockets. He fished it back out and put it on the chair. Unbelievable.

Somehow there was a kindness in him not to spread the money on the bed.

Chapter 4

After Abe had gone, I'm sure you can imagine what I tried to accomplish with the next client. Successfully, I might add.

I had heard about this thing before: a coupla sporting girls I met on a Boston omnibus were busting my ear with it, but back then I didn't believe them. Thought they were inventing their own tricks. Lots of girls do that, have special tricks like claim that they're a virgin or that they were Prince Albert's special courtesan before he got married to that stiff dowager the queen. I myself never had to lie because my face is pretty and I'm good at figuring what the gents want. Like Abe, for instance. He just wanted a woman to be kind to him and show him what makes boys men.

So the next fella was in his sixties, grizzled and reeking of tobacco. He didn't doff his hat or waste any words on me. He pushed me back onto the bed, positioned me the way he needed, and did his business like he was eating breakfast or mending a fence post. But I tell you what, I just started concentrating on what he was doing, 'stead of running numbers in my head like usual, and after a time it happened again.

I think I nearly sounded the death knell for this old fella's heart. His eyes bugged out and he looked down at me, amazed.

"What the fucking blazing spackle of tarnation are ye doing?"

"Well, I'm uh…just enjoying it."

"No need to pitch me to the roof, ye blooming hussy. I like a little bounce in a girl, but I'm an old geezer!"

"Then twist around and lie back," I suggested, gathering my skirts with me so I could kneel over him. "Mind you keep your feet on the oilcloth."

I'm not saying this is novel, to straddle a man. When we get customers that is handsome and young, we swivel and bend and give them a good time. But generally what you get in the cribs is someone who wants to lie atop you, ignore the fact you have a head, and pump until he puts the fire out.

When he was done, I charged him six dollars, just to see if he'd blink. He did. And grumbled too, but paid it. I guessed I'd better keep it at five, at least until I changed nationalities and became French.

Which of course gave me an idea.

I knew my workday was over when it had been black as a pot bottom outside my window for hours. There were a few lanterns bobbing in the dark, but most fellas by now were too drunk or broke to come by. I walked down the line and stopped at the French girl's crib. She was still busy, as I could hear through the door, so I bided my time scratching designs in the dust with the heel of my boot. 'Twasn't long afore her visitor heaved a huge groan and began tucking himself back into his pants.

"Mare see bow coo, miss ure: I 'ope to see you agane," I heard her say.

Well, the first part could have been spoken by a Chinaman for all I understood, but the second part was real pretty. It was just English spoken with a special spin on it.

The two of 'em appeared in the door, and as he wandered off I greeted her.

"Hello," I said. "My name's Nora."

"*Bonjour*," she said. "I am Yvette du Lac."

"You're a ways from home," I said. "Are you from Paris?"

"Where else?" she asked.

"Well, you could be from Lyon or Nice or Marseilles," I said, smiling. We had learned major European cities back when I was still a useless saint of a schoolgirl.

Yvette looked confused. "Just Paris," she said, but she pronounced it "Par-ee."

"I got myself to thinking..." I said, "and I have a proposal that might be of some benefit to you. Care to speak privily?"

She looked left and right and saw no men shambling toward us, so she motioned me into her crib. Inside she had scarves and velvet draped everywhere and the scent of heavy perfume. I sneezed, admiring her sign, which had quaint, French-looking letters and birds I didn't recognize.

"Seet down," she said, and I took the chair. She sat on her bed and sniffed. "Can you steel smell ze man? I use a parfoom to get reed of ze odoor."

"If'n he smells like a cartload of roses, I can still smell him," I joked.

"What ev you come to ask me?"

"I'm the kind of gal that's always thinking. I came out here 'cause I heard the girls like us are scarce, and I aim to make some good cash. And I know you French ones make the most of any of us."

"We desairve more," she said proudly.

"Huh. Well. In any case, my offer to you is that you teach me some French phrases and I'll pay you to do it."

"For what pairpose?"

"I'm after pretending I'm French," I said. "Nobody knows me from Adam— or Eve—out here and I might as well start out right. Won't be any competition to you; I'm stark down at the other end of the row."

"I am leeving anyway," she said with a smirk. "To a fancy parlor house on Pacific Street."

A parlor house. The way she lengthened the Rs of parlor made it so exotic sounding. Parrr lerrrrrr house.

I knew about parlor houses. Rich girls worked there. They weren't poked into cribs like chickens in a coop. They had room and expanse and jewels besides.

"You can just go there?"

"I should ev started there. When I came to America, somehow by some mees-take I am in ze crib although I am more elegant zan zis. Eet ees a meestake."

"Oh."

"Yas. I am reliefed to go whair I truly belong."

"How much will you make there?"

"I weel give ze man champagne and talk wiz heem, play ze piano and sing and spend ze hours een convairsation. Eet ees…how do you say…classy. And only later I go upstairs to a beautiful room and please heem. For all zis, eet ees feefty dollars."

"Fifty."

"Feefty."

"Oh sweet Jesus who dwelt with the apostles. How do you get into a parlor house?"

She laughed. I had to bite my tongue to keep from yanking her precious perfumed hair.

"Pleez don't tell me you are zinking of trying to become a parlor girl your-self."

"I'm pretty," I said stoutly.

"And zat ees all you have. You are not accompleeshed. With one queek look, I see you are poor and ze clothes are faded. You speek like a girl of ze streets."

I stared at her and then at her ceiling. Of the few prolonged conversations I'd had in this city, two revolved around the fact that I spoke like someone below my class. If Boston scorned fine speech, San Francisco reviled common talk.

"It's not like it's permanent," I said finally.

"I am finding zis hard to beleeve. How can a common mongrel dog become like a plush…how do you say…pureblood?"

"I ain't a dog," I said, heated. "And folks can change. I could work in any parlor house in this city!"

She laughed again. "Zey would call ze police on you," she said. "Zey would zink you are zair to steal ze silver!"

"I don't look like no burglar. I may be plain in my dress, but I know I look honest. I ain't no conniver."

"See ze four walls?" she asked. "Zis ees a crib. Zis ees all you can hope for."

"If I put myself in a pretty silk dress, all done up like Parisian-style, you'd say different."

"I do not argue that you are attractive. But zair is more zan zat. Zair is an *air* you must have. Of money, of accompleeshment."

"I'll work myself day and night to get that money. And as far as accomplishment goes, I was raised in such a household as prized feminine skills. I'm an ace at pianny and I sing like an angel."

These were lies.

"And what about ze *air*?"

"I'll breathe until my commoner lungs burst with it. I'll get it somehow. I'll study up! I'm a quick one at learning, always have been. Was a star scholar back East."

"I zink you fight ze battle with loss already ze outcome. But you ev asked me eef I weel teach to you my language, and I weel. For ten dollairs a lesson."

I swallowed. I had just argued and set a pig free over three dollars. "How long a lesson?"

"One hour."

"Only one hour?"

"I don't care eef you do or don't. Zis ees my offair."

"Done," I said recklessly after a moment.

"Now, I am off to ze tailor."

"At this hour?"

"When you are beautiful and have ze propair *air*, you will be surprised what ze common merchants weel do for you. And myself, even me, has to be fitted for all new clothes for ze parlor house."

I looked down at my simple cotton skirt and shimmy in the bold, exotic colors of gray and dark gray. "But they don't even look at our clothes," I said. "Just what's not covered by them."

As soon as I said it, I knew how cheap I sounded.

"Here in cowyard zis ees true," she said. "But walk along ze streets and you weel see finery—such as zat in my own Paree—that ees worn by the soiled doves."

Soiled doves. I hadn't heard that one before, but I sort of liked it. All birds get messy by flying about.

"All right now. Lesson one. To say good-bye, eet ees like zis: Oh rev wire," she said.

"Oh rev wire."

"Exactly."

"Oh rev wire. Now teach me a dirty thing," I said.

"Why, when ze men here weel nevair understand? Eet ees a waste."

"Aw, c'mon, Yvette. I gotta learn something I can use. Saying good-bye is only after the money's paid."

"Okay zen, hello: Bon jore."

"Bon jore. And what's the word for cock?"

"You are not ze parlor house material," she said firmly and with a snotty little laugh.

"Then what's the word for wrong? 'Cause that's what you are."

Chapter 5

"Bon jore, mis sure," I said through the open window. A gent with knees and elbows poking through holes in his clothes ogled me.

"You French, aintcha?"

"*Oui*. Wheech ees French for yes."

He looked down the row where a bold wench named Emma had left her crib and was standing in the dusty thoroughfare yanking her skirts above her head. "Yoo hoo!" she called. "Four dollars only. Forget the Frenchie and get a good homegrown woman."

Poor lass hadn't grasped any of the subtle ways of bewitching men and so sufficed herself by hauling petticoats so they blocked her face and let men judge the wares scientifically. Holey was brought up short by her hardihood, and he gazed befuddled down the twilit lane at her.

"Aintchew proud to be American?" Her voice was muffled but still carried.

"What be your charge?" Holey asked me.

"Seex. I can promees you a world of delight and unaccountable ecstasy, miss sure. Those two dollars will make all the deeference. Ev you not heard about all the delicious things the Frenchwomen know to do wiz zair men?"

"Like what?" He was turning his head between me and Emma, obviously torn like his trousers.

"I can wheesper all ze foul words of France into your ear," I said. I crooked my finger at him and began walking backward into the crib.

"Like what?" he asked, already heading my way.

"Like *J'aime danser sans vêtements*. Do you know what that means?"

"Nope." He was now inside and I reached behind him to close the door.

"It means I like to dance wizzout my clothes. Now, before we begeen, eet ees customary to pay."

"I ain't never paid beforehand! It's on the bed first, then with the wallet."

"I am understanding, yes, thees ees the way for Americans. But in France, we pay first." I wasn't about to let holey pants do as he pleased and then come up empty at pocket-time. Sure enough, he retrieved six dollars from his sock—his pockets dangled in useless wisps like a lady's scarf—and presented them to me. If I'd had the toilet water from my stolen trunk, I'd have sprayed the wilted bills, but instead I waved them about, to air them, before I tucked them in my bosom.

"Now zen," I said, sitting on the bed and raising up my skirts. "I weel show you the ways of *l'amour*."

"What about the prancing around?"

"That ees extra charge. You ev paid only for ze throw."

"Ain't nobody in San Francisco speaks the truth straight," he said. "Well, I don't need a dance. I just need a good time."

"My specialtee," I said.

He unbuttoned his trousers, although I'm sure he could have worked one of the holes around to the front and saved himself the trouble. He got into position and I helped him in. Then I began the French Onslaught, phrases delivered to his eager ears with a husky voice.

Now, Yvette had failed to teach me the dirty words I wanted, but I figured I could just use the everyday phrases and who'd be the wiser.

"*Vous êtes un homme,*" I seethed like a teakettle. *You are a man.*

A groan was my reward.

"*J'aime beaucoup votre…jolie robe.*" Damn! I had just told him I liked his pretty dress.

"Oh, yeah, keep it coming, Frenchie."

"*Vous êtes un….un…arbre. Avec un oiseau.*"

Ooh! I hit the mattress with my hand in frustration. Stupid language! The easiest part is when I fake the regular English, trying to use that lilt Yvette has—like saying "I em appy" instead of "I am happy"—but the worst is when I try to say the actual words. I forget halfway and then try to rush through with the rest of another phrase, so I'm saying things like "You are a tree, with a bird" and "You are such a beautiful weather."

Which would be fine—who understands French anyway?—but for the fact that I sputter and flub and make a stew out of the entire performance.

"You cursing me in that French language there?" he asked.

"No, mis sure, I em cursing myself."

"Do it on your own time. I'm still looking for that ecstasy I got promised."

"*Bien sûr.* Of course."

So I quit with the parlez-vousing and dug my heels in and did what I do best. I ain't never had a gent complain, and today wouldn't start nothing.

At the end he wiped his brow, said "Whoo!" with the scant amount of air left in him, and grinned, shaking his head.

"Aren't you pleesed you deedn't tarry with old skirt-head?" I asked.

"You French gals shore are something! I ain't converting to your way of talking, but the way you gits your carriage up and moving—hey, that's worth a trip across the seas."

"Oh rev wire," I said, knowing that was one phrase I couldn't possibly tangle up.

"Oh rev wire yourself, little filly! I'll be seeing you again."

Off he went, and I pulled the six dollars out of my bosom and put it under a loose floorboard. That was my "purse" nowadays.

Yvette had been teaching me French for a month, and I was making six dollars a throw, but I didn't feel any more elegant or closer to being a parlor house sort of woman. And she made sure to remind me of that each time I saw her. She sure wasn't a teacher who wished the best for her students. In fact, I was grateful she didn't carry a ruler to snap across my knuckles.

I'd been trying to talk more genteel in my *native* tongue, too, aping Mehitabel, but it's so frustrating when the folks I'm speaking to so lovely-like rolls their eyes and says, "Enough with the trap. Open your legs and earn your coin." So in a way I was almost getting worse, my perverse mouth pushing out *more* "ain't" and using them verbs like a crowd of people is one person.

I went to the window to spy for the next customer, thinking over my circumstances. I was a little more optimistic than the night my purse had foundered—which is what I chose to *remember* of that night. Things take time. Why, just moving Nora Simms from Boston to San Francisco took seven months and the cooperative restraint of several crocodiles who coulda bit our canoe into kindling.

It had been a month of surprises. I hungrily watched the ways of the fancy women I saw on the street as they paraded up and down in their gossamers and silks, hair piled all wind-worthy on top of their heads in coronets and chignons and interlaced pearls. I couldn't say as to whether some of it was paste, but they wore gems: huge brooches at their necks and diamond earbobs and rings. They were real showy and tried new ways of tailoring their chemises and patterning their skirts. And then I saw them timid Eastern wives mincing down the street and not looking nearly as fine. I saw them studying the way the Cyprians were kitted out, studying so as to copy them. Ain't this city a revelation: the Christian womenfolk imitating the harlots!

I was getting thinner, walking these steep streets when I wasn't working. Lord knows I had a nice proportion of meat on my bones, but this was all right. The parlor house girls I saw seemed to have the smaller waists, staved in with whalebone. One sailor brought me a whale tooth and I thought, "This poor behemoth had to die so my middle don't sprawl and I can light my lamp." I put the tooth under the floorboard, thinking it was my first thing I could consider precious. I could begin to accrue again, so I could lose again.

My expenses ain't been what I first reckoned that day I set my price. For one thing, when I paid my crib rental, instead of fifteen dollars a month like I was told, it was forty-five. For the linens, the owner told me, and the police bribe. I tried to fight, saying I'd pay off John Constable myself, but negotiations didn't go so fruitful. Since I fussed and raged, she kept the price the same but moved me into Yvette's crib, the prime placement in the row.

And I sprung shocked like cotton at the prices of simple dry goods. I saw on a lass of ill fame a foxy little duster I wanted made for myself, and when I went to the shop for the broadcloth, they asked ten dollars the yard! So I still wore the same dress I arrived to San Francisco in, washing it each day, which further degraded its fibers. If the weather was fair, I hung it to dry in Mehitabel's back garden. Oftentimes, though, I had to heat the iron on the stove to press and sizzle the thing dry. I was tired of its gray somber cut, but the dress performed its task. I planned that my first true expenditure would be a new one.

And despite all my trouble finding two cents to rub together, I'd decided to pay for another month at Mehitabel's. If nothing else, she was a good influence on me.

On my way home one night, I spied something familiar in my lantern's umbrella of light that made me stop short in front of a woman, blocking her way.

"Pardon me," she said and tried to pass.

"I don't believe I will," I said and grasped her sleeve. "Where did you get this?"

"What?"

"Your shirtwaist."

"I had it made, of course." But her eyes looked from side to side, as if judging whether there was room for her to escape. She was halfway pretty, with thick rolls of curls like alder twigs resting on her shoulders. It was a new style of hairdressing and made the most of her bland looks.

"Really? Did you have it made in Boston, at the Robinson Street tailor, from fabric he'd recently purchased from the Lowell looms?"

She made a bolt for it, but I was too fast and grabbed her by the curls.

"This is mine," I spoke into her hair. "And it was stolen from me. I imagine you have a whole trunkful of this stuff."

"Oh no, miss, no." Her face was scared enough that I released her. "It was given me, by a lad of my acquaintance. He seemed solid, miss, too young to be a crook, but I hardly know him."

"This is the only thing he gave you?"

She was silent. "See, he tore one of mine, miss. So he gave me this to make up for it."

"Tore your shirtwaist?"

"He was a rough one, miss." She lifted up her chin and looked me square on. I appreciated that. "I can see we're two of a kind. We have the same sort of relations with the menfolk. And I'll give you it back, if you wish, but I can't take it off in the middle of the night in the thoroughfare."

"You sure there ain't another few gowns he slid you, for instance, a day dress of blue worsted—"

"I told you what he gave me, and I'm wearing it now," she interrupted.

"Well, then, the next thing you can do is take me to him. We have a score to settle."

"I've no clue how to find him. He comes to me, not the other way around."

"Well, take me *there*. That's a start anyhow," I said.

"No, miss. This isn't my grudge. I ain't the kind to court trouble. He pays, and that's all I'm after."

"Wouldn't you ask my help if…Please, he stole everything I had: my dresses, my money, the daguerreotype of my dead mother. I have to wear this," I gestured to myself, "every single day! Can't yet afford to tailor a new one. I'm ready to burn it and walk the streets naked. This fella that gave you the shirtwaist, he *ruined* me practically. When I arrived here, I came as forlorn as a dog."

"Our kind don't help each other," she said with no more emotion than as if she were telling me the time. "Each girl fights for herself, you know that."

Then she made a resourceful move I had to admire, even as I cursed her for it. A cart was passing us, and she leaped for its bed. She dashed up its length, leaned next to the driver, and swatted the horse's rear so it took off running. I grabbed for her, of course, to no avail.

And although I was no closer to owning my trunk again, now at least I knew Thomas was still in San Francisco, and not in the hills panning for gold as I'd imagined.

Chapter 6

The next evening I started my workday as I often did now, by undressing in front of the crib window. This had two utilities. For one, it allowed me to discard the sole dress, which was now worn and sad from daily wearing. For another, it was attractive to the men to watch great flashes of my skin appearing. I act like I don't realize I'm in front of a glass pane fronting the street so they feel like they've caught me at something they're not supposed to see. Makes them a Peeping Tom, more lurid and stirring than watching yonder strumpet down the lane flapping her shimmy like a cupboard door.

I felt someone lingering to watch so I took my time with the buttons. Sometimes I think I could run that Fanny Kemble off the stage, so focused am I in my charading. A couple of inches down the button row, he was crossing the threshold, dropping his cigar on the chair still burning, and lifting me by the waist onto the cot.

He didn't look like a regular one. He wore a tie and a boiled cotton shirt, with a stiff sort of suit and shoes that had no truck with the dust this side of town. He took his top hat off but left all else on; no stranger to the cribs, I guessed.

During it I had to ask him—forgetting to use my French—what was digging into my poor crushed bosom, and he pulled out a golden watch and let it dangle off the edge of the bed on its chain. I listened to it tick while he thrashed around with me. I was too nervous to think about what Yvette had told me was called "*le petit mort*" and instead willed myself to pipe up with something intelligent. After all, here was my chance. This was the type of fella that would visit a parlor house. I could test out whether I was ready to please this variety of customer.

"Sir, your watch is very fine," I said. "Does it run with Swiss works?"

He faltered mid-thrust and glared down at me.

"The Swiss make a far superior product, don't you find?"

He didn't resume, so I gulped. "Sorry," I added. "Carry on."

"I'm here for a quiet lay," he said. "You don't need to talk at all."

"Afterward, perhaps," I said. "I'll just wait."

Then I got to feeling guilty because I wasn't giving as good as I could. So I ran my hands where he truly responded and got pumping far better than before I'd spake. I bit his earlobe and breathed a lusty gust into his ear. After I arched my back real good, letting him feel those recently-oppressed-by-a-watch-fob paps, he grabbed hold of the mattress and drove me into it. I guess them high-class men is more emotional at times like this.

"To what do I owe the pleasure of your visit here tonight?" I politely inquired as he used a monogrammed handkerchief to dry things off. I arranged my skirts, knees together, hands folded relaxed-like.

A smile appeared below his victory of a mustache and he chuckled like men do with each other. "I didn't have three hours to spend," he said. "More like three minutes."

"So…you came to me for a more speedy and…" I ferreted around in my noggin for another word that meant fast.

"Expeditious," he supplied.

"…expeditious social call?"

"Right. Parlor houses require quite an investment of time. Lots of long-winded discussions about literature and current events. And copious beverage consumption, which frankly I'm not always in the mood for."

"I aspire to be a parlor girl," I told him. "I'm learning the piano and how to speak French."

"Good girl. Let's hear a bit of that French."

"Je m'appelle Nora."

"I gathered that from your sign. What else?"

"J'aime beaucoup faire l'amour avec vous."

"You should really use *tu*, not *vous*, when you're talking about making love," he said. "And that's quite a lamentable accent. Who taught you?"

"A Parisian named Yvette."

"Paris, Texas, is it?"

I didn't understand at first. Then my jaw dropped and I pressed a hand to my cheek. "Oh no, sir, no! She's as French as they come. You ought to have seen the scarves and things she had in here."

"If you're assured, then I'm assured," he said. "And now, thank you for a splendid time and I'll be off. What donation might I leave with you for your excellent hostessing?"

"Ten dollars," I said without blinking.

"Well worth it. Good luck with your plans for the parlor house."

He had turned to go when I blurted out, "Won't I see you again?"

"Perhaps, my dear. You were a fetching sight in the window."

"Half-price next time. I'll remember you."

He laughed. "Money's not the issue. Good luck to you, Nora. *Bonne chance.*"

"Sir?"

His body was already framed by the doorjamb. A crueler man would have kept walking, but he turned and raised his eyebrows.

"What's *your* name?" A thing a woman like me oughtn't ask. He might have a wife or an important job, something that would make him reluctant for to say it. I waited for the sneer and exit.

"Professor Hugh Parkson."

"You're a professor?"

"No, that's just my given name."

"Devil in a frypan, I wisht my given name was Lady or Princess. You can change your whole outlook with a name like that."

"What a delightful turn of phrase, that 'devil in a frypan,'" he said, and tipped his hat to me. "And that was a *blague*, dearest."

"A blawg?"

"Ask Yvette."

"I won't see her for another fortnight," I said. "Tell me."

"A *blague* is a joke. And I am a professor."

The next evening Mehitabel put on a dinner for the boarders, asking only ten cents for the food. Because of the pinched way she'd invited me, I knew she'd fretted over it and worried I'd carry on my doings under the table or in the privy or such.

"I'm pleased to come," I said. "Shall I make a blancmange for dessert?"

"Oh no, don't trouble yourself. The sweet is the best part to make. Be ready to sit at seven o'clock."

I sighed. That meant a late start at the crib. But at seven I went to sit with my fellow roomers, some of whom I'd breakfasted with in companionable silence or greeted with a nod in the hall.

"This is Miss Simms, gentlemen," said Mehitabel, "in case you haven't formally made her acquaintance before. And this is Mr. Hobart, Mr. Holmes, Mr. Fleming, Mr. Quince, and Mr. Twomey."

They all seemed fine gentlemen—perhaps not miners but businessmen designing to make their profit off the miners, rather like myself.

"Good evening, Miss Simms," said the very deep-brogued Mr. Twomey. "'Tis a pleasure to be making your acquaintance."

Of the five gents, two would not meet my eyes. They all knew what I was. Although I'd started avoiding the rouge and darkening my eyes until I got to the crib, and then wiping it off soon's I got out the door, it still probably wasn't too hard to cipher what it was I did. I took it into my skull that I wanted those two principled gents to stop avoiding my gaze, so I picked on the one with eyelids that could barely cover his bulging eyes. Put me in mind of poached eggs, they did.

"Mr. Holmes, how come you to be here on this side of our vast continent?" I asked.

The chop Mehitabel had prepared endured his searing regard.

"I have set up a mercantile business and am getting things in order for the eventual arrival of my wife."

"Indeed. And will she come overland?"

After a silence, he reluctantly began his answer. "Her brother will escort her overland, yes. She has a powerful dread of the sea."

"And will your wife come to live with you here, at Mrs. Ashe's establishment?"

"Certainly not!" he said. He had still not raised his head, but I could see the flame rising in his cheeks. "I'd prefer we not speak of my wife, if you please."

"I beg pardon for my prying, sir," I said quietly. I knew his gruff request and my hurt tone made me the favored one to others at the table.

"You're being damnably rude to this young lady, Holmes," said Mr. Fleming. "She meant no harm in her conversation making."

"And this is scarcely a dangerous place for a wife," said Mehitabel, scalded by his earlier insult.

"Let's have an apology, then, for the lass," said Irish Twomey.

"Apologies," said Holmes, with ice tongs emerging from his voice.

"There's naught to forgive," I said, "but I thank you kindly."

Mr. Holmes let go his fork and knife on his plate with a tremendous clatter and rose to go. "Compliments to you, Mrs. Ashe, for the dinner. I'll be retiring now."

"Gracious, there's courses yet to come," she said. "You haven't eaten half."

"I couldn't abide another bite."

So he was gone and I had never gotten those bulging orbs to look at me.

"Don't know what chafed at his cravat, but the company's cheerier with his absence," said Twomey, smiling around the table. I blessed him with the ought-to-be-patented crinkle-eyed smile.

"His wife must be deranged or syphilitic for all he didn't wish to speak of her," I said lightly.

Gentleman No. 2 stood up. It was Mr. Quince, who hadn't looked me in the eye previous but now glared apace.

"Use your God-given wits, hussy. He didn't want the likes of you talking about a woman who has achieved the sanctimony of marriage. You aren't fit to frame the word 'wife' with that besmirched mouth."

The table rustled and bellowed with "Come now" and "How dare you," but the voice that piped the loudest of all was Mehitabel's.

"Mr. Quince, I will not brook any such judgment at my table. Shall you cast the first stone, you with your practice of charging ten times the natural price for flour when you could simply double the price and still see a fine profit? You rob children of their bread and peeve even me with the outrageous cost."

"I never thought I'd see the day an upright woman would ask me to sup with a whore."

"You count yourself better than our sweet savior? He supped with the Magdalen and saw what was good in her heart."

"Yes, well, Jesus Christ never had to come to San Francisco!"

He banged his fist on the sideboard, making Mehitabel's sole glass pitcher tremble, then pummeled up the stairs. Once he slammed his door and all was quiet, I reached under the tablecloth and seized Mehitabel's hand.

"Mr. Hobart, I'd surely appreciate it if you might send the plum butter my way," she said. "And please, sirs, take your fill of biscuits. They won't be fluffy by nightfall, and it's a shame to crumble them for the birds."

"It's excellent fare," said Hobart, passing the small pewter bowl. "Who would have ever thought we could have such an elegant dinner so far away from the producers of alimentary goods?"

"Securing the plum butter was certainly a test of will," said Mehitabel. "I had to request the plums months ago and set aside a bit of sugar each week. I've been drinking bitter coffee so we could have such a delicacy tonight."

"Marvelous! Excellent!" beamed Hobart. "I'm delighted your sacrifice bore such fruit. I haven't eaten so well in a year, and that's no exaggeration."

"'Tis more splendid than ye know, Mrs. Ashe," said Twomey. "'Tis a feast such as we'd have in the old country for a wedding or a wake."

Mehitabel released my hand so she could spread the butter on her biscuit, and I took up my fork again. The chatter continued around me, and Twomey told a funny story about losing a donkey in the Burren and having to pull a cart seven miles himself. I sat silent.

I always liked seeing tempers flare and being part of a dramatic tableau, but tonight I had ruined Mehitabel's dinner. Even the biscuits looked deflated. I wished Holmes and Quince were still at the table, even if they did smolder and refuse to look at me.

Afterward, I helped her clear even though she hissed at me that I had paid like everyone else and should simply go upstairs and allow digestion to occur.

In the kitchen, I placed my hands on either side of her hips, feeling the crisp tarlatan of her apron strings, and kissed her cheek. "You've made my heart ashamed with your kindness," I said. "I *cannot* tell you how miserable I am that I chased those men away with my wickedness."

Damned if that woman didn't tug me in, to embrace me with a mother's hug. "Nora, sweeting, you're young and still gnash your teeth. In time you'll want your teeth sitting placidly in your head."

Pressed tight against her, corset to corset, I smelled her peppermint soap. "Why are you so nice?" I whispered. "Your house would be respectable without me in it."

She stepped back, grabbed a napkin, and put three cookies on it for me.

"It isn't anything I think of," she said. "Our dealings with one another are just the way they end up."

"And what if you lose Holmes and Quince as boarders over me? You should tell me to find other lodging. Send me on my way."

"Stop with the blither. Now, head upstairs and eat these, then clean your teeth and sweet dreams."

She thought I was off to bed! Well, I'd climb the stairs to keep her ignorant.

"If they leave, I'll pay for their quarters for the rest of the month," I said. My hands twitched, wanting to seize the words back before they reached her ears. That would be a fair outlay of cash. Yet, she had done me a turn of kindness that was surely worth all of it.

"Everyone pays in advance, and I shan't refund anyone leaving for such a reason. Besides, there'll be ten men pounding on the door tomorrow looking for a space. And maybe they'll be better men."

I examined her, gray hair slowly progressing in with the black, and the right kind of wrinkles on her face: a few for frowns to show she'd lived as people generally do, but most clustered around her eyes to demonstrate her years of laughing.

"Good night," I said, not moving.

"Off with you, Nora! Good lord, you'd think every person you'd come to know in your life had beat you, and you're boggled to find me not doing so!"

"Thank you, Mehitabel, for what you said at the table, speaking for me."

She threw her hands up in the air. "Do I need to find the broom and sweep you out?"

I waited until her smile emerged. Then I scuttled out of the kitchen on tiptoes, like a child. "Good night, then!" I called sweetly.

At the bottom of the stair, Irish Twomey handed me a scrap of paper and asked me to write down the address of my place of business.

"I'll never sport with you here, understand?" I whispered in the lamp-lit dark. "This is a decent house and I won't have it any other way."

"My sentiments exactly," he whispered back. "But I've no problem with despoiling myself at other locales."

"I'm going there now," I said. "But be discreet. Wait a while and be quiet on the stairs."

On the landing, I had a similar hushed discussion with Mr. Fleming. He was indecent enough to inquire so far in advance what my price was, so I tacked on another dollar for him.

In the second-floor hallway I encountered Mr. Hobart, who was emboldened enough by the quietude of our faraway nook to propose we undertake business then and there.

"I'm scandalized at you," I said. "After such a meal, which you yourself praised like a bootlick, you'd affront our mistress by carrying on under her roof?"

"Perhaps it would be prudent to seek you at your place of business," he said.

"I'd warrant so! Now, here's a cookie for consolation, and I'll see you later this evening at the cowyard on Jackson Street, nearest Beckett Street."

"Farewell and good night, Miss Simms."

"Good night."

I passed the door of Mr. Holmes, he who had first abandoned the table leaving only the memory of his bulby billiard-ball eyes, one of which, I now had the feeling, was surveying from the keyhole. Whether true or not, I bent to it and whispered the address. His wife wouldn't be arriving for a while yet, and sometimes the men who seemed most offended were really the ones most intrigued.

My first fella that evening was Abe. He had become a nightly visitor, and sometimes more than once a night. He came with a gift, as he frequently did: a nosegay of blue salvia. Sometimes it was a length of fabric—never enough for a dress, but sufficient to sew a new purse so the space below the floorboard no longer had to serve—or a packet of nuts.

There wasn't a vase in the crib, course, so I wrapped the posies in a bit of hair ribbon and propped them up against the wall.

"What a glorious sight, that blue," I said.

"Their little stems was easy to break off. I just tugged."

"Well, I've got something else that's easy to tug—come and help me with my hose."

He liked undressing me, threw each piece of clothing in the corner with great relish. Then with the strong tip of one thick index finger, he pushed me down onto the bed. He spread my hair out on the pillow and pressed kisses onto my locks as if they were a living thing.

He kissed all the way down and all the way up. Most everywhere in between too. I never needed lamp oil with Abe—he got me slicker than a hen's fresh egg just by taking his time.

He slid in easy and stopped himself twice, just to keep things longer and better, afore he let himself blast his seed into me. I sighed and took a few more thrusts so I could get there too.

"If I hadn't met you," I said dreamily, "I'd never know about how downright majestic it can feel."

"I done that for you, Nora?" He seemed amazed.

"You did."

"I'm glad I done something for you after all you done in my sake."

"What have I done, other than show you what that fleshy device is for?"

"I talk a little better. Afterward, when we lie here and talk, it's a good practice for me. And you ain't never been mean like a schoolmarm," he said.

I had sorta noticed improved articulation with Abe. He ain't so slow once he's easy with a lady. It's like his brains grow a little once someone is kind.

"I think you are better, Abe. But that's your own doing."

"Nobody but Caleb ever gave me as much space for discussing. Ever'body else hustles place to place, no time to wait for me to put a thought together."

Abe reached into his trouser pocket on the floor to get a hanky to wipe his lip. Once, I had told him a little moisture had collected in the corner of his mouth—not drool, you understand, but just a little extra spittle—and that only happened the once. Since, every ten minutes poor Abe runs a hanky over his mouth just in case.

"I don't put much stock in the world," I said. "If folks are rushing away from you, they ought to ask themselves what they're after."

"Errands," said Abe.

"That's the literal answer."

"Literal," he repeated.

"But really, truly, what are they seeking?"

"Eggs?"

I saw this one might be beyond Abe's sphere, so I tickled him and got his goose to rise. Such a plucky goose, I loved it. Strong-necked, ever willing.

"Some mornings I wake up and I try to figure what I like better, lying with you or talking with you," said Abe a bit later, when we unplugged from each other for the second time.

"Which one do you most often land on?"

"Day to day it switches."

"Well, lucky I can provide both so you're not obliged to choose. How's it going at the livery these days?"

"Grand. Horses are another beast that'll let me talk. I just stands there grooming and talking things a horse would like, and they settles down to listen."

"What about the other men there?"

"They ain't bad. John what owns the stables is a good enough fella. Treats me like ever'body else, not like I'm lacking gears."

"And what do you do besides grooming?"

"I feed them, help them stretch their legs. There ain't nothing like being paid just to ride a handsome nag! I check them, make sure their shoes and teeth are healthy, take burrs out'n their coat. And of course another thing I do I won't mention afore a lady."

"It's scarcely something to shock me, Abe. I step around it every single day as I walk these streets."

"Well, it ain't so bad as that. John runs a tight ship. The second it happens— why, quick as darts we clean it up."

"Sounds like you found yourself a perfect job, Abe. I'm glad for you. And Caleb would be right proud if he could see you."

He whimpered at the mention of his brother's name and turned his face into the pillow. I could have boxed my own ears, but maybe it was good for him to have a little snuffle. I rubbed his back until he turned faceup again.

"He wanted me to get along without him but was scared to let me alone to try it. I guess fate wanted to see too."

"And look how well you've done," I said.

He repaired his eyes, kissed me all along my jawline, then stood up. "I have to go," he said. "I'll see you tomorrow."

I handed him articles of his own clothing and dressed myself as well. As I saw him out the door, my next man was standing there waiting: Irish Twomey from the boardinghouse.

"Hello, red," I said. "And farewell to you, Abe."

Abe glowered as he walked away and clapped his hat back on his head. Most men don't mind seeing the fella next in line, but things with Abe were a little contrary.

"I've been up half the night thinking of this moment," said Twomey.

"Really? Thinking of standing in the dooryard kept you sleepless?"

He laughed. "You've got the spirit, girl. And I'll show you a little of me spirit now too."

I could bore you with the yawn of a time he gave me and the forever it took to work himself to the state of being finished, but it's pain enough in the experiencing, and double pain in the telling. One tidbit did arise from the

encounter, however: the hair this man had in curls and wires surrounding his odds bodkin was bright red. And that's the first time I'd seen such a sight.

But it surely wouldn't be the last.

'Round midnight, in slunk Mr. Holmes, he who left the dinner table to disgrace me but then hovered at his keyhole with one bulging eye to watch my arse walk down the hall.

"Why, Mr. Holmes, the public library is on Washington Street," I said. "I believe you have lost your way."

His face got red as a shoe on the anvil and he puffed up his chest and blinked furiously. The latter made me think of trying to pull a blanket down over a pair of eggs to get them to sleep.

"On Washington Street," I repeated.

As he turned to hasten out, I saw the profile of his pecker pressing against his loose trousers. It was a jaunty one and he'd obviously been nursing it out on the street with the thought of what might be to come.

I laughed and trotted to the doorway to see his flustered walk down the line, for he was unfortunate enough to choose that route. Girls called to him, "Mister, that was quick!" and "You deserve some kind of ribbon for that performance," as he sped away from their jeers.

"What was it with that one, Nora?" the gal two doors down called to me.

"He mistook me for a prostitute," I laughed. "He was devilish ashamed when I set him straight on my righteous rules for living."

"You sent good money packing?" she asked in disbelief.

"Oh, he'll return," I said.

I got straight to work with a sailor, then his friends, then all of them again after they'd gone off for a few drinks. It wasn't until I'd considered concluding the evening that I saw from my window the humbled figure of Mr. Holmes heading back toward the cowyard.

He pulled his hat forward and kept his head down as well, but it was easy to tell him, even in the small light cast from his lantern. He had a rare air of furtiveness and mortification. One hand was fisted in his pocket and he shuffled along like he hoped no one was watching.

He had to look up sometime to fix his position, and I waved gaily to him when he did. He kept walking and came straight to my door. I was impressed by his fortitude.

"Did you find any volumes to please you?" I asked. "Did the library have that *Wuthering Heights* what came out a few years ago? Wasn't it outrageous that the lady there kept rapping at the window when she ought to be good and dead? And goosy Heathcliff, let's explore his features. Come on in and we'll commence our literary probe."

"You slut," he said. "You dirty, heathen slut."

"Oh dear, you're angry," I said. "Oh. Oh. I see now." I batted my forehead as if an idea had just busted out of that location. "And how could I have been so careless? Of course there's no library established here yet, nor would it be open at this hour if it were. I've sent you on a fool's errand."

"You're naught but a slut" was his unrelated answer.

It was time to stop hectoring him. I relented. "I am quite bad," I agreed and broke the button on his collar to wrench it off him. "I'm a slutty, dirty girl and I'll never be good."

His mouth remained open a small portion, like a fish served on a platter.

"Girls like me only want to do terrible, wicked things," I said and raised my knee to nudge his waterpump. My fingers worked quick at his shirt and soon had it dangling from his waist, still tucked into the trousers. I licked a path from just behind his ear all the way down to where the pants formed a barrier. He groaned.

"Do you want me to do the wicked things to you?" I asked. "Do you want a slutty girl to make you all dirty too? Get you sticky and hot and unfit for civilized company?"

"I...yes...make me dirty."

"Tell me exactly what to do. Tarts ain't smart; we never know."

"Just..."

I could tell it was hard for him. Being required to say the things, rather than just fall prey to them...this was putting a little too much responsibility back into his Christian heart.

"Just what, love?" I asked.

"Do as you were before."

"How?"

"Please. With the tongue. And..."

"And?" I asked, said tongue getting in the way of speech, as it was otherwise employed in the region of his waist.

"And..."

"And?"

"Oh fuck, you are making me crazy. Take my cock out and stick it in your juicy cunt and I'll fuck you on the floor and get dust up your ass and fuck you until kingdom come."

What a string of suggestions! I hadn't heard a sailor yet who could put such a sentence together.

"You filthy man," I said admiringly. I pulled him to the floor and yanked out his member and pretended it was hot to the touch, licking my fingers as if they were scorched, and thrust him inside me like throwing a hot meatpie back into the oven.

His eyes rolled up in his head and he studied the thoughts and memories engraved on his brain. I worked him with a lot of breathing and moans and of course the praise of how dirty he was, how debauched and smutty and crude. I exhausted myself with all the striving until he was little more than a boneless puddle on the floor.

"All right then, Mr. Holmes," I said after a few moments of breath gathering. "It's time to be tidying ourselves and paying up."

He pulled himself onto all fours like a dog and from there cranked his limbs until he was upright again. He reshirted himself and tried for a bit with the broken collar, then gave up.

"How much?" he asked huskily. I could see the hatred beginning in his eyes again. It was worse now: he despised himself too.

"Six."

He dropped the money onto the floor and I let it lie. I still had my self-respect. As for him, he could pray all guilt away.

"Next time you come," I said, "you have to talk a little more. I was plum stretching my mind out trying to come up with aught to say."

"Next time?" he asked. "This was a severe lapse in discretion and it was only your wickedness that caused it. I shan't fall prey to such lowly desires again."

"Suit yourself," I said.

"And if you injure my clothing again, I'll charge *you*, you destructive slattern. As a rag merchant, I know exactly what to charge you for this damage."

"Mrs. Mehitabel Ashe takes in sewing," I said helpfully. "And ain't collar-button busting a fair way to commence a friendship?"

"You're from the gutter, girl. The trash seeps from your mouth."

I had to stop to puzzle that one out. *He* was the one whose mouth performed as a gutter. Or did he refer to…my grammar?

"You mean—do you mean—" I was stammering, my hand itching to slap him.

"You're as common as they get. And I *ain't* going to allow you to despoil me ever again."

"Oh, *ain't*, huh? You have a terrible problem with this street slang, do you? Well, by god, I'd rather—rather be—"

Thundering volcanoes! Could I not complete a sentence?

"Look at yourself," he said. "Look at this sordid little shack and the mistress of all its glories. You're nothing. A rat is more worthy of admiration."

"I was educated!" I said, fashed at myself for even reasoning with him. "I learned proper English; I've just forgotten it along the way, is all."

"And it appears there are a few other lessons you've forgotten as well. I'm sure your mother is proud and pleased."

"Oh feck yourself!" I screamed. "Feck yourself and your slut of a wife! Don't you ever mention my mother."

We were both pure white looking at each other, myself offended at his mention of my mother, and he in scorched flames about his wife being called a slut. He left in high dudgeon and I was grateful, for the other road would have meant a bruise on my face.

The remarkable thing was I knew he'd return. He'd likely be as regular as Abe.

Chapter 7

The next morning, I wandered around town and thought on what I could do to make sure I was the kind of girl a parlor house would want. I stopped and bought a paper of horehound candy and popped one in my mouth as I resumed. I'd have to focus on my speech, that was clear as could be. Yet what else could I do to improve my chances?

I ground down on the hard sweet rather than letting it melt. I thought back to my first talk with Yvette. At the time I'd said I could play the piano. Well, well. The horehound had helped a whore hound down a thought. And now it was time to make a falsehood a truth. Mehitabel used to play piano for those snoots back East, so I decided she would be my schoolmistress.

I hied myself home and caught her in the kitchen, asked if she might teach me a tune or two.

"Oh!" she answered. "I would with great pleasure teach you to play. I had a certain aptitude when I used to enjoy it. But short of painting keys onto the edge of this table, I don't know how we'd do it."

"I know where there's a piano we can use," I said.

She said no, scrubbing with new effort at the tin bowls the boarders had eaten porridge from.

"No? You just said you would if you could."

"Any pianos you've found are in sordid quarters, I'm sure."

"Aw, it ain't—isn't—so bad. A hurdy-gurdy house during the day isn't ten-anted by nobody. Who'll see us? The girls and men don't show up until after suppertime."

"No."

"Honest, I'll take you there by back alleys and not a soul will see us."

"Buy some chalk from a timberman and we'll draw a keyboard on this table. That's the best I'm offering."

"You *know* what a bum lesson that'll be. I got to hear the sound the key makes or it'll be like learning to kiss by reading a penny novel."

"You're asking me to enter a hurdy-gurdy house? You're actually asking this of me?"

I sighed because I hated to lie to her. But I was going to anyway. "Mehitabel, this world ain't offered me too many box seats at the opry or gentlemen bowing from the waist. Now here I am, trying to become a proper lady and begging for your help in this noble endeavor…"

I watched her hands still and the thought bloom in her head. I had been humiliated at dinner the previous night; I had been persuaded by her Christian charity: I was preparing to change my stripes.

"How can you say no?" I continued shamelessly. "Why, ever'time you hear me creeping up the stairs in shame for what I am, your head won't rest easy on that pillow, I wager you that much."

Silence.

"Ain't it sorrowful to see me begging?"

Silence.

"And I'll pay you."

Reaction!

"You'll have to promise me you can safely escort me there without any eyes seeing," she said.

"Of course, Mehitabel."

"And I'll ask two dollars a lesson. That way I can relieve my bread baking a bit and rise fewer loaves."

"Yes, indeed!" I didn't want to tell her that was a tiny amount, less than half of a common throw. I comforted myself that protecting her from that unpleasant truth was almost redemption for the lie I'd told.

So there we were later that day, a slut and a disapproving former debutante, working through scales in an empty dance hall.

We could still smell the liquor, as no doubt it was marinating the floorboards, but I'd made sure that Joe Sullivan, the owner and grateful visitor to my fine one-room establishment, had run a broom over everything afore our arrival.

Mehitabel eyed the place carefully when we first entered. In her mind, probably, naked women were lying on the bar and all the men were whipping out their fleshy tubercles. She envisioned stabbings and shootings in the corners, murdered ghosts learning the pianny along with me.

In a scant half-hour, I was already twinning a certain sound with each finger. The two middle fingers rang the same note, just in a different octave—octave being a word that meant a set of keys. I told Mehitabel that it was a good thing the notes only went up to G since that was all the schooling I'd received on the alphabet. I could see she wasn't even sure it was a joke, and again I felt like a sham of a girl.

"Now I'll show you a chord," she said. "It's just a way of pressing a lot of keys at once to make a grand, single sound." So she spread her fingers in a different octave and I copied where they were on mine, and at a nod of her head we sprawled forth on the ivories together.

Glorious!

We both smiled at each other, like wee girls with peppermints in our mouths.

"This is surprisingly in tune for a piano in such crude surroundings," she said.

"It sounds like God's touching all the angels on their heads," I said.

"That's quite…fanciful."

"Meaning I shouldn't have thought it?"

Quiet were her lips, although her fingers now rippled up and down, making a sound like a waterfall.

"It's odd to hear you speak like that," she said finally, arranging my fingers into a new chord.

Woe is me, having to hide the grin that launched like lightning across my cursed face. She weren't only referring to my rough speech this time. She meant that, in her world, fallen women didn't think about angels.

Chapter 8

I'm not a girl for reading newspapers, but when you see one lying in the mud of the street with a picture of a face you recognize stretched across three columns, you tend to take notice.

It was an artist's sketch of the lass who'd caught wearing my shirtwaist. Her eyes were closed, but I knew her by the enormous rolled curls. What was she in the paper for? She must have been caught flagrantly practicing her trade.

I stooped and used my shoe to clear the mud so I could read the story. And wished I hadn't. The reason her eyes were closed was that the picture had been drawn postmortem.

This woman, known by her fair but frail companions as Nutbrown Nettie, was found murdered in her place of business at 8:30 in the morning of December 6. The harrowing discovery was made by a businessman who appeared to be of some standing, who made his report to the police anonymously and dashed off. The woman's throat had been cut from ear to ear, and due to the stiffness of her corporeal vessel, the coroner conjectured that the deed had been accomplished the night prior.

I crouched in the street, aware I was sullying the final inches of my gown, and clutched at my own throat. She was the second to go in such a manner.

Whenever I thought about that woman in the ship's hold—which I tried not to—I figured that she had paid the price of a lover's quarrel or a debt she had skirted. That she died for who she was, specifically. And that it was an isolated instance, to be forgotten.

Now it seemed that women were being murdered for being prostitutes.

Nutbrown Nettie could have been me. I could have been the one to usher a gent inside to tear at my skin with his bowie knife. And it still could be me...today or the next day or thereafter.

"Whoa!" shouted a man, his voice seemingly in the air, as if he floated above me. Simultaneously I heard the quick clip of horse's hooves and felt a tremor under my feet.

I looked up. Into the terrified face of a horse, its jaw flaring back with the yank of the reins. He was only a few yards from me, and his huge feet lifted dull silver shoes and then clamped them down into the mud, thrusting and thudding the earth so jarringly I felt it through my own stout boots. I screamed.

This massive horse bore down on me as I was stooped to look at the newspaper, showing his teeth like a lipless skull in a casket while his master frantically stood up in the wagon and used his entire body weight to pull the leads.

"Whoa! Whoa!" he yelled. "Miss, move yourself! He's barely broken!" I heard men shouting from the sidewalk, only adding to the horse's disorientation.

Those hooves were huge as irons, and if they landed on me they'd stamp me clear down to China. I scuttled sideways.

"Go then, *haw!*" yelled the man. I saw the prancing legs respond chaotically, according to some equine architect's grid. One hoof planted a mere inch from my splayed hand, descending on Nutbrown Nettie's eternally reposed face.

Whumshd. I screamed again, for the horse was back to running. He sprayed up divots of mud that spattered into my open mouth.

With a jolt, the wagon bounced into action behind me, and I threw myself sideways to avoid the wheel that came so close it in fact pinned my skirt. I was pulled a bit by its revolution, and then it released me and the long wagon passed above, darkening my world. The second and third wheels on that side also abused my skirts, tearing and bruising them, before broad sunshine again hit my head.

I stood up, trembling and mud-built, and watched the wagon churn down the road. The driver was still attempting to pull up the reins he'd dropped, which now dragged beneath the horse's feet. He turned his head, once, to see if I still lived, then attended to his own emergency. The whole time he was shouting "whoa," but the horse, bent on some agitated journey, ignored him.

That was almost a ticket to the crypt, I thought, breathing raggedly. *I'm lucky to be yet of this world.*

A man put his arms around me and led me to the board sidewalk. "Miss, you must be careful in the streets," he said. "These aren't civilized thoroughfares like back East. Are you all right? That was a tremendous sight to see. I had my pistol drawn and was ready to shoot the horse, except I feared it would drop upon you and make things even more calamitous."

"O, 'twasn't the horse's fault, sir," I said. "I'd chide and batter you if you shot him. No, it was the man's error for not breaking it properly."

"You'd think differently if you'd been trod on by it!"

"I wouldn't. It was a noble creature, just not ready for his harness."

He shook his head with an admiring smile. "You've recovered well, miss. Fortitude of spirit. And you're all right?"

I looked down at myself and sighed. Not a single trespass of my skin, but the horse had ruined my dress. It was smeared with mud and torn where the wagon had run over it.

"I'm fine, sir."

"Do you require…any other assistance? Might I help you with…" His voice died, but he was pulling a purse out of his waistcoat.

This was kind of him but made me aggrieved to think I looked as poor as I was. Could this soiled wretch ever hope for a place in a parlor house?

I curtsied and took the money, though I couldn't look at him or it.

"Mind the horses from now on," he said. "And the best that fortune can offer you: may it be delivered to your door."

"Thank you, sir," I mumbled and turned to make my way back to Mehitabel's. I looked at the bill finally and stopped short in disbelief at the man's charity. I turned my head, ready to thank him proper, but he was making his way with dispatch, unwitting of how sore happy he'd made me.

And then I remembered that Nutbrown Nettie was dead.

In the kitchen, I tossed my purse onto the table and took off the battered dress. I threw it into Mehitabel's wooden washbasin and boiled water in the kettle, standing only in my shift. I poured kettleful after kettleful onto the dress, making a brown stew, but the stains were stuck fast to the fabric. I scrubbed and rinsed and willed the stiff mass to loosen.

The benevolent gentleman had given me enough money for a cheap dress, and with the money I had saved I could pay for the tailor's skills. But I wouldn't be able to get a dress for tonight's proceedings, not with it being already late afternoon.

I would need to borrow a gown.

Mehitabel was not at home. I knew neither her errand nor the hour of her return. As I used a stick to stir the dress in its bath, I thought about what to do. If I asked her to lend one, she'd surely refuse. She held such distaste for my whoring, she'd think her dress would be forever clouded by being worn under such circumstances. She'd picture men's grubby hands caressing me through it, and for her the dress would be dirtier than the one I now stirred.

If I could wear my own dress, I could walk to the cowyard, shed it, and then just be shamelessly naked all evening. But the gown was now sopping wet and

I didn't relish the thought of the hours it would take, even with the iron's help, to dry it. I should have gone straight to work from the horse's hooves; why had I come home with the faulty thought of cleaning it?

I had to work tonight, despite the unexpected donation. Money. An ever-present absence.

I thought of asking the kind Irish Twomey to loan me a shirt and trousers. But I'd be a ridiculous spectacle. What woman ever appears so dressed? Maybe I could go in the absolute dark of night, and carry no lantern, and stick to the shadows. But the girls of the line would see me when I arrived, all pressed against their windows and lounging in their open doors. And they'd hoot. A girl with a fair face like mine arouses petty jealousies. I don't know what I ever did to make God angry with me—perhaps it was that small matter of not treating my body like a temple—but He was smiting me again and again.

"Are you finished with me yet?" I wailed to the ceiling.

"And who be ye talking to, lass?" asked Twomey, coming into the kitchen behind me.

"The creator of all evil," I said glumly. "God. The fella that invented mud."

He stood next to me and looked down at the dress I still fruitlessly stirred. "Your only frock?" he asked. "Is that why there's a tantalizingly undressed miss in the kitchen?"

"I'm decent in my chemise," I said.

"Decent forever," he agreed. "Such loveliness."

"You don't happen to have any dresses lying about, do you, Mr. Twomey?"

"Sadly, my wardrobe contains only masculine apparel. But even if it didn't, I'd hide the fact from you to hinder your covering up this lovely physique."

He was nice. Bright red hair and a bright red smile.

"If'n I can't locate a dress, I can't go to Jackson Street," I said. "And I must go."

"How about if I act as your customer all evening here?" he said. "I'll pay you as if I were ten men. Twenty? I don't know how many you are able to...accommodate of an evening. I'd be hushed as a spider and Mrs. Ashe would never know."

"What an offer!" I was astounded. That would be over sixty dollars at the minimum, and he was willing to pay, *calculate quickly, Nora, twenty times six...* one hundred and twenty dollars! Parlor house prices!

I nearly tossed the laundry stick and challenged him to a race up the stairs. But there was that mention of Mrs. Ashe: Mehitabel. I couldn't bear the thought of the smallest murmur or bed wrench drifting down to her ears. She'd be so shamed. And she had been unfathomably good to me.

"Oh, we mustn't," I said.

"Are you certain? I really can be quiet."

Which would be worse: carrying on with Twomey under Mehitabel's roof, disregarding her clear intentions on that matter, or borrowing a dress from her chamber? Both would have horrible results if discovered. I would not only have to secret the dress away, but also sneak it back. And wash it, and dry it, all without her knowing. It seemed too formidable an undertaking.

But if she thought I were using a room of her boardinghouse to entertain men, why, she'd boot me out the door, and there I'd be shivering in my shimmy in the streets. And trying to make my way to my crib without attracting notice from the police or, even worse, attention from the wild, drunk packs of men who would surely see my *déshabillé* as an invitation.

"No," I said. "I can't do it to her. Please let me alone and I'll remedy the matter myself."

"Lass, how about this? I'll pay you for a throw in advance, and next time I come you can remember it."

"That's a help, sir, and I won't spurn it."

I took his coins and he gave me a quick buss and left. One throw. An entire evening and only earning six dollars. I would starve. I had to get out there somehow.

I dumped the washwater in the back garden and clodded the dress together and hid it behind a large rock. It was far too wet to carry up the stairs to my chamber, leaving a slimy trail like a slug. It was getting dark already and I wondered where Mehitabel was. I would have to ask her, I just would have to. Maybe she would pity me.

I went back into the kitchen and stood there forlorn, waiting. *She would never say yes. She never would. She wouldn't. She won't, Nora.*

I willed her to come home. I imagined her commonsense step at the front door, now her hand on the knob, and she treading down the hallway.

You have time to visit her room and make your own decision.

I hated myself, hated that horse finally. I went and opened the door to Mehitabel's chamber. There was still enough light to look without a lamp. It was simple and tidy, without much ornamentation. A dresser, a stuffed chair, a chest, and the bed she'd once shared with her husband.

I walked over to the chest and opened it. If there was a dress in there, it'd be one she didn't often wear, and would hopefully not notice the absence of.

How I had fallen!

There were two dresses, and I pulled out the one that was on the bottom. That way, if she opened the chest she wouldn't see it missing unless she looked closely. The fit would be tight in the bosom, but even if the buttons didn't close it would be enough to get me to Jackson Street. It was a black silk and braid gown with a severe cut. It might have been her mourning dress for her squabbling husband, but I couldn't stop to ponder the sacrilege of that.

I closed the chest and threw the dress on, working the buttons as I scurried back to the kitchen. I grabbed the money from Twomey and the nice stranger. I'd go out the back door and sneak through the yards. If I went on the street, she'd surely see me.

In the garden, I passed my wet snag of a dress and felt the tears spurting from the corners of my eyes. Whatever my sins, I'd never stolen before.

The dress was indeed tight, reprimanding me with each breath I tried to take without bursting the threads. I hoped the natural vapor that seeped from my skin did not eternally transfer to the textile.

I hastened block to block, sure my face was betraying my theft. The little street urchins in Boston had worn wrenched-up smiles that were a clear indication of their intent to pickpocket, and crooked men in alleyways spoke polite felicitations that did no work to mask their villainy.

I knew I meant to return the garment, but until I did so, my resolution would appear insubstantial to others. If Mehitabel were to denounce me to the police, not a one would believe me. A thieving whore.

I thought of how she'd defended me at the dinner table and embraced me in the kitchen afterward, and a sick vat of shame boiled up and over within me.

At Jackson Street it was a busy night, all the girls indoors, so I reproved myself for not slinging on Twomey's clothes. I went into my own crib and immediately disrobed and sniffed the dress.

Foolish girl! Even if every smidgen of my odor was cleaned from the dress, it would still be defiled. I groaned to think of Mehitabel wearing it. I folded it carefully and set it in the corner. The least I could do was ensure it was far from the bed where I did my foul craft.

Never forgetting for an instant that Mehitabel was likely back at home now, opening cupboards and rearranging items, perhaps even hunting for something in the chest at the foot of her bed, I entertained a gray-haired sailor, several men of general trade, my sweet friend Abe, who came with nutmeats and was puzzled by my distracted manner, another sailor, and then a miner so fresh from his diggings that he carefully leaned his pick up against my wall.

Not only was I obliged to feel guilt for my misdoings, I was also still beset with the more meaningful worry: perceiving the murderousness within the men's eyes, if it indeed existed. Nutbrown Nettie might have been some man's first assassination, but perhaps not his last.

And the men looked warily at me too. I could carry a disease, I could skim money from their pockets while they were thickly engaged in the act of fornication, or I could be crazy.

"*Bonne nuit,*" I said to all of them but Abe. "*Avons une pomme de terre merveilleuse.*"

Each man was dismissive as soon as he'd spent himself, barely grunting a farewell. It was because of my thievery, I knew it. They could feel what a low slut I was, scraping to keep life and limb together.

Not one of them was capable of killing me, but maybe one should.

After my seventh fella left and there wasn't one waiting in the dooryard, I curled up in my bed and let myself cry a wee bit. To not even have a dress! I was worse than the heathens of Africa who slapped a bit of lionskin on their parts on the days they were feeling particularly shy.

I believe five tears were shed, two from my left eye and three from my more emotional right orb, and then I sat up and wanted to slap myself and good. I wasn't paid to cry. Crying did not bring cash through the door; in fact, a reddened face might make a fella choose the next girl in line. So I stood, looked at my fine sign, adjusted it although it was already straight, and went to the window to see who I could entice.

I breathed relief that I had altered my mood, for here was the customer that could help me improve my *self:* the professor. I threw open the door.

"Just the one I was looking for," he greeted me, his boiled cotton shirt gleaming in the dark boulevard. "Might I have the pleasure of your company for a moment?"

"I'm happy to indulge you," I said and led him inside. "Oh! I mean, *je suis heureuse*…well…I em appy to eendulge you."

"Bah, don't bother with that," he said. "And excellent, you're dressed—or rather, quite undressed—already."

For him, I pulled back the covers, inviting him into the crisp sheets. On my small cot we twisted like acrobats in a dazzling circus display, and truthfully I felt like I was high above the air, with a blazing light trained on me and my body looping and presenting to the crowd. I didn't have to peer into his eyes to know that he was safe, that this was the most upstanding fella I'd ever had in my life. And he had sought me out!

Underneath him, I lifted my hips up, up, like the circus girl who creates a bridge out of her body, and pressed my hands backward next to my ears against the bed to support the weight, and this was the finishing of him.

"Gracious!" said he. "I do enjoy your machinations to bring our frolicking to a quick and pleasurable close."

"And I regret the close of it," I said, "for it was not work but pleasure."

"Ten dollars, was it? Well, I'll leave you twenty."

Under the sheets I clenched my hands. Such goodness, and at a time when it was absolutely required!

He buttoned up his trousers, handed me the money, and sat back down on the bed. "You really are quite beautiful, Nora. Your large gray eyes, the down-turn of your mouth: you look petulant and flirtatious at the same time."

"Jaw like a shovel," I said. I was just coaxing more out of him.

"Not at all! A strong jaw, certainly, but feminine and ovoid."

"Well, that is praise I will cherish." I had no idea what "ovoid" meant.

He leaned in to look at me closer and I almost shivered at the raw way he peered. It was almost like he was looking through the skin down to the plate of bone beneath.

"Might I draw you?" he asked.

"Draw *me*? I ain't nothing to draw," I blurted in surprise.

"Spoken like a true crib girl."

I winced. "I'm worth drawing," I said. "You just surprised me." I sat up and leaned against the wall, the sheets pulled up to my bosoms. I didn't mind him drawing my face, but he'd have to pay if he wanted to draw the rest.

He chuckled and pulled out a little pad of white paper from his pocket. I tried to look while he did it, but he held the paper such that the image he created was hidden from me. A scant five minutes later he held it out, and I twitched backward to see a mirror contained in such a tiny piece of paper.

But it wasn't a mirror; it was just a rendering so true to life that it was frightening. There was the dark shadow under my chin, the slightly uneven line of my hair across my brow. My eyes were my eyes, my earbobs dangled just so, and he had captured what my mother called the "devil's wings" of my eyebrows.

"What a marvel," I breathed. "And you did it with just a quick brushing of your pencil."

"I learned to do this rapidly," he said. "I draw for the newspapers now and then, for a little cash and the enjoyment, and I have only a few moments to capture the likeness before the constables need to clean up the scene."

"Clean up the scene? What do you draw?"

"I draw the hapless victims of crime. If you see a drawing in the newspaper of a person deceased unfairly before their God-given time, odds are you are seeing my handiwork. Of course, the papers only publish the portion of the drawing that doesn't display the gore."

I sucked my breath in. "You drew Nutbrown Nettie."

"Indeed. What an end."

"Is it terribly awful to...do that?"

"It puts a soberness in one's self."

"I saw a corpse once," I said. "She had been cut in the neck, like Nettie, and left in the spoiling pool of her own blood. I think on it now and then but, well, it's cruel to say…I try not to. Our lives are so short."

"The faces of the dead urge us to forget them. In their vacant eyes I see the wish that I should nourish my own vital spark and leave them to the worms."

"Oh, it's horrible. And sir, I'm sure every one of my type across this city is taking a special, second look at all her men today." I touched my ovoid chin distractedly.

"How can you continue? You must not feel safe."

"I can size up folks pretty well. I look at you, for instance, and don't even hesitate a second. Sometimes, though, a fella just gives you a sickened feeling in your gut, and you know that's one to avoid."

"It's too bad there is no description of the perpetrator, so you can back up your own fine-honed system of decision."

"If Nutbrown Nettie could talk, what she'd say…You know, I knew her. Or at least I met her, a bit before she went. I almost hit her, in fact, because she—"

I was interrupted by a rapping at the door. "Pleez to wait!" I yelled. "I am with ze lucky one before you."

"I'm sorry," came the voice through the door, which was, oddly, female.

"I ought to be off now, Nora, and I wouldn't want to deter your business dealings," he said.

"Oh, stay a bit, sir. That ain't no client out there; that's another one of me."

"Nevertheless, I'll be on my way." He tucked his drawing book in his pocket and kissed my shoulder.

"Please come again, any time, professor. I cherish your company."

"You'll see me again," he said, and let himself out.

A few moments after he left, while I lay there still luxuriating in the compliments the professor had paid, the feminine knock came again. I went to the door clad in the blanket from my bed and stared at the wisp of a child there.

"Miss Nora?" she asked.

"Yes?"

"Sorry for rapping whilst you was with someone. I listened at the door but didn't hear nothing."

"Well, you did just chase away my chance to learn how to culture myself for the parlor house, but what do you want?"

"I wanted to know if I might come inside and ask you a few things."

I frowned. "What variety of things?"

"Can I come inside to ask?"

I stepped aside and let her in. I saw as she passed that she was older than I'd first thought but still very petite and thin. She sat on the chair and I took the bed.

"My name's Charlotte. I ain't ever done this afore. My husband brung me here two days ago and bolted plain away. I ain't worked yet, stewing over my question, and I ain't got a cent."

Her fingers twisted in her lap. I'd never seen such frailty. They were like hands off a churchyard skeleton.

"I'll take you along with me and we'll get something to eat," I said. "I was just getting hungry myself and thinking of bobbing along to find some victuals."

"It ain't that," she said, raising her head and looking angry. "I ain't hungry. The day I beg a meal is the day I put Prussic acid atop it. Here's what I need from you, miss. I got to know how to stop the babies."

I thought of the small slab of cheese I hadn't finished the previous day. Shame I'd eaten the bread, but I reached under the cot and got the leavings. I made a point of biting off exactly half and giving her the rest. I looked toward the window as she tried not to wolf it down.

"How'd you keep from having them with your husband?" I asked.

"He ain't never touched me. Married a year ago and I thought my wedding night would be a real shake-up. But he drank himself to sleep and didn't even scoot over to my side. Truth is, I think he's a one that doesn't cotton to the ladies."

I raised my eyebrows.

"I don't want to say no more on that theme, but I seen some things in the smokehouse that he and our neighbor ain't never wanted no one to see," she said.

"You saw?"

"I saw through a crack in the wall. Trousers down by their boots. But I ain't gonna talk about that. I said that already." She scowled.

"Well, I use a tincture made of birthwort," I said. "A midwife mixes it up for me. I met one shortly after getting here, and thank goodness, for my trunk with all its birthwort bottles was stolen as soon as I arrived."

"Midwives will do that for harlots?"

"If they don't know what it's for. And sometimes if they do. *They* use it for women who are having a hard birth. It eases the babe right out. And if you're quickened with one you don't want, it'll expel it from you."

"But it keeps you from growing babies to even start with?"

"Ain't it a miracle? It also cures snakebite."

"When do you drink it?"

"Right after. A few swigs throughout the day. I'll give you a bottle to start you right."

"I ain't no charity case. I just wanted to know, not to get."

"Well, how are you going to work if you don't have it?"

"I thought I could make a pessary, I guess. Don't hold much stock in them. My sister used them and she's got a passel of children."

"I can't stand them things. What could be worse than pulling some drenched clog of herb out of yourself?"

"It's free anyway. Just gather some seaweed and soak it in vinegar. Ain't no precious bottle."

"Do whatever you like," I told her. "Take the bottle I'm offering you"—and I thrust it right into her hand—"or eat the seeds of Queen Anne's Lace, or willow bark or cypress root. But stay away from pennyroyal. It'll do the trick but clutch your stomach and pain you."

Plus, anything with the name "penny" in it I can't abide. If it's not at least a dollar, I'm not interested.

"What else do you know?" she said quiet. She was holding on to the bottle still, but I could see the fight in her face.

"Well, I've heard some daft things," I said with a smile. "Like jumping seven times after being with a man, making sure your heels hit your ass each time."

"How could that fail?" She almost laughed, but her skinny throat couldn't manage it.

"Or wearing an amulet or spitting in a frog's mouth. Some women close their eyes and hope that fate will do some kind looking in their stead. But I make sure none of these gents leave me with anything but some coins."

She nodded. "I don't know what I'd do if my stomach swelled with child."

"Birthwort will keep you barren."

"I'll pay you back for this, every cent," she said. "I ain't like that kind of folks that takes a charity and that's all. I'll pay you for it when I can."

"That's fine." I named her a price for the bottle, the amount I had paid for it. I wasn't going to take the five cents off her like the midwife suggested. "Which is your crib?" I asked.

"Four down. You know why I picked you to ask?"

"'Cause my crib's the first one in the line?"

"No. 'Cause two days now when I was watching things here, and trying to figure if this was how I could settle myself, I seen you take that simple man. And I seen you be friendly to him as he leaves."

"And you better be agreeable to him as well if he comes to you," I said. "That's Abe."

She nodded. "Because of that I thought, 'There's a kindhearted one. She'll tell me all she knows.'"

"Well, the other thing I know is that two prostitutes got their throats slit. Make sure you watch your men and decline them if they don't feel right."

"Here in this row?" she asked, her eyes instantly alarmed.

"No, elsewhere in the city. But that ain't no call to slacken your nerves. You be careful."

"How can I know?"

"You have to survey them, and trust your own feelings."

"Well, I married a bugger," she said bitterly, "so I'm clearly no fair judge of character."

"Well, a bugger won't be visiting you, now, will he? Just pay attention to a fella's demeanor. Watch him closely, and if he seems strange, never be afeared to say you're done for the evening and that he should move on."

She was clearly scared, which was a good thing. "All right," she said quietly. "I'll look them over like buying a slab of meat, checking for the rot."

"That's good."

"Well, I thank you for this," she held up the bottle of birthwort. "And I'll be paying you back for it, never fear. Just as soon as I can."

After she left I counted my money. With the professor's grand tip, Twomey's advance payment, the assistance from the gentleman who escorted me out of the street after I'd nearly been trampled, and what I'd earned, there was enough to visit a dressmaker in the morning and a little besides.

I put on Mehitabel's fated dress and walked to Pacific Street, where there was a late-night grocer, and bought a chicken, potatoes, apples, brown bread, and a bottle of ale. When I returned, I counted four shacks down, dropped the bundle so it made a noise, and scampered back to my crib before Charlotte could see me.

I had forgotten to tell her about condoms, but who can afford them anyway? I personally can barely stand the thought of sheep intestines being snaggled right in there, but if a gent pays extra—for they're mightily expensive—he can bear down on me with nary a worry. I always have to suppress a smile when I see a fella outfit himself that way, tying the little ribbon at the top like a schoolgirl with her apron.

I realized Charlotte hadn't asked me about what to do with men. If her husband never touched her, odds were she had never known a man that way before. I winced thinking how her first maneuver might go. But she'd be too proud to ask; it had been hard enough, I saw, for her to ask me something so terribly important as how to keep her womb empty. The mechanics of how to please a gent were probably lower on her list.

I was sure regular women were also curious over what women of my ilk do with men, if we knew special things they didn't. And we did. Why, a regular woman couldn't even let her ankle show on the street, and there we were disrobed before God and San Francisco. We were more lax with what we let ourselves do and say. Mehitabel told me about an entire set of rules over ways to sit correctly, hold a fan, let a fella know his remark was crude. And none of that had anything to do with us soiled doves. We were lawless when we were standing and even more so on our backs.

This Victoria lady, who sat on the throne over across the sea, set the standards everyone followed for proper social intercourse. Whose vile idea was that? Seems to me in Massachusetts we had learned about how only eighty years ago we hated the Brits and chased them out with buckshot and bayonets.

One time a gent with an accent like he'd stuck his nose into his throat came to me for a throw, and I tossed on my cloak like I was all off in a hurry to be elsewhere. That was one of the few times I ever cut a fella loose. It wasn't like I'm so deeply patriotic, but my grandmother did tell me her mother was raped by one of them lads in redcoat soon after she arrived here from Ireland. For her honor, I wouldn't let any of 'em touch these Simms goods.

Chapter 9

After dropping off the food for Charlotte, I went to the window, displaying my wares for the rest of the evening's indulgence. I noticed a figure come out from the shadows behind a parked hack and without hesitation move straight to my door.

He didn't knock but plunged right in.

He made the contents of my stomach curdle, just as I'd told the professor. Pressing my hand against the cold glass of the window, I understood this was the time to ask him to withdraw.

"Sir," I began.

"You're a good-looking one," he said in a strong German accent. "I have seen you in the window and waited until that other one was finished with you. You left and put food at some other whore's door, and I waited then too." He had a mole at the top of his left cheek. His hat was of old, slouchy felt.

"You were outside all that time?" I didn't even pretend to be French, I was so unnerved.

"Didn't you feel the eyes burning on you from the window?" He pronounced window with a V. He smiled slowly, showing thick teeth crowded together like sheep huddled at killing time.

I jerked my head around to look from his perspective at the bed hulking in the small room. He laughed. "I have scared you, now, haven't I? You don't like to think about somebody watching you when you don't even know it."

"Fine with me," I said, trying to sound airy. "That way you know you'll get your money's worth. But we'll have to do that evaluation later. I've got some drudgeries to perform, and so I'll have to ask you to leave. I'm off myself into the night, for tasks such as can't be put off."

Next time I'd have the door locked and do my negotiating before I opened it.

"Oh no, Liesl. You didn't like that thought at all. You feel like my eyes are seeing every little bit of you."

"It ain't Liesl. It's Nora." I nodded my head to the sign, without letting my eyes leave his face.

"For me, you will be Liesl."

"I don't want to be no Liesl."

"You are under my spell now, little girl. You vill do the things I say, and you vill be glad to do them." He was biting his lip so hard I saw blood rise from a minute gash.

Oh, dogs that admire wolves. It was time to back away.

"I don't work that way, mister. In fact, I think my evening's over. One of the other girls in the row can help you out." I walked backward to the door. I wanted him to follow, but wouldn't turn my back on him.

"You are scared of me."

I tried to laugh.

"Was that strangled bit of noise supposed to serve as a laugh?" he asked. "Of what are you scared?"

"Not a thing," I whispered. "I just want you to go."

"You are acting timid as a rabbit when the farmer waits with his hoe. Come on back. I want to talk some more."

"Time to go." My voice was soft as mice steps behind the wall.

"Come now, Liesl. You have got to help me out with my problem here." He opened up his trousers and pointed to the "problem."

I considered what to do. I could escape the crib, but that might make him more angry. But at least there'd be other girls around to protect me.

What a joke! I thought to myself. No one would intervene and help me. Hell, that girl wouldn't even give me back my shirtwaist; who'd leap on this man's back to stop him? Every one of the girls in this row would sit on her cot gnawing her nails at the sound of my screams while I was murdered in the street.

"Take your trousers all the way off," I said. I was thinking if he had a knife in his pocket I'd at least get it away from his hands.

"Since you have asked so sweetly." He flashed the yellow smile at me again and did as I asked. Maybe I could talk my way through this ordeal. Oftentimes the men just wanted a woman to reverse the roles, to order him about.

"Now throw them here," I commanded. I was regaining my voice again, getting louder.

"No, Liesl, you come to get them." He held them up in front of him.

"Shake them first."

"Shake?" He frowned, perplexed. He shook them in his arms and looked like a palsied wife working with the laundry.

"No. Upside down."

"Oh, I am understanding what you wish. You want that the contents of my trousers should fall out. What might you think I have in there, little one?"

I said nothing, just motioned that he should do it.

A knife hit the floor. He laughed.

"Are you thinking about the same thing I'm thinking of, Liesl? That girl in the newspaper there, who had her face drawn up so pretty?"

I was still by the door but frozen in my steps.

"She was a beauty, but someone cut her up and ruined what she had. This must be making all of you whores frightened."

He knelt down and picked up the knife. I tried to open my mouth to scream but I was truly stuck.

"It gave me a good idea, that article did," he said.

And in a second he had jumped across the space between us and grabbed my arm. He yanked me onto the bed and pressed one hand against my mouth. The other pulled up my skirts and then held the knife to my throat.

"I am pleased you had me take the trousers off. I am ready to go, Liesl, and there is nothing but air between us."

I wanted to close my eyes but couldn't. I wondered if Nettie had seen her own blood fly from her neck. Had it happened that fast? Or was it a slow slitting that had her gurgling in her own blood?

He entered me and began thrusting as hard as he could. "Do you like that?" he grunted. "You are such a whore I cannot even hurt you. Too wide open. Too many years slutting around."

I'd had hard before, but this was bad. The tears welled in my eyes and he laughed at the sight. "I spoke too quickly, Liesl! I guess you are a little tighter down there than I thought."

I kept trying to burrow my head into the pillow beneath me, to get some distance between my neck and the knife, but he kept a steady pressure.

When he had his finishing, seizing and bucking, I pleaded with my eyes, for I couldn't speak with his hand on my mouth. I knew it was now, the knife's moment was now. How cruel for my mother's eyes in heaven to look down at me in this last sordid circumstance, killed by a man I'd fucked for money, with a stolen dress folded in the corner. I'd have to beg her forgiveness up there. If I was allowed up there.

Oh sweet Jesus, I never meant this for myself. I only wanted to be good.

"What do you think, little Liesl?" he asked.

I sobbed.

"Will you be the next prostitute to appear in the paper?"

He bent his face to mine and I almost feared he would bite me with those thick teeth. "Who will draw your picture? Are you not embarrassed to think of some man sitting at the foot of the bed drawing you, with your blood

everywhere and your female apparatus on display?" He finally lifted his hand, and I dragged in a huge gust of air.

"Go on ahead," I whispered. "But stop talking about it."

"Shall I bring to you some carrots, and a little cabbage to nibble on, little Liesl rabbit?"

Why was he calling me that? Why?

"You did not answer, little rabbit."

"I don't want carrots," I whispered, appalled that my last words would be so absurd.

"So then, you just wish for the knife?" He pressed it in a little farther and I thought it might be drawing blood already.

"Who's Liesl?" I asked wildly.

"She is bride-to-be who did not wait for me to come home across the sea. She married the son of the biergartener and told so in a letter."

"She's a bitch," I said. I don't know what I was thinking, I just thought I should agree with him, whatever he said, be sympathetic. Somehow. Anything.

"That is right, rabbit. And now that you know who Liesl is, it is time for you to be saying good-bye."

My body slackened and I almost fainted. So this was really how it was to end with me. Far from home. Finally, I was able to close my eyes.

Varying shades of blackness, a blessed void. The sound of our own ragged breaths. The thin blade tipping its steel edge at my throat. I kept my eyes closed and waited like a cornered animal.

And I didn't open them when he rolled off of me, nor when I heard him fumbling back into his trousers.

I waited what must have been hours before I finally opened them.

"Girls! Girls!" I yelled in the middle of our row, naked as shattered Eve but for the blanket I pulled about me. If I was destroying any idea of theirs that I was French by my plain shouting, I couldn't care less. "Come out, all of you. We're in trouble and we've got to talk. There's a man killing prostitutes!"

"We all know that, you dumb feck," came the reply from one of the cribs.

"But he was here tonight! He—he almost killed me. Let me tell you what he looks like so you won't let him in."

A few women came out, holding candles, with scared faces. The small group of us stood in our tiny circles of light, the black night all around us.

"Is this all of you?" I shouted. "Are you daft? I can tell you his looks, to keep yourselves safe."

"If it's him, how come you're still alive?" shouted the same voice.

"I don't know. He changed his mind somehow. But he was dangerous and it's only by a slight shiver of fate's shoulders that I'm here talking to you now." More women were now trickling out into the street.

"What does he look like?" ventured Charlotte. She was among the ones assembled to listen to me.

"His hair is brown and his teeth are very yellow and close together. There's too many teeth in his mouth, they're all cramped together. He's yay high," I gestured. "He has a mustache but no other facial hair. There's a mole on his left cheek, and he's German. Speaks with a thick accent. He called me Liesl; she's a woman back there who didn't wait for him."

"That's all?" said one of them.

"That's a good report, you dolt," said another to me. "German with a mole and yellow teeth. If a man here ain't a Fritz or a Mick, what is he? And which of our fine men *don't* have yellow teeth?"

"It's something to start with," I said. "At least. You can relax with the blond men and the dark men. But the Germans with brown hair—please be careful."

"What did he do to you?"

"He teased me grievously. He took pleasure in frightening me, called me a scared little rabbit. I say, that part was as bad as feeling the knife at my neck." I rubbed my throat vigorously while the other girls tried to stare beneath my hand.

"When did he pull the knife?"

"He had a knife in his pocket and he held it to me the whole time he used me."

"Oh, poor Nora," said Charlotte. She alone came forward to comfort me. She put her thin arms around my shoulders.

"When'd he leave?" asked one of the girls, looking around like he'd grab her next.

"I couldn't say. I lay there like a slab of stone until I mustered enough vim to start up again. Now, let me think. We should all…Let's see. We should have a plan. First of all, we should all stand at the door, and if you see a brown-haired one approaching, lock it. Don't ever wait at the window or farther inside."

They nodded.

"And if'n we hear a girl screaming, we should all pledge to come to her side. I know in our trade it's general to not hear the things we don't want to hear, and to keep our own counsel. But if there's a man wanting us ripped open—girls, we have to help each other!"

"I would have in any case," said Charlotte. "What kind of girls don't help each other?"

The other ones shifted uncomfortably.

"Are we promising?" I asked.

They all nodded.

"And those of you still holed up in your shacks, do you promise?" I shouted.

"Quiet yourself!" came a male voice. "I didn't pay to hear all this racket!"

But above or underneath him came the female voice: "I promise!"

And it was echoed down the line.

"Now, this is for true, girls. If you hear someone calling out, you can't forget and lose your courage. We'll all have to move."

"For true," said Charlotte.

I slept that night in my crib for the first time, not able to risk going home in Mehitabel's dress. I locked the front door and pulled the chair in front of it besides.

All night, through the thin plank walls I heard the jostlings and shakings of the girls who were still working, who charged less than me and therefore had to work longer, or were less pretty and took the men whenever they agreed to settle for them. It was restless sleep and I don't believe I dreamed.

I thought, *This would have been my life all along if I hadn't found the respite of Mehitabel's boardinghouse.* It was her dignity that allowed me, somewhat, to escape my own fate. A prostitute in a house that doesn't brook prostitution is somewhat salvaged.

At first light I rose and unfolded her dress again. It felt worse to wear this time, for I was in no hurry and could savor the extreme soreness of my swindling. I took the compressed breaths the dress required, moved the chair from the door, and stepped out into a foggy San Francisco morning.

The line was finally silent. Everyone asleep, and all the gentlemen satisfied. I moved along the cold dirt as quietly as I could, hoping the women had been paid with money and not bloodshed.

I stopped at three different dressmakers until I found one that would accept the payment I could offer. He had some odd rags, leftovers from a nearly finished bolt, and so I chose an ugly, dingy pink plaid, the best of the lot. He measured me and muttered things like "No special tucks for that price" and "It won't be pretty but it'll do to cover you."

He wanted me to return in the early evening for it, but I insisted he sew it while I waited. His glance moved to other fabrics on the shelf, and I saw he wanted to do other ladies' dresses first, but I said, "I'm your first customer walking through this door today, and you'll appease me first."

He grumbled and indeed sewed a monstrously plain dress, but it was enough to cover me and let me inhale as fulsomely as I wished, so that was a task accomplished. He had some plain brown paper that other bolts had arrived in, and I asked him for a length. He charged me two cents, and I used it to wrap up Mehitabel's dress.

I left, feeling poor and slovenly in my distressing shade of pink, and went to complete my next task. I knew it would do no good, but I wanted to make a report at the police station. If I could help that German brute pay for his crimes, I would gladly usher him to the tribunal.

So I sat down with an officer and described the man's appearance, voice and accent, and what he had done to me. The policeman, who wore a quaint cap and seemed to be taking his job quite seriously even though he was only a volunteer, listened quite intensely and shook his head in sympathy as I told the more harrowing parts of my story. He wrote down all that I said, and even had me sign at the bottom of his report.

"This will go on file, miss. And I hope he'll be of no trouble to you or your kind again."

I stopped in the middle of standing up and hovered in a strange half-crouch. "You do?"

"Of course."

He had nice hazel eyes, and teamed them with a genuine smile. "I'm sorry you had such a deplorable experience, miss. It isn't right. And we'll do all we can to stop him."

I wanted to invite him to come see me at Jackson Street, and without pay; he was so rare with his sweet nature. But I thought maybe he didn't consort with my kind. Maybe that's why he was so nice; he didn't know how mean and small our lives were. I wouldn't want to be the one to corrupt him. It occurred to me that I was just a criminal reporting a larger crime; the evidence of my theft sat there in my lap as we spoke.

I bustled out before I could become emotional, and walked the streets with vigor to get my mind on other topics. Kindness is sometimes as hard to bear as cruelty.

Chapter 10

I had no sooner stepped inside the boardinghouse front door than Mehitabel raced in from the kitchen.

"Good morning!" said she, her eyes intense like a crow watching the farmer. She knew. Or did she?

"Good morning," I said.

"What kept you away all night?"

"It was a cold night and I already had a fair fire going in my stove. I decided to just stay," I said.

"I see. And you're in a new dress."

"Yes," I laughed uneasily. "I was finally able to manage the purchase."

"Brilliant coloring and needlework," she said.

"Oh, it's plain as a tree stump. Don't spare my feelings."

"So now you have two dresses," she said. "You are replenishing the goods of your stolen trunk."

Was it my guilty imagination that she emphasized the word "stolen"?

"No," I said. "My other dress is destroyed."

"In what manner?"

She *must* know. Why else keep me in the front hall asking question upon question? While my mouth mechanically answered her with a truth, I was already using the other side of my mind to concoct a future lie. "Muddied in the street, and torn as well. I tried to wash it to no avail. We'll burn it in the stove and its last usefulness will be as kindling."

"Is that why it's clumped in the backyard?"

"Yes, of course. I threw it out there for frustration," I said, shaken to think she had found it.

"It's odd to think that, as it appeared to be hidden."

Lucifer's cloven hoof! She knew, *she knew*. I worked faster to get my lie ready. "Well, I was frustrated and threw it, then kicked it into a sort of shape behind a rock back there, so it wouldn't bother your eye."

"You mean you didn't want me to think it messy?"

"That's right. You keep such a tidy household, I knew a garment tossed in the yard would offend."

"I see." But what she *really* saw was straight through my biters and chompers to my lying little tongue.

"But goodness, I have to count my blessings that I had this dress made yesterday before that one was ruined." I shifted the brown-wrapped bundle that was her dress from one arm to the other. The first segment of the falsehood had been told.

"You had the one you're wearing made yesterday."

"Yes. And wouldn't you know how the world works against people who try? As I was walking home yesterday, wearing this one, excited to think I now had two dresses, a wild horse came by as I crossed the street and in sheer terror I flung out the package I was holding, which was my old gray dress, and it landed under his hooves and he smashed it for dear life in the mud, and his shoes must have been new with sharp edges for they dug and tore at the fabric."

Mehitabel nodded but her face remained puzzled. "I held up the dress and it did look like a horse trampled it into the earth, now that you say it."

"Yes." The only thing remaining was: had she looked through her own wardrobe?

"Nora, I still require an explanation on one matter."

"Require? You sound like a schoolmarm."

"I knew that was your only dress, Nora. And when I saw it in the backyard, well, instantly I thought the worst. That something had happened to you and you'd been spirited away by some dangerous man."

I hung my head.

"But then since it was only dirty and not bloody...I began to reason with myself about other states of affairs. And, of course, I wondered what you were wearing. And so I looked," her voice faltered, "in my own room, and counted one gown missing." She looked at me miserably. "Did you wear my gown because yours was ruined?"

I straightened my back to launch into the next half of the lie. I would have to sound surprised and hurt. "Wear your gown? *Without asking you?*"

"Well, if yours was ruined you had no other recourse."

"If mine was ruined I would wait naked until I had your permission. But I *had* a dress to wear. And there's a reason yours is missing, but first I want to express my horror and indignation that you would suspect me of such a deed." It was necessary to say this.

"Oh, Nora, I'm so sorry!" Her face blushed red as a chokeberry and tears even appeared in her eyes. I nearly doubled over in shame. "I knew it couldn't be true, I was certain in my heart that there was an explanation, but without seeing you here in this pink dress, oh Nora, how I've suffered these last hours. Please don't think ill of me. But honestly, this is what I saw: your only dress in ruins, and one of mine missing. I surely thought—"

"Don't cry, Mehitabel," I dropped the package and gave her a Judas embrace. "Oh, now I'm after crying too! I don't blame you for thinking that; anyone would make that association." The two of us sobbed like sisters, me prickingly aware that I hadn't even delivered the full lie yet, and she had already believed the whole of it.

"Do you want to know why I have your dress, even if it means a lovely surprise shall be spoiled?" I asked while I wiped my cheeks dry.

"I do, Nora, I do!"

"Well, after I went to have my dress made, I thought of you and how you've been so kind, and Christmas is but weeks away, and I thought to have one made for you too. So I carried away this one," I knelt to the floor and picked up the package, then peeled away the ribbon and paper to show her her own gown, "and took it to the tailor for measuring and copying."

"Oh, I'm so shamed, I'm so shamed," she cried and actually sank to the floor. "How I hated thinking badly of you! I hated every second of it!" She was crying so vehemently that she was now gulping for air and breathing in a crazy, hitched disrhythm. "I'm so sorry, sweeting. How foul to think you stole my gown while you were preparing me such a kindness!"

I was like to grab a knife from the kitchen and slit my own throat. This woman was worth a hundred of me. How dare I? How *dare* I?

My other impulse was to dash to my room and be free of this scene, but I knew that was unforgivable. So I crouched down and gentled her. "Mehitabel, we barely know each other. It is not so unforeseen that a girl in this rough town might steal from you when she herself has no frock to wear. I'm not hurt and I won't brood over this, I promise you. It is all a mix-up and we'll laugh about it tomorrow."

"I shall never laugh at thinking badly of you, Nora," she spurted in her hampered voice.

"Well, I'll laugh enough for the both of us. Now then, let's rise, and won't you brew us some tea to be friendly again? I'll place your dress back in the chest and we'll be done with this interlude."

While she fetched water in the kettle, I went into her room and banged my fist against my temple as hard as I possibly could. It did make me reel, which

I welcomed. I performed the hand-flog a second time, then opened the chest and put the damned dress back in. I had never washed it, and I prayed the scant time I had worn it would not have left some essence of me behind.

"It smells musty in there," I told her as I came out into the kitchen. "My mother used to put cloves in our linens."

"That's a grand idea," she said. I went to the cupboard, shook a few cloves out of a glass jar, and tied them into a napkin to make a pomander. Then I stepped back into her room and tossed it into the chest. I hoped it would cover the stench, the absolutely overwhelming rank, fetid odor that was making me gag: the stench of my deception.

Chapter 11

I contrived over the next few weeks to forgive myself for abusing Mehitabel so. I was back in money trouble again, since I would have to deliver the dress I'd promised. I'd have the tailor fit it to my size and just deduct a few inches in the bosom. If it didn't fit correctly, I could tell Mehitabel he was a defective tailor and my own drab pink gown wasn't comfortable either.

Luckily, the professor visited quite frequently during those weeks, always paying far higher than my asking price. And daily Abe always tried to get me to take the contents of his pocket, more than the six dollars, but I refused him, for I knew he was offering something he shouldn't.

Besides the worry of making brass and enduring the pained look I saw on Mehitabel's face each time we conversed, there was still that murderous villain all us soiled doves had to scout for. Fear is something my kind lives with anyway. I passed the December nights at the door, hands poised ready to close it, with the wind chilling my cheeks.

"What's with all of you?" asked one fella. "Every single harlot in this city has a look in her eye like she thinks I'm going to slice her open ear to ear."

"Ev you not seen ze newspapers?" I asked in my false accent.

"So one girl was killed. It was probably someone she owed money to, or made jealous some way."

"I don't zink so," I said. "I know ze murderer and I zink he chooses randomly."

"Well, if you know him, why are you looking at *me* like I'm him?"

"It ees hard to trust men when zair ees one like that. If ze world produced one, why not more?"

"Fair enough. But you got to tell the girls around here to smile at a man for once. It's taking all the fun out of whoring."

The other thing pumping the amusement away was the blasted cold weather. I'd heard California had naught but fair weather and orchards, but here by the

95

bay a wind rose at night and howled through the chinks in the crib walls. The trade became a necessity to warm my body: without a man's smoky furnace heat, I shivered. When I beckoned in customers, I was truly fervid.

The little woodstove was proving to be of great necessity. Abe always brought wood and stoked the fire before he put out his tentative hand to caress me. One evening, he brought a kettle and some tea. We drank with our hands cupping the hot mugs and our faces growing rosy from the steam. We got to talking and drinking and never even did the feat he'd come for. A knock at the door reminded me that there were others I needed to tend to.

"Gracious, Abe, time's a-flying. I ought to set you loose so I can make some money here tonight. No charge since we didn't bounce the bed."

"I'll pay anyway," he said.

"No, honestly, it's all right. You got me warm on a cold night and that's all I can ask."

I led him to the door and opened it. "Plees just to wait a minute, sir," I said without bothering to look outside. "Let me only to send zis one on his way."

"Certainly," came the reply.

I gave Abe a peck on his cheek. "Good night, Abe. You have your lantern?"

"Do I? My, it's dark."

"Mind you keep it tight. It's like pitch out there."

"I will, Nora. Thank you for such an evening as I'll think on 'til I slumber."

"Same to you. Night, now."

As he left, he gave a glare to the next customer, who I saw with delight was none other than the professor.

"Hello, sir! What a pleasure to see you again, professor," I said.

As he entered, he bowed to me but wore a scowl.

"Good lord, Nora, what was that?" he asked.

"Don't you mean 'who'?"

"I'm not certain. Was that human?"

"That's Abe," I said, flushing. "He's one of my most frequent men."

"I shudder to think of you in his arms. He seems brutish."

"He's got a feather's manner of comportment. I think you'd be more likely to hurt me, professor, than him!"

"I've noticed, however, Nora, that persons of such limited mental capacity often lack the typical measure of empathy most of us are guaranteed."

"Meaning?"

"Meaning he might not realize he is hurting you. You would make the grimace and exclamation that would make most people cease whatever form of aggression is wounding you, but it would not register with him that you were in pain."

"That's a whole lot of words to talk about something that will never happen," I remarked.

"You seem quite confident."

"The only person I need to worry about is that German beast who's slitting girls open," I said.

"Pardon? Who?"

"Well, you know about Nutbrown Nettie. The man what did it is still loose, and I actually had the misfortune to meet him, sir. It was a hard scene, but I didn't want to bother you with the knowing of it."

He looked absolutely alarmed. "What happened?"

"I almost became one of your drawings in the newspaper. He pinned me down and put the knife to my throat and I closed my eyes, thinking my next sight would be either Satan in horns or God with a halo."

"And you say he's *German*?"

"Yes. Thick accent. A mole on his cheek. I told the police all about him. He was addled in the head, and kept calling me some other girl's name."

"German. How remarkable."

"Why is that, sir? Do you find Germans not so generally violent?"

"Why, I heard the police talking about the suspect, and I didn't recall they thought he was…" His voice trailed off.

"Well, bless their batons! How would they be able to tell if the suspect was German or Swedish or African or anything, unless if he left his native flag at the scene or some letter in his own language?"

"Quite true, Nora, quite true. Now, I beg your forgiveness for seeming slap-dash but I did come to see you for a particular reason."

"Quite true, professor, quite true," I parroted him.

He smiled and gently pushed me toward the bed, where he plowed through me as briskly as any of the men who don't have fine gold watches.

"Do you think I could be a parlor house girl?" I asked afterward.

"To my way of thinking, you are far surpassing the skills of a parlor house girl," he said gallantly.

Chapter 12

I spent Christmas Day with Abe. A huge fire had cut through the city, and the stench was awful, so he rented a trap and brought us all the way out to the other side of San Francisco, where you stand and see all the endless ocean that don't stop 'til you get to China or somewheres.

It was a whole other land. Not a sign of city or people. Just long beach grass and the gulls sallying forth on the chill wind.

"How 'bout here?" asked Abe.

I sat down, but the tufts of grass were rankling my behind. "You be on the bottom, sir," I suggested.

We tried for a bit, but I couldn't ignore the pained look on his face. "You eejit," I said. "Down we go to the sand." As soon as the words were out my mouth, I wished them back in, holding court with my tongue. Plenty of cads on the street call him idiot; he don't need it from a woman of ill fame.

But he took it in the teasing manner I intended it, and carried me like a threshold bride down to the beach.

"It's purdy without no people," he said.

We were like Adam and Eve, except our garden wasn't too lush and the only snake there was controlled by Abe. This time I let him dress down to his skin and myself as well, all clocks stopped for Christmas Day and not a soul waiting for seconds or thirds. We got sand *everywhere*, and not just little bothersome grains either. I thought if we shook ourselves down we could make our own neat beach back on Jackson Street and charge admission.

The sand didn't squeak like that old crib cot, and the firmness supported me, kept me closer to the root of evil. Weren't long until my breath was gasping like the waves heaving up on the beach, and the salt wind battering my skin let me prickle into that feeling: *le petit mort*.

"The little death" is how that translates. If it's a death, I guess I'll keep dying until they actually bury me.

Afterward, I pulled a hairbrush from my reticule and Abe raked the sand from my hair, slow and calm-like.

"You do this with other fellas," he said.

"No one's ever stroked these locks but my mother," I said.

"No, t'other thing," he said. "You lie down with men."

"That's what I do," I said. I decided to be gay about it. "Ain't you glad I bring all that joy and excitement to the men of this city?"

"I wisht you were only for me."

I took the brush from his hands and made a swift braid, sweeping my hair up with pins I'd piled in the sand. "Are you trying to make a courtesan of me, darling? I don't know whether livery boys are allowed to have courtesans."

"Ain't no reason we can't hitch it up."

I laughed and the wind took the sound and dashed it against the rocks. Here 'twas, yet another marriage proposal. And he no better than the other lacklusters who offered it before. "Abe, what do they pay you at the stables?"

"I've got enough to keep you like you want."

"And where will we live, in a flophouse with a hundred other men?"

"You got a place, dontchew?"

Which meant that he had sought me out some late, late evening after he'd already visited once and saw no lamp at the crib.

"I can't bring you there. That's for single working women." Mother of the infant born today, why am I always fibbing? I was the only female in the boardinghouse besides Mehitabel, and I was certain she had no prohibition against married couples.

"I'll build something. I know a fella what's got a hammer. Maybe right here, way away from ever'body, we can make a little house and eat clams. You can look for them clams during the day while I'm a-working."

"I'd die of loneliness out here!"

"With all them birds to keep you company?"

I let a little silence set between us so he'd start to understand this weren't going how he wanted. Then I pressed a kiss on his shoulder and said, "Abe, I've already got me a plan. I want to be a parlor girl. Them girls make money like those men who was at the river first to pick up the hunks of gold big as carp."

"What's that?"

"A parlor girl?"

"Yep."

"It's a lady who does what I do, just fancier. And not in no single tiny hovel of a room. No, thank you, these girls live in palaces with velvet sofas and staircases and a madam to take care of them."

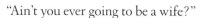

"Ain't you ever going to be a wife?"

For some reason, I had a sudden picture in my mind of that watch-fobby professor. "I don't know," I said.

"I can give you all the purty things you want, them sofas and stairs and all. I got the cash. And you know...you know I need a little something too."

I propped my feet on his shoulders, still naked as a heathen. "This?"

"Well, yeah," he grinned. "But also someone to...you know."

"What?"

"You know."

"I don't know. What?"

"Think for me."

Course, I don't have to tell you how I slathered him with kisses and let him know what a fine instrument his brain was. Honest, he's smarter than some of them that are set on regular speed. I got him thinking he was a Pythagoras or Socrates, and then we walked down the beach. After only ten steps we returned to put on our clothes, teeth already clacking from the wind. Then we set out again, making firm prints with our bare feet.

"Abe, how much cash *do* you have?" I asked idly. And when I say idly, I really mean with bright, intent eyes, like King Midas toting up the day's take.

"Enough for sofas and steps," he said stubbornly.

Hmph. He'd given up on gold panning just like every other no-account. Maybe he had a purse laid by, but it certainly weren't nothing like the contents of my long-lost steamer trunk.

We saw a fowl the likes of which I never could have imagined. He stood on the beach as tall as my hips, his beak drooping. I hid behind Abe as we walked up to it.

"Careful!" I hissed. "He could knock us down and eat our eyes afore we have a chance to peep an alarm!"

Abe weren't afraid. He was gentle, like he was with them flash-eyed stallions who'd take the bit from only him. "He's thinking the same thing of us," he smiled over his shoulder at me.

"Tits of Jezebel, I wouldn't never eat no eyeballs!"

"Be quiet," he said, "or he'll startle." But my voice had already made this bird spread its mammoth wings and wheel off on them, slower and more graceful than sparrow or dove. I felt again like it was the Garden of Eden, like this was some magic beast that stayed when we got pushed out. Larger than a kite and dark as a coal hod. I wished I could flap down the sky like that.

"Don't you like beast and fowl?" asked Abe. I thought of the bull and bear fight, and how Abe would probably unload a tear or two for the fate of the bear snapped from his tree to fight a creature he didn't recognize.

"I do," I said. "Anything that can't talk, I want to help it out."

"I don't talk so well," he said. "I'm probably no brighter than that there bird."

"You're smart as a goat," I said. "Them can make a living off of tin cans and clotheslines."

"So you'll help me?"

"I'll lend the famed assistance of a harlot's hand," said I. "Not too clean and not completely mine, but I'll stretch it your way."

We walked with the sea tossing surf across our toes and watched a crab amble, pincers clicking, into the shadow we cast. It got so the waves spilling their spray were timed to the breaths we took, the pauses in our talk. Then we turned around and made our way back, seeing the bundle of our belongings as miniature on that vast beach as smoky San Francisco must be in the California landscape.

Abe had brought food tied in a cloth: veal, biscuits, and a mutton elbow. I ate until he started plucking things off my lap, knowing a man's appetite is more than a woman's.

"Merry Christmas," I said to him, handing over a bundle tied with a silk ribbon. Inside was a boiled cotton shirt. I had brought a man Abe's size to the tailor and had the shirt fitted to him; his dummying work was paid, of course, with fair trade. The cotton and the tailoring, sure enough, were expensive, as was the dress I had yet to present to Mehitabel. After buying my pink dress, I had set by for the holiday, just like she had saved sugar for the plum butter at the disastrous dinner party.

Abe immediately put the shirt on, grinning foolishly. "It's so soft and so fancy," he said. "Makes me feel like a lawman or a banker."

"You look handsome," I said. "You're too good for homespun."

I took the brush he'd been using on me and combed his locks into some sort of order. If I squinted at him, I could almost pretend he *was* a man from an office. I undid the button closest to his heart and pressed a kiss there, then buttoned it back up.

"I ain't ever taking it off," he vowed.

"We'd sure appreciate it if you'd abide by washday rules," I said. "Once a week at least."

"You're hard on a man," he said.

"And of course here I give it to you in this most hazardous of spots," I agreed, smiling in the blaze of sunshine that had just pushed aside a cloud to be the sky's victor. "You'll get sand on it and ruin it afore you even worn it an hour. Now, what'd you get me?"

His smile sorta left and he pouted like a little boy. Men like Abe don't control their emotions that good. "You don't want it but you oughta take it anyway," he said. Presented in the middle of his large mitt was a delicate diamond ring.

I loved that little ring, with its diamond pegged in the middle of the gold circlet. I picked it up and slid it real easy onto my ring finger. Fit like it were fashioned for me only. I twisted my hand here and there and let the gem catch the light. This was no paste diamond; it was something a rajah woulda loved to get his brown paws on.

I glanced over at Abe, who had started smiling when I slipped it on. He was a Roman candle between the sheets and I held infinite affection for him, but I'd be casting my dreams into the surf if I accepted his proposal.

"Where'd you ever get it?" I asked.

"It was my mother's."

"She's not living?"

He shook his head. "It was passed to my brother, Caleb. He was oldest. And he had a gal he thought he'd marry. With all the gold, he was gonna go back and ask her."

I put my head in his lap and listened to the waves spraying up a mist onto us. Abe cried about Caleb, sniffling elegantly in his new formal shirt.

"How old was Caleb?"

"One and twenty."

"And you're how old?"

"Nineteen. He was my only living kin."

"Did he go fast or slow?"

"Slow. His head was so hot, I'd put a cold cloth on it and next time I checked it'd be like I took it from the oven."

"Did you say good-bye to him?"

"I said it but his fever was so bad he never heared it. Ever'body told me not to touch him and just leave him be, but I fed him and took care of his natural things."

"And you never got sick yourself?"

"No."

"I'm glad of that," I said. "Who else would be my friend in this huge city?" I sat up and used my sleeve to catch his crying.

"Caleb was smart," said Abe. "And he had a girl what would marry him. I shoulda been the one that fell with the fever."

"Ain't for you to decide the divine plan. You're on this earth for a reason."

He nodded. "You gonna keep wearing the ring?"

I looked down at it and bit my lip. Who knew what that genteel mother thought, glancing down from Heaven at the ring that sat on her finger for all those years, now worn by a six-dollar tart that couldn't rid herself of "ain't"?

"This is your family's ring," I said. "Someday you'll get a girl you'll want to marry, and she should have it."

"I already met her. You keep it."

"I tell you what. I'll wear it until things change for us. If you meet some filly that says yes, I'll slip you the ring back all quiet-like so's she never knows I wore it."

"Long's you're wearing it, it might sway you," he said.

"You're a good man, Abe," I said. "I don't scarcely deserve to be sitting here with the likes of you."

"You're good too," he said. "And ain't for you to decide no divine plan. You're sitting here nexta me for a reason."

Hmph.

Chapter 13

It was a sight to behold, as we traveled along the land used by nobody, the horse picking her way through the withers-high grass: San Francisco sitting there smoldering, half undone.

"We're part of something new, Abe," I said. "We should write down our history so's people generations down will know what it was like for us."

"You'd be a fine one to do it, you speak so good."

"Maybe I could keep out the part about what I do, and just write about what I see."

"Would you put me in it?" He lifted the reins so his arms were fixed in sharp angles and he sat up straighter, trying to make himself look more worthy of being in a history, I suppose.

"You bet, page one. Actually, I'll put you in the title. 'Nora's History of Abe.'"

"'Nora's History of Abe,'" he repeated.

"Chapter one. The small boy is born, and his first words are 'I love taking harlots out for holiday excursions whilst the city dampens its embers.'"

"You should start it when I met you. Nothing's important afore that."

"Aw, flip, Abe. You'd feel this way about Mealy Mel if it was her crib you entered 'stead of mine."

"Nope," he said stoutly.

Oh well. Arguing with a post.

If I was to write my story, maybe I'd start with how I got here. I saw crocodiles and birds of such plumage that the Cyprians should copy them in their dress! And visited another country, Panama, something the Simms family would have never foretold for itself. But that's interesting now, I reflected, and won't be much longer. Because more and more people will be coming here—each day the ships bring thousands—and everyone will have my same story. And years hence, my tale of being paddled up the Chagres River, battling mosquitoes the size of Abe's hand, will be everyone's story. In the year 1949, a century from now, why, who *won't* have made this journey and seen the Panama men and their funny monkeys?

I'd no time for writing anyway. All spare hours were devoted to my lessons. Mehitabel was now more easy at the hurdy-gurdy house (and with me, as the memory of the dress debacle faded). Together we filled the empty dance hall with popular tunes rollicking as when it was filled, and classical songs as somber as if every person who ever passed through its doors was now dead. Mehitabel liked the excursions and even suggested them on afternoons we had not planned for them. As we played, her face would occasionally grow thoughtful—remembering the days she played at genteel parties—but never regretful.

As for my French lessons, well, I could only practice what little Yvette left me with. It'd been quite a while since I last saw her. She explained she made so much at the parlor house 'tain't worth the bills I gave her.

As Abe pulled us down Market Street, we saw a crowd had gathered and was frothing and spewing like what comes from a rabid dog's mouth.

"Stop," I said. "Let's see what's the matter."

"They're loud; they'll scare Minnie," he protested.

"Pish! Pull the trap over to the side and we'll keep her out of danger's way."

Abe pulled over so far I almost couldn't see, but it was good to be up in the air 'stead of on the ground, so we could see over all the heads. And what I saw was the beam and crossbeam of a gallows. A man stood next to it with a noose around his neck. His hands were behind his back, doubtless tied, and his head was bowed.

"Mary's virgin tailfeathers, this city's rough. Do you see what I see?"

"Yep."

"Doing it right out here in the square like this? Wish they'd do it in the jail cellar. Wonder what he did."

And then we were told. Another man stood on a crate, towering above the condemned man, and read a proclamation in a loud voice. The crowd hushed for that.

"The concerned gentlemen of San Francisco have assisted the overtaxed volunteer police force in righting the wrongs of society. The charges against this man include carousing with liquor in his gut during the daylight hours, visiting the fair but frail of this city, and slitting the throat of not one, but now two of these, leaving the body of the most recent murder abandoned on the floor with no more thought than toward a soiled handkerchief. And this on Our Holy Savior's birthday."

My heart ran to steel and I clutched Abe's hands. Another one of my kind had been fated to die like that?

"Press in closer," I urged. "I want to see his face."

Minnie took a few steps, nodding her head like bobbing wheat. I stood and craned forward. At that moment, the condemned man raised his head and I saw it was *him*. What a surge of blood to my heart! I could have buckled over the side of the carriage with the odd weight of my distended, filled-to-busting heart. I never had to worry again! No one did. The girl of the row could take a man without thinking.

"Ha ha!" I thought across the crowd at him. "You put your knife at my throat, and here you are now with rope to go at the same place. Meet your atonement!"

"I knew that fella," I said gleefully to Abe, sitting back down. "And I'm glad to see him wearing his fine hemp necklace."

"We have captured this foreigner, this monger of vice, named Franz Oberstein. And now we set San Francisco free of the pestilence he has brought from overseas," continued the man reading the crimes. He never said the name of the girl who'd been killed, however, and I kept my mind closed like a book to that thought. Wasn't nobody I knew.

The folks in the crowd hissed and spat on the man. Myself, I would have had the distance not been so great. Then the orating man stepped down and the headsman leaned a ladder against the crossbeam of the fresh-built gallows.

He grabbed the rope around Oberstein's neck and began climbing the ladder, pulling on the noose. Oberstein was forced to follow, like a dog on a leash. On the second rung, Oberstein paused. The orator, still on the ground, conked him on the back of his head, and he nearly fell sideways. The headsman yanked on the rope to keep his balance.

"Must be hard to climb a ladder without your hands to steady you," I said.

Near the top of the ladder, the headsman swung the rope over the crossbeam and secured it, keeping a few feet's worth loose. He stepped around to the other side of the ladder so he faced Oberstein and turned his back on the crowd.

"Your face is high vengeful," said Abe. "Did he hurt you?"

"Not a bit of it," said I. 'Twasn't right to tell Abe; 'twould be like telling a child.

The two men paused there a moment on the ladder, as if one had been bringing a pot of whitewash to the other, and lingered to examine the work. Then the headsman lifted his leg and thrust it through the rungs, kicking Oberstein off the ladder.

Oberstein pitched out into the air with a lurch, like a bag of potatoes, and dropped the length of the slack, and now taut, rope. He bobbed and swung heavily. They hadn't covered his face, and I saw spurts and jerks cross it. He wriggled like a fish until the headsman changed sides of the ladder, clamped onto the crossbeam with both hands, and stepped upon the man's bound hands, jumping up and down to quicken his death.

The heads in the throng followed the swaying twosome, looking like they was performing a strange, mostly motionless, dance.

Oh, I got quiet. Mistake me not, I was relieved for his passing, but there was also a sideways feeling in me I couldn't identify.

"That's about the worst thing I ever saw," I said.

"I seen worse," said Abe, and I imagined he probably meant his brother Caleb, dying slow in some godforsaken mining camp.

"Merry flaming Christmas," I said bitterly. "Guess they did it today to make a point."

"Would you have spoken for him to live?"

I almost laughed. "He stuck some woman like a slaughterhouse pig, so he should die for it. But not on the street like this."

"Let's go," he said. "I never like them bunches of people."

A straw bed was being prepared for the hanged man to be laid in, afore his removal to the dead-house, but we turned our backs on that gruesome display before they could cut him down. As Minnie slowly wended around the side of the crowd and headed us for Kearny Street, I saw a figure I recognized. It was Yvette, craning her head for a better view of the swinging unfortunate. I bent down to poke her on the shoulder. She whipped around, startled. Her eyes was bright and feverish and wide.

"Did you see it, Nora?" she asked. "That fucker killed one of the girls from Jackson Street."

I stared at her like I'd never seen her before.

"I'm glad I'm at the parlor house where the likes of him wouldn't make it past the gate. What?" Her face took on a look of horror. "Did you know her very well, Nora?"

Although I knew I'd grieve later for whatever woman had fallen in such an evil way, my shock was more for the words coming out of Yvette's not-so-Parisian lips. The professor had been right.

"You ain't French?" I asked.

She threw her head back and whinnied like a horse. "I'm from Champaign County, Illinois. Ain't that a French place?"

I stood up, furious. "Give me back my money, you filthy skank of a liar!"

"Sit, you'll spook Minnie," said Abe.

"You pay me this minute, you fool of a hussy!" I said. In my head I was trying to calculate how many lessons she'd given and what the sum total was. I reached down and grabbed one of her curls so she couldn't run. I was in a rare state of passion, most likely worsened by the tableau of a swinging man behind me.

"I don't care," she shouted back. "I'm flush with it! I shit gold coins! Here's your stinking money, you vulgar crib girl. You'll die in the cribs, just like her, and you'll never see the inside of a parlor house." She opened up her purse, which from above I could see was fat indeed, and grabbed a handful, throwing it up onto the floor of the carriage. It was certainly more than she owed me, and it was gold, not paper. "You had a dreadful accent anyway!"

Then I let go of her hair and she was off through the crowd. I jumped down and picked up the coins that had fallen on the ground and clambered back up to get those on the floor of the trap.

"Did you see how much was in her purse?" I asked Abe in awe.

"Don't ever talk to her again," he said.

"I don't aim to."

"She's bad. She said you'd die like that girl and she were happy at the thought."

"Honey, they caught the man what did it!"

"That don't change the meanness in that one. And I ain't gonna let you alone, never, from now on."

I rolled my eyes at him, even as I was piling up the coins in stacks of five on the slat seat to count them. "So what are you planning to do, Abe, sit at the foot of the bed and coax the gentlemen along?"

"I'll sit in the corner. Put the chair there."

"Start Minnie; this is too much money to be counting while we're stopped. And that's a very handsome offer, darling, but I don't think many men would like to have you listening and waiting a few inches away."

"You ain't working the cribs alone no more. That's firm."

There was fifty-five dollars there, and she'd only schooled me for thirty of it. I made a profit! Then it sunk in what Abe said and I leaned over and kissed him. He was slow, sure, but his spirit wasn't.

"Don't worry, Abe. I ain't gonna work the cribs no more. If'n she can shoot me fifty-five dollars without a thought, and there's more than that in her purse, and more like than not plenty extra in her trunk back home, I'm going to be a parlor girl without a doubt. I can fake them fancy accents—and something even better: I can play piano!"

He kept threading Minnie through the carriages in the street, not saying nothing. Then he said, "You think about money too much. You got to think about being safe."

"The parlor houses are safe as can be, Abe! The rooms for sporting are upstairs, so a fella has to come and stay for a while in the downstairs, while the madam looks him over and makes sure he's an upright gent. And there's all kinds of other girls around, and everyone'll look after me."

"Where?"

"I don't know yet. I ain't going to try for Yvette's house, that's for sure, and if I see her I'll spit. But maybe if I walk around and look hard I'll be able to tell which houses are parlor houses. I mean, after all, the gents have a way of knowing, don't they?"

"I'll go with you."

"No, Abe, you can't. Nobody'll take me with some gloomy miner hanging on. I have to go alone."

"What's gloomy?"

"Dour."

"What's that?"

"Mad about something."

"I'll wait outside so's they don't see me. Now, I'm taking you back to your crib so you can get your things, then back to your quarters to be safe."

Well, well, well. Somebody telling Nora Simms what to do. But I guessed I could use the ride. He pulled up at the top of the line there on Jackson Street. I climbed down and got my things out of good old Number One, tucking my sign under my arm.

Turning around inside, I looked one last time at the dark wood boards and the piddly light coming through the window in the front. "This is the last time I hear these tired old springs," I said, and bounced on the bed to hear the sad jangling. I ain't too sentimental, and that place sure wasn't anything to get the waterworks going for, so I turned my back and loaded my gear onto the carriage.

"Just give me a minute and I'll let the lady know I'm gone," I said.

She had a shack across from the line, not too much bigger than a crib, really. I poked my head in the open door and called for her.

"What?" she asked, coming with her hands twisting in an apron. She'd been washing.

"I'm leaving," I said.

"Cause of what happened with Charlotte? They hanged that fella today, and there ain't any better cowyards in this city. You'll get charged triple what I ask for rent."

Charlotte.

"It was Charlotte?" I asked stupidly.

"Right, the new girl. The one skinnier than a board turned sideways. I'm surprised she even bled, but lord she did; I tell you, the floor in there was like an abattoir."

I leaned against the wall and pressed my hands to my mouth. Poor, proud Charlotte. She had begun slipping bills under my door, so I had stopped leaving her food. I figured she had it all running smooth.

I whimpered behind my hands and felt my legs trembling. My heart physically hurt with the panicked blood squirting, as I imagined, through the wrong passages, and some veins constricting with no vital fluid at all.

I drew a few more breaths and then let my hands fall to my sides.

The woman cocked her head. "Were you friendly with her? You look like you're going to tip over."

Oh, I wished I hadn't counseled Charlotte and helped her join this pitiable profession. I ought to have slammed the door in her face and made her go to the poorhouse in desperation. She'd be alive today.

"I don't keep smelling salts, but I could dash some water in your face," she added.

I moaned with the image of slight Charlotte fighting that man off, with his eyes gleaming and his intent so foul. I wanted nothing now but to have Abe's arms around me.

"I must go," I said.

"Well, tomorrow things'll seem different."

"No," I said. My voice was unrecognizable to me. "I ain't coming back. I'm going to a parlor house."

"Well, let me figure up what you owe me and we can part our ways."

I reeled. How could money be mentioned when Charlotte had been left on the floor in a spreading lagoon of her own heart's blood? That poor wretch that life had treated so basely? I wanted to smite down this savage proprietor. She had no more thought for the girls in her yard than a housewife has for the fly.

I straightened up my shoulders and slapped the wall with my palm. "Well, I'm paid up for December and this is only the twenty-fifth, so maybe it's you doing the owing."

"But there's the crib-clean fee. Whenever a lass leaves, we have to get the crib respectable for the next girl, and that's twelve dollars right there. Plus the cost to seek a new girl for your spot."

If they could capture the cold in my voice, men would never need to cut ice again. "Crib-clean fee? Why, when I moved in to the initial crib, there was spiders turning their own tricks there! And I didn't pay when I moved to Yvette's spot."

"We make it as clean as possible," she said, moving her hands to her hips and looking kind of hard. "You didn't pay when you went to Yvette's spot, 'cause she paid for you. A courtesy."

"That's a lie through and through," I spat.

"I'll need eighteen dollars afore I release you."

"You're more of a whore than all of us put together! You aren't worth Charlotte's fingernail!"

I spun on my heel and dashed out to the carriage. "Go, Abe!" I yelled as I ran. "Let's go."

He reached an arm down and pulled me up quick, then turned Minnie and we was on our way out. That fishwife came out in the road to holler at us but got a mouthful of dust for her trouble.

I calmed as Abe and I drove. I nestled against him and he tucked me in between his arms, holding the reins in front of my chest. It was the warmth I craved, but I couldn't tell him about Charlotte. This was one I'd sit in my room and ponder until I was ready to let her memory slip away from this earth.

I directed him up the hill to Stark Street, where Mehitabel boarded me. We parked in front and I showed him my window.

"When are you going out tomorrow?" he asked.

"Not sure."

"Well, how will I know when to come get you?"

I sighed. "Abe, I already told you. You can't come. Nobody'll take me if you're there."

"I'll hang back."

"No. It won't work; just try to understand." I climbed down and he handed me my Nora sign. The diamond ring flashed in the sun, and I thought since my circumstances had changed, it was probably time to give it back. I started tugging—despite all horrors witnessed, it was already in love with my finger— but Abe stopped me.

"You and me ain't done yet," he said. "Keep it."

"Good-bye, dear Abe," I said. I stepped on the platform to deliver one last kiss. I was suffering in every ounce of me and just wanted to be in my room with the door closed. I wasn't so sure about what was done and not done with Abe, but I knew I wouldn't be seeing him for a while.

Chapter 14

Mehitabel caught me on the stairs with my sign tucked under my arm and looked at it delightedly. "Can this be a portent of things to come?" she asked. "Starting a new year with a new life?" Her face was so gay. It was like she couldn't possibly be a citizen in a town where one neck felt the blade and another the noose.

"No more crib for the likes of Nora Simms," I said. For all the flair in my voice, I could have been an afterlife companion to Charlotte and the hanged man.

She gave me a hug, the sign digging into her waist. "You're too good for that life," she said. "And it's never too late to change yourself and become an honest woman. I'm proud of you, dear."

I coughed a bit and arranged my skirts, feeling the stirrings of guilt penetrating through my daze. "Was it a merry Christmas here, then?"

"A delightful feast and we all missed you. Of course, I'm pleased to see you spend time with such a nice—" She spied the ring flashing in the dark hall. "You're affianced!"

I was mumbling something about "gift" and "hard to promise" but she overrode me like a coach and four rumbling down the thoroughfare.

"Ah! What better way to start this new life! You'll be such a fine, handsome bride. I'd love to play the wedding march for you, mightn't I? And we could decorate the parlor and bring in some lilies. What's his name?"

"We ain't sure yet what all we'll do. Lilies, now that sounds pretty! If'n you'll just let me up past you, I need to lay my spinning head down; I'm all fluttered about things."

"Darling Nora, let me do just one thing before you retire."

"Anything. Yes. Immediately."

"I'd like to give you your gift," she said.

Beetle in the teacup! In all the hullabaloo, I'd forgotten that I wanted to give her the newly made gown that was purporting to have been made weeks ago. "Of course!" I said. "And I can't wait for you to see…well, you know what you're getting!"

"I ought to get a jabbing from a pitchfork for what I thought of you, but let's be glad today and set all that aside. Run up and get it and we'll exchange our goodies in the front room."

I smiled and nodded and climbed one step before I felt her tugging at my sign.

"Well, you shan't be needing this any longer, will you?" she said. "Husbands generally know their wives' names, I believe. Mine knew mine! Let's put it upon the fire and put an end to this…this…"

Oh, small ache that started up when I looked at the purple pansies with their yellow centers, and the butterfly just spreading its wings atop the A of Nora. Ache atop of ache. What would happen to Charlotte's sign? Did she even have one?

"This what?" I asked.

"This…way of being."

I looked her straight in the blinkers and stifled what was starting in me. Mehitabel had no part of this wrath, but I nevertheless felt like that bull Ricardo Oro, leading with the horns and ready to plug into real flesh.

"Take it," I said harshly. "Burn it, but I won't watch."

"It'll be a great Christmas present for me. Honestly, I've become so fond of you I can scarcely bear to think of what it is you do all day."

"Ha ha ha, those days are over," I said over my shoulder as I kept climbing. I simply let go the sign and it remained in her paws.

I hate to lie. I hate, hate, hate it. And I get mad thinking I ain't so good a person as I ought to be. The respectable women hiss at me on the street, "You're worse than dead," but I can berate myself even further.

Ah! It was a baneful life. Lying about my future as a married woman, going upstairs to retrieve a false dress. But far worse: the pitiful way that Charlotte had gone.

I reached the first-floor landing and began redoing fate: sliding a knife under Charlotte's mattress so she had something to defend herself with, having another gent waiting just outside for his turn, so he would dash in and protect her. Or me. I would have come running like a gazelle if I heard her peep. I'd be in that room afore another breath was took. I was strong; I could batter that fiend until he plunged out and chose another woman to introduce his blade to. Yet where was I? I was walking barefoot along a beach and getting sand in my recesses.

And what of the other girls of the line? Had they not come to her rescue? And after they had promised each other that they would. Yet maybe Charlotte had not had the chance to scream.

I flounced myself onto the bed and threw the ring across the room. For a few minutes I buried my head in the pillow, like a sparrow keeping its head warm in its feathers, and thought about what Abe wanted and Mehitabel assumed. I saw myself living in the shack Abe'd built and making bread or sewing hems to keep us in clothing. I imagined opening my legs for himself only and not being so sore and sticky all the time. Women would nod their heads to me in the butcher shop and I could order my meat without the counter fella wagering my price and asking where I worked.

I'd never meet another fellow I had to look up and down and assess for whether he'd hold a stropping razor to me. And I'd never have to encounter another Charlotte again. I'd be apart from that society.

Was that possible? I longed for a glass of brandy. I rooted down into the galley mate's trunk, which I was now using as if it were mine, because I had once received a tip in the form of a bottle. There it was, at the bottom, with a full draught of forgetfulness. I uncorked it and swallowed all I could.

Oh, come fast, let me out of this mind I'm in, I thought. I wanted to be cheerful and thoughtless as the mouse that prowled behind these walls.

I sat up to take another long drink from the bottle and looked across the room to where I'd left a smidgen of cheese by the dresser leg for that creature. It was gone. And of course, as I had fed cheese to Charlotte as well, that little beastie would doubtless end its life with a torrent of blood wetting its fur.

Was it possible? I asked myself as I tipped the bottle to a radical angle. *Had I moved myself across oceans to marry a miner with a slow wit?*

Thus fortified, I grabbed the dress I had the tailor make for Mehitabel to cover my lie and made my way back downstairs.

Bulby-eyed Holmes was in the front room now, pouring a glass of champagne for Mehitabel, but upon seeing me he set his own glass down stiffly and exited the room. He was keeping up appearances; he had been a steady patron of my depraved establishment.

"Oh, how that gentleman makes me seethe!" said Mehitabel. "He is so unpardonably rude."

"Guess he won't be able to scorn me once I'm a married woman," I said. This was the liquor spinning out a lie, not me.

"What's your intended's name?"

"Abe."

"That's a good name, illustrating simplicity and no nonsense," she said. "Will he come to live here? I can move you to a larger chamber."

"Oh, no, Mehitabel, we'll have to go live at his house."

"Where's that?"

"Well. It's...Over across the bay. In the oak groves."

"So far? I wanted to remain close companions."

"I know. It's heartbreaking to me too." I wanted to give her a kiss but worried she'd smell the brandy.

"After all we've experienced together, it shall be painful to say good-bye," she said. "I hope when you wear this, you will think of me."

She handed me a bundle that was my Christmas present. I opened it to find a large tortoiseshell comb, curved and decadent and such as a society lady would wear to an elegant engagement. I ran my fingers along its arch, feeling the drag where the hand-cutting of the design had been made. I knew nestled in my brown curls it would gleam and catch the light.

"This is so beautiful," I said in a tiny voice. "How could you ever spend such a fortune on me?"

"Who better to spend it on? I knew once I saw it that it could grace no finer nor handsomer head than yours."

I brought it to my lips and pressed a long kiss into the ornament's cool surface, knowing Mehitabel would take it for a kiss to her.

"I have never been given anything nicer," I said.

"Oh, pshaw! What about that diamond ring Abe gave you?"

I put my hands in a cupped prayer position so she couldn't see I had taken it off. "Still," I said. "It is still the nicest thing." Then I stood and carried over to her the package that contained the ugly dress I could afford.

She opened it and made great sounds of rapture and amaze, entirely sincerely, but I knew the gown was of poor quality.

"Nora, what a sacrifice it was to you to make this," she said. "This is without a doubt and a hesitation the best gift *I've* ever received, for I know the thoughtfulness behind it. You could have used the money to make two dresses for yourself so you wouldn't have to spend each morning washing yours, but with the unselfish spirit I have always seen in you, you chose instead to bestow generosity on me."

"I hope you like the pattern; it reminded me of tiny birds on the wing," I mumbled. The pattern was white darts on pale blue, hardly a striking design.

"I do like it, I do! And I would like it if it showed baboon posteriors, for all the goodness in your heart that it represents."

In my alcohol cloud, I struggled to decide if she thought monkey asses were a representation of me.

"Mehitabel, I love you," I said. I was besotted with brandy, but this was factual.

"And I love you. Bless the ship that brought you to this shore!" she said. She stood, walked over to me, and pressed a kiss onto my forehead. I smiled up at her, rendered back to some purer form of myself...really, like a child.

Next morning, I shook my head to clear the brandy fuzz. I was fixed in my mind again about what I wanted. Charlotte was gone and the man who killed her was gone, so the world had to carry on. I washed up, sprayed some toilet water behind my ears, put my hair up with the new comb Mehitabel had given me, and dusted off my boots. I was whistling on the stair, as coarse as that sounds, and didn't even pop my head in to see if there was bread or tea for me.

I emerged into the light and clamor of Stark Street only to see a carriage sitting there at the curb. My presentiment about not seeing Abe for a time was pure folly, for it appeared he'd sat there all night to not miss me. I stepped delicately, hoping perhaps he dozed still, but he heard my boots on the wooden sidewalk and his eyes flew open.

"Where's your ring?"

Good night, his eyes were sharp even if his mind weren't. The ring still lay where God's will had plunged it, and I hadn't remembered to seek it out with the yawns stretching my mouth. But with the course of business I had to do this day, an engagement ring was probably a wise thing to leave home.

"Pawned it," I said crossly.

He climbed down, eyebrows becoming pitch-roofed shanties. "That was my mother's ring, Nora. What'll I—"

"It's upstairs, you lunk, sitting fancy on my dresser."

"Upstairs?"

"That's right. It's safe and solemn. Now then, why don't you get Minnie her oats this morning and care for her?"

"First I care for you."

"Abe, you can't help me today. I'm explaining and explaining until I'm like to bust, and you still don't listen."

"Choose not to."

Hands on my hips, I stamped my foot. "Not too long ago we didn't even know each other, and today you're behaving like my keeper."

"I'll hang back, like I said. Jes' do as you wish and I'll be looking on."

"I'm off without you," I said and resumed walking.

"Mostly."

"Altogether!" I spun around and glared at him, which facial posture made my head hurt. I hadn't come unscathed from my sojourn with the bottle. "Now, ain't you got a livery job where the horses are weeping for their Uncle Abe?"

"They'll get looked after."

"I won't be talking to you or looking at you or even understanding that you're planted on this earth."

He nodded and motioned to the carriage.

"I ain't riding! Foul mouths of sailors, it's like talking to a rock."

So he tied up Minnie and followed me on foot. Ever' now and then I turned around to see him skulking a few lengths back.

For a moment, I considered that it was right strange that he should have such an overwhelming interest in me. Surely I knew his motive could not be reproached, for he had not the mental facility to think of harming me. But usually when women are so repeatedly followed by a man, after her own protesting, there is malefaction afoot.

Yet his face was so bland. The brain behind it was no more capable of a wicked thought than a spoon has hopes of cutting meat.

I crossed Pacific, Jackson, and Washington, heading south, thinking the finer things were far from my little corner of San Francisco. Yvette had said she was going to Pacific Street, so I knew I'd avoid that like the Rue Merde.

I peered up at windows, thinking to see the women looking out like they do in the cribs. But this was different than I was used to. The men knew where to go already, and they picked their women once inside. So how was I to figure it out, other than sitting on the stoop to watch the comings and goings?

Abe and I wandered until my feet started to hurt and my bosoms heaved with the exertion of our jaunt. Then finally I saw a silhouette in a window that made me think of how us crib girls use our front window. It was a handsome form with a wasp waist. But mayhap it was just an honest lady, a wife or aunt. How could I know this for a parlor house? I looked up at all the other windows and saw no signal. But just then the front door opened and a gent stepped out, replacing his hat to his head. A woman bid him adieu and closed the door behind him. Their farewelling had the smack of a transaction completed; she was a madam, I wagered.

I watched him step down to the gate. He wiped sweat off his brow and gave a deep sigh.

"That's it!" I said triumphantly to myself. He passed me at the gate and gave me the surveying stare, which further strengthened my surety.

I marched up to the door and rapped upon it. "Yes?" It was the same woman who had just said good-bye to the gentleman.

"Bonjour, madame. My name ees—"

"Oh, please, you sound as French as my poodle. Your likes aren't wanted here." She slammed the door in my face.

I took a giant step backward, amazed. I'd been treated unfairly before, and in fact saw more of that than its opposite, but I hadn't even finished my sentence!

"What'd she say?" called Abe from across the street.

I made no reply but bustled myself out the dooryard. My French was fine! I'd fooled all manner of men. And look at Yvette: *she'd* found placement at a parlor house through her falsehoods.

At the second parlor house that I managed to identify (I saw a flood of men emerge after the luncheon hour), things went a little better. The woman at the door listened to me for quite a while.

"So, you see, I em vairy much eenterested een locating anothair parlerrr house to live in, such as I ev been used to een my home country of France," I concluded.

She plucked at my dress. "Is this what women are wearing in France these days?"

It was the dim plaid, and what else could it be?

"*Oui,*" I answered.

"It looks a lot like a cheap piece of stuff made by someone who had not so much to spare."

I laughed. "Ah, ze American women who do not know the fashions of Paree! Zis ees truly en vogue. And pleez do not find offense, but sometimes as I travel through ze streets of San Franceesco, I em laughing to see ze styles here! You see, eet ees only a bit of one country not recognizing what the other values."

"Let me see your hands."

I took off my gloves and offered them.

"They are coarse. You have not been massaging cream into your hands like a lady."

"Again! A difference of our lands. We French vimmin nevair use cream on our hands."

"The brand of cream this house uses is imported from Paris."

"What ees the use of hands? For ze men, ees eet not the prettiness of ze face? Regard me: em I not fair?"

"You're pretty, but we need pretty with class."

"I have class! I have eet! I play pianny!" I had dropped my French accent in my haste.

Her eyebrows raised and she smiled snidely. "This is why the madam has me do the preliminary interviews," said she. "For you girls connive and wrap yourselves in lies."

"You ain't the madam? Can I talk to her?"

"No, I *ain't*," she mocked. "And you can't!"

Ach, find my voice and set it afire! *Are not—am not—is not;* why can I not remaster this bit of language?

"You're right, missy, I'm not from France and maybe I'm not even so cultured. But I'm a hit with the fellas! They love me and I have return business like you can't understand. Just let me talk with the madam, please. See my face? I'm pretty and the men like me."

"All our girls here are pretty. But they're also cultured." And she closed the door.

Pickled viscera of the saints! All this time I'd been arguing with the maid—she who should have been cleaning my shoes and making my bed.

I tried one more house that day, with Abe trailing behind me like an unheeded ghost. "That's it," I said finally when that last door had been closed nearly on my fingers. "I give it up for today."

"I'll take you home and be back tomorrow morning for the searching," said Abe.

"Take me home, yes, and thank you. But Abe, what use has today been for you? You're restless and tired."

"I want to see where you end up."

"I can send you word!"

"I want to see with my own eyes."

"Fine. Come back at ten tomorrow."

At the door of Mehitabel's I gave him a light kiss.

Upstairs, I kicked the trunk. "I'd have money for a finer gown if you were the right trunk!" I said. Then I hissed at the mirror: "And you—what good does your prettiness do? Tame your tongue and talk right!"

Chapter 15

The next morning, I was washed and ready to go at nine, thinking I could relax if Abe weren't with me. Maybe that was why I hadn't been successful.

But the lad was perhaps wise to my knavery and was there waiting for me in his trap an hour early. I looked at him in disbelief. Maybe he wasn't there an hour early. Maybe he had waited all night.

"Why are you dogging my footsteps? I'm a grown woman," I greeted him.

"I'm bigger than you and I can protect you agin the bad ones in this city."

"What if you're one of the bad ones?"

"Nora, no!" He was shocked and I felt ashamed. I examined my boots as he climbed out of the carriage.

He took me in his arms and gave a right good hug. "I wouldn't let a bee sting you or a cat scratch you. I ain't bad. I'm good."

I smiled against my will. "Why, Abe, you always get me bright without my say-so. I know you're good; it's plain as gold in the river."

"Today you'll find you a parlor house," he said. "I don't know what was wrong with those people yesterday. I couldn't believe they was turning you down. You!"

"I have to concentrate today on how I talk," I said. "I have to be as elegant as possible."

"You're the most elegant thing I ever saw. And the prettiest. No parlor house even deserves you."

So we began walking again, he several feet behind me. I walked, and strolled and bustled and sauntered, all without ever seeing any signs of a parlor house.

An hour and a quarter later we had crossed Market and were down below the cemetery. We had walked quite a while on Price Street. I was just about ready to turn and yell at Abe, thinking he was jinxing me, when luck appeared in the distance, dressed in watered silk and Parisian bonnets.

It was two of 'em, brazen as foxes, arms linked and heads proud. I tell you, some days my chin is as high as those, but these gladdies looked like their chins never came down! They passed me, giggling much too hard to notice me and my dour shadow. I watched where they entered a gate and climbed the steps of a fine building with a turret and woodwork that looked like lace.

Fair enough. I cast one look back at Abe and lifted my skirts to climb the steps myself. I rapped at the door without even thinking what I'd say.

"Yes?" a colored woman answered the door.

"Hello, good day. I'd like to speak with the woman what runs this establishment."

"She's out, miss." And that door was clanged in my face. I knocked again.

"I'll sit and wait if you don't mind," I said and pushed into that house. The housewoman, unsure what to do, stood there with the door open, Abe framed in its view, on the sidewalk gaping.

"Who are you? Cain't just rustle your way in here."

"I'm Nora Simms and I want to wait for the lady of the house." I opened up my reticule and sprung a small coin on her. That clammed both her mouth and the door behind me.

"Sit down here, miss. Actually, I'm thinking that's the back door I hear and she's coming in now."

My keen ears ain't heard anything, so she was a fibber like me with Mehitabel.

I took a seat, opening my eyes in awe at what I saw. Gleaming wood that was oiled like a fine brunette, and carpets stacked up against each other, and dozens of portraits and paintings in gold frames, hung with long wires from the moldings. Every seat was overstuffed and plush, and sure enough, there in the corner was the piano I'd be hopefully playing to a finer brand of gent.

There were even books with golden writing on the spines, and antimacassars (a word Mehitabel had taught me), and an umbrella stand seemingly made from an exotic beast's leg. This latter I disapproved of even as I appreciated the large amount of money that had obviously been paid for it.

This was a parlor house, and it was even better than Yvette had described.

Then I began listening to the noises from upstairs. They weren't the noises I was used to, the springs and the men squawking with sheer bewilderment. No, these sounded like trouble. I heard female murmurings and, after I listened hard enough, a girl crying. Footsteps pacing across the floor. Water being wrung out of a cloth into a basin.

My stomach curled up into itself. Then the screaming started and I dashed out of my seat and up the stairs, tripping on the way. I staggered into the room above the parlor, where I found a bed built of blood.

It looked that way, but there was a girl posted on her back in the middle of all that red, screaming and banging her fists against her stomach. There was another girl there, hands dripping with it, who ran to me. "Can you help? Do something to help her; it went wrong somehow."

I stepped to the bed and wailed a wee moment, helpless and knowing not where to put my hands.

"Help me!" the girl screamed. "I ain't fucking leaving this world for this rotten slip of prick I didn't want!"

"Hush, Patience, soften yourself, you're only making it worse," said the other girl.

It was true. A gush of blood accompanied her shouting.

I took a cloth from the dresser and wiped where it was all coming from. The minute I saw her woman's parts, they was instantly covered again in blood.

"Fucking help me!"

I put my fingers in and felt the hunks of flesh left in her passages. They were big pieces. "You ain't supposed to wait so long," I said to the other woman, shocked.

"She hid it, keeping her clothes loose. I guess she thought it'd go away if she didn't think about it."

I pulled out what I could, but I knew this blood was from Patience herself, that her insides had been cut at the same time as the makings of a baby were.

"Can you stop the bleeding?" asked the woman.

As easy as I stop the seas from pitching boats against the rocks, I thought but didn't say for Patience's sake.

"Of course," I said. "I'll just stanch it with this and it'll all calm down in a minute. The worst is over. I'm seeing less already. Patience, dearest, I know it still hurts but it won't by and by."

Patience stopped screaming to listen to me, and grabbed at the sheets. They were so wet it was like wringing the laundry on washday. "It hurts so evil. Can't you do something to make me rest easy?"

I hunted for a fresh cloth to put on her forehead but they were all red as poppies. "Did a doctor get called for?"

"Won't come," said the other woman under her breath.

"Well, what's in the house we can give her? Any whiskey or port?"

She was gone so quick she stirred a breeze. Patience commenced a horrible sound that brung the tears to my eyes: she sobbed and then shrieked. It was like the devil himself was teasing at her nerves.

"I'd take it from you if I could," I said. I pulled a chair to her bedside and took one of her hands in mine.

She didn't hear me, rocking with her own weeping and screaming. But her hand did squeeze mine. I looked down at the blood stuck under her nails, as if she'd been scratching a sore.

The other woman clattered into the room with a brown bottle and we set it to Patience's lips.

"She never liked the drink," said the other woman.

"Well, she needs it today," I said. I lifted the bottle again and poured as hard as I could without making her choke.

"That's enough, I think," said the other woman.

"Not yet," I said grimly. Every few minutes, I tilted the liquor, until finally Patience's sobbing became quieter and her breath oozed as much odor as the bottle.

"Now cover that up," I said. "It's enough to kill a soul just to see all that happening down there."

The woman stripped the sheets and bundled them off, bringing fresh linens to cover Patience again. "I'm not supposed to," she said. "Bridget's so particular about the bedding. And this'll be ruined as soon as I set it down." But she tucked it in nevertheless.

"Bridget? Who's that?"

"The madam of the house here. She's quite strict with us."

"Where's she now?"

"She's waiting it out. She hates things like this. I smelled cigar smoke under her door, and she'll just be sitting there waiting until Patience's one way or another."

"One way or another. Cold blood in this house, ain't there?"

"Cold enough. But then, it isn't Bridget's fault this one here hid her belly so long. It would have been easy enough if she showed us earlier."

Patience's eyes were closed, but I still shook my head fierce at the other girl. "Shh, now. Speak only kindly."

"Who are you anyhow?"

"I'm Nora Simms. I'm here to take a position."

"What house are you from?"

I couldn't reveal I was straight from the cribs. And if I had a rat to shake, I would have, because I had completely forgotten to pretend I was French.

"I'm from a house in Chicago," I said, not sure why I lied about my place of origin. "A bit nicer than this one, but I knew San Francisco would be a little rough."

Already the new sheets were red.

"Any family to this one?" I asked.

"No idea where she's from. She didn't get along with the other girls so no one really knows her."

"Maybe that's why she hid her growing."

She nodded. Downstairs we heard knocking at the door, and she looked right out relieved. "I'll handle whoever that is. Thank the saints there's no more screaming."

Cold blood, indeed.

"What's your name?" I asked before she scattered herself.

"I'm Patience too. Good thing there'll be one of us to carry the name."

After she left, I bent my head to Patience's chest to feel the breath still struggling through the liquor and the blood. She twisted a bit but didn't wake. I was still holding her hand, and mine was going numb with the effort.

I looked around for the first time. The room was posh, with mirrors all over draped with silky cloth and velvet framing the windows. The carpet was a thick affair that would have made me take off my boots if the situation wasn't so very dire.

How was it that I, who knew this girl least of all, was going to be the one to sit with her when she drew in her last breath?

No sign above her bed, but her name was known. Patience: a girl dying essentially by herself, no visitor that mattered or knew a whit about her, young as a gosling still yellow and fluffy.

I wished for a clock so I could know how long I'd tarried with this mess. Eventually, Patience's eyes opened a squidge and she gazed up at the ceiling.

"Want some whiskey?" I asked.

"Will it make me die any faster?" She pulled her hand out of my grasp and tried to pull the sheets up closer to her chin. I had to help her. All the blood must surely be out of her body now; her face was wan, as if the veins carried no freight. She breathed shallowly, making a gaspy sound as she did so. "I'm going to die right here, I know it. I just wish I could let go a little hastier."

I had to fix my eyes to the foot of the bed, to avoid her face.

"What about some morphine? Isn't the doctor here yet?" she whispered.

"We're just waiting," I whispered back. "Seems like he ought to be here by now."

"I'm scared to look down there. Is it bad?" She had to pause after each word, to muster the air to utter the next.

"No. It's no worse than other girls I've seen. And they're all up and on their feet today."

"Don't lie," she said. "I'm going."

I made the mistake of looking at her face. Her eyes reproached me, even as her thin coloring assigned her the visage of a corpse. She was young and tearstains crossed the soft landscape of her unwrinkled cheeks. She stretched her mouth open to assist her breathing, and I saw the tiny pearls that were her perfect teeth.

And then I let out a little sob, against my will, my strong Nora Simms will, because I was so set on calming her in the last moments. "I'm sorry," I said in a voice I'd never heard from my lips.

"I'll take a little more whiskey," she said. "It did help ease me." I succored her, then sat down again.

"You've been right nice," she said. She tried a grotesque smile that made my breath hitch in my throat.

"Do you...want to say anything?" I faltered. "Should I send word to any-body?"

"I don't want my mother to know how I ended. She can imagine something better than this. Maybe she thinks I eloped and live in a palace with a prince."

"I bet she does."

Then Patience began to shake and her throat issued forth some horrible tone. It was the death rattle, and I set my head in my hands and cried full storm, for it wouldn't affect her now.

An hour later I heard steps at the door. I rose and covered Patience's face, then faced the visitor.

"Maid says you're seeking a spot here," said the woman who must be Bridget. "Said you were pretty too. Well, luck is on your side—we have a room that just this minute opened up."

Chapter 16

An undertaker came and took Patience's body later that morning. Bridget sent me to the back garden, where the mattress had been dragged, with bucket after bucket of water to help the kitchen boy. Other girls might've complained about such a loathsome duty, but that was to be my mattress and so I watched the cleansing of the ticking with a very watchful eye.

"Won't ever be like new," said the boy.

I made him go through three more rinsings after he was first prepared to stop. "What'll I get for it?" he asked slyly.

"Reprieve from an ear boxing," I said.

Near the noon hour, Bridget took me to her wardrobe and picked out a gown for me. I was fit to swoon for the darling tucked sleeves and embroidered bumblebees. The thread-made insects made me think of the fat, satisfied bee that wheeled off from a flower on my burned sign. Maybe he had flown from the ashes to come adorn this dress, and invited other callers as well! What a delicious, fanciful gown after the dowdy pink I was wearing.

"Your hair's good but you ought to dress it differently," she said. Opening up a drawer in a tiny bureau, she pulled out a paper of pins, but not before I had seen the tiny pistol sitting in there.

"Have you ever shot that?" I asked.

"Never, darling. Simply an insurance to help us all sleep."

She lined up a row of pins in her thin lips and reworked my head 'til it nearly sank under the new weight. She tossed kid boots at my feet, so light they were hardly there, and I took off my brown ones with grim satisfaction.

"Did you wash today?" she asked me.

"Of course!"

"My girls wash between each visitor," she said. "I don't know your background, but each visitor needs to think he's the only one you're visiting with today."

Visit. What a funny word for what really happens.

"In Chicago, ma'am, we made *him* wash too. No girl would touch a fella 'til he'd laundered up his John Thomas."

She looked at me so doubtfully that I busted up laughing. "I'm only jesting with you," I said. "By the way, I can speak French. Ought I to fool with that?"

"With a name like Nora?"

"Well…I could be Yvette or Marie or something."

She surveyed me and I surveyed back, looking at the heavy shading she'd done around her eyes, and how she'd taken a piece of coal to make her eyebrows twice as long.

"We do a lot of conversing in this house," she said. "Our visitors will talk and debate the issues of the day, sometimes for hours, before coming upstairs. Can you talk long enough in French to do that?"

"What I dew," I said, putting on the bluffy accent, "ees I talk like thees. Dew you zink zis ees eenough for to convairse a long time?"

"I think you will drive us all stark raving mad," she said. "Keep yourself what you are. And by the way, if you don't hold up to our standards or we get complaints from the visitors, you'll be out on the sidewalk without a howdy-do."

"And what are these standards?"

"We've developed techniques not available at other parlor houses. I myself or Alice, one of our best, will train you. Some of our visitors come every day, moving through the rank of girls one by one and then starting over again. Our repeat business is the strongest in the city."

"I play piano too," I said, thinking I'd make the gents prefer only me, not move through the girls like a clock working through the hours.

"Grand! That's what you'll have to do today at the lunch time. I won't trust you with a visitor until you've been trained, but you can sit and discuss and play a few numbers."

"All right."

She bustled into the corner and tossed a small broadsheet at me. "The *Alta California* carries the news of the day," she said, "which our visitors enjoy discussing. Oftentimes the publisher, Mr. Gilbert, comes 'round and tells the tales not fit to print. Gloss through it and prepare to sound versed." It was the same paper that had carried the news of the murder of the shirtwaist girl, along with the fine drawing of her the professor had made.

"Yes'm." She was just about to leave me in peace with the paper when I cleared my throat and smiled a serpent smile. "I believe we ought to mention particulars, oughtn't we?"

"The house takes care of that and distributes your share to you."

"He don't pay me?"

She stared. "What kind of parlor house were you in, child? Our visitors would never do anything so base and coarse as paying directly. No, when you and he adjourn upstairs, it's all magic and skill and…good conversation."

"We used envelopes," I answered, thinking as rapidly as ever I did. "He'd leave it on the dresser."

"We allow no reminder whatsoever that you are not an absolutely willing and riveted participant."

I strove to figure if this was a con. If I never saw the money, how'd I know what he paid?

"So is there a house rate? All girls the same?"

"No, of course the finer girls earn more. You've quite a face, so you'll do well."

"How well?"

"Sixty, ninety," she shrugged. "Depending."

"On what?"

"His financial circumstances, mostly."

"What about the lodging cost?"

"One thousand per month. You'll make it up quickly."

"One thousand!"

"What was it in Chicago?" she asked.

"Deucedly less! And what about odd costs like linens?"

"Nora, Nora. You are asking such a volume of questions! Now, are you interested in being part of the most illustrious parlor house in California or not?"

Although she smiled, I saw the steel flirting with her face muscles.

"Oh, do I! I'm only asking in the spirit of finding all the wonderful details of my new situation."

"When's your next monthlies?"

"Not for a fortnight."

"You must tell me and we keep you out of sight. Eventually you'll regularize, but 'til then 'tisn't good business to have a visitor ask for something he can't have."

"But today you'll have me in view although I can't work?" I asked.

"You're new. The visitors understand there is always a breaking-in period. Like teaching a horse to take the saddle."

"Oh, I already know how to ride," I said proudly.

I was starving, never having eaten all the day. I waited down in the parlor with the other girls, hardly noticing them so's I could read down the four fat columns on each page of the newspaper. At length the door began knocking, and the men—pardon me, *visitors*—began to seat themselves upon the velvet cushions.

I was ready to faint when finally the colored maid brought in a salver of meats and bright yellow cheese. I ate as much as I could but tried not to be unseemly. Finally, I looked around. The girls here was lovely, made me feel like a hayseed. Oh, certainly I had bumblebees fetching ingredients for honey all over my bodice, but *they* looked like the bees had been buzzing around them for years.

And, I'll confess it, the gents almost scared me. They looked like the professor, only smarter. Not a one of 'em ever set foot in the itty horse stall we call a crib. Nor had anyone they knew, I warranted.

"Were any of you ladies in danger from the Christmas Eve fire?" asked one of the men. I knew now from reading the newspaper that the fire had been quite close to the Jackson Street cribs. On Christmas Day I had been so upset about the hanging—and learning that Charlotte was the dead man's victim—that I barely registered the smoulders from several blocks away.

"No, we were here all evening. We climbed to the roof and tried to see what we could," said a girl I recognized: she was one of the ones who'd tripped lightly down the sidewalk and keyed me to the character of this establishment.

"Hardly wise," said I without thinking. "The paper reported that a gentleman fell from a roof and won't recover."

She made a moue at me and I realized what I'd said.

"Outspoken!" said the fella approvingly.

"This is Nora, gentlemen," said Bridget, keeping her back to the room and winking her anger at me. "Fresh from Chicago, that delight of a city. She's an accomplished pianist. I shivered to hear her play earlier."

Which I hadn't.

"Well, you're a perfect fit with all the other ravishing beauties who reside here," said a gent with extreme wayward whiskers.

I bowed my head and tried desperately to blush—a hard trick to master when it don't come easy.

"What I found appalling," chimed in another girl, "was the final paragraph of that article, which stated that the men who assisted at the fire were requesting payment."

"Quite so," someone agreed. "Are some of my fellows so vile that they must ask gold after we've saved lives and property?"

I liked the way he worded it, so's it sounded like he was one of them that helped, although judging by his pallid architecture, he'd have been hanging back and letting women and babies climb ladders with their buckets.

"Isn't it scandalous the Dennison's Exchange had a painted cotton ceiling? Why, they might as well have hired a hawker to broadcast the news that fire was highly welcome!"

The woman who said that was sipping coyly at a glass of champagne. My head flapped from side to side, spying for the bottle. God's molar, everyone had a glass but me. Bridget must have poured and left me out.

I've learned in life that you have to push a little sometimes, to make sure the lovely arc of the horse's shoe don't wind up impressioned in your backside. So I rose, stepped to the sideboard, found the bottle and filled a glass for myself, then sat again.

"Is there really powder stored in the Parker House, as the crowd feared?" I asked.

Two of the gents nodded. "Indeed. The loss could have been far greater if that ignited. Fifty buildings burned, though," said one.

"Ashes and smoke everywhere," said the other. "The smell is horrible. The good news is it stirred the citizens who were fire men on the East Coast to form an official fire department."

"What was the total loss?" asked a girl with curls so profuse I wondered her head wasn't rolling around in the air, wheeling on them. Whatever her precise name, I'd be calling her Curly in my head from now on.

"A million."

Oh, how I cherish that word.

"San Francisco is always on fire, it seems," said Curly. A wise statement, for it got the men on about insurance and having axes handy to break down walls.

I rose and had another glass.

"And what did we think of our new governor's address?" asked another girl. She had earbobs that broke my heart, so shiny and delicious, and a comb like a señorita's holding her bun in place and looking like a crown.

Now, this was the article I'd read with the greatest interest because it said that one of the first things the legislature should do is set up a way to tax us. I couldn't speak for anyone else in that room, but I earned my money and was quite happy with the way it sat undivided.

"This Burnett character wants to give the right of suffrage to Negroes," said one man with obvious disgust.

Suffrage? Who cares? What's a vote?

"Wasn't it interesting how Burnett wanted collectors to receive taxes in gold? He was thinking of the miners!" I contributed.

"It's certainly a bold stand to take," said another man.

"Indeed! I'll pay 'em in paper if I pay at all!" spake I.

"Er, I was referring to the suffrage issue," he said to me kindly, then addressed the group as a whole. "California could lead the nation in this. We could be the example for all the other states to follow."

All right, I had a third glass but it weren't so brassy this time since I'd brought back the bottle to my seat and poured all meekly. The meat was long devoured, and I willed my stomach not to complain in any voice the assembled company could hear.

A full hour later, we went to our dinner table and ate oxtail soup and savory pie. There was red wine and I became heady. "Why didn't she ask me to play the piano?" I wondered. I giggled perhaps a bit inappropriately during the meal, responding more oft to the expressions on people's faces than the content of what they'd said. But I got some looks that let me know the "visiting" would begin with a vengeance when it began.

After all plates were emptied, a solemn thing happened. A gent would catch a lady's eye, extend his hand to her as if asking for a dance, and she'd give a certain filly-like wiggle and precede him up the stairs. So that's how. I knew the fellas got to choose, but I didn't know how they'd do it with all the girls gathered together.

Two girls was left over, and they shrugged at Bridget.

"Now, then, miss!" scolded Bridget. "I see how you are with the liquor. We don't tolerate that in this house."

"I was hungry!" I protested. "I haven't eaten all the day long. And helping Patience with the leaving of course made me weakish."

"You should have spoken before the visitors came, and you'd have eaten. To my infinite regret, I can't look at a girl's belly and know whether it's full or not."

The unpicked ones laughed. I thought of Patience and her unforecast stomach.

"It's been so fast and all," I said. "I barely knew where to locate that belly, I just knew it was hankering."

"Well, you got some good eyeing from the visitors. So as long as you understand not to drink like a crib girl, we'll be all right."

An insult I wasn't eligible for no more.

"Why didn't you have me play the piano?" I asked.

"You had too much champagne. You would have sprawled over the keys and fallen asleep."

I smirked at her. "You wait. I've got a few lively tunes to make you tap your feet and nod your head."

"I'll be glad to hear them on another occasion. Now, Liza and Thomasina, since you're not busy, why don't you instruct Nora in our methods?"

Grand. Taught by the two no one wanted. We all stood up, Bridget left, and the lesson began at the foot of the stairs.

"You move your weight side to side as you ascend," said Liza. "That way your hips sway and he can hardly wait to get you upstairs." Liza's hips swayed in the manner of a barge knocking against the dock.

"That looks so smooth," I observed, and Thomasina looked at me suspiciously.

"Now you try," said Liza, halfway up.

Since Liza ain't worth describing, let me tell you instead about the stairs. I hadn't noticed them much on my scamper up to find the source of the screaming, but now that things was as they was, I ran a hand over the fine mahogany banister. It was glossy and sturdy, yet had a curvy beauty like…well, like hips when they ain't Liza's. A thick carpet ran down the steps, pegged in with carpet tacks that looked to be made of gold. I wouldn't have been surprised.

I ascended that stair in queenly manner, letting my hips rise as they would.

"That is surely natural," said Thomasina from below. "You don't need any practice. Up to the landing you go."

At the door I learned that the visitor turns the knob, not me, and that it had been found to be successful for the girl to cover her mouth as if having a slightly shocked inkling of what was to come. Then flash the eyes, they said, and glide into the room.

"Glide?"

"Like this." Thomasina plunged into the room like she'd heard the shout of fire.

"Or like this," said Liza. She minced in, knocking into Thomasina.

"Or like this?" I asked. I glided.

"Not really," said Liza. "Back up and try it again."

Well, over the course of five and twenty minutes I learned how the monkey feels when the organ-grinder is training him to hold the hat for alms. I glided back and forth across that threshold like a ghost of no essence while the girls tried to coach me back into a clunky, corporeal body.

When we'd reached accord, things got more interesting. I started to asking questions 'stead of waiting for the limping instruction.

"Who takes off what clothes?" I asked. I saw no oilcloth on the bed.

"We keep a list downstairs," said Liza. "We all memorize the preferences. Some men watch you disrobe; others'll do it for you."

"And some want you to undress them and some don't," I added.

They looked at me, blank as September slates.

"Oh, we never do that," said Thomasina. "They're men. They don't want womenfolk fiddling around with their clothes."

"They just take them off and put them in this chair."

"Would it be blasphemous to yank a man's shirt off and toss it in the corner like you're mad to get your hands on him?" I asked. "Or play like you're frustrated with the trouser buttons because you can't wait a moment longer?"

"We don't really do that," said Thomasina. "Let's continue. You'll get into bed on this side, and he'll get in on the other. You meet in the center."

"You don't go together? Clutching each other?"

"I think that would frighten a visitor," said Liza.

"Now, Bridget's rule is you must let him touch you wherever he wants. Even if it's uncomfortable and makes you wonder what type of gentleman he is."

"What kind of touching do we use?" I was eager to learn the techniques of the parlor house, although I was having the sinking worry that these tutors were not armed with a courtesan's arsenal of skills.

"You can hold his shoulders like this while he…"

Thomasina demonstrated the shoulder grip on Liza, both of them standing a foot apart from each other.

"Nothing more fancy than that?"

"This is really all you need," said Thomasina. "The men tend to do what their bodies urge them to, and we're there to support them."

"Do you ever use your mouths?"

Theirs gaped. "There's one girl who does. That talks about it, anyway. Patience."

"The one still living?"

"Yes."

We all bowed our heads a minute, thinking of the girl who didn't like anybody enough to confess she was *enceinte*.

"And does Patience have a lot of visitors?" I resumed when I judged the time respectful.

"Such a lot!"

"Why don't you assay her technique? Then maybe you'd be behind closed doors with a paying fella 'stead of playing headmistress with me."

"That's simply unpleasant," said Liza. "I think what we do is unpleasant enough."

"You don't enjoy the work?"

"I'd be in a poorhouse now if a madam back East didn't scoop me off the street," said Liza. "My mother was a laudanum addict and ran off with a man one night. I was eight. But I'm only one step above that. I'm not too happy with my station. I like the girls here, though. If only nobody ever visited."

"Sometimes I like it," said Thomasina. "When they act like you're pretty or whisper things into your neck, that part's good."

"Do you like it?" asked Liza.

I said, "I don't like the drunks or the rough ones, but—"

"Your Chicago house admitted those? Bridget doesn't even let them past the door."

I gulped. *Slow down, Nora.* Lying is a slow art, like needlepoint.

"Well, sometimes, you can't smell it on their breath but it's there. And they seem all cultured downstairs, but upstairs they're bestial rogues. Those are the ones I just work my hips for, to make them come faster and leave. But if he's handsome or his shirt smells clean, why, it's right enjoyable. And if you can manage the thing they manage, that feeling when you—"

"That's a lie," interrupted Thomasina flatly.

I was all set to retort something that'd make clear my private thoughts on her, but remembered this was just my first day. I'd been wanting to be in a parlor house for a long time. I had to make friends, not knock sense into the mental cabinets these two kept impaired thoughts in.

"Actually, it isn't. But I'll leave you to make that journey yourself. Now, anything else I need to know?"

"Encourage him to return. Say you'd enjoy another visit."

"Where do I wash?"

"This basin here is for your regular washing. Under the bed—and don't mistake it for a chamber pot—is another one for…that kind of…"

The skunk that enriched the forest! If they couldn't even talk about these things, how did they ever bring themselves to do them?

"You wait here while he goes downstairs," said Liza. "You can even stay undressed until he leaves if it's not too cold."

"So what about the money?" I thought maybe I could find some information through the back door.

"Bridget handles that."

"How much is it?"

"Each girl is different, and it counts on the visitor's stance in the world as well."

Well, they were little parrots any pirate would be proud to have on his shoulder.

"In general terms, how much would you net each month?" I persisted.

"We don't talk like this," said Liza. "It's vulgar. We do our work and she pays us out."

"Apologies for the vulgarity. It's just that in Chicago the visitor would put money in an envelope upon the dresser, and out of that we'd pay the madam. See, rather than her paying me out, I'd pay her out. Isn't that a grand way of doing it? Maybe if other girls thought it was a good idea—"

"You talk too fast," said Thomasina. She was frowning. "And you're trying to change what runs already."

I could see their patience was gliding through the door graceful as a trained whore, so I let my mouth droop and confessed to a false weariness. They understood that and forgave me, I saw, as they led me to my room.

"Oh!" said Liza. "The mattress is gone."

"It's drying in the yard," I said. "It may take a day or so. I believe I'll go to my old lodging and tarry the night there. I need to move my belongings anyhow. What's the hour?"

It was three o'clock. Lunch had been an extended event. Perhaps all the men had finished while we talked and were now back at their desks, rolling their sleeves into arm garters and blotting their pens.

Liza and Thomasina saw me downstairs to the front door. "Ought I to tell Bridget?" I asked.

"We flit here and everywhere without call to tell anybody," said Liza proudly. "Bridget only cares that we're back for the lunch and dinner hours, and that there's always at least five girls home."

"Fine, then. I'll return in the morn."

I stepped outside and nearly fell down the front steps, for there was Abe waiting for me, leaning against the iron fence. After all the events, I'd plumb forgotten about him.

"Are they taking you?" he greeted me. "Are you a parlor house girl like you wanted?"

I began walking briskly, knowing he'd follow. I didn't want any girls looking out the windows and seeing him. "I'm in," I said. "But I'm returning home for the evening and I'll come back tomorrow with all my earthly goods. I'll say good-bye to Mehitabel and that'll be that."

"Tomorrow I'll see the inside."

"Oh, I don't think so, Abe. It's enough for you to see the outward. And thank you mightily for waiting on me, although you shouldn't have. Did you eat?"

"Caught a loaf off a peddler," he said morosely.

"You must be sick unto death of this street, and hungry besides."

"Why cain't I see inside?"

We were now several blocks from Price Street so I stopped and put my cool cheek against his hot shoulder in its stiff boiled cotton. "Abe, sweetheart, it's so fancy inside. There's velvet and every chair looks like the stuffing from another chair besides was pushed inside. Little knickknacks and things you'd break. It's just too fancy."

"So you won't let me in?"

"Not *me*. You know I'd let you in anywhere. But it's the woman what runs it. She'd be upset."

"Cause'n I look like I ain't smart nor rich?"

"Not that, cherub. It's more like…" I let my voice trail off and pretended to notice something absolutely ordinary. "Why, goodness, Abe, has that barber pole always been there?"

Abe kept his jaw closed the entire rest of the walk back to Mehitabel's, and I babbled to cover that.

At my gate, I kissed him. "You're such a good friend to me, Abe. I will always remember that you are a good man."

He didn't say a word, just climbed into his carriage, clucked to Minnie, and rode off.

Chapter 17

At breakfast, I said good-bye to Mehitabel, letting the reclaimed ring speak for me and my supposed nuptial happiness to come. The damn woman cried and I felt more and more like I didn't know what the hell I was doing. I was making Abe quiet and Mehitabel sob—all to learn sexual folly from the likes of Thomasina and Liza.

I popped my head to the window to see if Abe was there for me, but he wasn't. So I stood in the street and flagged a truck, and got the man to carry my things down the stairs. Mehitabel pressed a heavy kerchief in my hand, and I opened it to see the return of my extra rent. I handed it back like it was a hot coal.

"No, I don't want it," I said. "You won't be able to rent for the last few days of December anyhow. It's yours."

She tried to refuse but was no match for me. I kissed her and she didn't even flinch, so convinced was she that I now had the lips of an honest woman.

"Thanks for the piano lessons," I told her. "And if you need to go to the hurdy-gurdy house on your own to flap your skirts around, I don't think anybody would mind."

It was just the right teasing; it got her to laugh as I walked out the door.

As the driver took my things into the parlor house, I saw how sorrowfully shabby they were. The galley mate's steamer had the long gash down the side, and the lockplate was gone from when I'd attacked it with the poker. The other girls watched the procession up the stairs with little tight smiles. I'm sure behind my back those cats snickered, but she who snickers last, they say...

Up in my room the mattress was back, leaned against the wall with toweling beneath to catch the drip. The entire bottom half was rusty with blood, and the driver kept his head turned away from it. I did the same.

When he was gone, I closed the door and sat on the floor, looked around. This room was too pretty for fecking, I thought. Seemed like wood made good, solid walls for good, solid bodies. I didn't know how I might behave in such a chamber with florid wallpaper and mirrors everywhere. There was a rap at the door, and I opened it to see a girl with deep dimples in her cheeks.

"I'm Alice," she said. "I've been here the longest of any, and Bridget sent me up to continue your instruction."

"I think I got everything worth knowing from Thomasina and Liza yesterday," I said, winking broadly.

She laughed and was thereby my first friend in this brothel, other than Patience, who lived on in my cot stain.

"Well, perhaps I can elucidate on what they provided you," she laughed.

Elucidate. I remembered misspelling that one and setting back down on the schoolroom plank.

"They was—were, I mean—kind of vague on things, like specific things."

"Specific things? What do you mean specifically?" She cocked her head.

"Well, like, do you girls do anything special under the sheets? Tricks a Chicago girl wouldn't know?"

"Well...do you know about clamping?"

"Oh yes."

"Tickling?"

"Where might that be?"

"Underneath. You know. And not so much a tickling as a...like using your fingernails like feathers."

I nodded vigorously.

"And speaking of feathers, I'm sure the girls yesterday showed you the contents of your top drawer?"

I looked at my own bosoms, confused.

"No, silly," she laughed. "Your clothes dresser." We crossed the room and opened the drawer. "The other three drawers are for your effects, but the top one is the house's. From time to time, you'll find new things in here as Bridget learns of them."

Inside was an array of long ostrich feathers, going the entire length of the drawer, and cock rings, vials of oil, and condoms. There was also a strange device with a bunch of pins coming off it, and I picked it up.

"That's for Elmer Clapp," said Alice. "He likes to be pricked with it. All over."

I pressed it against my arm and yelped. "Elmer's an odd one," I said.

"The harder the better for him," she said. "Don't be frightened to draw blood. He pays more when you do."

I rifled around the drawer some more, finding daguerreotypes of ladies naked to the skin and doing naughty things. "These are for…?"

"Show them to a visitor if things aren't going right. You understand my meaning?"

"Not precisely."

"If you find he's not really ready for visiting."

"Oh!" That had never happened to me. In the cribs, things was fast and rough and a gent already had a poker by the time he stepped inside the door.

She explained the other things in the dresser to me, then had me strip to my skivvies to see how things looked. "Your garters are loose," she observed. "They make your stockings sag. I'll get you some from Bridget's chamber. There should be a nice firmness as if the garter doesn't want to let go of your thigh. The visitors enjoy tugging."

She judged my bosoms all right and admired a beauty spot in my cleavage. "You're a good package then," she said. "Nice and fat in all the right places."

"Do you think so?" I asked. "Walking all these hills I've lost my nice roll of a belly."

"It's fine," she said. "The belly is less important than the ass. And that's still intact."

We talked on certain visitors' proclivities and methods and body positions she knew: parlor house girls really did service the men better.

"I'll take you downstairs to read the log book," she said. "That makes it easy. And anytime you please a man particularly well, go record it in the book to help us when he's ours."

"What about the mouth?" I asked.

"Do you do that?"

"I might," I said. "A few girls in my Chicago house did but everyone says it's dangerous."

"Right; there's the risk of syphilis. But you can use a condom; it just tastes bad. And the visitors strongly prefer the feel of a girl's mouth. You just have to look him over and see."

"So you do it?"

"It's quick and doesn't make you sore," she said. "There's only one thing I won't do and that's Greek."

I had no idea what she meant. I imagined her in a toga shaking her head vehemently.

"So the mouth is easy," she said. "Just make sure everything's really wet all the time. If you think it's too wet, it's probably just wet enough. Keep working up the spit and use your hand for what you can't get in your mouth."

"So it's just like using your mouth in place of your...other part."

"Well, you can be a little more fancy. Quick with the tongue, slow with the lips at the same time. Or change the rhythm, or work along the outside for a bit, like you were presented with a tasty cob of corn. And of course, don't neglect the boys."

"Pardon?"

"The boys. The boys." She laughed. "It's easy to talk bold with the visitors—they like that, you know—but with a pretty lass like you it's making me squirm a bit."

"Are you referring to the sack?"

"Quite so."

"Every miner has to have a sack to carry his gold," I said, and we laughed together until I realized suddenly that she had probably never dallied with a miner. 'Twas only professors and clerks and magistrates for her.

"Alice, do you ever experience this thing, *le petit mort*?" I asked over the laughter, finding it easier to ask than in the blank quiet.

"I do," she grinned. "It's easier with some of the visitors. Some of them actually work you toward it, with busy fingers and sometimes tongues."

I gaped at her. This was indeed a different perspective.

"But with all of them," she continued, "you must *appear* to have experienced it. They all expect it. So if he seems at the end of his line, you just start bucking and sighing and...you know, make it like the end of the symphony when all the horns and drums and bells are blasting out. Get loud, scream it out. Breathe hard. Here's a tip I'll pass to you since I like you: try to sound like you're speaking a language that doesn't exist, with lots of pauses to breathe roughly in between. I can't tell you how many visitors request me over and over just for that."

There was certainly a range of ability in this house. I thought of poor Liza and Thomasina lying down no better than a wife, unaware that in the other rooms girls were mouthing men and feeling the explosive bolts of sexual death.

"Thanks for all your plain speaking, Alice," I said. "When will Bridget consider me fully trained?"

"I'll tell her you seem ready to me. You're so inquisitive and wanting to talk about these things. Some girls come here and just bow their heads throughout the whole speech."

"I'm raring to begin," I said. "No use flopping around here without a cause."

"The only thing is your mattress," she said. "Each room is full now."

"Anyone with their monthlies?"

"How long were you in your Chicago house?" she asked.

"Uh, two years," I said.

"And you never noticed something funny about that?"

"About what?"

"Well, I've been working in three different parlor houses," she said. "And a thing of many marvels always happens. Even though each new girl arrives with her own time for making her blood, in a year or so we all get so we're together on it." I remembered Bridget saying "Eventually you'll regularize."

"Do doctors know about this?" I asked.

"Who knows? But it makes for a vacation for us, the ones that don't get the horrid female convulsions. Bridget puts a sign on the door and we eat cookies and take outings if we like."

"It's beyond science," I said. "Someone ought to study it."

"Oh lackaday, it's just women. Who'll study on us?"

"I don't know," I said. "But the day I bleed with twenty other girls, I'll be pickled about it."

"You don't seem scared of anything," she said.

So there you are, Nora Simms, delivered a compliment by a one not possessing a John Thomas. I felt rosy indoors of my heart and flashed her a smile that got my earbobs swinging and rioting.

"Nor you," I said.

Well, Alice must have spoken honey into Bridget's ears because Bridget took me aside and showed me the room I'd use for the day. "I'm letting Thomasina visit her baby, so you can sport in here," she said.

"Where's her baby, at her mother's?"

"At the poorhouse. She left it at the door, and every now and again she pretends she's a lady looking for a child to raise and goes to look at it."

"How can she know it for her own?"

"Birthmark on the brow, like a vat of lye was spilled on her."

At noon, when I heard the bells chiming, I bent and snapped my garters to make sure they was decently tight, gargled peppermint oil to make my breath sweet, and went downstairs to take my place among the lovely, talkative girls.

There were several young'uns among the troops of gents that called, including one that scarce looked fourteen. Made me think of that other youngster I'd had dealings with: the galley mate that spirited off my trunk.

I thought this boy'd choose me, no doubt, since I'm gentle-looking and don't spook horses, but instead it was his father, apparently extending his son's schooling beyond academia, who bowed his head to me in that significant way after dessert.

I climbed the stairs without thinking of my hips and entered Thomasina's room with nary a glide, simply the step of a woman who's good at what she does.

I put one leg up on the bed and pulled my skirts, demonstrating the wound-up nature of my garter.

"Keep them on," said the fella roughly. He seized me from behind and pushed me facedown onto the bed.

"Ease up," I called over my shoulder. "Stop behaving like an omnibus."

"Shut it," he snarled. "I'm paying for this."

"I'll scream high murder if you don't stop smashing me, and how'll you explain that to the snot-nosed brat you brung with ye?"

He twisted the flesh on my buttock and made it smart but did let me up so I could bring some gusty air into my lungs. I have to say I was disappointed with my first go-round of "visiting"—it weren't no slower or prestigious than what happened in the cowyard.

After he left, I washed up just like I was told, in the fancy bowl beneath the bed. I was just making things dry and tidy again when there was a rap on the door.

"That was certainly fast," said Bridget when I opened up. "Did all go well?"

"Well enough," I said. "I'd be curious to see what it says in your log book. I'm sure it ain't a haven of praises."

She looked at me and I looked at her. "Isn't. *Isn't* a haven of praises," I continued.

"He generally doesn't go so fast."

"I think I made him mad with passion. Is his son still visiting?"

"Are you daft? He finished before the father! Those young ones practically spill coming up the stairs," she said.

"So I'm free until supper?"

"Yes." She peered into the room behind me, as if trying to divine news from the state of the sheets.

"Have I passed the test of quality?"

"He did pay well," she admitted.

"See? He wanted a quick little turn. Your regular girls just move too slow."

"Mayhap. Well, settle yourself and we'll see how the afternoon runs."

I shut the door and did a little turn of rapture in front of the standing mirror. I had done it! I was a parlor house girl. I ran my fingers over the thick, packed bodies of the embroidered bumblebees on my new dress. The men might not be any different from the crib fellas once you got their starched expensive clothes off.

But I was.

Chapter 18

After dinner I climbed the stairs with a skinny thread of a man, thinking I could knit him up into someone bigger. I undressed him, letting my tongue write words like "isn't" and "mayhap" on his skin.

But when I looked at his bobbing tomkins, I plucked his trousers from around his ankles and shot them right back up. "Sorry, lad, no visiting today," I said.

"What do you mean?"

"I mean it's supposed to be pink, not red and pustuled! As the laywoman puts it, your dick is sick."

"That's not so," he said. "It always looks like that."

"Then it's always been sick."

"Since I was a babe in arms. Now, let's get back to the tongue, miss." He pulled his pants back down and stepped out of them. He motioned me to the bed.

"No," I said, knowing him for a liar. "I'll defrock and let you handle things yourself, if you're understanding my meaning. Here's a hanky to keep your hand out of the mess."

"I came here for fucking, not my own damn hand."

"Well, come back when things are smooth and pretty again."

"I'm paying quite a lot for this," he said. "I wasn't aware you were allowed to cast me off."

I looked at his skinny feet, archless and hairy, and began to think they didn't look so right either.

"I'll tell you one thing, and then we can quit arguing like cousins at a wake. I ain't letting *that* touch *this*."

"We'll see about that," he said shortly. He put the pants back on but left his shoes by my bed. He went into the hall and I moved the shoes to outside my door as he walked away. I didn't need to have any further truck with him.

A few moments later, when I heard the knock at the door, I sighed and called out, "They're at your feet! Look down."

"Nora, it's me," said Bridget's voice.

"Oh. Come in."

She closed the door behind her, but not before I saw Ill Willie's visage out in the hall.

"You can't say no to a visitor," she hissed, her color high. "That's a rule of this house."

"But he's got syphilis or something near! His cock's all oozing and red."

"So clean up after."

"That's like closing the window after the fly's sitting on your pie."

She jabbed a finger into my chest, hitting whatever bone holds my skellington together. It made me straighten up. She weren't no piece I could work around with boldness.

"There isn't any arguing with the madam of this house," she said, each word sounding a curse. "If you want to be in the finest parlor house this city has ever seen, you live by my rules. Have him wear the skin sheath, and you wash harder afterward. I told him this throw's free, just to keep him happy and coming back. So do your damnedest to please him. If anyone spreads infamous word due to your ninny-acting, you'll be packing your bags back to Chicago with a tear in your eye."

I tossed my head and flounced down on the bed. I heard the brickwork in her voice and knew I couldn't argue. So out she went and in came himself, smug and unbuttoning even as he walked. I took off my clothes without looking him in the eye. From the top drawer I took a cock's nightgown and handed it to him. As he tied the bow at the top, he kept his pinky fingers sticking out like a society lady holding her teacup. The preservative didn't cover everything, so the whole time we romped I tried to keep him from striving too deep. I knew I weren't completely successful though. Sometimes flesh hit flesh and I burned to think what particles was bouncing off his body onto mine.

"Thank you kindly," he said when he was done. I knew I was supposed to wait until he left to begin my hygiene, but I couldn't. I yanked the pot out from under the bed so fast it slopped water onto the floor. I soaped up good while he watched fascinated.

"Get out, you're done," I said. I could have hit myself as I saw that he was getting worked up again.

"That one was free. Maybe I ought to pay for a second go."

"I've got a gent already lined up," I lied. "Bridget would kill me if you detained me."

I stomped to the dresser and yanked out drawers to see what else might help me out. Thomasina had a bottle of sipping whiskey, so I poured that all down my female parts, biting my lips against the sting.

"Go on, git," I said.

He finally padded to the door, where his shoes still waited, and bowed from the waist.

"Hope it don't fall off on you," I called as the door shut.

I hustled myself over to the mirrors and tried to look at how things sat down there. When I heard the rap on the door I almost fell over for I had one leg braced against the wall in an unsturdy manner.

It was Bridget again. "Are you washed up?" she asked, sticking her head in the door.

"Indeed. Care to check?"

She narrowed her eyes at me. "There's a latecomer downstairs and I'm sending him up to you."

"Really? Is his dick black with plague?"

"You've a mouth on you, girl, and you'd do well to sew it up. Your place here is not guaranteed."

"Send him up," I said. "I eagerly await his tubercular cough."

Well, guess who it was. The professor!

He recognized me as well, even though I was dressed finer than last time and with my hair done different. He gave me a surprised smile and I bounced a little and clapped my hands together to show my pleasure.

"*Bonjour*," he said.

"*Bonjour!* And you were correct, sir, in your assessment that my instructor wasn't French at all."

He chuckled. "How is Lady Fortuna treating you?"

"Can't argue. Look at my circumstance: in a fancy house screwing men with…" I stopped myself. If I told him I had just slept with a syphilitic visitor, then he wouldn't touch me.

"Far cry from the cribs," he said. "I applaud your rise in ranks."

"It's a whole other world here, professor."

"And now you can be free of that idiot you seemed fond of."

"Oh, I won't abide any harsh words on him, even from you who I admire like nobody else."

"I beg your pardon." He took off his cufflinks and laid them on the dresser.

"Not at all. But I must say, I feel safe from the dangerous type of man who frequents cowyards."

"No repeat of your horrible experience with the German, I hope?"

"No, although another girl there…well, she…"

"I know," said the professor, pausing in his unbuttoning. "I had to draw her."
We regarded each other for a quiet moment.

"What a relief not to have to say it," I said. "But professor, the story has a brilliant ending, for I watched him be hanged not days later."

"Indeed." He was now naked from the trousers up, his waist slim and muscular.

"I ain't spiteful, but that was a good one to release to the vaporous otherworld." And then I smiled for a second because I had figured something out on this professor. "I see your plan now, professor."

"Pardon?" His frown was sudden and overly dark.

"You don't like the talking that parlor houses require, so you conveniently 'missed' the dinner meal and arrived late, so you could simply tread the stairs and get your lay. Am I mistaken?"

"You see through me like the glazier does the glass."

"Have you been back to the cowyard on Jackson?" I asked.

"I did seek you but found other comforts in the stead."

"Who?"

"How am I supposed to know the name?"

"Well, it's bloody printed on the board above her head, isn't it?!"

"It is, but I didn't notice. She was fragrant, womanly…Let's get on with the merrymaking, shall we?"

"What's my name?"

"It's Nora," he said without hesitating.

All right then, so that got me out of my clothes. I liked Professor Hugh Parkson, and soon I felt like we was the only folks in Christendom, twisting our limbs to get each other closer.

"You're my favorite," he whispered.

"You're mine too," I whispered back. Then I remembered Abe was supposed to be my favorite and buried my face in the professor's neck.

He didn't leave afterward. He propped his head up on his arm and played with the heat curls back of my neck.

"Want to talk?" I joked.

"You know I'm not here for that," he scowled, but with twinkling eyes.

"Professor, if there's any field of knowledge you're weak in, just report it to me and I'll assist you. I have vast amounts of knowledge tucked up in this neat, tidy head."

"Phrenology," he said.

"Speaking of heads…Well, if your forehead's all bumpy, as yours is, it means you have a predilection for not talking. This broad space back of your ear, that has to do with your capacity for tenderness."

"Thanks for all that," he said. "Tremendous assistance rendered by a trollop, something I certainly was not banking on."

"Is that what you are, a professor of phrenology?"

"No, that's a tawdry science. My sister's got all the same head features as me and we're alike as a baboon and rat. I'm a professor of mathematics."

"And which are you, the baboon or rat?"

"Now I'm stuck in an unpleasant metaphor of my own invention. Perhaps I ought to have said, 'alike as a mountain lion and a...' Help me, darling."

"A majestic Black Angus cow," I said.

"Fine. So I'm cattle. I can sit with that."

"You're handsome," I said and rolled back toward him, knocking him off his arm perch. "Want another one? Just quick. I won't tell Bridget."

And he did, and I didn't.

Chapter 19

Three days later, and still no sign of the bubbles on my nether regions. Every morning I checked with a hand-held mirror I purchased from a shop on Broadway for three dollars and fifty cents. 'Twas shocking to see the lay of the land at such close quarters. I promised myself if I ever saw that fella back at the dinner table again, I'd make sure Bridget knew my blood was sudden flowing and I'd be out of it for the next five days.

So it was the eve of the New Year, and that night there'd be special sporting with musical entertainment and dancing, followed by Year 1850 fecking. But for the afternoon, I was out getting measured for new gowns, buying on credit from Bridget, and seeing the city.

The tailor on Columbus had few fabrics in spring green, the color I was most admired in, so I picked a pale blue lawn with a sprig of ivory and a lightly striped crimson wool twill. He was a funny man with some mannerisms that made me think he was the bugger type, but he made supreme suggestions about the tucks of the bodice and even showed me some sheer tulle to stretch across my bubs; he knew my trade, I'm sure of it.

The millinery store was a delight. I brought the milliner a length of crinoline to fashion a bow to match the lawn. The sample hats on display were frothy like meringue and carried feathers of every color.

I called at the jewelers too and got a chain of pure gold links with a flower encased in glass as a bead pendant, and a string of jet beads.

Only someone who has spent weeks in one dress can imagine the heady pleasures of this sort of shopping. I could scarcely keep from laughing aloud at the feel of true silk or the sight of bows and furbelows that could make the worst girl comely. Oh! I was in a blissful state, gorged with beauty and color and the ability to purchase it. Bridget was fair with her monetary disbursements as far as I could figure. At the end of the week, she gathered us and gave the report for our number of customers, delivered compliments or censure taken from quotes of our good gentlemen, and then counted out the money—minus expenses—into each girl's hand. She did this payment in front of us all, so there was no question of amounts.

Having only been in the house a few days, I was surprised to see I made more than any girl, but Bridget, noticing the spiteful glances I received from the others, made a short speech about how each girl had once been the chief earner when she was new in the house. "Remember, novelty only lasts so long, girls," she'd say. "Patience, don't you recall how it was your palm that once held the most? Things will settle out, so stop your catty eye-rolling and be sensible."

I kept as much track of the expenses as I could, for just as the crib owner swindled me with the linens fee, so too did this Irish madam with thin lips tax me for each glass of champagne I drank and each pastry I slipped on my plate. It was a marvel she could keep count of all the girls and their tabs, but sure as the fat sizzles in the pan, she did it.

But I wasn't as affronted as I was with the crib owner. Even though the charges were extravagant (I paid nearly as much for champagne as a visitor did!), I was living finely. After my tasks were done, I simply walked the streets to see the men bustling at their duties, the fruit vendors shouting their prices, and the horses shaking their heads through the gray vapor of minute flies. On one particular morning, the bay was especially blue behind the clutter of abandoned ships, and the air was good and clean. I bought a sweet biscuit and ate it as I walked, dripping crumbs into the dust. Before I knew it, I had wended my way back to the cribs on Jackson Street.

As I looked at the line, I wished I was wearing my new frock already, with the feather of my yet-to-be-made hat nodding in the breeze. I hovered, waiting for somebody to see me and ask my business.

I had never really looked at the cribs like this, as a man might stand and think about entering. I had always been on the plank sidewalk or in the window enticing my own selection.

I saw how flimsy the shacks were, and how small. *The air must be close in there*, I thought. There was a repugnance in me, as if they were simply sordid dollhouses for little girls who had been bad and whose dollies were made for them with frowns and missing limbs.

One of the doors opened and a gent emerged. After he had taken a fair number of steps, the door opened again and the girl of ill fame came out. I recognized her. She had been one in the crowd when I told the girls what the killer looked like.

"Lassie!" I called to her. "Remember me?"

She came over and nodded. "How goes your trade?"

"I've found me a spot at a parlor house. It's a new life now. But I wanted to ask—"

"About Charlotte," she said flatly.

"Yes."

"That girl said nothing. I would have helped her if she'd screamed or crawed; I even had a hatpin under my pillow should the need arise for me or another."

"That's a foul fiction!" This bark came from behind me and I turned to see a girl who was returning to the cribs after some errand. Her eyes were small and hateful. "She screamed like he was raking her insides with a tool fresh hot from the forge."

"Shut your trap, you hussy! I ain't heard nothing that night," the other girl returned.

"Bloody murder, it was, and not a one of you came out. I rushed out and was at the door when he brushed past me. The deed was already done."

"So you have better ears than the rest of us. Congratulations!"

"Better *something*, that's for certain. When I close my eyes at night, I feel like God is shining a special ray on me, 'cause I tried to help her. And some of you even had men with you—couldn't you have asked for their gentlemanly assistance if you were too cowardly to act on your own?"

I stood speechless, watching the girls snip at each other. I knew who I *wanted* to be the truth-teller, but feared she was the liar.

"You're making the whole fib up, to make yourself look fine," retorted the other prostitute. "Charlotte was silent as the tombs."

"I hope that 'silent' cry rings in your ears for eternity, you heartless scrap of shit. And better than that, I hope he comes back for you. Serve you right if you scream into the night without anyone stirring."

"He ain't coming back for nobody," the other girl said. "He became very good friends with a rope."

"That weren't him! I saw the fella they hanged, went right and looked at him full in the face, lying in the straw afterward with his neck broke, and it weren't the one that brushed past me that night."

I gaped at her, as the other girl did.

"That's right!" she crowed triumphantly. "I wasn't going to tell a one of you, since you didn't give a pin about Charlotte. But he's still out there, the fella what done it."

The other girl was white as bone china, and I figured myself similar.

"So what did the murderer look like?" I asked.

"I'll tell *you*, since you was nice and told us what you knew that time." She whispered in my ear: "It happened so quick-like, miss, I barely saw him. But I know he had no facial hair on him; his cheeks was all smooth and empty. He had no mustache or dark mole like the German fella."

"What'd she tell you? What's he look like?" screeched the other one. "I'll have you arrested for not speaking the truth we need."

"The citizens grabbed that German fella," she continued. "Based on some police news that he was hassling our kind. Hassling, not killing, though."

"What's she saying?" howled the other girl. "It ain't right to not say. It ain't right!"

"You've got to tell everyone," I said to the girl. "I'm ashamed worse than I can tell that nobody came to Charlotte's side, but I don't think she would want others to be killed the same as she was!"

"Why not? Eye for an eye."

"*I'll* tell then. And you tell the rest on the line, Little Miss 'I Didn't Hear a Sound.' It was a fella with no beard or any hair on his face," I said.

"Smooth-shaven—and that's the only word you have to give?" the other girl asked.

"That's it. It was dark and that was all I saw."

She left with a look that was half fearful and half angry, and the witness gave me a wry smile. "She won't tell a soul. The girls here care nothing for each other, not a whit. You keep yourself safe, Nora. You were good to try to get the girls here to help each other, but it's a task for a passel of saints."

Then she turned on her heel and walked to her crib.

I swallowed the last of my sweetie and was prepared to walk on when I saw the roof of one of the cribs trail a bit of smoke, and then appear overtaken in flames a moment later.

I closed my eyes. Ah god. The cowyard was a tinderbox, all the shacks built sharing common walls. And most of these girls kept all their earthly goods inside, not having the luxury of another home for boarding.

"Fire!" I shouted.

There was nary a peep.

"Fire! Girls, get you and your gents out! The line's on fire." And then it was a madhouse of doors opening and fellas sticking themselves back into their trousers, and girls running with crooked skirts, moving teats back into halfway-buttoned shimmies. They piled out onto the street and looked for the flames. By now the fire had a voice, speaking with a crackle and a spit. I hated myself for liking the smell, instantly embraced as a comfortable kitchen fire.

"Mary's mewling son!" yelled one of the women, someone I hadn't seen before. "'Tis Emma's crib!" She grabbed the man nearest her. "Go inside and fetch her, sir! She'll die!"

Emma was the trollop in the habit of pulling her skirts over her head, not so subtle in her solicitations, but likeable nonetheless.

"'Tis none of my business," said the snake, and he tossed a coin at her and began a jaunty step back toward Dupont Street.

"You contemptible villain!" I called after him. The woman dashed to the door of the shack in flames with myself at her heels. 'Twas locked. The heat pushed out of the wood to press against us.

"She smokes a pipe," said the woman to me. "I fretted her about it, but she don't listen, so deep in her cups all the time."

I threw myself full weight against the door, thinking I was certainly stronger than this pasty cut of wood, but I didn't even shake it, although I was shocked how hot it was to the touch. The other woman took off her boot and tried to use it to break the glass of the window.

"Harder!" I yelled. A bit of flaming roof fell past me and I stamped it out afore it could get the sidewalk going. I turned back around to see the company assembled and doing naught to aid the cause. "Fellas! Bring axes! And Nancy there, go sound the alarm! See if you can rouse any of those brand-new fire men."

A man I recognized from past days of sporting walked right up the window, pulled the woman aside, and kicked it out. A huge whoosh of black smoke came out and the fire smell became even stronger. There were still jagged bits of glass, but he kicked them out too, and then stepped inside. He was invisible in one step.

"Emma!" I screamed.

"Do you know her?" asked the other woman anxiously.

"I surely do," I said. "She drinks herself to puking and works her pipe like a smokehouse. I have oft thought to bring a ham and leave it with her a week to flavor it." There were tears streaming down her face and we both began to cough with the smoke. "He'll bring her out and she'll live to lift another bottle," I said.

I stepped back and cast my regard to the roofline. Already the two cribs on either side were crackling with flame, and no fire men were here as yet. "It'll all come heaving down," I said to myself, then turned and yelled at the motley collection of harlots and gents who stuck around just for the spectacle. "Get buckets! You can save your own crib if you quench the fire."

"I ain't no fire man!" one girl shouted back at me. "And I've got me sign and me clothes and that's all I'm after."

I scanned the crowd for the owner's face, despicable as I had last found it, thinking surely she could organize the girls to save the place they needed for their livelihoods. Yet I couldn't clap eyes on her.

It had been too long. Why wasn't the fella back out with Emma? I saw no shack now, only its shape created in yellow and red flames. The other woman was still by the door, weeping disconsolately.

Fecking noose of Iscariot! I tucked my hair under my hat, for I'd heard tendrils of human hair ignite as no other matter, and stepped inside the window, into the pure black pit of Satan's smoke.

Each crib was built exactly the same. My feet knew the measure of steps from the door to the bed. Afore I got there, I kicked into the man, who groaned in response. I kicked a second time, as hard as I could, and heard him stirring there. I wanted to tell him to make his way back out, that I'd take care of Emma, but was keeping my lips pressed together as hard as possible to remind me not to breathe.

A few more steps and I was at the bed. I leaned over, grasped Emma's body, thought for a second how fortunate 'twas that she was of the skinny ilk, and hauled her across my body like an overgrown baby. I stepped back across the room and didn't feel the man. At the window I tossed Emma and then leapt through myself. The smoke was out in the world now, and I still battled in the dark to drag her body free of it. Then I coughed and cried and slapped her.

Someone pushed a ladle of water to my lips and I drank half, motioning for the rest to be given to Emma.

"Did the gent get out?" I asked.

"He did, and he's bleeding from the glass that scraped him as he clambered through."

The contents of the ladle poured out in rivulets down Emma's face. Then I felt someone hugging me from behind. "You're the best and only lass! Oh, miss, how bold you are! I'll pay for prayers for you each and every week until I quit this earth."

It was the woman who had tried to get help for Emma.

"Don't be blessing me yet," I said. "Her eyes are clamped like the dead and she ain't even twitching from my slapping."

She came around from behind and laid her head on Emma's chest. "She ain't moving."

I put my fingers by her nose and tried to feel the suck of air. "Come on, then, Emma! There's a girl. Breathe and shake and let us know you're grateful. Come on, lassie!"

The other woman made a flat of her hand and walloped Emma on the side of the head. I grabbed skin and twisted. The person with the ladle returned and splashed the whole of it onto her face. It moved the ashes off her visage but didn't shock her back to opening her eyes.

"Did anyone fetch a doctor?" I called out into the melee, but it was too far gone. The flames were roaring like sailors now, and everyone was doing what they could to break down the walls and make a firebreak. I heard the axes chopping like this was suddenly a lumberyard, and the fire men shouting orders to each other.

I pulled Emma up to a seated position and her arms and head flopped like that cursed doll I had been picturing not so long ago.

"I think her spirit has fled," I told the other woman.

"No! She's just drunk still. She's in a stupor. I'll sit with her and you can go, miss. You can always remember this day as the one where you saved a soul. When I saw you stepping into that smoke, I thought 'God is smiling upon that one.'"

I was beholden to her for her suggestion that I go. I'd been a deathbed sitter only days prior, and I didn't think this one was ever going to shake off the dusky veil that sat upon her.

"She'll be waking from that liquor soon and be frightfully surprised when she hears the story!" I said, offering a false smile that was doubtless more of a rictus.

"What's your name, miss? She and I will remember you in our prayers."

"Nora Simms."

"Bless you, lass!" She clasped me across Emma's stricken body and kissed me soundly. "You're bolder than all this lot! You're better than a man."

"I hope good fortune clears a path for you always," I said. As I walked away, I wondered what her fate would be without a crib and without fine looks to get into a parlor house. She'd go to another cowyard and start life again. She'd need a new sign fashioned.

I joined the bucket brigade, saving steps for one harlot who was dancing across a gap too wide to simply hand the bucket across.

"Thank goodness, miss!" she said and, unbelievably, threw me a curtsy. "You're a kind one, to come here and assist with our set."

I took a bucket from the lad on my left and passed it to her, water spilling over the edge. *With our set?* I was part of that set! This filly thought me too fine to be a prostitute. I passed the buckets until my arms were clear ready to drop off. The heat was such that I wiped the sweat from my forehead in between handlings.

"More water!" a fire man yelled unseen from behind the wall of smoke. "Gentlemen, use your hats."

Two horse carts pulled up with their backs full of bay water, and a cheer went up. We worked with renewed fervor, passing hats—their felt trembling with the weight—and Congress boots and even a chamberpot.

Hours later, it was over and the fire men shook hands all around and left. Most of the line was gone, burned to the ground, but there were a few cribs at the top end left standing: including mine and, as I counted, Charlotte's.

I suddenly thought of her face, all tight and worried about getting a baby. She had been so terribly used by life.

She who felt a knife plumb her throat, and Emma who died with a pipe in her mouth, and Patience who brewed a viscous stew with the remains of a child in it, and Nutbrown Nettie who must have bled all over my shirtwaist, and the poor lass in the hold of the ship...

God almighty, I've seen some sights and narrowly escaped a similar fate for myself. Life and times ain't a ride on a joke pony for us.

I thought I'd rescue Charlotte's sign for her memory if it was still there. Probably some other girl had taken over the crib minutes after her body was carried out, but perhaps not. There was superstition over such things. I walked up and pushed open the door. It opened with a loud creak and I thought, *By god, what a sham establishment. Oil the hinges!* I stepped inside and sure enough the board still hung above the bed. I looked at it a while sadly. It was a plain plank, with her name written in crooked black letters. Not a single flower or color graced it.

Then my eye fell on something halfway under the bed. I knelt and reached for it, then screamed. I dropped it like it was made of spikes and poison.

'Twas a bonnet, simple pink but tinged with rusty blood from the flow that had been on the floor. A gruesome remnant of Charlotte's life, certainly, but the true reason I screamed was unrelated.

What frightened me about this bonnet was that it was *my* bonnet. Last seen in my stolen trunk.

"Oh, feck, she was right, they *did* hang the wrong man, they did!" I blabbered to myself, crouched in the dark crib, smelling the smoke still drifting from the crib fire. "The German was just copying the real killer; he told me so himself. He said he'd seen the picture in the newspaper and it gave him an idea."

It was clear. This hat represented a link between me and Charlotte: the galley mate.

Chapter 20

I went back to the police station, hoping to find the same nice man who had taken my report before, but he wasn't there. In his stead was one who looked at me like I was rotten cabbage animated and on foot.

"I have valuable information," I said. "That German fella what got hanged for killing...uh...soiled doves, sir? He wasn't the right one. And I know who truly did it."

"Justice was meted out, miss, and you notice not a murder has occurred since then."

"It's been only six days!"

"What do you have to say, then?" He looked at me but without interest.

"Ain't you going to get a notebook out? Write down what I say?"

"I believe I'll be able to commit it to memory."

"But then I have to sign it, official-like? Why not do it all now?"

"Just say what you have to say. It's New Year's Eve and the clock is about to tell me I can go home."

"All right, then, all right. I'll be swift. The German fella was strange, sure enough, and I thought he was going to kill me, but he wasn't the one killing the prostitutes. No, the one that did it is a galley mate from a ship, *The Lady's Peril*. I was on that ship and he stole my trunk and replaced it with his, which was ratty and full of nothing of worth. But how I know, see, that he's the killer, is that each of the girls that died wore something of mine from that trunk. The one they call Nutbrown Nettie? She was wearing my shirtwaist and said someone had given it her. Then Charlotte—"

I stopped and swallowed. The police officer yawned.

"Charlotte, well, she was sweet, sir. She was one that—"

"That what?"

"Oh...that didn't earn what got visited on her. She had my bonnet under her bed. And here it is. I thought maybe you could find clues on it?"

He took it with ginger fingers.

"There was a third one. She's still in the bottom of the ship."

"And was she wearing your corset?" he chuckled.

I froze.

"Well?" he prompted.

"You're laughing, sir? These women went the worst way possible."

"In my line of work, we have to keep a sense of amusement handy. With what we see, day after day, miss, without a laugh we'd all be sunk through to the basement."

"What *you* see, day after day? A desk clerk?"

His eyes narrowed.

"She was killed probably just after my trunk was taken," I continued. "And he didn't court her like he did these other women. She received no gifts afore he claimed her life."

"All right, I've got all the facts. Thank you, miss, for your concern, and I'll make sure this is duly recorded."

"Well, I've got some evidence besides the bonnet, sir. I've a trunk full of that galley mate's belongings. You should send someone over to look at it. There are clothes and some letters. I read them after the theft and found no clues, but a detective could find information there, I'm sure."

"What's the address?"

I recited it and asked, "Ain't you going to write this down?"

"I've a memory like an abacus."

"Is there some other officer around? Last time I was here I talked with this nice fella who—"

"I took his position; he headed for Sacramento. And everyone's knocked off already for the holiday. If you might take the trouble to recall, we are volunteer officers and receive no pay for our labor, so when it's a holiday we're all raring to be off celebrating. If you'll kindly direct your eyes to the clock, you'll see it's time for me to be quitting."

"You don't believe me, do you? You think I'm just some ranting piece of dross."

"To the contrary, I'm quite impressed by you and your high carriage."

"Oh feck you sitting at your stupid desk! If you were worth anything you'd be out stopping crime. I swear, a monkey could do your job and do it better!"

"And from what I hear about your abominable lot, a monkey could do *your* job and do it better!"

Hateful, hateful man! I scurried out of there half ready to commit murder myself. No one would listen to us. The women of ill fame existed only from the waist down.

I bit my lip and wished to find a low hurdy-gurdy house where the men would buy me drinks and wish me well. But I had a higher, more cultured evening ahead of me. It was New Year's Eve and I had to celebrate with the lawmen, bankers, and businessmen who took only tiny sips of their liquor.

And I had to be careful again. In the shadows might hover a young boy, one who would take a moment's chance with me to drain my life's blood.

New Year's Eve in the parlor house: something I had wanted desperately and now surveyed through glassy eyes.

These moneyed gents ought to figure out how to buy themselves some spirit, for they only danced like stiff puppets and still carried on the lousy slow discussions of news of the day.

At one point in the evening I squinted across the room and saw someone who made me smile to myself. It was Holmes, the man from the boardinghouse who insulted me at the table and then proceeded to visit me at the cribs as oft as possible. I pushed across the crowd to him.

"Why, you've found me!" I said. "I knew I would only have to bide a short while."

"I certainly wasn't seeking you," he said. "But I've not only found you, I've *caught* you—in a lie. Where's the bridal veil, Miss Simms?"

"Say a word to Mehitabel about this and your wife will hear plenty about your romping!" I said. I wasn't worried a bit.

"So you've worked your way up a bit in the world," he commented. "Still a regrettable whore, but with finer trappings."

"Regrettable? Bite your tongue," interrupted another gentleman, one I had tarried with a time or two. "This is *Nora Simms*, the finest of the parlor house girls. Show your respect!"

Holmes turned and bowed to him. "Mr. Marshall. I concede to your wise evaluation. Shall we step inside the antechamber and discuss your case?"

"Exactly what I'd hoped to hear. Pardon us, Miss Simms, but I'm desperate for the counsel of Mr. Holmes. My last attorney took my retainer and vanished," said the gentleman.

I looked at Holmes's distended, spherical eyes. "I can think of something else I'd like to discuss with your wife when she arrives, Mr. Holmes," I said quietly. "I think it best you not tell Mehitabel you saw me." That surely sealed our deal.

The two men turned and walked away. Holmes was no attorney; he was hoodwinking the gent. He had last been described as a mercantile man: a rag merchant, specifically.

I watched the two of them confer as an idea grew in my mind. Why, Holmes might be just the person to ask about my stolen clothing! Perhaps he had even trafficked in the vestments and could remember the galley mate—and then who he might have then sold them to. Once Holmes had extracted himself from the lawyerly confidences, I approached him.

"You're a rag merchant, Mr. Holmes, and I have a very pressing matter to ask you in that regard."

"I'm not a rag merchant," said he. "I am an attorney."

"Kittens of Gomorrah, sir, I've heard your history reported all around the boardinghouse table. It's no use lying."

"Perhaps I ought to amend my response," he said. "I was once a rag merchant and *now* operate as an attorney."

"Funny how you found a one-month law school," I observed tartly. "When you passed the bar exam, does that mean you merely sauntered past a saloon without entering?"

"I am a graduate of Harvard's esteemed law school," he said.

I snorted.

"When newly arrived here, yes, I did dabble a bit in the rag industry. It is thanks to my industriousness that the *Alta California* has paper to be printed upon."

"But you sold rags to others as well," I stated.

"To private individuals, yes, when garments were intact and wholesome."

"Did you ever buy a trunkful of women's clothing from a youth? A boy?" I asked eagerly.

"A boy? Perhaps that sounds familiar. Perhaps. And why would you care?"

"Have you heard about the soiled doves being killed?"

He smiled and I shivered. "'Tis a method for Christ to bring these women to their penance sooner. Abbreviating the length of their potential sins."

I adjusted my necklace and rubbed at the goose pimples that had suddenly appeared on my arms. "It is a sin that involves two," I said. "To be just, the killer should be likewise marking attorneys and…rag merchants."

"But one actively tempts, Miss Simms, and the other passively succumbs."

The professor was at Holmes's elbow suddenly. "What's the topic?" he asked. "Such secrecy."

I nearly leapt upon him, glad to know someone whose eyes fit into their sockets properly.

"We are remarking on how women have learned nothing since the folly of Eve," said Holmes. "Instead of a proffered apple, today's temptresses make an exhibition of their bodies. And just as Adam was helpless before that delicious redness, so are men hardly accountable for the wildness women elicit in their nature."

Unaware of the dire question I had earlier posed about the soiled doves and their desperate ends, the professor laughed lightly, not seeing the flay marks Holmes's speech had written on my face.

"We'll have to wear blinders like horses," said the professor. "And harness bells to warn women away, like the cat wears a bell for the birds."

"Except that birds don't attack cats," said Holmes. "Otherwise, a serviceable suggestion."

"Anyway," I seethed. "If I visit your place of business, can you look at your books and give me information on this particular personage I just spoke of?"

"And a connection between that request and the slatterns being killed?" he asked.

"Never mind," I said tightly. "I would prefer not to take you into my confidence and will simply pay you for the information."

"No," he said. "I cannot have the likes of you visiting my office. It is a respectable business venture."

I raised my eyebrows. "Respectable? With your false Harvard diploma—inked by your own hand—on the wall?"

The professor laughed uncomfortably.

"Truly, Mr. Holmes," I pressed. "Tell me where I might seek you out."

"Miss Simms, I cannot help you, and indeed, I do not think anyone matching your description has been any part of my business enterprise."

I stared at him through slitted eyes until the professor grabbed my hand, clenched my waist, and pulled me into a waltz. As we whirled I watched Holmes turn and walk away.

"What was that about, Nora?" the professor asked.

"Ah, the man's such as would make a maggot shiver in disgust. Let us simply enjoy each other, professor."

I danced with him, drank the champagne he brought me, and listened as he described some mathematical problem that had him all vexed.

He described, and this wasn't no quick conflict to outline, no, the numbers were so terribly horrid-behaving that he had to spend all evening telling me about this one mathematical quandary. I tried to be bright-eyed but instead took glum pleasure in watching Thomasina and Liza clomping about in the name of dance.

Finally, I could stand it no further and blurted out in the middle of his discourse, "Eighteen fifty! Can you believe it? That's the number *I'm* thinking of tonight, my kind patron. Good riddance to 1849!"

To his credit, he laughed and didn't mind. Upstairs, we trysted and publicized our regard for each other with sighs, moans, and cries that must have drifted down the plush velvet hallway.

"When I'm in your arms, professor, it's like the rest of the world just vanishes clean away," I said afterward.

"And this is a good thing? I count myself intriguing and a fair companion, but I certainly should not be a surrogate for the world."

"Well, with you, nobody is getting her throat slit. And with you, I get to speak my piece and get heard as well."

"Why do you still think on that murderer, Nora? They hanged him."

"Oh, professor, it isn't so. You'll have cause to draw another woman of ill fame again. They hanged the wrong man."

"That's absurd. What makes you think this?"

"I just learned it today. One of the Jackson Street girls saw the one who dashed out of Charlotte's crib and said he was clean-shaven, not the German with the mustache that was seized. And then I went into her crib and saw a bonnet that belonged to me once, that I was robbed of by this young galley mate I met aboard my ship. It's possible he's the killer because he's just a lad; he hasn't any facial whiskers as yet. Although I'm pondering the more likely possibility that he sold my garments to a rag merchant, and that's what I was asking Mr. Holmes about earlier this evening."

The professor's jaw dropped at this long and breathless speech. Then he settled the sheet around my waist and appeared deep in thought. "A galley mate robbed you of a bonnet?" he asked slowly.

"My entire trunk! Which was filled with my earnings from the voyage. He switched it with his. I still have it."

The professor sat up and whipped his head around, looking. "Where? For heaven's sake, Nora, there could be clues in it. I insist on looking in the trunk this minute."

"Wasn't even a shadow of a clue inside. I looked, believe me."

"But the trunk, Nora? Where is it?"

"It was a bit shabby looking so Bridget hied it up to the attic."

"May I be so bold as to request a visit to the attic? Seriously, you may be missing some evidence."

"Professor, I assure you, there was nothing in it but dirty shirts and effects."

"Nothing that gave his name?"

"A few letters that call him Thomas and no more. How many Thomases might we find in this city?"

"And what did the rag merchant tell you downstairs?" he asked.

"I didn't confide my thoughts to him. He's beastly. But since he's here tonight, he must be in Bridget's logbook, so I'll learn his address and pay him a visit whether he wants me in his establishment or not."

He sighed and lay back down.

"I thank you kindly for your diligence and concern, professor. Why, you're a thousand times more protective than the rotten police."

"So you've gone to the police with your information?"

"Yes, and they discarded it promptly. But I did warn the cowyard girls and said a few words to Bridget as well. If the killer is indeed the galley mate, it should be easy to avoid him. Boys are not among our usual visitors."

"That is an oddity," the professor said.

"Yes! Can you imagine one who has barely mastered his own body and is now holding women down and gleefully slicing through their necks? It's an aberration of nature."

"A coarse one."

"Oh, feck," I groaned. "Feck, I'm tired of thinking on it. It's a new year tomorrow, professor, what shall you do with it?"

I watched him make a gallant effort to change his mood, which was distracted and worried by our discussion. After a time, he conquered his frame of mind and answered me gently. "My aim is to defeat the arithmetic problem I talked of earlier before you lost your patience with me."

"Fie! What a plan." I made a programmatic demonstration of laughing. "And I'll respond in kind. For me, it's to have seven dresses, one for each color of the rainbow, and to be the girl always picked first after dinner."

"You'd stay in your profession?" he asked.

"What else can I do?" I asked. "I'll never be a mill girl or a teacher or a wife."

"Why not a teacher? Your evolution has been more…shall we say fine-tuned?…than those around you."

"I didn't mean I don't have the ability to become any of those things," I said. "I don't choose them."

"Whyever not?"

"I don't like children. They're smarmy and bratty and a nuisance such as to take your head off. I remember my own schooling days and the smart talk we gave the mistress."

"Well, you discipline them. You make them better citizens and then you can easily instruct them."

"I'd rather instruct men."

"You're a character, Nora," he laughed. "You're accomplished and clever and, above all, beautiful."

The "accomplished" part was being thrown at my portrayal since I'd played two logy bits on the piano as part of the evening's earlier entertainment. I had watched my fingers on the keys with a bit of melancholy, thinking of Mehitabel's kind tutelage and the other friend I'd left behind, Abe.

"Now, you did say you'd never be a wife, yet you don't despair of men as you do of children. So what's your reasoning on that line?"

"From what I've seen," I said, "a wife is like a child. She has to listen to her husband and do as he says. She can't leave the house without an escort, and she's stuck making all his meals and sewing his suits and laundering them— all work that ought to be paid for but isn't. The only thing she gets paid for, really, is for lying all limp and fishy in the bed for his pleasure, and that I do with flair and get paid for it. Without any loss of liberty, I might add."

"What if you found a man who enjoyed your spirit and allowed you all the liberties you wish for? And could make sure you got a dress in every color, and more besides?"

"And picked me first every night?" I asked wickedly. From my experience, husbands visited us and then picked their wives second.

"Of course."

"Such a husband may be a figment of your imagination, professor."

He bent and kissed me and I started to swoon a bit, not like the lasses who sink to the sofa and can't be revived for a time, but so that I felt floaty. His kiss seemed to be a message to me. Was he…?

Dismiss the thought, Nora, I told myself. *A professor wouldn't care to marry such as you.*

And then I heard the horns champion the changing of the year and all the crowd crying out their excitement. Out in the streets, men ran their canes along the wooden fence railing to make a clatter and stretched arms to ring their horses' bells. The tumult came in through the window and still the professor kissed me, lips warm and newly of an 1850 flavor.

Hours later, I awoke as the professor dressed, lit by the guttering, almost-dead candle. "What time is it?" I asked sleepily.

"It's five in the morning. I'm going home."

"I've never had a man stay all the night," I yawned. "It was nice to feel your warmth and never think of exchanging it."

He finished jingling his cufflinks and sat down on the bed, holding my hand and looking strangely serious.

"Nora, did you…have relations with that galley mate?"

I shifted uncomfortably and rearranged the pillow beneath my head. He was such a sweetheart. All night he must've tossed, thinking of me in the killer's embrace, unwitting as a lamb.

"I did," I answered. "And I treated him lightly, professor. I had no conception that he had such a corrupt and depraved character. How I wish I could turn back the clock and—Oh, I don't know what I'd do!"

He kissed my hands and stared at them, as if the kisses left stigmata there. He seemed so deep in reflection that my breath began to catch in my throat. After his abstract talk of marriage last night and this incredible display of concern…my tattered soul began a hopefulness that was almost dizzying.

Finally, he stood and resumed dressing. "Do you think you could have killed him, Nora, knowing what he was to do?"

"My blood is sour at the suggestion. I'm not a type like that. I help things, sir, not harm them. Why, I can't hardly look at a cat with a limp without tears springing to my eyes."

"But he killed people you knew."

Charlotte's thin face came into my mind and I thought of how earnestly she had promised to help anyone who cried out for it. And nary a hand had shifted for her. "Perhaps I could," I said. "I lose my temper sure enough; maybe if I could lose myself in the passion of the doing of it…"

"It must be that way for murderers," he mused, sitting back on the bed. "It must be a blinding passion that envelops them and cloaks them from insight of their deed. Perhaps it is even a pleasurable blindness."

"Pleasurable?"

"I only dare imagine. Why else perform such low acts?"

I nodded. "The one they hanged, the German man…he was happy with his knife at my throat. You're right. He taunted me and…well, he had his slow enjoyment of me."

"And you a slow enjoyment of him, remember? You saw him twist and contort for what he'd done."

"I didn't find amusement in the watching of that, professor. In fact, it made me miserable to see."

"A hollow revenge, then."

A *revenge*. I hadn't really thought of it that way before. More of an atonement between him and his god. But I did directly benefit from his hanging. And also—bleedin' cockles of a mockingbird's heart—also contributed to it.

I sat up straight in the bed. "Oh, professor, I just realized something horrid. It was my report to the police that got him hanged. I was the one who told them it was a German fella with a mole on his cheek."

"What of it, Nora? One like that is of no benefit to society anyway."

"But maybe he was playacting and had no idea how much it frightened me."

"Don't start the year of 1850 with telling lies to yourself, Nora. Keep yourself safe and I'll see you by and by."

He kissed me rather coldly and strode to the door.

"Professor?" I called. I knew he must have heard, but he made no reply. The door clicked shut behind him.

Chapter 21

A week later, on a Sunday evening, my dinner visitor had just left and I was squatting by the bed to redeem my hindquarters from his milky onslaught. I patted dry with a cloth and walked over to the window to dash out the water. My workday was done. Satisfied, I knelt and leaned my elbow on the windowsill, inhaling the sweet twilight wind. And from below I heard someone whistling on Price Street, a tune I much admired. It was the one about Irish girls and their mischief:

Reproving Peggy, who says she cannot in Connaught
Or wretched Siobhan, who let me dangle in Dingle—
And let us not forget the wicked, restless troublin'
I had with twins who doubled up on me in Dublin...

I hummed along lightly, and when the whistler had just passed underneath, I finally craned my head to see who it might be. He was a skinny lad but wearing a man's hat, moving with a fairly jaunty step.

Oh!

I screeched and knocked the basin off the sill, where it plunged to splinter just at his feet. He jumped back with a curse and looked up at the window, confirming what I thought. That bland child's face again: it was none other than the galley mate!

He recognized me too and shot down the street with his heels so fast they pummeled his arse as he went. And I screamed from the window and called and begged passersby to stop him, but he was gone as quickly as a report of thunder, leaving only two puzzled gentlemen lifting their hats to me and politely inquiring how they might assist.

"It's too late, you bummy snot-noses," I muttered, sinking back down to the floor. Below, I could hear them scraping the basin shards into a pile to protect horses' tender soles, talking amongst themselves in a surmising matter about why I had been yelling.

My second look at the child had me musing. He was, no doubt about it, still just a boy. And the expression upon his face to me seemed more like that of a petty thief seeing again the one he burgled than that of a malicious killer. He was young, young, *young*. And the girl at Jackson Street would surely have mentioned that the killer brushing past her was a boy, yet all she had said was that he was clean-shaven. Could anyone's eyesight be that bad?

I could now hear Bridget outside speaking with the gentlemen about the pile that had been my basin. "Screaming out that window, madam..." drifted up to my ears.

It was possible. Few whores bothered to spend money on spectacles. Many was the woman I'd seen with wrinkles festering around her eyes from squinting to focus her vision.

The most important thing, I felt, though, was that I was merely angry at missing the galley mate—not terrified. That sensation I'd talked to Charlotte about, that prickling unease, the shadow's claw extended toward one's spine...I hadn't felt it. We women had to trust our intuition, listen to the whispered messages of our knowing souls. If the galley mate was indeed the killer, one would think I'd be fighting for breath now, trembling and undone.

Still, based on his spurting away, he was doubtless guilty of something. But perhaps it was simply the exchanging of his trunk for my trunk. Perhaps someone else's hands had been on my shirtwaist and bonnet.

By mid-February I already had all the things I'd told the professor I wanted on New Year's Eve. If he had solved his math problem as well, we were having a ripsnorter of a year.

The orange dress, first of the rainbow gowns, was the talk of the town as I paraded myself down the slant of Columbus. It was made of chintz dyed with cochineal and orange peel. The man who dyed the chintz was set against making it, thinking me gaudy and foolish, but I explained as to how orange was one of God's colors too, and the poppy and Indian paintbrush would be sore at hiding their lively heads, and he still harrumphed. Then I quoted a passage from the Bible at him, which had absolutely nothing to do with the color orange but rather about Paul scolding the Galatians, and he folded.

Then I took the dyed bolts of fabrics to a fancy dressmaker, instead of the one who made the wretched sackcloths for Mehitabel and me. I paid him handsomely to ensure all the odd ends would come back to me—I wanted no one else to wear this color—and had a dress made with neat bell sleeves and a gored bodice. Not to mention the bird's eye view of a bosom; this dressmaker catered to the parlor house set and didn't give a speck about decency.

I had to buy a new trunk to hold the dresses, spangling in their violets and lemons and robin's egg blues. There was a rainbow in that trunk, and also the money I'd earned—a fair lot, although now it seemed my high-class way of living required me to spend it as much as save it.

As for the second part of my New Year's wish, I was still the belle of the parlor house. For a time I was always picked first purely for the curiosity, as Bridget said, but now it'd been nearly two months and I still saw the men getting edgy around about dessert time and sliding her a pre-payment coin as a bribe. The other lasses weren't too happy about that; Alice was the only one who seemed supportive. She was always friendly after the day she trained me and we saw we were kindred spirits. She even gave me a good nod and smile the day Bridget announced that my earnings, including a fair-sized Valentine's Day take, had set an all-time record for the house: seven hundred dollars counted out in gold and paper into my hand. I couldn't prevent myself from pummeling my nose into that pile, to smell the juices that must surely arise from such fortune.

'Twas grand here, no doubt about it. The men, with the exception of Mr. Sick Snake, who never came again, were well-mannered and good comrades in the bed. And no, I never found the blisters upon myself and finally stopped seeking for them.

There were moments when I thought of something funny I wanted to tell Mehitabel, or lonesome trysts when I wished the fella working me over was the thoughtful and ardent partner Abe. I wondered what he was doing after sulkily grooming the horses: instead of coming to me, he was probably standing drinks for the world's riffraff, craving some kindness. I pictured him watching a faro game, confounded by the array of cards, and his so-called friends trying to get him to bet since they knew he'd lose. I missed his tender regard for me, and Mehitabel's mistaken conviction that I was someone better than I was. But I realized any change in life had its downsides, and being at the parlor house meant I had to leave those dear ones behind.

For a bit, I watched the front door each time it opened, expecting to see that fresh-faced demon from the nursery of hell—or whoever he had sold the clothing to—but maybe he was frighted that a man had hanged for his sins and remedied himself. Bridget, all the girls, and the colored maid had been warned not to open the door to any that was a lad. Somehow Mr. Holmes had avoided getting his name into Bridget's logbook, probably fearful his wife would somehow learn of it, and he never returned, so I had no way to learn anything about the rag mercantile.

Yet days continued to pass, and the regular small wants of life reasserted their clout. I laughed once or twice, and then severally, and then I was sharp side up again, like a righted milk saucer. I wouldn't say I was easy in my mind, but I was starting to think the menace had passed. One cannot tremble with every inhalation, and so all of us soiled doves began breathing steadily again.

I had a go with Elmer Clapp and gnashed his ass with the prickle device. He was clean spent afterward and looked like a puppy who loved me despite the kicking. Another gent had me tie him to the bedpost and lash him with my undergarments. What a time I had of it, trying not to titter in the midst of his carrying on! I had to tell him in a schoolgirl voice how they were soiled and smelled like the naughty girl I was.

I've done the mayor several times. I can't wait for the governor to come to town so I can ask him about all that taxation nonsense. The constables are so funny when they come in. They act like they're only here for the bribe Bridget slides them, and then embarrassedly stay for dinner and the after-treats—as if the former mission were more noble than the latter! After my doings with their department, I have a high disdain for them that they seem puzzled by. I told a few officers about the galley mate, since perched on a pillow I had their undivided attention, but one complained to Bridget that I was mixing business with pleasure, and after her fuss I didn't dare raise the topic again. She of course had me pay for the basin I'd toppled from the windowsill.

I helped decrepit old men with the removing of their clothes, making a game out of whisking away their bent-up fingers, and I was the inaugural throw for many a first-timer who stammered and hid his face from me. In late January a visitor from France chose me, and I learned all the dirty words from him that Yvette couldn't teach.

One fella spent two days straight, and one evening pulled me into a doorway on Cohen Alley and did me right there. Other times I was licked in front of the mirrors, bent into positions I felt were undignified (yet gratifying), tickled, squeezed, washed, made dirty again, kissed, and slapped. And I gave back as fair as I received.

But the one visitor I really wished to see stayed away. My scheme was to marry him. Hadn't he been hinting in that regard on New Year's Eve? Surely it wasn't idle conversation. I wondered if he was getting his affairs in order, so that he could return and pledge his troth.

It wasn't until late February that he returned. In an effort to impress him, I brought a slate to bed and showed him some powerful hard arithmetic I could do. There was carrying of numbers and quite a few nines, which are famously hard to work with. He was mad with passion but did take the time to check my figures before he drove himself into me. To my relief, I had done it all correctly.

And afterward, he sat back up with math still on his mind, asking me the square root of some atrocious number.

"I only do the ones up to 81," I informed him.

"Wise of you," he said. "I never thought to limit things that way, but it would certainly ease some of the tough ciphering."

He pulled off my stocking and ran his tongue along my arch.

"Professor?"

"Um hmm?"

"These last few months passed so slowly. I wondered where you were."

"I was embroiled in other matters."

"I missed you dreadfully."

He said nothing but continued to nibble.

I decided to change my tack. Perhaps jealousy might be the way to awaken his emotions. "One time another visitor took me out. We went to dinner and he gave me the business in an alley."

"Must have been good fun."

"Not like with you. But it got me to thinking, maybe the professor would want to squire me around like that."

His tongue wiggled around my kneecap and into the sensitive space behind. I giggled and kicked free of it.

"As if I was courting you?"

My heart stopped, but his voice was mocking. Nothing serious in it. "Well... I suppose it might look that way to folks who didn't know us. Know me, I mean."

He lifted my skirts, pressed both hands down on my pelvis, and let his thumbs trifle with me.

"Who doesn't know the girl in the orange dress?" he asked.

"Well, then, we ain't—aren't courting," I stumbled. "Just a girl of ill fame and a professor having a spin about town."

"How's that feel, darling?"

I could have screamed at the change of subject. I didn't care right now about the bodily response he was creating in me. I wanted to talk about the idea of courting. I took a deep breath, though, and responded as he wished. "Well, it's about perfect. You do better with your fingers than most men with their tongues."

And then his face was buried in me, fingers and tongue and even the ridge of his nose. Men of science are very empirical.

And despite my resistance, my heart swam down my body to lodge atwixt my legs. I helped him with his cravings, and then it was time to say good-bye or talk some more. I waited.

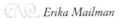

"I'll take you to a place I know," he said. "Up in Chinatown."

"What kind of place?"

"An opium den."

"Are you an opium smoker, professor? But you have a job and can do all this math in your head."

"I indulge now and again. Like I indulge with you and your frail sisters."

I sat with my legs curled under me and pondered. Most of the wickedness I saw in my profession was not from the relations we had with men but from the girls drinking their money away or sleeping whole days from laudanum until their lives were a crust of curd the pig would sniff at.

But he had said "now and then."

"You don't get so you can't stand not to have it?" I asked. "The opium, I mean?"

"It's gentle and dreamy, and won't send you to the poorhouse. I promise."

I guess all wives smoke opium with their husbands if they have any sense. So I pulled on my clothes and said, "Yes. Let's go this minute."

"This minute? Well, certainly, I can accommodate you, Nora. But allow me a few moments to leave word to be sent to an associate of mine. We had plans for this evening and I will let him know I won't meet him after all."

I put new color on my lips and looked at myself in the mirror wickedly. So I was important enough for the professor to rearrange plans for me!

Dupont Street was from another country, with ducks hanging by their necks in the windows and the men wearing their hair in one long, thin braid down their backs. The smells were at times delicious, of strange spices, and at times wretched, like a corpse had rotted right alongside a cabbage. I gathered from the looks I got that white women didn't walk down this street too often.

The door we entered I could never have identified again, for it was part of the melee and arched awnings that all buildings here had. We came into a dank hallway and went down a flight of steps. I had a sense of foreboding such that my heart began to tilt.

"Want to hear something horrible?" he asked me.

"Is it about how a professor knifed a sweet, young prostitute in the bowels of Chinatown?" I joked nervously.

"No, it's about how the Chinese prostitutes wish that someone *would* knife them."

My ears pricked up. I had heard bad stories about these girls, that they were treated rough. I once heard they came over the ocean in crates, like animals, and never did the door open. I pshawed the story at the time.

"What do you know?"

"Well, the girls are sold into prostitution to pay for their passage here. The problem is the contract they are under says that for each day they don't work, another two weeks are added to their length of indenture."

We went into a room and closed the door behind us. There were low couches and a table in the center holding a large brass device with a tube coming off it and several pipes next to it. I sat down and tried to figure out what was wrong with what the professor had said. It seemed fitting to me if a girl shirked a day's work she might be fined. It wasn't nice, and certainly two weeks was overmuch, but it would probably keep her from dodging her obligation.

He sat down next to me. "Do you see why it's a terrible deal for the girls?"

I shook my head.

"Don't you miss several days of work each month yourself?"

"No."

"Really? I thought women had a particular monthly complaint."

"Oh, snail's shortcut! You don't mean?"

"I do. So each month she essentially adds a month or more to her time. After a year, she owes a year, so you see she can never get free."

"Is this fact? You know it to be true?"

"Indeed." He handed me a pipe. "Relax and lie down. If you recline on your hip, you can smoke and dream comfortably."

"Dream my ass! What are we going to do about these girls?"

"It's epidemic, my dear Nora. It would be like trying to put all the gold back into the hills and streams, and asking the miners to kindly go home."

"But that's slavery!"

"Go ahead and smoke now, things are cooking here so don't be wasteful." He actually put the pipe to my mouth and I took in the smoke while still thinking which police officers who visited Bridget's might be induced to take action against the Chinamen.

"Professor, there's another thing I've heard."

"What's that?" He was now settled on his own cot, legs stretched out like a sassy cat's.

"I heard the Chinese girls are young."

"That's also true," he said.

"Like eight years old."

"Not unheard of."

I inhaled again and let the smoke tarry a bit inside my body before I let it out in a long, sinuous stream. "Can you imagine grown men who think it's decent to do that with a girl of that age? I'd stuff cotton down their throats, douse it with kerosene, and send a bit of flame down there."

"There's damnably little we can do about it."

"Can't you tell one of them newspaper reporters about it? Get the citizens riled up?"

"There's a fairly strong anti-Chinese sentiment in this town, hadn't you noticed? Chinatown would end up in ashes and those girls would burn in their cages and be no better off."

"So there *are* cages! May Christ return and smite me!"

I stood up, prepared to run throughout the streets and gather a mob, but I found I was very tired from that action and sank back onto the cot.

"It's working an influence already, I observe," said the professor.

My skin was warming and felt as if it was shedding like a snake's. I focused on that sensation and then was surprised to see the professor on his cot a few feet away. How had I forgotten he was there?

I lay back and placed my lips around the pipe again, as slowly and deliberate as I'd do for starters with a gent. That was a lovely cloud of bliss I brought into myself. I closed my eyes and drifted into thoughts of snakes licking my skin off and coiling and uncoiling in my hair. Then I saw an orange snake and knew it was the one that ate my dress. I brought the pipe to my mouth again and again, until my hand couldn't lift it and rested on the mat.

A man came into the room and there was certain alarm in my head, but I couldn't seem to let my body know it should react. I simply watched, my eyes the only thing moving in my entire thrashed stack of a body. He picked up the pipe and brought it to the table in the center of the chamber. Then he went over to the professor and spoke with him. The words trembled and blurred as they came across the room to me, like murmuring in another century. I couldn't hear it and so I closed my eyes again and let the bumblebees arrive, having flown off my dress from back…where? Irish woman's thin lips and spittle and bees resting on my lips and my skin prickling from all their little legs walking and the wings brushing against me.

Roar! Woosh! Such a sound as the door opened again and a little girl entered. She was the girl I'd envisioned when I thought of the eight-year-old. Her eyes were dark and covered with a heavy lid, and she walked like a man to the gallows. Then I was swinging on that rope and clutching at my neck, and she climbed onto the bed next to the professor. While my feet kicked out into space, he moved her under him.

I couldn't focus my brains. I was surely dreaming. Bumblebees flew from me to her but couldn't stop his hips from bucking into her. I whimpered and he looked right at me, but nothing stopped. Words. Priests murmuring prayers in the lofted cathedral and me not catching the Latin. The humming was in my ears but I couldn't arrest it. My skin was not on my body but on hers instead, rocking and twisting.

I woke to find him smoking a regular pipe, the more familiar smell overcoming the sweet one.

"What time is it?" I asked.

"Time to get you home. Does Bridget keep account of your coming and going?"

"No. But what time is it?"

"It's ten."

"How can it be ten?"

"Ten in the morning, Nora. It's Wednesday."

"Oh, feck. I'll have to scurry home and wash up for lunch."

"Did you enjoy yourself?" He smiled at me with the pipe gripped in his teeth.

"I'm not sure. 'Twas lovely while it happened, but now I feel so old and wiped. Like I lost a decade in one night."

"Nice dreams?"

My head was heavy on my neck and I remembered snatches of the imagery. "I think I was dreaming I got hanged," I said.

"Not so pleasant at all! Distressing to hear."

"Oh, and lots of bees making honey, and snakes in my hair. And…" I stared at him, starting to feel dread visiting under my corset.

"And?"

Oh, now it was coming to me. Had that happened? Certainly there hadn't been snakes removing me of my skin, but had a young girl been here?

"What, Nora?" He clicked the pipe against his front teeth.

"I dreamed about you," I said slowly. "With a girl. A Chinese girl of schooling age."

He grinned. "Did I get into her cage with her?"

"I…I wish I knew if that were real. Was there a girl here, professor?"

"Only you, if you think you still qualify."

I was dragged down with despair, for I couldn't know whether to believe him. How could I have created a girl out of thin air with such clearness?

"Nora, I have a proposal to make to you," he said.

Aha! The fog cleared out of my mind and I prepared myself. I sat up straight and reordered my skirts, then lowered my head and lifted my eyes. If he were to draw me now, he could call the scene "Shy girl modestly awaits the proposal."

He said, "I have an associate who is seeking a wife, and I'm happy to introduce you, one to the other."

My fingers clenched the velvet lounge and I hoped my nails dug rents in it. "An associate? Professor, I hardly know what to say!" If my mouth couldn't say it, my eyes could, and I know they were launching arrows and bullets as fast as the artillery could ever supply them.

"Well…you can thank me for starters."

"Thank you? I'll *hit* you. I'm not some fish dinner you can just pass around."

"I thought your kind wished to be recommended."

"Well, I hope to have some power of selection. This is just absurd! And insulting!"

"I showed him the drawing I made of you when I first met you—remember? He was absolutely charmed and captivated and said he couldn't wait to make your acquaintance."

"What about showing me a drawing of him?"

"It doesn't work that way, dear Nora. He has the money, you have the looks. And I can assure you he is devastatingly wealthy."

I sat back down, my chin high lifted, as bristled as any hornet.

Something was ticking in my mind, though. If he was a friend of the professor's, then he wasn't such a stranger. And he already liked my appearance, and he was rich. *Problem solved, Nora, yes? No more worrying about your throat being slit. At least meet him.*

"I'll think about it," I said stiffly. "What's his name and what does he do?"

"It's Cleveland Hopkins, and he's an architect."

"That sounds like a made-up name."

He laughed. "You're so suspicious!"

"How old is he?"

"Thirty-eight."

"His looks."

"He's taller than I, about six feet one, I'd wager. Delicate cornsilk hair, but a robust mustache of the same hue."

"Eyes?"

"Blue."

"Interests."

"Researching early druid quail-raising techniques, and collecting the false teeth of deceased famous persons."

"Now this *really* sounds made up. Are you inventing me a fiancé?"

"Darling, if I were making him up, he'd be far more sensational. I'd create a veritable prince for you."

I sat and digested that.

"Be wary, professor, I don't take kindly to condescension," I said in a brittle voice finally.

"Nor can you spell it."

I rose again and this time kicked over the little table that had held the opium pipe. It clattered over and I put my hands to my ears and cringed.

"Nora, you're being exceedingly foolish," said the professor as he grabbed me from behind and propelled me out into the hallway and back up the cramped staircase. "Just come meet my friend, and you'll be delighted by him, I promise."

He packaged me into the carriage, where I fumed and stared at my hands in my lap. I had thought the professor had designs on me! On New Year's Eve he had asked me all manner of questions about what I sought in a marriage. The whole time was he asking only for his associate? I found it hard to believe. When the professor looked at me, there was a tenderness, as much as he might try to bury it deep inside himself.

I had a sturdy back. I was used to speaking my mind, hardly ever blushed. If I wanted something said, I should say it. For how could I walk to the altar with some other fellow when I knew that it was the professor I wanted to exchange vows with?

"Professor?" I asked.

"Good! She is finally speaking to me again."

"Have you ever heard the story of Miles Standish?"

"Every schoolchild has."

"Well, then I ask of you: why do you carry forward another man's proposal when it is actually yours I hope for?"

There! As much as I wanted to stare out the window, I forced myself to look right at him.

He smiled at me and his fawn-colored glove brushed my cheek. "Nora, I hold you in the highest regard possible. I tenderly cherish all the evenings we have spent sporting and pondering mathematical issues together. Your face is as beautiful to me as any queen's."

I frowned. That Queen Victoria was downright dowdy.

"In fact, I hold you on such a pedestal that I do not dare to sully your charms with my professorial soot."

"Pardonnez-moi?" It felt like a good moment for French.

"In short, I love you too much, my dear, to marry you." He bowed his head over my hand and kissed it.

Yet, I was sure there was something in me that wasn't up to his standards, despite his polite little lie. *Oh feck, Nora Simms, you're a tart in fine clothes, but a tart nonetheless.*

I sat stonily the entire length of the drive home. We parked in front of the parlor house and he held my hand to speak a few words while I shivered in the chill morning air.

"Don't be a frost maiden, Nora. It doesn't match your warm face. Now, I'll send for you next Saturday evening and have you brought to my residence. Eleven Orchard Street. A delightful part of town; you'll be pleased at the vistas. My associate is actually my roommate as well, and we will all dine together."

"He's your roommate? Professor, I don't like the idea of coming to live in a two-man household. Especially since you and I have had our own history together."

"You'll of course move into a new home if you marry, and I'll be stuck with the searching for a new roommate. Not that I require one anyway. He is a long-time family friend of mine, and I offered him my lodgings as a courtesy and for the company."

I nodded and prepared myself to step out, without his assistance. I didn't know if I'd come to his little dinner party or not. I needed to muse over it and would send word if I declined.

"Nora?"

"What?"

He took a deep breath and appeared sorry. It was the first time I'd ever seen such an expression on his face. "I've enjoyed our trysting. I shall be regretful to see you wed and bound up tight to another man."

"There were days, professor, when I looked forward to your visits as to none other. I wish your esteem for me equalled mine for you." I said it miserably; I had naught to win nor lose by speaking of my hopes.

"Sweet Nora. Farewell." He kissed me on the lips lingeringly. My eyes opened again long before his did, and I watched the odd sorrow that crept across his visage like a quilt being pulled across a bedstead.

"Professor? Why are you so sad?" I asked.

"I shall miss you. Now, then, steady down, let me help you." He dismounted and then stood on the ground below me with his arms outstretched. So painfully did I wish to be embraced in them! But I simply allowed him to help me down. "Get safely inside, Nora. I'll send a coach for you at seven next Saturday. And I'll alert Bridget."

"All right," I said. "And professor?"

"Yes?"

"I shall sorely miss you too." His look of regret didn't shift, and with confusion I walked away, feeling he cared for me more than he would allow himself.

Chapter 22

The door was locked, and so I had to ring as I heard the professor drive off behind me. The maid opened it and shrieked in my face. I shrieked back in pure startlement.

"Get in, Miss Nora, get in. Quick stepping, now!" She pulled at my skirt to bring me across the threshold. "What's the matter?" I could hear footsteps running back and forth upstairs, and the hysterical voices of the girls.

"Miss Thomasina was killed. It's the same way as the crib girls in the newspapers! Now the monster is after parlor house girls as well…Meaning no lack of respect, Miss Nora, but I'm glad, powerful glad, I don't do the work you do!"

I sat down on the little stuffed chair just at the side of the door, splaying my hands out like I had just dropped something.

"Shall I fetch smelling salts?" the maid asked.

"No, I just need to sit a bit." She scampered off.

He knows I'm here, I whispered to myself. *It's a message to me. Oh, why didn't he kill me when he could? Because I was his first ever lay…or is it because the cook was there the whole time? Am I only breathing today because there was a rude and thoroughly ill-bred cook moving pots and pans around us? Bless his awful heart! The food was wretched and I couldn't keep it down, but…*

Or was it some stranger I had no connection to? Some opportunist who had purchased the trunk and its contents?

I knew what I must do. I had to climb the stairs and see what article of my clothing was in Thomasina's room. What would it be this time? My woolen cloak? My beribboned corset?

Upstairs, I could hear the gruff questioning of the police men. I wished I had an opportunity to enter her room without their interference, but they were, by the sounds of it, already swabbing things up. I had to look now or it might be too late.

I climbed the stairs still fighting the tinge of dreaminess from the opium. I trailed my fingers along the textured velvet wallpaper of the upper hallway, passing each girl's room until I reached the door that was wide open.

Inside three police men were busily taking notes. "Out, out, miss!" one called when he saw me.

So I stood in the doorway and looked. Thomasina was halfway on her bed, halfway off. Her bedspread was blotched with blood. I saw a little motion at the bottom of my vision. I gasped and looked down. A thin worm of blood rolled toward my right foot.

I jumped backward and the trail pursued me into the hallway, faster now that the slope of the floor was assisting it. A quick step to the side and it ran past me, coming to a halt and pooling against the hall runner.

I then straddled that thin river, thin as the vein it had once run in, and looked again in the bedroom. Thomasina—what was left of her—really brought nothing to mind so much as the whole cow hanging from the butcher's hook. I saw the knife had skipped down her throat sideways, cutting her clothing and exposing several ribs on the way. She had been reduced to meat. I put my fist in my mouth to keep from gagging.

"You should step away, miss," said one of the officers. "There's no call to be looking at this."

I nodded but instead stepped into the room. "I need to see what she is wearing," I rasped.

They all three stopped and looked at me.

One step, two steps, an unsteady third. And there I was at her bedside, looking down at the jellied gore that was once a woman. And tangled up in all the blood were ribbons, floating now in a sense, pink furbelows that laced up the front of my favorite corset.

"That's my corset," I said woodenly. "A man named Thomas stole it. He's the connection to all the murders."

One man nodded, but it was the nod you give a child when she says she saw fairies prancing amongst the buttercups. He put his hands on my shoulders and firmly walked me back to the door. "We know where to look," he said. "We spoke at length with the woman of the house. Rest assured, miss, we are going to bring him to justice."

"Bridget knows," I said. "Yes. I did tell her about him. Good."

I stumbled over the rivulet of blood, down the hallway to my bedroom. I laid down in the crisp linens, eyes wide open, trying to stop my heart from racing. Until Bridget banged on my door and entered without waiting for my response.

"Wake up, Nora! I can't believe you're sleeping when the house is in an uproar like this!"

Somehow I snapped into clarity without a hesitation. I thrust aside the sheets and stood up. "Why did you let a youth into the house, Bridget? I warned you all about that. The maid knows, all the girls know. No one under that particular age."

"Don't you blame me for this, you hussy! It might not be a boy child. Plus, that scamp smuggled him in herself. None of us knew."

"How is that possible?"

"She confided in Liza, who let us know everything in tears a few hours ago. Thomasina was upset how she was never picked at mealtimes and felt her attractiveness was waning. So, to pick up some extra money and not pay the percentage to me, she was whisking men up the stairs when she could for secret dalliances."

"And getting these men how?"

"Common streetwalking." Bridget's lip curled. "Worse than crib work."

"Did she scream?"

"Not a bit of it. The police think, based on her blood's congealment, that she was killed last night. We didn't even discover her until this morning when she never came down for breakfast. And nor did you—but thank God I see you are intact."

"And why did you say it might not be a child?"

"The girls have noticed a carriage that sits outside for hours at a time, with a man—not a boy—simply sitting there staring at our front door."

"Was that carriage outside last night?"

"No one reports seeing it, but we aren't in the general practice of dipping our heads out the windows."

I glanced toward those windows now, shivering. "You're right, it may not be a boy. I'm all flustered at what to think! What madness, Bridget. But there is a connection here, and even if it isn't the galley mate, it's someone who—"

"It's none other than the man in the carriage, Nora! He gawks like a scarecrow. One day Alice asked him rather saucily what he meant by simply staring at our door, and his reply was so crippling slow and half-witted that it sent daggers of fear to her heart. Her exact words? 'There's something wrong with that one.'"

Ohhhhhhhh. It was Abe.

"Oh, Bridget, he's a simpleton and doesn't mean anyone any harm. He wouldn't hurt a flea. He's a good-souled one. I even know his name."

"Please tell me you are joking," said Bridget icily.

"He's fine and has a respectable position. He doesn't dress fancy, but he's fine. He's not even close to being the killer."

"Then why is he hovering at our dooryard and making all the girls uncomfortable?"

"I didn't know he was doing that. I'll tell him not to."

"Is it safe for you to have contact with him? Nora, it's best fixed by the police. I've instructed the girls that next time they see him they should make an alarm."

"That's like making an alarm on a bunny rabbit!"

"Why are you so convinced he's harmless? He sits there like he is waiting for his prey. It's menacing and evil."

"I'm sure if this was the Dark Ages you'd recommend him for the auto-da-fé. Take me at my word: He's harmless. Let me speak with him before you involve the police. For certain, he's got more wits in his noggin than the entire police force combined."

"You have doings with a lot of strange characters, Nora. Don't make me regret taking you into my house."

"Hasn't your business mightily improved since I got here?"

She lifted her chin but wouldn't reply.

"So. Well. The house is closed for the day?"

"Certainly."

"I guess you'll bury her, Bridget?"

"The girls are taking up a collection. I can't cover this expense alone. Things are not as financially glorious here as you might think, Nora."

"But we have all the mirrors and champagne and velvet."

"All of which gets more expensive by the day. Feeding a houseful of hungry girls and their gents, paying the bribes and the rent for this monstrosity of a house and…well, everything costs these days, Nora. And I never went prospecting for gold and only get what the men see fit to hand us."

"Raise our prices, then."

"So many women are arriving here each day, Nora. Floods of them. More and more beautiful. We no longer have the corner on the market."

Even this dream was ending badly. Cross the world to get what you want, and then watch it crumble into fire ash.

"I should get married," I mumbled. *But I wouldn't be a professor's wife. Only a professor's roommate's wife.*

"If you can secure that circumstance, you'd be smart. Now, rise, say a prayer for Thomasina, and find me a new girl for her room."

"What?"

"'Tis hardly puzzling. Just walk the streets and find a pretty one and talk to her a bit. See if she's willing. We don't want crib girls, though, so mind about that."

"And why might that be?" I asked out of pure contrariness.

"You can never get the roughness out of them. Those women are used to an entirely different breed of men."

"You'd be surprised what those crib girls are capable of," I said. I rubbed my face with my dry hands as if they held soapy water. Trying desperately to gather my thoughts through the soup of the opium's residue. I thought of Abe in the carriage and what the three men in the other room were told of him. "I'll get you a new girl if you promise not to call the police on Abe—the man in the carriage—without first calling me."

"Done."

She left. As I stood before the mirror, preparing myself to go out of doors, I thought that there was no one in the world I truly trusted now. I could never feel the same about the professor, for even if the vision in the opium den wasn't true, he had brought me to the part of town where those things happened. And he didn't want to marry me!

And after all, was he as wealthy as I might want? When he said he needed to go to his offices, what did that mean? He never spoke of any students, so where was he a practicing professor? He could be a sham in a tie for all I knew.

And Abe. Harmless Abe. Or was he? I hadn't realized he'd been trailing my steps so heavily still, keeping vigil on my life. It gave me an eerie along-my-spine feeling. That day he'd trailed me as I tried to find a place in a parlor house: well, that was unnatural. I should have put a stop to it.

The only one who had never done me an ill turn and seemed on my side, why, that was Mehitabel, someone I was too shamed to see.

I threw my gloves across the room, then walked over to each of them and kicked them. I kicked the bedpost as well. Godammit! I was not helpless. If the wretched police were too ignorant or lazy to look through the galley mate's trunk, well, then I'd *make* them. There were men on the premises right now, and they were here for business rather than for pleasure.

I opened my door so forcefully that it banged into the wall behind even though Bridget had placed a stuffed doily there to muffle exactly that effect. I strode down the hall as strident as any pirate on a surrendered vessel's deck, muttering a little as I went. Alice stood outside Thomasina's door, watching the men inside. I brushed past her, tipping her off balance, and entered the room. The second sight of Thomasina made me wince, but I kept an anvil in my voice.

"Sirs, I must insist, with the very most fortitude that a woman can muster, and with the feminine dependence that a man must honor, that you accompany me to the attic to investigate a trunk that may have clues to this and other murders," I spat.

I knew my color was high and my gray eyes were blazing. All men are tea cakes inside, and they crumple when women issue truly heartfelt challenges.

"Uh, miss, we certainly...honor that...uh...dependence," said one of them, holding a magnifying glass still to his eye so it appeared an outsized, morbid marble.

"Do it!" shouted Alice. She stood next to me, and together we fairly bristled. I thought of the steam mechanism I had once seen in the Lowell factory, how its pistons shook the floor.

Gallantly, one man agreed to come up and look, for the others were expected elsewhere.

Alice and I brought a footstool to the attic and sat upon it while the lone officer knelt in the dust to look through the trunk.

"Typical clothing here," he mused. He had the odd habit of bringing each garment to his nose and sniffing it. It was obviously an investigatory maneuver, but I couldn't figure out what he might determine by such a nasal inquisition.

"Sir, why do you sniff the objects?" I asked.

"In case of...smell," he said.

"Truly?" asked Alice. "What might a smell tell you?"

"I'm looking mostly for neighborhood smells," said the officer after a pause. "See, if your sailor is still down by the docks, it ought to smell of fish, right? And salty air?"

"But it's been in the attic now quite a while," I pointed out. "The smell of the garment doesn't change with the whereabouts of its owner."

"It's something we were trained about," said the officer stubbornly.

Alice wheeled her head around and we shared a look of dubiousness. I noticed the officer sniffed no further clothing after that discussion.

He wrote out a list of each garment. There were three buttonless shirts, one buttoned with porcelain, two pairs of trousers mashed into terrible crinkles by being flung pell-mell into the trunk without folding, a soft cap, a pair of leather suspenders, and some socks—the last items, I am certain, arousing gratitude in the officer that we had embarrassed him out of his whiffing tendency.

Then he examined the packet of letters.

"Thomas is the lad's name," he said aloud after a few minutes of reading. "These seem to be a mother's letters, urging him to remain safe and all that."

"An excellent lead," said Alice with the tint of sarcasm in her voice. "Do we know any Thomases in San Francisco? Replete with mothers?"

The officer chuckled without looking up. "He is a young one; you were right, miss. His mother is worried about him because of his lack of years." He moved to the next letter. "She promises pumpkin pudding when he next returns home...yes...yes...and so forth...she misses him terribly..." He read the next one. "She's frightened he might not be receiving her letters because she receives none in return. She has been bothering the shipping company asking for progress of his ship—oh, miss, it's not *The Lady's Peril*; he's on a vessel called *Betsy Malone*. What do you make of that?"

He lifted his face from the letters and looked at me.

"What do you mean, what do I make of that? He was on the flaming ship!" I said.

"Is it not customary to switch at the isthmus?" asked Alice. "I hardly think this is a wrench in the works."

The officer surveyed me a moment longer.

"What?" I sputtered. "Do you think I'm now the killer? Stop giving me that look."

"I just find this information curious," said the officer. "I'm going to make a note of it." And indeed, he scrawled a little message on the garment list to the effect that I had not had the ship's name correct.

"May we please continue?" asked Alice. "I'm sure in the next letter you'll learn that the lad has transferred to another vessel…perhaps, can we wildly guess, *The Lady's Peril?*"

"We *may* continue," said the officer. "I'm just trying to situate myself with this newly unveiled information."

"Steaming flapjacks, mister! How do you think he got these bloomin' letters anyhow? He obviously changed ships in Panama, just as I did, after crossing the isthmus. How else would the mails catch up with him?" I asked. "I hardly think some Saint Bernard paddled out to the middle of the ocean with mama's letters in the keg!"

"Actually, Nora *is* the killer. You should arrest her this moment. Quick! Before she makes her escape!" said Alice drily.

"Perhaps you'd like to sniff me, sir?" I asked.

The officer responded to none of this folly and simply continued to read through the letters. "Here, then," he said after a bit. "She mentions he is going to stay with a gentleman in San Francisco, his sponsor, but she neglects to name him."

"Mothers are deplorably inexact creatures," observed Alice.

"So we're searching for a Thomas being sponsored by an anonymous bloke. Cheers to the police man who could solve that," said the officer.

"But it does mean something," I said. "It means he had plans to meet up with someone, not to go to the hills for gold."

"Or at least that's what he told his mother," chuckled the officer.

"'Dearest mother, the angel of my nursery,'" said Alice in a funny voice meant to imitate a letter. "'I am going to San Francisco to be quite dull, and stay under the charge of my chaperone, and never do what all the lads around me are doing. I think gold is wicked and I'll do far better to study my lessons and be polite to women.'"

The officer rebundled the letters and set them to the side. We all three looked into the utter bareness of the trunk.

"Well, Nora, it was a good idea to look here," Alice said. "It's no fault of yours that there was nothing useful."

"Well, what about the ship's register?" I asked the officer. "Can you investigate that?"

"Before this gold boom, the registers were neat and tidy, listing even the rats, practically!" he chuckled. "But you saw back East how ships' crews were gathered up, sometimes mere moments before setting sail. The likelihood that a mere galley mate, especially after the scramble in Panama, had his name recorded is slim."

Together, the three of us discussed the idea that my trunk might not still be in the hands of the original thief.

"Perhaps the galley mate simply tipped it overboard and as the garments reached shore, various hands stretched in to pluck them out, dry them, and use them again," the officer suggested.

My already low opinion of this man plummeted. Had he never seen a bonnet? Touched the head of his wife or sister? Clearly he had never witnessed the labor of the strong-fingered milliner, who sewed and tacked and starched and molded with extreme precision. These were flimsy confections, held together only by a woman's adoration. And her hatbox.

"I hardly think the bonnet could have survived an odyssey in the bay," I said.

"Well, it may be that the whore's—oh, pardon me, miss," he said.

We regarded him chillingly.

"What was the name again, of the lady with your bonnet?" he asked.

"Charlotte."

"It may be that Charlotte's possession of it had nothing to do with her eventual murder. A coincidence only. She finds a pretty hat being pushed along the street by the wind and claims it as her own. Later, and unrelatedly, she falls prey to a monster who…does what he does."

I appreciated that he didn't use gory words.

"Maybe he *did* sell the trunk, and can describe the rat who bought it," I said. Much to my surprise, I was beginning to be persuaded by the arguments against the galley mate's being the killer.

Bridget's head appeared at the top of the steps. "Officer, your fellows have sent for you," she said. "And Nora? I believe you have a task yet to perform this afternoon." She sneezed.

The officer looked at me, shrugged, threw all the effects back into the trunk, and closed it.

Chapter 23

I wasn't exactly clear on Bridget's meaning. Was I supposed to find some girl of honest virtue, and then simply by speaking earnestly persuade her to open her legs to the whole of San Francisco? I warrant I'm a decent convincer of men, but when it comes to the fair sex, what tools could I use?

I thought about it not too long afore I remembered how the crib owner had sent men to the wharf to meet my ship and assess its women. I could do the same. What was the difference between meeting a woman on the street and meeting one with fishes spurting beneath her feet?

I wore my newly fashioned yellow dress, the color as light as a pat of butter. I carried a parasol thinking that if I had to use plain language, I could hold it sideways and gain me and my protegé some privacy.

I felt protected in the bustling streets, but I still watched each face carefully. Lively stepping brought me to the wharf while I was still practicing in my head what I might say. "Miss, you look the type of female what is always popular with the menfolk"; I'd get her all goosy with a compliment. Or, perhaps I'd use a comic touch: "Lovely dress, miss! I know just the place to take it off!" A pert comment like that could be just the thing.

There I was, back at the place where it had all begun, where the fiend had stepped onto San Francisco soil to do his misdeeds. But for the first time, the wharf shined in the light. There were no dark skillet clouds and high winds like the day I arrived, or a sly moon like when I returned to look for my trunk. No, instead there was industry at the docks, sun and men working in tandem.

Well, my timing certainly wasn't what it is in books, meaning that there was no fresh ship there debarking passengers, just the loading of an outgoing vessel. I waited, spying at the horizon, getting anxious.

When I saw a fella who came close by with a coil of rope, I hied my way to him. "Sir, I've been awaiting a ship for a quarter-hour or more. When shall one arrive?"

"Look yonder," he said and pointed over my shoulder. I spun to see a tall pole on a hill with several wooden arms on it.

"It's a signal, miss. When a ship is due, the arms are raised. The position even tells you what type of vessel. That there's called Telegraph Hill, and it's visible from all points in San Francisco. It'll save you another trip."

"So that's what that fool thing is for," I said. "I always wondered. Looked too high for hanging laundry."

"It's an excellent method. And good day to you, miss."

"Thank you kindly."

He scooted off with his rope and I quit the docks and marched up the streets instead. In the four months since I'd arrived, it seemed the city's population had nearly doubled. There were more people, more horses…and more women. I examined each one's face, looking for that spark or glint that meant she'd be willing to set aside her shame during a few shakes of the clock. But they were all walking purposeful today, like they couldn't spare a thought for me. I thought I oughta have worn my orange just to capture their eyes, but alas.

I had a hankering to step myself up Stark Street and see Mehitabel. I was wearing Abe's ring, just on the wrong hand, so I moved it as I walked. Could I do all the lying that visit would ask me to carry? Perhaps I'd say, "We fought a bit last night, Mehitabel, so I'd prefer not to speak of him." But she and her husband had fought, so maybe she'd be more zealous than not to talk about the wherefores.

Where did Abe and I live? What kind of meals did I cook for him? How did I feel about wifing? All of these would demand answers already perched on my tongue.

So I stood at the intersection of Stark Street and sighed. The fact was, I could go live at Mehitabel's again. Leave the parlor house life and see if I could take in some honest work like she did. The galley mate wouldn't find me there—or would he? Maybe he knew I lived there previously.

But to live there, I'd have to tell Mehitabel the truth: that I hadn't married Abe, that I was still a soiled dove.

From this distance, the boardinghouse looked the same as always, except that one prior lodger was scared to knock at the door.

Then that door opened and Mehitabel stepped out. She had a basket of what looked to be fabric over her arm, so I thought mayhap she was delivering back some mending. Her long, refined fingers grasped the edge of the basket, and I remembered how they'd looked positioned on the piano keys. I gnashed my teeth from the impulse to rush over and kiss her upon the cheek.

She was coming up the street, so 'twas time for me to stop my gaping. I turned to go and heard her call from two horse-and-cart lengths away, "Nora! Is that you?"

I widened my legs and tried to lurch a little so my stride looked to be that of some other woman's. "I must look like Liza from the back," I thought. I swung my arms briskly and popped back onto Stockton. Once there, I gathered my skirts in my arms and ran for all the world like I was a thief.

Rough going for a girl wearing new high-heeled boots to come down a street upright as a shovel left in dirt. I took a left onto Pacific Street, which wasn't as steep, and slowed to a walk. I had nothing to be ashamed for. I had paid Mehitabel all I owed her, and if I lied about what my plans were, that was only to protect her. Little lily-handed good one, anyway, the kind of girl that would have told a teacher on a prankster. I spat into a spittoon stationed just outside a public house and considered going inside for a bit of absinthe, to keep me sturdy for my mission. But a glance inside revealed the surly nature of the bunch, so I continued on. Certainly I had tarried long enough and could go back to the boats to greet the city's newest residents. I looked up to the hill to see that the device for informing on ships had in fact changed its position.

Then, of a sudden, I was cross and wanted only to go back to my bed, safe or not. I could tell Bridget there were no girls of ill repute to be found, and what *was* found was only the vermin that works in the cribs. Plus, I had to admit in the rice pot of my mind there was a grain that was saying, "You'll get a girl for the parlor house, and she'll end like Thomasina. You'll have her blood on your hands."

Who would go look at Thomasina's birthmarked child now, and assure that the growing was happening correctly? Who would keep Liza company when she wasn't picked?

I did all I could, I told myself. *I told the police, I told all the girls. Not my fault Thomasina took a chance.*

I thought of her dancing on New Year's Eve, so clunky she practically tore her partner to the ground. And she wasn't even drunk, just one of those that couldn't move right.

I shouldn't get another girl. Let someone else do it and have the guilt.

Still, I went to the docks and sat on a huge steamer trunk to watch the folks coming down the gangplank. Rascals, all of them, I thought. They were all here for gold and to screw each other. They of course shouted over to me, the first filly they'd seen not bracing her legs against the rock of the ship, and I shook my head at them.

"'Nother time, Sallie?"

"When pigs spread their wings and the goblins offer to serve you bread pudding in hell."

"You've a mouth on you, Sal, and you don't ken what you're missing. This here's prime cock from the ironworks of Salisbury, Connecticut."

"Oh really? Did they cast that wee bit of pipe for you? Shame the mold was so woeful small."

Eventually, the first female appeared. She was fourteen or thereabouts, pretty as a turnip rose. I thought I'd leave her alone. Although girls did start so young, I didn't need to be the one that showed her that road. A moment later I saw she was accompanied by her mother, too dour for our line of work, and what appeared to be an aunt. Had the aunt been alone, I would have spoke to her, but what a perilous thing to pull her from a family.

The next girl was certainly frail, though the kind of frail that happens in cribs, not parlor houses. Her look was a bit too hard for Bridget's eye. Her mouth was set in a sneer and her eyes squinted suspiciously. She would've been good for the likes of Elmer Clapp. She walked past me looking out of the corner of her peepers. She recognized me for my type.

"Good day and welcome to San Francisco," I said.

She stopped.

"Know ye a place for me?" she asked.

"I'm surprised the men ain't here already fetching for you," I said. "The only place I could send you already burnt to the ground."

"So where are you then?"

"A house."

"A parlor house? Take me there."

"'Fraid I can't. I ain't the madam." Lord, how my voice was sounding like it did afore all the cultivation and manners!

"Ain't you here meeting boats?"

"Not really. Sunning myself."

"You fucking slot of a cow's ass. You might help a girl and yet you sit judgment on me like a crusted feckled magistrate."

"Why do you need anything from me? I only wished you a good day."

She spewed more complaint and vexment, but I didn't listen for I'd seen a girl on the gangplank who looked just right. She was willowy but with a set of bosoms that seemed like they was presenting the brooch on them to a gentleman five streets off. Underneath her hat was a red that nature couldn't have given. She looked around the docks like she was waiting for guidance.

"Pardon me, and good luck," I said, standing and walking toward the other lass.

The redhead nodded to me as I came right up to her. "Are you seeking a situation?" I asked.

"Indeed."

"Are you accustomed to the parlor house life?" She undid her glove to show me the bracelets and gewgaws. "From Connecticut, are you?"

"Yes. Raised in New Haven. Well, Milford actually, down the coast a bit." She had a New England accent that made my ear shirk a little, but her long eyelashes undid that damage.

"What skills have you?"

"I'm a soprano."

"Sing something."

She opened up and let some Italian operatic loo-la spill out onto the wharf. She pressed her hand to her chest and looked skyward, immediately carried away with her own reedy voice.

"That'll do. Show your hindquarters."

She circled for me and I was satisfied.

"Name?"

"Frances."

"I'm Nora and I'll be pleased to present you to my madam, Bridget. Shall we engage a boy for your bags?"

"That's already paid for," she twittered, like a schoolgirl being tickled.

I felt the knelling of an ancient bell in my gut.

Then she pointed a distance away, and I was relieved to see the man with her baggage was full grown.

"Faithless pilgrims, Frances, I did the same when I arrived. We might be two of a kind."

"Except my hair's red," she said.

"Not by any natural deed," I said. Girls like this, you have to keep a tight rein.

"Doesn't it look real?" she asked.

I reached out and touched a lock. "Honey, it don't even *feel* red."

Coming back by way of Jackson, who did I practically slam into but Abe. And this time, there weren't no way to adjust my step or be some other person like I had with Mehitabel.

He said nothing but gave me plaintive, beauteous eyes.

"Who's this?" asked Frances.

"How are you, Abe?" I asked him softly. In response, he dropped the bag of oats he was carrying. I bent with him and tried to sweep up with my hands what was still unsullied.

"Don't need to," he said.

"I'm sorry I made you drop it," I said.

Then we both stood up and I put my hand on his shoulder. "They tell me you've been waiting outside all the time in the carriage."

"I have to. I'm worrying about you."

"But Abe, that's an oddity. It makes me feel…strange…that you're observing me and my doings, and I don't even know it."

"Why?"

"Because we don't know each other well enough for you to be watching so hard."

"Leave her alone, you bad man," said Frances. "Can't you hear what she's saying? She doesn't want you around."

"Hush, Frances, that ain't what I'm saying."

"Nora, I ain't hurting nobody. I just want to make sure you're faring well," he said.

"But Abe, you're getting yourself in trouble. We've had a—" Shit! I didn't want to tell him there was a murder at the house or he'd never let me alone.

"A what?"

"Nothing. See, the girls at the parlor house, well, you're scaring them. They see you skulking outside and they think you're out to seize them or harm them or something. The madam said she'd call for police next time she sees you."

He started to cry and dropped the oats a second time. "Don't mind them," I said. "I'll buy you a new bag. Frances, let us alone for a bit." I pointed to an alehouse. The fella holding her trunk sighed and shifted his weight from foot to foot.

"How long?" she asked.

"Drink a couple each and come back out."

"All right, but then we'll make speed to the parlor house, right? I gave this gentleman a good time but I won't own him the entire rest of the day."

"I don't mind a quick swallow," said her porter, and so with a shrug she preceded him inside, holding the door for him as he squeezed through with the steamer.

Tears were coursing down Abe's face. "Did I hurt your feelings so bad, sweeting? I'm so sorry," I said.

"I miss you," he choked.

"I miss you too." And it was true. In the back of my mind, hadn't every visitor, excepting the professor, been unfavorably compared to the fella who took off his hat for me and lay there in a sweat wanting to know my history?

"I was hoping you'd come find me, but you never did."

I used my lemon sleeve to collect up all the crying. "How could I?" I asked. "They keep me so busy I scarce get a moment to check my particulars in the mirror." A falsehood: my room was naught *but* mirrors.

"I just kept thinking, today I'll see Nora tripping up the street wearing the ring."

It was awkward on the sidewalk, with everyone weaseling around us and his face still wet.

"Abe, you should have forgotten me by now."

He looked like I'd slapped him. "Forget you? You're my true love."

I had misspoken and was thankful he hadn't put together the other half of the sentence: that I ought to have forgotten him by now as well.

"Ain't there other girls you like?" I asked.

"Who?"

"Well, other girls you visited with. You know. Like you visited me that first day."

"I ain't never been back."

"You oughta, it's a good thing. You took to it real easy."

"And then, Nora, I walked past it one day and a lot of it was gone." His eyes got all saucer-shaped and he clutched at my arms. "They had a fire. And I knew if'n you was ever to try to find me, mebbe it'd be there, on account of we met there. And if'n it wasn't there, mebbe we'd never meet again."

"But you know where I live, Abe. You saw the parlor house."

"But you spurned me."

Hang all the public for staring and snickering, but I opened my arms and folded Abe in a hug and kissed at his ear. "Poor Abe," I said. "I never meant for you to feel so bad."

"Poor Abe," he echoed. "And now the girls is scared of me. I never lifted my hand to nobody, ever."

"I've got me an idee. How about next Tuesday, March fifth, I'll meet you here at this exact spot and we'll take a ramble about town together?"

"We could go now." He pulled out of my embrace and I saw how bright his eyes were.

"I've got to run this girl to the parlor house," I said.

"You promise you'll meet me? What time?"

"Three o'clock. I would have to get back for the dinner hour, but we can walk quite a ways in that time."

He groaned in so much ecstasy. A girl like me knows what it's like to have power over men and own them brains, heart, and all, but this one was such that he owned me a little too. The heart part. I could scarce keep from plunging at his shirt and nestling myself there.

"Nora, don't forget. Don't forget. Three o'clock, right here."

"I won't forget."

"I can't wait until March fifth. Meet me tomorrow."

"March fifth." I reached in my bag for a gold coin. "Here, for the oats." He wouldn't take it. "I can't stand the idea you'll have to pay for them yourself. Come, take it."

"No, I don't need it. Nora, I love you."

I thrust the coin into his hand and clamped it closed with a kiss. "See you soon," I said.

I ducked into the alehouse for Frances and her man, and when we came out Abe was still standing there, with the bag spilled at his feet and oats all over his shoes.

"He's thick, isn't he?" whispered Frances. I recoiled at the scent on her breath. She smelled like she'd let the tap run open into her mouth the whole time she was in there.

"A lot smarter than the half-wit that makes her hair look like something a child would have drawn," I said tartly, pulling her down the street as I looked back over my shoulder at Abe.

"Why're the girls scared of him?"

"Because they don't know him. Mosquito's tusk, lass, you smell like a brewery!"

"You told me to have a couple," she slurred. "I did that and some more besides."

"Well, that'll make Bridget happy! Now there's one thing I want you to know. Bridget will tell you as well, I'm sure—she's the madam—but I have to tell you myself. You've just embarked in a city where there's a killer of the girls of ill fame."

She frowned and stumbled. "Why us?"

"We're easy to get alone, I guess. We have intimate dealings with strangers."

"How many have been killed?"

"Four. And here's the part that's rough to tell you. The fourth was just yesterday, and she was one of our girls."

"At your parlor house?" She stopped short and swayed a little.

"Yes. Thomasina, the girl who died, she didn't listen to me. I know the killer and he—"

"You *know* the killer?"

"Not in a friendly capacity, certainly, but you see, when I—"

"It's him! I guessed that already. You two work in concert. He dropped the oats because he was excited you had a new one for him. Well, it won't be me! I've been warned about the friendly folks waiting to welcome young girls. I'm not some foolish hayseed ready to trust any seemingly civil persons!"

I cast my eye onto the man with the trunk, who grinned. "She drank 'em real quick," he said helpfully.

"The killer isn't Abe, Frances. Do you even think him capable?"

"You brute! Preying on girls as they arrive! I knew from the second I looked at him he was the type to delight in bloodletting! Those freakish men who never learn to speak properly, never sit up right in society: they're the ones that don't know killing is wrong. I might've known there was a reason you had me go drink a few to get drunk, while you make your terrible plans for me. Well, bless the saints I keep my wits about me when I drink. And you'd perform your treachery in broad daylight too, you unnatural couple!"

She spun and indicated to the trunk-carrying fella that they would retreat. He gave me a sailor's salute he hid from her.

"Frances!" I called. "Wherever you go, don't sport with anyone who makes you feel worried. Tell all the girls you see."

"What I'll tell them is a pretty girl is luring other girls to their doom with a idiot murderer!" she called over her shoulder.

What an astounding turn of events! Now word would spread that Abe was a killer, and the girls in my parlor house, coming across the rumor, could indeed agree that he had made them feel uncomfortable, and soon enough he'd be hanging from a rope on Market Street too.

I rubbed my face in my hands and smelled the odor of the oats. Abe was no killer. But why did everybody have such dubious opinions of him? I saw something in him, for some reason, that nobody else could.

Or maybe…I was going to allow myself just to try out this thought, and then discard it. Maybe everyone else saw something in him that for some reason I couldn't.

Chapter 24

Woke up the next morning and threw my pillow across the room, then the glass of water from the windowsill, which made a right fine chinkly sound. I had left it there so if the galley mate or any other malfeasant came in through the window in the middle of the night, he'd knock it over and wake me. I set to cleaning up the shards, thinking it was worth the mess to throw something.

I wished I hadn't seen Abe. I almost felt like he was mine to take care of, since he doted and spent his first-ever seed here in my Nora garden. But he was part of something I'd left behind. My men didn't wear linsey-woolsey and a damaged felt hat. Nor did they sit outside in a carriage like some Angel of Death.

Bridget hadn't been pleased I couldn't bring a girl home, but I told her I was too distraught over Thomasina and she said she'd send Alice instead. Since I'd tried, though, our agreement about Abe still stood.

After the glass was off the floor, I sat on the edge of my bed and wondered if I was becoming a snob. I'd hated the gals growing up that was all delighted with themselves and their studdy jewels. The phrase "nose in the air" doesn't even do it—it's not just the sniffer but the entire countenance.

But I wasn't being a snob about Abe: I liked him. And I knew myself to be no better than him. The only thing keeping us from being out-and-out friends was the company I kept.

And why would I keep such company? Because of what I set my sights on, all steely and determined—to be a wealthy woman, to not have to worry about myself and my finishings. For I knew how other girls had finished. Nora Simms would not be found staring at cold space by strangers, and laid to rest with the other purseless failures in Potter's Field.

I washed and pulled on my stockings, thinking today would be a good one for all the Elmer Clapp types, since I'd wallop and thrash them all without an ounce of rue. I jabbed the combs in my hair like I was an Injun scalping myself, and slapped my cheeks for color. God help the timid milk-drinker sent my way today!

I spent the rest of the day jolting whenever the front bell rang and watching from another room as the maid opened the door. The other girls did the same. At one point, as five of us sat around with no visitors on the premises, I decided to introduce the topic. Since Liza was not there, the one who mourned the most, I thought it would not be too uncouth.

"Girls, are you all as anxious as I am?" I asked.

They looked at me warily and nodded. "I know you think it's the fella out in the carriage. But it's not him. You've heard him speak; he's not put together enough to pose harm to any of us."

"So say you," said one girl.

"The one to fear…well, as I've told you before, the one who stole my trunk was just a boy, barely of pants-wearing age. But maybe we need to look out for others besides just those that are youthful. The trunk, you see, might have been sold with all its contents intact, maybe to a rag merchant or some other interested party."

"You make this connection based upon your bonnet, Nora. But couldn't it have been a bonnet that only looked like yours?" asked Curly.

"That was mine with no doubt," I said. "He must have given it to Charlotte—the crib girl that died—in lieu of payment. A barter since she was so stone-poor."

"And tell again how you happened to be inside of a crib?" asked Curly with distaste.

"The fire, girls, remember the fire? I was helping the fire men with water and only poked my head into a crib."

"This is what I don't understand, Nora," said Alice. There was a gleam of suspicion in her eye, but I could see she was trying to overcome it. "How do you know it was the crib of the girl who died?"

"We're getting off the topic at hand: how to protect ourselves from now on. I'm only urging you to watch for a boy. And I must tell you something more. Only Alice knows this: Thomasina too had an item of my clothing."

"I think you should answer Alice's question," said Patience. She was wearing lots of paint on her lips, something she constantly had to reapply, given what she did with her mouth.

"Certainly you have heard of the crib girl's custom of having her name painted on a board above her bed?" I asked. "I poked my head in, saw her sign, and on the floor the bonnet that once belonged to me."

"But I would not have known that—Charlotte, is it?—was the name of one of the unfortunates," said Curly.

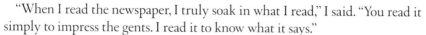

"When I read the newspaper, I truly soak in what I read," I said. "You read it simply to impress the gents. I read it to know what it says."

Curly rolled her eyes at that.

"Forget the newspaper and the news," said I. "One of our own was taken from life…in a bedroom mere inches from ours!"

"It's strange how much you know about this murderer," said Patience.

Except for Alice, they all gleamed their eyes at me, looking like cats in a half-lit room.

"Please, girls," said Alice. "Are you truly insinuating that Nora has anything to do with this? Why, of her own volition she pulled a constable upstairs and I watched as he ferreted through her things."

"But do you *know* the man in the carriage—" began Curly.

Just then the bell rang and I sucked in some air to repair my lungs. Rather than helping the girls, I had done foul work to myself. They now thought me dangerous. And what would I do if they all, separately, went to Bridget with their fears?

I had to be wise. My days at the parlor house might be numbered. I really ought to focus myself again on the purpose of getting married. I didn't much like the idea of taking the professor's cruel offer; how it would please me to be able to tell him I'd found another husband, one that wasn't a miserable pity offering from him!

My mother used to have a saying about keeping the silverware in different drawers, to not keep everything staked in one location. It wouldn't hurt to see if anyone else was marriage-minded, so I could get out of this parlor house and out of this life altogether.

The most handsome man I'd seen in San Francisco yet was Rudolfo deLucca, so I told him that day I looked forward to seeing him as no other visitor. I began coaxing him for facts about where he lived and how lonely he was.

"Well, I'm not lonely so much as I'm bothered with too many people," he said.

"Oh? Too many servants?" I bent my head so he wouldn't see my smile. I couldn't wait to have a houseful waiting on me.

"A wife and five children."

So I worked on Simon Bogart. "Wouldn't it be fortifying and wholesome to have a wife waiting at home with a hot supper each night?" I asked him.

"You would think," he said glumly, "but the reality, I can assure you, is just not that way."

So, Richard Blake. "Sometimes I dream of wifely pursuits," I confided in him.

"Sometimes I dream my wife will cease pursuing me."

After all these unfruitful forays, I got aggressive. "Marry me!" I said to Archibald Jenks.

"Make me a Mormon and I'll be right glad to service that request."

As if to spite me, Curly, the girl with the thick hair and a long neck to boot, announced that afternoon, after the men left, that she was marrying a visitor.

"Who?" I shouted.

"Elmer Clapp."

We all hooted. "'Twill be a lifetime of pain and agony—literally!" said Alice.

"In the stead of rice, we'll throw needles and daggers!"

"Will you promise to love, honor, and always hurt him?"

Ah, it went on like this quite a while. After we tormented her to the extent she became cross, Bridget cleared her throat and caught my eye.

"Professor Parkson paid for your services Saturday, Nora. You're off to dinner at his house."

I was puzzled: how did she already know? "Did he send payment?"

"No, he was here Tuesday while you were out. Working with the constables."

Oh. He had to draw Thomasina. Bridget cleared her throat. "You know, if he marries you, he'll have to pay me five hundred dollars."

"Excuse me?"

"That's the rule here. Any visitor who takes one of our girls permanently has to pay for that privilege. Elmer Clapp will pay it as well."

It was a relief to feel anger, an emotion easier to handle than sadness and confusion. I bit down on the sensation, my teeth tight and hard and relieved. "Sounds like something you just decided on, since the situation arose!" I spat.

"Oh, no, Nora, we told you about that clause the first day you came," said Liza.

"Well, that's foolish. You don't own me. I pay rent and a percentage, and that's what you get."

"We embraced you and brought you into our family," said Bridget. "We made accommodations for you, and the five hundred is a way to readjust ourselves."

"So, not only do I have to convince someone to marry a prostitute, but now I have to break the news that he'll pay a heavy surcharge to someone that's not even my relative?"

"Precisely."

"Which means I'll probably not marry and instead keep living at the parlor house and bringing you income."

Liza laughed and Bridget tried not to.

"Shut up, you peahen," I said. "I'm getting myself out of this life, and if I have to pay the five hundred dollars myself, I will. Too much blood gets spilled! I know there's a day that boy will walk through this door again, and it's me he's looking for!"

"So maybe Bridget can get the five hundred from him!" Liza crowed.

Both of us glared at her, plumb out of words to respond.

"Thomasina was your best friend, you lizard. How can you speak so lightly of her butcher?" I finally demanded.

"I didn't mean anything," she mumbled. "I don't know what I'm saying. I'm just talking. Babbling. I'm sorry."

"Well, you ought to be," I said. "The day we joke about any of our gullets being cut is the day we lose what small amount of dignity we have."

Chapter 25

The doorbell rang at ten a.m., too early for the lunch gang. Perhaps a fella burning from his first-thing barn raising, if you follow my thinking. I was at the top of the stairs when I heard the maid greet the visitor.

"Get out of here, you! You're not welcome here."

My nails dug into the banister. It was him, it was the galley mate! In my mind, I was already in the kitchen snatching up a big knife and plunging out the back door. Yet my body was, as it had been in the opium den, not under my control. I breathed shallowly and willed my feet to lift up from their cement fixtures.

Then I heard the quick rustle of skirts and Bridget's voice: "Sir, I must demand in the most imploring manner that you remove yourself from my doorstep."

"Ma'am, I'm here to see Nora."

Shoenails of the saints, it was Abe. I collapsed onto the steps, sitting down and fearing for how Bridget'd deal with him.

"I think you are mistaken, sir. Good day."

"No, she lives here. I brung her that day. She's the real pretty one, what with curls and nice eyes."

"Nonetheless, you are mistaken."

I heard a thwack, which I imagined was Abe's strong paw on wood, keeping her from closing the door.

"Just call for her," he said. "I seen her on an outing just the other day."

"You are not welcome at this home," said Bridget. "Please leave before I make an alarm."

"An alarm?" I heard the panic in Abe's voice. "I ain't nothing bad, ma'am. I count Nora as my friend. Just tell her Abe is asking for her."

"Nora isn't friends with your type. She's an elegant woman of class and high carriage, and you are surely mistaken about any acquaintance with her. Pray leave the door this instant and never return. Robert!" Bridget called out the man's name in a loud voice. There was no Robert on the premises; she was only fooling Abe with that.

"I'll go round to the back," pleaded Abe. "Nobody will see me. I washed myself yesterday; I'm as clean as a boat's oar.'"

"Robert!"

Then I heard a sigh and slow footsteps, and imagined Abe trailing down the steps, wounded as a kicked dog.

I stood again quickly, my delicate, golden rosebud bracelets making a sweet symphony against each other. Bridget closed the door below me and I tried to listen to my heart. I had told him I'd meet him in a week, so why was he not satisfied? It wouldn't do to encourage him. Bridget's unstated objection was true: if our regular visitors saw the likes of Abe's homespun and suspenders— or heard his slow and tortured manner of speaking—our reputation would instantly plummet and our visitors would visit elsewhere. Moreover, the girls were frightened of him, and I knew from experience what befalls people who are accused of things they did not do.

Yet, even while thinking this, my feet was drumming down the steps, my body flying like it used to fly when I was a crib girl and didn't worry about modulating myself.

Bridget was standing with her back to the door, as if holding it closed. "No, no, Nora. Don't go chasing after such a one as that."

"Bridget, I'm sorry. But I can't be cruel to him. He's got nothing. His brother's dead, he has no money—"

"He may have nothing, but you have something, and it'll all vanish if you carry on ties with his sort. Thank our sweet virgin that he didn't come at a time when our men are arriving."

"Just let me catch him. I'll explain it all, and he'll never come again."

"That's already been accomplished." Bridget didn't shift. The only way to move her would be through trickery.

I bowed my head and sniffed, bringing up my handkerchief to carry off crocodile tears. "Oh, you're right, you're right," I said in a tiny voice. "He has to understand I'm not of his world any longer."

"When were you ever?" asked Bridget sharply.

Stupid Nora! You were never in the cribs, always of parlor house quality, always. "On the ship," I stumbled. "I met him there, and although I had a first-class ticket, he came to think we were of the same milieu."

"You will lose your position here if he darkens our door again," said Bridget. "He is a risk we simply can't take."

She looked out one of the windows on either side of the door and stepped aside, apparently not seeing him in the yard.

"Of course, of course," I said. "It shan't happen again."

She gave me one last look and then swept off. I began climbing the stairs, so she'd see me do so in the corner of her eye. But when we were out of each other's view, I skipped down silent and willed the door to hold its tongue as I opened it. Then I scampered down Price Street, looking for the trudging back I knew I'd find.

"Abe!" I called when I spied him.

He turned around and nearly knelt with happiness. Then he ran to me and I caught him up in a hug and a kiss to soothe his mournfulness.

"I came for you and this lady said, she said…Nora…"

"Shh, Abe, I can imagine what she said. No call to tell it."

"I ain't good enough to be with you no more. I wisht you was still in the cowyard, and I could come see you ever'day like I did afore."

"She's a snotty snip, Abe, and she's wrong. You and me are the same, we just dress contrary to each other."

"I love you," he said. "Ain't nobody as good as you, and that's me too. I know that."

"Pish!" I said. "Now, why was you after me when you know we're meeting on March the fifth?"

He sagged against me, exhaled. "That's why I come, Nora. I didn't remember the day. And I didn't want to miss it."

"It's the fifth, Abe. Want me to write it down? Then you won't have to keep knotting your brain like that." I glanced around, wondering what I might write on, and with what.

He shook his head. "I've got to remember. The fifth. The fifth. If'n I could just remember the day, it's an easy thing to ask anybody if it's the fifth yet. Well, if they don't lie to me in a funning way because I'm like I am."

"Folks do that? Make sport with you?"

"I don't mind. I'd mind if I was smart, but I ain't."

Flap! I imagined my fine, lofty boots with a blade stuck in the toe, and I'd go around kicking anybody who dared harm such a tender soul as he. Everywhere I went I'd trail a dribble of blood from my shoes.

"How about this, Abe? Here's a way to remember it. Give me your hand."

It was indeed clean, as he'd told Bridget, with clear white crescents showing under his fingernails.

"Now, you have five fingers here. One, two, three, four, and five. You know your numbers, don't you?"

He nodded.

"Well, pretend your hand is the month of March. Count a day for each finger. When you get to your pinky, that's the day to come see me. So. Your thumb's today, then the second, third—what lovely hands, Abe—then the fourth, and here's the fifth, when we meet. Can you remember that?"

"This here's my favorite finger now," he said gravely, lifting his pinky like a smidgy lady having tea.

"Mine too," I said. I kissed it. "I'll have to return now. And Abe, you shouldn't go there anymore."

He nodded, morose.

"I mean it. I could lose my place there," I added.

"Because of me?"

"It's not my choosing," I said, "but I have to obey the rules at the house. I'm making a lot of money finally, and that's what I always wished for."

His face lit up and I was surprised he smiled. Somehow he skipped on over the insult that his mere presence could cost me my job.

"Money's what you wish for? Why, Nora, I've got plenty from mining with Caleb. I'll give you all I got."

"No! Abe, you need that money to put bread into your mouth. It's good to have a stockpile for whatever comes your way. Maybe some day you'll be sick and can't get to the livery for a week or so. Then you can turn to what you've got and use that. I wouldn't take it in a million years."

"Honest! It's a lot. I don't need it."

I pictured him counting on ten fingers and concluding the assessment. "No, sweeting, keep it for you'll need it."

He took those ten fingers and pressed them into my back, drawing me to him. His eyelids got all heavy-hung and he started breathing like I was boosted up on him, plying my trade. The scent of his neck was better than Parisian perfume, and my bones started to warm. I pictured my skeleton glowing rose color.

There in the street we kissed like curtains kept us from view. If simpleness makes lips soft, then that's an explanation for the mouth of Abe, a grand, brimming, heated mouth that stole my breath and tucked it into his body.

He moaned against me and I felt an upsoar of my spirit. Nora Simms, a firecracker in the sky, through the hills, turning at the Golden Gate, and going out to sea. Brushing off birds as slow and childish. Me: faster, brighter, the sky's best champion.

How can you fight against feelings like that? But I pulled back from the indulgence, for I knew I'd best be preparing for the noon.

"I'll see you on the fifth, then, dearest," I said, smoothing down my bodice and tucking stray passion curls back into my chignon.

"This day." He held up his pinky and I waved with all five of my fingers.

"Wait!" he called, but I was already down the street. "Wait! What about my gold?"

He drew strange looks from passersby for that one, and I shook my head at his foolishness. Hopefully no one would follow him home and clear out his basket.

"I wouldn't take it!" I shouted back.

"Marry me and it'll be given, not taken."

"We'll talk about it on the fifth," I yelled. "I must hurry now."

Chapter 26

When I returned, Bridget wanted to send me up to Broadway and Stockton to pay a house call. She said the gent was nine and ninety if he was a day, and I had to wonder how he'd gotten out to California anyway.

His son, a robust sixty or so, had thought me a delightful young woman and wished to pass the stimulation on to his father. I won't comment on the decision to share a woman with your own pappy. Suffice it to say, back in Boston I did read that Greek handwringer about the fellow Oedipus.

But I guess I didn't count as a Jocasta or a real person. For men, my type of woman is just property. It's like Bridget's customer was simply saying, "Esteemed father, this bottle of vintage Madeira is absolutely scrumptious and I must insist you imbibe with me." Or, "Bring your fork over and I'll load it with this juicy steak that I myself am eating on."

It was bad enough for the professor to wish to pass me to an associate, but when there's a family tree involved in the transfer, it's even more distasteful. Makes you wonder what variety of sap courses through those boughs.

When Bridget described the details to me, I was understandably distressed. "He's bed-bound. You'll have to be gentle and not put any weight on him. Yet he won't be strong enough to mount you either, so you'll have to be creative, Nora."

"How about just the mouth?" I asked, although the thought of some limp, ancient sausage hardly made my eyes shine.

"The son is requesting the standard. And paying triple."

"Does the ancestor even know I'm coming? Or is this some seductive surprise?"

"Well, you're supposed to make it seem as if you're merely making a delivery. Bread or cheese or something. Then you're to *notice* him and become overwhelmed with lustful feelings."

"This makes about as much sense as asking a mule to draw the bath. Isn't he up in his bedroom, and don't deliveries usually happen right at the door?"

"Creativity, Nora. He won't think much when he sees what you're offering."

Great. So here I was climbing the stairs, let in by a butler that already looked a hundred varieties of suspicious. I had apples in my basket.

I pushed open the door at the top of the stairs and looked in to see an old man sleeping with his mouth open. The loose skin of his face jiggled with the snoring he was apparently hoping could be heard by his kin back on the East Coast.

"Fresh apples for the fresh of heart!" I singsonged, coming to sit on the edge of his bed. I'd like to say his eyes flew open, but it was more like tiny goblins sat in his eyelashes and pushed with all their might.

"Aaaeeeaaahhh," he said. This was a language I was unfamiliar with.

"Apples, sir, apples! Can I slice one open for you?" It had occurred to me back on Price Street that his teeth would not be sufficient for a vigorous bite, so I brought a knife to make thin wedges with.

"Ssssss."

Wow. He was addled. Like Abe, only worsened a hundredfold because he wasn't handsome or earnest.

I cut as thin as I could and hoped it was mealy rather than crisp. I put one end of the slice in my mouth and leaned over the bed to let his lips take the rest. His eyes were absolutely terrified, so I withdrew and let him gaggle it down alone.

"What a handsome one you are!" I remarked. "A simple fruit girl like myself rarely sees the raw, scalding good looks you have."

No response, just chewing with wide eyes.

"Do you find me attractive as well, sir?"

"Aaaeeaaahh."

"If you'd like to see me titties, blink your eyes."

He did so and I unbuttoned myself. Just as well. The air was close in his tight wooden loft. I rubbed the next slice across both nipples and delivered it into his gaping mouth.

"Chew then, that's a love," I said. I leaned over and let my bubs hang down, each as ripe and rounded as the apple before the knife spoke to it. "You ain't paying attention," I said. "Keep on with the masticating." He had, predictably, stopped chewing to watch the dangle of my bosoms.

As soon as he swallowed—which I knew had to happen before I did anything further, to keep his mouth from spilling forth half-gnawed pulp—I stood and undid my skirts. They dropped to the floor and I felt a shudder move through me. This wasn't an easy way to earn my money today.

"When I see a fella like you, I just want to throw myself on top of him—er, rather, to the side of him, cautiously—and grab up his manhood—lightly, of course—and pump away like a wanton woman. Gently."

His lips formed into a grin and I counted how many teeth were left. Definitely a sum Abe could easily figure.

I pulled down his sheets and saw his wasted legs, but also an uncommonly stiff rod. Did this part not age with the rest? I moved next to him and pressed against it. It bounced a little.

"You're in tip-top shape, sir," I said. "You can probably please me in a manner of minutes."

Which was my little hint to him. I didn't want any long-winded, gaspy, slow, pulling-an-anchor-down-Market-Street feck.

"Aaaaeeeah," he said cleverly.

Demned if he didn't roll himself on top of me and shove in like putting the scoop in the coal hod.

"Bless me!" I blurted.

I could practically hear the bones withering and the veins busting, but he thrusted well anyway. I looked at all his wrinkles and the horrible half-toothed grin and kept my hips moving. *Triple pay,* I told myself. *Bridget said he's triple pay. Tomorrow you'll meet the associate and this could all be over.*

His breathing was labored and rusty, and all of a sudden its similarity to the death rattle made me think I might be bringing this gentleman to his maker. And, further, it occurred to me that maybe the son had hoped for that, that he wished his lingering father to head on home so that he could read the will.

"Slow down, there, sir," I said. "No use of getting all chop-chop."

He wheezed out some vowels at me and I started watching the pulse under the rice paper skin of his neck.

"Easy there…it's better if you just let me do all the jostling and pushing…"

His face got red. Redder. A vein in his forehead gained the thickness of kindling. His eyes lost their yellow tinge and got whiter against the ruddy field of his face.

Without realizing it, I began muttering, "Our Father, who art in Heaven, hallowed—"

"Aooooyyyyy!" He glared down at me.

"Sorry! Sorry! I just…wasn't doing that for any particular reason; I'm sort of a religious prostitute. Don't mean a thing."

He didn't recommence his movements and I saw I had offended him. "Oh, sir, 'twasn't last rites or nothing like that. I'm just fond of that prayer and you see, I…"

He balanced on one hand and brought t'other up to smack at me. Property, you see. Badly behaving property.

But it was that action, I believe, that sealed his fate as a sinner in this sphere. Poised on one spindly arm and swinging the other up in the air, he must have crushed the veins leading to his heart, giving it nothing but sour bile to do its work. He spasmed and fell on me. I skittled out from under and rushed on my skirt while watching his mouth work its way through soundless, violent prayers.

Buttoning my chemise, I scrutinized his face. I would be wise to run. My kind never fare well when police officers are probing a situation. He had closed his eyes now, although he still shook somewhat. I looked longingly out the window, but knelt back on the bed and took his two hands in mine.

"Never fear," I told him. "'Tis a good land you go to. A place of rest."

I pressed down the bulging forehead vein with the flat of my cheek like a mother. "Can ye hear the angels yet?" I asked. "They're plucking at the harps for none other than you."

His nether regions looked forlorn and so I pulled the sheets back up to his chin to afford him some dignity.

"Sorry your last sight is of a tart like me," I said.

He never opened those eyes again but finally his body slowed and the pulse in his neck registered nothing.

I had no idea why I'd started the Lord's Prayer for him. I liked him no better than the poor lass Patience whose death came between her legs, or the one I drug from the fire. They were words that hadn't been on my lips for a long time. Sitting on the tawdry bed, I thought of my mother's voice in the tight confines of the First Congregational, speaking her prayers with those in the other pews, but her voice ringing loudest. If I closed my eyes I could see light beaming through the apostles' glass bodies, lovely amber glass making up their halos. So long ago I can scarcely think who I was then.

I'd no use for such thoughts. I left the apples where they lay and went down the stairs, hoping the butler was hard of hearing. As I opened the door, I began to inhale with relief at the sun beaming right straight at me, but then saw a gentleman sitting on the stoop and froze.

"How'd you fare in there?" he asked. I recognized him. He had been to the parlor house on many occasions.

I couldn't speak.

"That's my father in there. I'm the one that arranged it for him. He used to be such a great one for the women. Sad to see him bedridden and unable to chase after 'em."

I brushed past him with my head set as if I hadn't heard him.

"Miss?"

He stood up and dashed into the house, and I kept on my steady pace, down Stockton, taking a left on Stark Street. I needed Mehitabel, wanted to lay down a burden and fix the lie I'd told to one who deserved far better.

I walked right up to the door of the boardinghouse and made my knock without giving myself a moment to decide otherwise. Mehitabel came to the door and her face bloomed like a morning bud. She pulled me into the house with an exclamation and a fast, solid embrace.

"Nora! Praise be. What a sight to open the door to."

I looked her clear in the eyes but was unable to reply with her level of gaiety. I had still said nothing by the time she had brewed tea, set it afore me, and smiled like regarding an infant in his cradle.

"Nora, I've wanted so desperately to know you were happy. Why haven't you come?"

I set my head down on the table and sobbed, my cheek abutting a muffin. Instantly her warm hands were rubbing my back. I cried like I hadn't for years, and didn't shift even after I realized a spoon handle was denting my forehead.

"Is it the fighting?" Mehitabel was murmuring. "Oh dear, I hoped you had the type that wouldn't."

I didn't even bother to shake my head, buried as it was, but just let the tears come. I worried for a moment my rouge and paint would mar her lace tablecloth, but then had to dismiss it. She'd never mind. She'd want me to keep crying until there wasn't an ounce of misery left in me.

After a while the hands left my back and I understood by the scraping of chair legs that she was just sitting there patient. I could imagine the look on her face: bewildered and pained.

I cried just a bit more and then gave it up. My lungs were exhausted from all the tights breaths I had to take, and I looked a mess. The distress hadn't left my soul, but I was at least ready to talk. I lifted up and Mehitabel actually laughed at me.

"Oh, how can you?" I begged her.

"You look a sight," she said. "With the spoon and lace all impressed on you, and color smeared on top of that."

I teared up newly and she laughed yet again. "I don't mean to be adding to your woes," she said. "I'll either fetch a mirror or you tell me what the matter is."

"I didn't marry Abe," I said. "I'm still practicing my depraved craft, at a parlor house. And I hated to come to you with that lie still in your mind."

She opened her eyes wide in shock. "What happened?"

"I never intended to accept him. I moved out to take the position in the parlor house."

She nodded, face grave.

"I wouldn't have lied to you except you caught me with my sign and got all excited, and there wasn't room to explain," I said.

"But that fellow—Abe—gave you a ring. I saw it."

"He asked me, and wouldn't accept my refusal. I'm keeping it only until he meets some other lass. He wouldn't take it back."

"All this time I thought you were married," she said. "I can't hardly believe it isn't so. I had pictures in my mind of your wedding day and the good times you must be having."

I hung my head. "I'm sorry."

"I wish you had been honest. I wasn't judgmental with you, Nora. We were close companions even while you admitted you were a prostitute. In fact, a few times I halfway wished you were still one so I'd have our friendship still."

"You're making me more miserable than ever, Mehitabel! I oughtn't to have told the falsehood and I regret it more than I can muster words for."

"What's done is done," she said with a pained sigh. "Apparently the parlor house doesn't make you happy if you come here and cry like someone's dead."

I blew my nose into a handkerchief. "That's just it," I said. "I've seen so much dying since I left you, Mehitabel. The very day I stepped out your door, and the very day I stepped back in."

"Today?"

"Not an hour ago."

"Poor dear lass! Tell me everything and settle your mind."

"Well, it was all deplorable, no matter if they went by way of murder or not. I've witnessed such unbearable scenes, Mehitabel! I've seen a woman with a cut in her neck so broad it looked like another mouth trying to talk, and I watched a man twitch in the gallows and a girl who tried to stop herself from having a baby with crude means, and that meant she bled to death and the child as well, and Thomasina was wearing my very corset with the ribbons twisted up in her life's essence, and just now some old man wheezed his last into my face. And those are just the ones I've *seen*, Mehitabel! There was also—"

"Stop, dear, take a breath. You're going faster than a runaway horse team. We've got all the time in the world to sit here and untangle the ruinous past."

"But I want to tell you and have it all said. There were two other women died, Mehitabel, with items of my clothing in their possession. Do you remember how a ship's mate stole my trunk? How I asked to be released from the rent agreement we had? *Charlotte*, oh, I feel the worst for her. She never got one minute of happiness, not from what I ever saw. But she was true of heart nevertheless and swore to help the others. And before her there was Nutbrown Nettie. Oh, Mehitabel, it's been such a heavy load. And the boy that did it is still out there. He could be slaying someone this minute for all I can tell."

"Darling, dear Nora. Oh my sweet!"

"I'm not sure when it will end, either! I have a potential offer for marriage, Mehitabel. From a fine gentlemen who is an architect and has a bundle of money. I've never met him, but it may be my only answer for getting out of this horrible stew."

"But what about Abe?"

That opened up Niagara Falls again.

"I can't believe you've got any more left to cry, but you prove me wrong," she said. She handed me a fresh handkerchief, shaking her head.

"Why aren't you with Abe?" she asked gently when my sobs subsided.

"He's a no-luck miner," I said. "I'm here for gold, money, cash, dresses, all of that."

"Really? That's what you want out of life?"

"Yes."

"That's a worse lie than the one you told before."

I screwed up my face. "How can you possibly know what I want?"

"You aren't made of that crass material. Your heart is undisguisable."

"I do want money," I insisted. "Who else will take care of me? I set money by for the future."

"No. You want better than that."

"And a slow-witted miner who gave up on the hills is better?"

"You're wearing his ring."

"Rolling yule log! Didn't I just get finished explaining he forced me to wear it?"

"Someone forced Nora Simms to do something? I find that difficult to comprehend."

That was a good thing for her to have said. It was true. What was it about Abe that made me relinquish to his desires?

She got up and reheated water. She was making me sit there and listen to the echo of what she'd just said. What kind of power did Abe have over me? He could barely articulate a word—

Oh. There it was.

All my life I've rescued the dumb things. A bird in the garden that had broken its wing. A bundle of cats about to be drowned: I lifted my skirts to whorishly save their wee lives. I escorted spiders outside rather than dashing them with a broom. I caused the bear Triumph to be shot, to remove him from his mortal wound and the jeers of the crowd. And Abe was all of this to me.

"I have to take care of him," I said.

"Fragile, is he?" She was sympathetic with a hot rag in her hand.

"It ain't a sacrifice," I said. "He's dear to me."

"If providence has set him in your path for you to guard him, it's your duty to do so."

"Duty? Fiddlesticks. He makes me laugh. We twitter like children. And under the sheets he's a rollicking good time."

She cleared her throat.

"Sorry."

"You can live comfortably without being dead rich," said Mehitabel. "Take in some sewing. Or teach piano; you learned it quick enough. And I'll help you anytime you're ready to put on your pauper's cloak."

"There's a tiny bit of gold in my trunk," I said. "I've been frugal."

"A good trait, Nora, a good one!" Mehitabel beamed.

I ain't going to paint an untrue picture; it wasn't like the clouds rolled back and there was a sky laid out for me. I was still sniffling into the handkerchief and thinking about what my life would be like if I did what she urged.

But I was thinking I could tyrannize anyone who dared to treat Abe shabby, and I could make a home for us where we greeted each other with skin ready to touch skin, and kisses that made our lips sore. And I'd know I had made amends to any higher power that might think my profession of the last few years was less than honorable.

I'd made a splint once for a beagle, replacing it with fresh, soft wood each time he gnawed it down. He yipped at the beginning but soon submitted to my ministering hands. A sweet dog, owned by no one, a street pup that lived on scraps. And one day, when I judged the splint was ready to be abandoned, I released the dog once and for all. He didn't even limp. He flew off down the street chasing an insect and I knew I had done something that would earn me favor later.

Chapter 27

I sojourned with Mehitabel all the rest of the afternoon, knowing Bridget wouldn't miss me until dinner. Mehitabel'd gone back to the hurdy-gurdy house many times without me to play its piano, a fact I could scarce believe. She told me more and more "honest" women were arriving here daily. "It's getting to be less of a wild place," she said. "The ladies arriving are laundresses, schoolmistresses, milliners, wives."

"You want it to stay wild," I teased. "So's you can lift your pinafore and show your pretty ankles."

"The days of shivering in my bed listening to the mayhem under the window may end," she said. "And that'd be a fine thing."

"I don't know," I told her. "There's more kinds of people arriving, but still there's greed and men with knives in their boots."

"I cherish the hope this city may become as civilized as those on the other coast," she said.

"Foolish hope," I said carelessly. "Anybody out here is hardy and speaks his mind and does as he wants. The timid ones stayed home, even our governor said that."

"My darling, bravery does not necessarily preclude being civilized."

"Well, you keep brewing tea for the population and we'll soon temper ourselves and settle down."

"Quite likely," she said dryly.

"And what about the boarders? Is Irish Twomey still here?"

"Yes, but he's the only one left of the ones here before. It's all new tenants now. Remember Quince and Holmes, who were so rude to you? You'll enjoy these stories. Quince got his comeuppance for calling you a hussy: his business already failed and he had to return to the East Coast, tail between his legs. And Holmes, he of the bulging eyes: his wife came out to meet him and then quick as a cat returned back with her brother, claiming her husband was visiting houses of ill repute!'"

"I can attest to that," I said.

Mehitabel's face stretched to encompass both horror and amusement.

Impulsively, I leaned across and kissed her. "Mehitabel, it's right good to see you. Thank the heavens I cast this falsehood from my shoulders so I can visit with you again."

She smiled and took up my hand. "I've no cause to reproach you, Nora. You're in such a spirit. Yet I've often wondered about why you chose this profession. It's so clearly below your station."

"It's easy capital," I said. "I warranted I'd never stand at a machine for ten hours a day, snatching my fingers from the mechanism every few moments to make sure I kept them, and faring no better than the least dullard. I don't mind what I do, exceptin' for today and other days when the gents were less than bonny. I do hardly anything, and yet my pockets fill."

"Do you remember the first time you ventured forth?"

"I do. I was out dancing, which my mother abhorred but which set my mood a flying. My feet would beat a tattoo on the floor and I'd dance each set and have to turn down a gaggle of boys each time. I suppose I made a spectacle, somehow, not being quiet and ladylike like the other girls. And at length, after weeks of visiting a particular dance hall, a woman drew me aside and whispered in my ear. She told me what she did to make money."

"And you adopted this idea readily?"

"Not exactly so. I pondered on it and a week passed until I stopped at the cribs she'd told me of."

"And your mother—does she know of your fate?"

"No, thank the saints. She died of typhus while my sisters and I were young. They went to the mills and I to the men. My youngest sister died of it also, a week after my mother."

"Your father?"

"After the youngest was born, Emmeline, he shot out into the world and we have nary a report of his whereabouts. I guess he didn't like the squalling she did in the cradle."

"Do your sisters know of your profession?"

"Of course. You can't keep such as that from the girls who bounced on the sofa with you. I'm as good as dead to them, like our father."

"And you never thought to marry high, with your looks?"

"How was I to meet the men like that? Even the ones at the dance hall were shoddy-shoed. I've only met the wealthy men out here, Mehitabel, and believe me I tried my hand at swaying them toward the nuptial bower."

"I can't believe it wasn't successful."

"There was this professor who seemed interested, perhaps. But…well, not for keeps, I guess. In fact, he's the one who is introducing me to the fella with the offer."

"Forget this offer. You don't even know him! Go with Abe, who is virtuous and who you have some true feelings for."

I sighed.

"Are you prepared then, to leave this life? To leave the men to their wives, and the bachelors to their courting?" she asked.

I toyed with the tablecloth.

"Come now, Nora, it oughtn't be hard to decide. Picture your poor mother gazing down at you and wishing she could have stayed alive long enough to steer you different."

"It's not the profession," I said. "It's the money. I'd miss the money."

"Fie!" She scowled. "It's harder for the meek to enter the kingdom of heaven—"

"You've spoiled the saying in your ire. The meek are the good ones. All the New Englanders who didn't dare come to California…well, heaven'll be full of them, carrying their wooden buckets of maple syrup. It's the *rich* that are poised for posthumous trouble. If you believe in that sort of thing."

"What does money buy you, Nora, a pretty dress? But someday your face will be wizened and you'll not wish to dress so flagrantly anyway. Money has never bought you safety, I might strongly point out. Nor has it purchased you a home, nor friendship, nor love; all those things you purchased with your own wit and smile."

"I don't want to end up in the poorhouse, or buried in Potter's Field."

"I pledge to you now, Nora, that I will never allow either to happen. I'll keep you if need be, and I'll buy you a headstone when it's your time, and even engrave upon it."

"You'll die afore me," I said sulkily.

She laughed. "You never stop dumbfounding me. I'll earmark money in my will for a fine funeral for you, Nora, finer than my own. Six horses draped in mourning crepe, and flowers strewn as thick as the coffin itself."

"What will the engraving say?"

"'Here lies Nora Simms, the girl smart enough to listen to her old boarding-house mistress and abandon a scandalous life of lewdness so as to adopt finer ways and live in bliss until the day the mason was obliged to carve this stone.'"

"That'll cost a pretty penny, all those words."

"But I've gotten something wrong. It won't be Simms, will it? What's Abe's last name?"

"I've no idea," I said. "I suppose I ought to find him and learn it."

After a visit to the privy, occasioned by all the cups of tea Mehitabel sent down my gullet, I set off on an odd mission: to find a man whose last name I didn't know, who lived in a location unknown to me, and was perhaps to be my husband.

I knew I wouldn't find him in any cribs; he'd told me of his misplaced loyalty to me. I wasn't sure if he liked music, but I poked my head into all the hurdy-gurdy houses I passed.

I liked the shouts of welcome and interest I received. Somehow I'd forgotten the roughness of regular men after all the dandy manners of our parlor house visitors. "Sister, sit on your brother's lap and let him buy you a tipple," they'd say, or "Bless my bones! Did the devil shine up a demon and send her here to break my heart?"

"Anyone know a miner name of Abe, works at a livery?" I'd inquire.

"You don't need him, lassie. I'm five times the man he is!"

"Nevertheless I'll continue my search, thank you kindly. Where might I find a livery?"

I saw as many horses as men that afternoon, and they all blew a kiss through their rubbery lips at me.

I walked Stockton, Pacific, Kearny, Washington, Montgomery, and up to Broadway by way of Columbus. I went into a public house for a drink to rest my feet and catch my breath after all those hills. Maybe I'd have to wait until March the fifth to see him.

The man two seats over leered at me, as I saw reflected in the mirror behind the bar, and moved to sit next to me.

"I'm looking for my fiancé," I told him before he could start any dirty prattle. "A miner named Abe who works at a livery; do you know him?"

"The simple one?" he guffawed.

There was no response to that but to take a swallow of the ale.

"How'd he hook a belle like you? Maybe that's my problem with women: I'm just too smart for them!"

"Dubious reasoning."

"If he's yore fiancé, why don't you know where to find him?"

"We've carried on a very traditional courtship, with he coming to my parents' door to escort me, as is respectable. I'd die of shame if I'd seen his lodgings before our wedding night."

"I don't believe you. You got the look of a whore."

I was grateful I hadn't had more than a sip, for I twisted my wrist and let him have the rest of the ale in the face.

The bartender chuckled but made his way around the bar quickly. "Just go, miss, don't make trouble," he urged me quietly.

"But he knows Abe," I said. "Where is he?"

"I'd sooner tell a snake," said the idiot, sputtering off his eyelids. "In fact, next time I see the bastard, I'll knock him around a little."

"Off you go, then. Drink's on the house," said the bartender, pushing me in the small of my back. He walked me all the way to the front like a police man. "Check Swansen's Livery on Beckett Street," he said. "And don't worry about yonder cad; he'll drink another keg's worth and forget the threat he made." He closed the door behind me.

I bolted down Dupont Street, with all the Chinamen looking at me as curious as I looked back at them, then zigzagged over to Beckett Street. There was an enormous wooden horseshoe hanging from a second-story peg to serve as a sign, with "Swansen's" written around the curve of it.

"Good luck! The horseshoe brings luck!" I said aloud like a child, but no one heard me. As I ran I held out my hand in front of me and newly admired the diamond. Maybe Abe's mother was looking askance over at my mother in heaven, the two of them shrugging. So what?! La!

I battled through the horses' bodies, heat, and straw until I saw the hat of one I loved. "Abe!" I called, and the man jerked around and clambered under a horse's gut to reach me.

But it wasn't Abe. "He's off today, miss. Can I help you with any matter?" said the man, who was about as handsome as they come.

"I didn't come about a horse. I'd like to see Abe. Can you tell me where I might find him?"

"No."

"You can't?"

"Who are you?" he asked.

"Goodness, what a tone. I'm Miss Nora Simms," I said. "Pleased to make your acquaintance."

He pulled me aside and hissed into my air, "Hurt one freckle on that boy and I'll make sure you pay, lady or not."

I put my hands on either side of his jaw and kissed him smart on the lips. "I wouldn't hurt him, sir. That's my whole purpose."

"Enlighten me further."

"Abe and I are friends, and I'm simply wanting to see him."

"Him or his money?"

"Oh, please, sir. I'm sure what scant amount he has, I've triple."

"So your relationship with him is…?"

"Well, I'm wearing his ring, ain't I?"

I showed him. He broke into a grin and pumped my hand up and down. "Don't take offense at me, miss. I've gotten so I think I have to take care of him."

"Me too," I said.

"I'm John Atkins. I'm his boss here."

"I'm glad he has such a watchdog. I'm the female rendition of you."

"Far better looking," he commented. "But I won't be bold enough to compliment another man's woman."

"So may I have the address now?"

"No. I know Abe has a surprise for you and I won't ruin it."

"A surprise?" But Abe didn't even know I was willing now. Maybe he was making me something for our meeting on March fifth?

"That's right. I didn't know your name, but if you're his intended, he's got something going that you'll be happy for."

"Have you the time?"

"It's four o'clock."

Axle of the hearse! It was time to be getting back to the parlor house for the dinner crowd. "Pleasure to meet you, Mr. Atkins."

"Call me John. Shall I tell Abe you were looking for him?"

"Ah, no. Let this be a surprise as well."

The men were already in the parlor drinking champagne when I arrived home. I went upstairs to change my gown and wash, then returned to the gay scene downstairs.

All the while that I spoke of the news and played a few melodies on the piano, I thought of Abe and of the professor's roommate. Mehitabel had certainly talked fire into me, but I had to take care of myself. What if I married Abe and two days later a horse kicked him in the gut and he died? Then I'd be destitute again. It simply made more sense for me to at least *meet* this Cleveland Hopkins.

"How did it go with the older gentleman?" Bridget murmured to me at one point.

I wondered whether to lie. Would the son ever come to Bridget and tell? Perhaps by that time I'd be married and long gone. "It was not so bad, Bridget. I thought it would be distasteful, but really he was sweet and his skin not all that loose."

"Excellent. It's good to have a girl I can depend on to do these special sorts of missions."

My fella for the evening was earnest and wished to treat me like I was a lady. He kissed with a noble sort of feebleness and asked my leave for every little act he did. I wondered if, when we got to it, he was going to ask permission for each stroke, but thankfully he took my blanket assent and carried forth.

When he dressed, I handed his shoes to him.

"Why do you look so sad, sweetheart?" he asked.

"I'm unsure of my life's course," I answered.

He was wise enough to leave that alone, and departed with a timid smile. I placed my water glass on the windowsill and made sure the sash was locked. Then I peeked under my bed and locked the bedroom door.

Time to sleep. Tomorrow was Saturday, the day I'd dine at the professor's. I was pleased I hadn't left word at the livery for Abe. I could make my decision about Cleveland, and then deal with Abe if necessary.

Chapter 28

I woke to feel a hand clamped over my mouth and nose. I began twisting and thrashing and using my fists to hit at his face. I tried to draw my legs up from under the sheets, but they were tucked too tight. Instinctively, I lowered my chin and hoisted my shoulders, to keep him away from my neck.

And all this time, my eyes were trying to scry through the dark to see that hated face, just a shadow above me.

I pulled at his hair, swatted his face, trying blindly and helplessly to wound him. But he was so huge, such a monolith.

Not like a boy at all came the dim thought penetrating through my own slow darkness.

I began to see sparkling lights in front of my eyes, flickering on and off like the wicks were magic. I couldn't breathe with this heavy hand blocking my nose, and my chest was painful, my lungs fit to explode for lack of air.

I'm going to die, I thought. My hands drifted down, too tired to fight him. And not in a slaughterhouse way, just quiet-like. With the stars and blinking lamps.

Still my eyes had not adjusted and my eyelashes fluttered down, ready to close without knowing who my assassin was.

Then, without warning, the hand was removed and I sucked in air gustily, trustingly, like a child after running the length of the yard with all her might.

"Jest don't scream, Nora, promise?"

Suddenly the hand was cradling my cheek, sweeping hair out of my eyes. Gently.

I continued to breathe raggedly, wanting to speak, but first attending to my body's wants.

"Abe," I said finally in a thin, air-starved voice. "You almost killed me."

Now my eyes were accustomed to the dark. I turned my head and looked at the open window, with the silvery outline of the glass of water still on the sill. Somehow he had moved past it without disturbing it.

"I didn't do such a thing!" protested Abe in a whisper. "I was just making sure you wouldn't scream."

"Or breathe."

I pushed him backward and sat up, pulling my legs from the sheets and setting my feet on the floor. Things still didn't feel right, and I wanted myself primed for escape.

"Oh, Nora, no, I'm sorry. Couldn't you breathe through your nose?"

"Not with a huge, hairy hand clapped over it. Jesus with a satchel, Abe, what are you doing?" I kept a good two feet of bedspread between us.

"I'm here to rescue you. I just found out about the girl killed here, and I'm demned if I'll let you stay another minute. You come home with me and I'll take care of you. You can have all the—"

"You can't steal me in the middle of the night, especially after nearly making me expire!"

"That's my clumsy hands and I'm sorry. But Nora, we got to leave."

"I'm going to, under my own steam. Tomorrow eve I'll be meeting a fella I may marry."

"No, Nora, no! No, no, no, no, no!" His teeth flashed in the dark and I saw the mottled crimson of his tongue working vehemently behind them. He looked like he could clamp the hand over my face again. I couldn't believe I had sought him throughout the city in mind of marrying him. The Abe I thought I loved did not resemble this man.

"Abe, it couldn't ever be right between the two of us." I was looking out of the corner of my eye for something I could use against him if he got dangerous again. There were long hatpins on the dresser, out of reach.

"Why couldn't it be right?" he asked. I saw the individual lines of hurt on his brow.

"I've got to be *safe*. And not just safe from the galley mate or whoever bought the trunk—safe from poverty. I won't ever wind up in the poorhouse and that's a promise I made myself."

"Who's the galley mate?"

"Maggots' dinner, Abe, I never expected to be telling long-winded histories in the middle of the night to a man who almost smothered me."

"You tell me this second!" There was steel in the face that had previously presented only soft rabbit fur. This was a different Abe, certainly.

I embarked on the tale, my heart beating faster again. "When I arrived here, a galley mate switched my trunk. And three women died with items of my clothing in their possession. So either he's the murderer or knows who the murderer is."

"He switched your trunk, so you have his?"

"Yes, that's right."

"Where is it?" He looked around the unlit room.

"In the attic."

"Up we go," he said grimly. "Step soft to keep the house asleep."

"Why? The police already looked all through it and there isn't anything there."

"You mean it was empty?"

"No, there were shirts and letters and the like, but we looked through it all already."

"I want to satisfy myself," he said. "Let's light a lamp."

It was an odd circumstance, to be following instructions from Abe. Suddenly he was smarter and more domineering than he had ever been before. And I had been thinking to wed him, to take care of him as if he were a mute beast.

"Yes, sir," I murmured, and lit the lamp on my dresser. The flame flickered in the breeze from the open window before I put the glass hood down.

As we crept along the velvet hallway, with its frequent mirrors reflecting my pale, worried face, I whispered to him, "How is it you just found out about Thomasina? This is delayed news."

"Thomasina is the one killed here?"

We were just now passing what had been her room. I nodded.

"I do read the newspaper, word by word," he whispered. "But it's slow labor. Just this evening I finally read about her."

"And saw the professor's drawing," I said. I pointed to the tiny door that led to the attic stairs, and Abe opened it with just a slight creak, no more than a rodent would make in its nocturnal journeys.

"You know the fella that does the drawings for the paper?"

"The crime scene drawings. My friend, the professor." We were creeping up the steps now. I held the lantern as high as possible to light both our paths. "He's the one recommending for me to marry his wealthy roommate."

Behind me Abe made a strange sound in his throat but said nothing.

"I'm so sorry, Abe," I said.

"If you'll marry for money, not love," he said at the back of my neck, his breath stirring the curls there, "I can't stop you. But I would give you everything I have, Nora."

"You need what you have, Abe," I whispered back. "And maybe I will love this man."

Glad to get his heated breath off my neck, yet still trembling with the awareness of him, I stepped onto the unfinished wood planks of the upper story and looked for the ugly trunk. There was a dim bevy of items up here: abandoned lamps with glass globes, lengths of fabric, and dressmaking dummies.

"Here it is," I called softly. I lifted the lid and stared again at the clothes of a mere child.

"Where's those letters?" he asked, picking through the ephemera and easily finding the bundle of papers. Tucking it under his arm, he continued to root through the trunk. He put his hands in all the pockets but came up with nothing, just as I had.

My arm began to ache holding the light aloft, a tiny pool of illumination in the musty attic, but finally he closed the cover and stood.

"All right, then, let's go," he said.

On the second floor, I tried to walk back to my bedroom, but he led me to the stairs.

"How did you know which was my room?" I asked.

"I studied," he said.

I swallowed. He hadn't sat idly in that carriage; he had watched the windows and seen which girls went where. Including me. I had been observed and hadn't even realized it.

"Well, Abe, thank you for reading those letters," I said by way of good-bye. "You're kind to take such an interest."

"You're coming with me," he growled, "and we'll read them together."

"No," I said. "I have an appointment, to meet my possible fiancé."

"But you aren't safe here," he said.

"Look, dawn will be coming soon. The worst of the night is over. I'll be married quick enough and far from here."

He put his paw on my arm and it felt like he was going to take me away by force.

"Take your hand off me," I said, "or I'll scream loud enough to wake the Injuns on the plains and throw this lamp down the stairs all a-clatter. I ain't going with you."

"Don't you trust me, Nora? I'll let you go meet the fee...feeance...whatever that fancy word was. I won't stop you if that's what you want. But at least let me deliver you from this house. They say a snake always comes back until the mouse nest is empty."

In the dark hallway, with my mouth still sore from his hand, I wasn't so sure who the snake really was.

"I ain't going with you. Here, take the lamp down the stairs with you. I can get back to my room without it."

"This sorrow weighs heavy, Nora. You don't trust me, and it's a dire load to put on my back and carry."

"I'm sorry," I whispered.

"What's the name of the man you might marry?"

"You don't need to know that."

"But I do."

"Why, so you can follow me some more? I don't like that, Abe."

"If you've ever cared for me, you'll answer me."

"I did care—I do. But it's time for us to be parting. And there's no point to you knowing anything about this other fella."

"I'll say it again. If you *ever cared for me*, you'll answer me."

He was tugging without laying a hand on me. I felt like I was looking at a kitten about to be drowned. And it wouldn't hurt to tell him; the two didn't travel in the same circles and would never have any truck with each other.

"His name is Cleveland Hopkins," I said through tight lips.

"Just like Ohio. I'll remember that. And where does he live?"

"Abe, no! You're going to park your carriage there and make everything strange again."

His eyes implored.

"I won't tell, I won't," I said. "I've a chance to make myself better, Abe, don't you want that for me?"

"If we married, it would be for love. But you're bent on money."

"I'm so sorry, Abe. But now it's time for us to be saying our good-byes. Take the lamp now." As I handed it to him, the diamond on my finger sparkled. "Here, take this too. I'm sorry but I'm certain you'll find another girl to wear it."

I twisted it off my finger and after a few seconds where I thought he wouldn't take it, he did.

"If you won't answer that one, then tell me the professor's name, the one introducing you to Mr. Hopkins," he said.

I obliged with a gusty sigh, for I knew it would help him naught. "Professor Parkson."

"Anything I do is for love of you, Nora. Remember that," he said. "Be careful with anyone you meet. Please."

I had to glance away, and when I looked again, he was at the bottom of the stairs, a frightening silhouette looming over the flame.

I returned to my chamber and listened to hear the ponderous creak of the enormous front door opening. After a bit, I told myself he had slipped out so silently I hadn't heard it, or maybe my rustling in my bedsheets had masked it.

Yet I had the feeling he was still in the house. I went back to the top of the stairs and attended to the slumberous emptiness down below.

My feet grew cold and I shivered in my nightgown. He was gone and I was being foolish. But then I heard a sound that convinced me he, or someone, was yet abroad.

I went stair by stair, bending to crane my head down around to see any gleam of light from the bottom floor. I used the banister and trusted my weight to the next step with hesitation, for I was moving through pitch.

Maybe it was the galley mate, fetching me in the middle of the night. I pictured his slim frame walking through the darkness in search of my room. Sullen and childish, he was come to finish me. I'd meet him on the stair if I didn't hurry.

I inhaled quickly at the thought of tussling on these steep steps, and hastened down. I'd make my way to Bridget's room. She had that lady's pistol and could end all this city's fearfulness with a shot to his evil heart.

I nearly tripped on my nightgown when I heard more of the sounds, rustlings as of paper, and I grabbed the banister to steady my faltering body. *Paper.* Of course, it was Abe, reading through those letters.

How odd he was reading them here. I was on the ground floor now and creeping past the gilt and velvet sofas. I could see the vague yellow now seeping from his lamp and headed toward it.

I turned the corner and saw he was at Bridget's spindle-leg desk, turning pages of the logbook.

For long moments I watched him. He used his finger to move down the page, infernally slowly. Eventually his finger stopped, and he smiled.

It was so silent, and I dared not twitch a hair. And then he tore the page from the book, which blasted like a shot and made me cry out.

He turned and looked at me.

"I know where he lives now," he said.

I swallowed. The grandfather clock ticked behind me in the dark, and I wondered how long we stood there while his words echoed. He kept looking at me with that smile.

"I knew I'd find something on him if I just looked long enough," he said.

"Don't," I whispered.

"I only want to know so I can keep you safe," he said. He folded the page twice and put it in his pocket. "Professor Hugh Parkson, Eleven Orchard Street," he said.

"No, Abe, you mustn't. Give me the page and leave now, or I'll shout and rouse the house. And you know what they all think of you. Bridget'll shoot you."

His face cracked open with pain, like the winter ice that splits on the pond when warm weather comes. "I'll go then," he said.

I wished I hadn't said the last thing; it was too cruel. Abe brushed past me with the lamp and walked toward the front door. He knew the floor plan of this house, that was clear to me. He'd studied and studied and was far more shrewd than I'd ever counted him. Sly, even.

Then the door opened, the cool night air rushed in, and he stepped out, setting the lantern down and showing me only his back.

In the morning, of course, it all seemed like a dream, except my bedroom was frigid from the window I'd never closed.

I had been just plain lucky that Abe hadn't been there when I'd stopped at the livery for him. All jumped up by Mehitabel's convincing, I might have become affianced to the man who crawled with great cunning through my bedroom window. And then he'd have a legal right to block my breathing, night after night.

I knew how Mehitabel would excuse this, too, if I were to seek her advisement. She'd say, "He had no idea the amount of force he'd exerted. And once you informed him, you could be assured he'd never do the same again."

I ate breakfast with the loud girls, deep in thought picturing Abe poring over the galley mate's letters, slowly. How long would it take him to get through the packet?

And then I pictured a younger Abe, learning his alphabet at school, squirming with his slate. The other students probably ridiculed him. In fact, I could imagine the pretty girls who would do it, their eyes flashing. And the boys would shove him and make him stumble. Worms in his lunch bucket, the class snickering when the teacher made him stand and recite...

I put down my fork and rubbed my face when the image came into my mind of Abe in the white dunce cap, embarrassed and confused in the corner. Doubtless he'd worn it. And repeatedly.

Our world was so cruel!

Poor Abe. He was doing the best he could with the wits God gave him. And I should feel honored he was so custodial toward me. Who else had ever, ever, *ever* looked after me that way?

Besides my dear mother, of course. Whose face I could barely recall. Glumly, I left the yolk on my plate.

"Nora? What do you think?" I realized all the girls were looking at me, awaiting an answer.

"I'm sorry—what did you ask?"

"We're arguing over whether herself should wear white when she marries Elmer Clapp. She doesn't really earn the color, do you think?"

They all erupted in giggles while Curly, despite a broad grin, pretended to look angry.

"Why not wear black, to mourn Thomasina?" I asked tartly.

There was silence and I immediately bowed my head in shame. I was no better than any of them. I too forgot her for long stretches, and I too looked forward to a wedding day of frivolity and, yes, a white silk gown.

Chapter 29

The carriage the professor sent for me elicited much jealousy from the other girls. "I've not seen something so grand," said Liza. "Look at the scrollwork on the door. Why, Nora, are you fit to ride in it?"

They were all gathered around the door, looking past the coachman.

"Elmer Clapp has a fine carriage too, girls, and white horses as well. These are common nags pulling the trap," said Curly.

"Hush, all of you. Aren't you pleased for Nora? She may marry out of this livelihood," said Alice.

"It's just such an ostentatious carriage," said Liza. "I feel bad for her future husband's poor taste."

"Off you go and good luck, Nora! Don't forget to say yes when he asks," said Alice.

The coachman led me down the walkway and opened the carriage door for me. He started the horses and I looked out the small opening at the parlor house and the girls still clustered in the door. Only Alice waved.

During the ride, I thought about what this Cleveland might look like. I remembered the professor had said he was thirty-eight—twice my age—so I hoped he was still youthful looking. I wouldn't stop myself from marrying a man I didn't find fair in the face, but it would certainly make things sweeter. I checked my rouge and lip paint in a tiny mirror as I bumped along in the carriage.

Once we arrived, the professor greeted me with such a melancholy face that I stood frozen in the doorway a second.

"Donkey's funeral, professor, what is the matter?"

"Your pretty face renders me rueful, dearest. Shall I not be authorized to kiss it further?"

"Well, you'll have to ask your roommate that, won't you?"

"Ah, the perpetual sauciness that makes the face even prettier. Come in, Nora."

I walked into a front parlor that was as elegant as anything at Bridget's, yet the appointments were of heavy, dark wood, and the fabrics of the midnight family. Fine. He and Cleveland were indeed wealthy. The lounges and chairs were covered with sable paisley, and the velvet curtains kept out any carriage lamp gleam that might defiantly try to enter. I smelled the opium immediately upon entering and saw smoke still rolling from a tabletop.

"Oh, professor, not opium again. I just want to meet your associate."

"You're so feisty, Nora. It will help calm you."

"I want to have my wits about me, thank you."

"Sit, darling. Cleveland and I planned an evening of relaxed debauchery. It won't please him to see you refusing."

"Well, I'm not going to—we never talked about…Oh, professor, I thought I was just going to eat dinner! With none of the parlor house tricks." I sank into an armchair.

"Why would he want to marry you without sampling the goods?"

"Can't you recommend me? I thought that was why I was here to begin with."

"Fine, Nora. Your high morals win out. We shan't do anything you don't wish." His eyebrows' slant, however, illustrated that he didn't feel what he said.

"Thank you. Now, where is he?"

"A bit delayed by business. Actually, that is a falsehood. He is hovering in the back, gentlemanly giving us a last chance to say our adieus."

"I thought we did that already."

"You're so unromantic, darling! Allow me to kneel at your feet and gaze upon your luminous beauty one last time, before I pass you to him."

He did kneel, and I tried halfheartedly to luminate.

"Your eyes are so cold, Nora. How have I offended?"

"You're a professor. *You* mull it over."

He solemnly kissed my hand, then said, "You are hurt I have not selected you for my eternal love match."

"I suppose there's a little bit of that in it."

"You'll be happy with him. He can offer you so much more than I can. What he does for women; well, the severity of his passion is extraordinary, remarkable. You will never wish to trifle with another; he will wipe you clean."

"Is he a man or a mopping product?" I asked irritably.

"What a delightful parlay! The gems that emerge from your mouth…"

"*You're* the one I know best, professor," I said. "And I'll be honest: we would make a good pairing. I don't know why you insist I choose some man who is nothing to me."

He laughed, and the tone of it made me wish to raise my boot and knock him backward. He rose and lit a cigar for himself, then paced back and forth in front of the fireplace.

"A good pairing. You think? A professor and a slut?" he asked.

"How dare you! I'm not some common whore. I'm a parlor hou—"

"Aren't you? I recall meeting you under some very penurious circumstances."

"And yet you think me fit for Cleveland?" I was sure my face was a hot, bubbling red.

"He's impetuous, like you. And not in as elevated a station as I am."

I couldn't believe I sat there to hear that. I stood in a fury and shook my finger at him. "Someday when you marry, professor, I'll visit the little ninny and tell her all the sordid things you ever did with me. She'll be denying you her bed and keeping the cradle empty of bairns. A good thing too! The world needs your issue as much as it needs monkeys wearing britches."

"Jolly image, my sweet! But your threat means nothing. By the time I marry, why, you'll not be…"

"Not be what?" I shouted.

"Not *be*. Period."

I felt like he penetrated a filmy hand into my chest and squeezed my heart so it would not operate.

I understood finally.

The danger was here in this very room. I bolted toward the door but he grabbed me. "Don't look so shocked, Nora. I'm not wishing it on you. But we must be frank. Dynamite and explosives men, horse breakers, prostitutes— these are all people with dangerous trades."

I writhed in his grasp and kicked with my boots, thrashing as hard as I could. *What a fool I had been. It was the professor all along.*

He hugged me so tightly that my arms were of no use, and then pulled me out of the parlor into the back hallway. Midway through he paused, and there it was.

There was no attempt to hide it; it was just stuck in the passageway blocking me like a cart in an alley. It was of sturdy manufacture, and the brass on it gleamed in the light from the fixture above it. In fact, its placement seemed intentioned so that it would catch the light, like a singer on the stage spotlit by the largest lamp.

"I found it for you," he said triumphantly. "And mostly intact. Only a few items missing. A bonnet, for instance."

He pushed me to my knees, grabbed at the key I still kept between my breasts, and inserted it in the lock. With a click and a lift, I was staring horrified at my pelisse cloak, my dresses and chemises and sashes and millinery. He took my right hand, still held in a fever grip, and pushed the garments aside, mockingly frantic, until I saw the long-ago-painted Nora sign and the tumbled bottles of birthwort.

"Oh no, dear me, no," he said in a high-pitched girl's voice. "This is my trunk. And what does that say of the professor? How can I interpret this terrible evidence?"

The Nora sign splintered my finger as he dragged my hand across it. His breath was hot against my neck and I was thinking furiously, furiously, what I could say to him. He cared for me, somewhat, I knew that. I had to, had to—

"My sweet bride, are you rifling your dowry?"

I shrieked at the new voice, and the professor released me. I jumped up. There he was: the galley mate. He stood at the end of the passage, blocking the door to the outside while the professor blocked the door back to the parlor. I was caught between them in the narrow confines of the hall.

The professor had delivered me up for more than marriage. I made a low sound, halfway between a moan and a gasp.

"Don't be spooked," said the boy. "You're like a horse!"

I turned and sprinted down the hall toward the parlor. I would have to dash past the professor. My feet clattered and I prayed not to trip in my skirts. I had all of five brisk steps before I collided with him.

"She's reluctant, Thomas," he observed. He held me in a grip so hard my veins must have been bursting inside and the cartilage cracking. I used my elbows to dig into his belly and kicked at his shins, all without outcome.

"Thomas? Who's that?" said the galley mate. "I go by the name of Cleveland." Behind me I could hear him coming, taking his ease, down the hall. "Now, my beloved, wouldn't you like to climb inside your trunk? It's just the perfect size for a corpse."

In desperation I bit the professor's arm muscle, feeling the warm flesh through his thin shirt. He swore and released me.

How I bolted then. My eyes must have appeared wild and flaring like a runaway horse's, just as the galley mate had said. I reached the parlor, saw the overstuffed chair I'd recently vacated, saw the door and felt the first twinge of exhilaration from escape—but then felt a yank of my skirts and tumbled hard to the floor, smacking my head as I went.

I was dazed for a second but I quickly pushed up to my hands and knees, twisting my head back to see the professor grasping my skirts. It was he who had brought me to the floor.

I pulled and crawled, trying to release myself, and he came with me like a child pushing a wheelbarrow, laughing delightedly.

With my face against the floor, I began to cry. "How could you betray me like this?" I sobbed.

"I felt betrayed as well, my dearest. You gave your charms to the one person I can't share you with. It would be an Oedipal disaster," said the professor.

Although he laughed, I sensed some underlying truth to that and seized upon it. "But professor, I didn't know you yet. I wasn't even…"

My voice trailed off. It was too hard to think when I was fighting to get free.

"Wasn't even…?" he prompted politely.

"Not in…San Francisco yet. Hadn't met you. Still on the ship…" I heard the pathetic, frail nature of my voice and despised it. I rose onto my knees again, turned my head to the professor and spat at him. The sputum landed on his waistcoat, and he brushed at it, unaffected.

"You were right," I heard the galley mate say behind me. "She is a fighter."

"Yes," agreed the professor, barely out of breath despite my own raging lungs. "She'll provide a good evening."

The galley mate knelt down next to me and put his lips only inches from mine. "I love the ones that fight, Nora," he said. "The ones that go white and freeze and don't try to knock the knife out of your hand, they're no fun at all."

I brought my fist up and smashed it in his throat.

"That's a girl," he crowed a moment after the spasm of pain crossed his face. Then the professor jerked my skirts again and I fell on my side, curled up like a fiddlehead fern. I scuttled backward and he let go.

"Let's see what she does now," the professor said.

I got to my feet but kept low to the ground, hunching in some instinctive defensive crouch. The two of them grinned at me.

"Just let me go," I said in a rasp that scared me almost as much as the looks on their faces.

"You're the one that arranged all this, Nora," said the professor. "If you hadn't told me a galley mate stole your trunk, I never would have shown him the sketch I made of your likeness."

"We never would have guessed that we both loved you, Nora!"

"Thomas is so enamored that he gives each girl something of yours to wear, recreating the moment he first yielded his flesh to the pleasures of adulthood."

"I'd killed before, but never ravished," said the galley mate. "I thank you for opening that door to me."

"And under my guidance, you have certainly grown," the professor said approvingly. "I never wield the knife, Nora, but I do *so* enjoy the aftermath. After*math*, see? I'm a mathematician."

The galley mate laughed, such a childish sound that I pictured him momentarily with five tumbled jacks in his hand and a wooden ball ready to bounce. "I never thought of that, sir!" he choked.

I was confused by the change in temperament and nearly laughed myself in this hideous bedlam.

"Math! Aw, that's too much!" the galley mate said.

"Darling, I feel we ought to provide you with an explanation," said the professor. "It is only courteous."

"Tell her!" agreed the galley mate. "You'll like this one, miss. A story I never could have invented meself if I wasn't fortunate enough to be in it."

My back began to ache from my crouch, but the two of them were wound up tight as an overdone clock, and I thought if I moved a shiver, they'd be on me.

"Back East I began my career of drawing crime scenes for the police force," said the professor. "Young 'Cleveland' here was the son of a friend, and I habitually took repast at his parents' domicile. Although I had no intention of ever sharing my portfolio, no boy would consider himself proper if he didn't do some snooping, and soon enough the lad had wide eyes and an accelerated heart rate at what he had seen in the family friend's sketchbook."

"It was like the professor went inside my mind and drew what was there," crowed the galley mate. "Blood and stab wounds and flesh all a-fluster…"

"We held a rather circumspect discussion, he and I, on the front stoop as his mother washed dishes inside. He managed to stutteringly convey to me that he could—how did you put it?"

My thighs were trembling at the effort of keeping myself on my toes, ready to fly at the least sign of their distraction. But they kept their eyes trained on me, bright and beady and overwhelmingly fascinated.

"I said I could tell him where to find them…*before* the police did," said the galley mate.

"It doesn't take a professor to decode *that* perplexing message!"

"No, indeed! And soon enough, of an evening I was saying, 'Sir, get your sketchbook and we'll be off!'"

"It was jolly fun but we were nearly caught," said the professor. "Had to kill a constable and knew that was an exercise in watching the sands run out the hourglass. So I booked myself a passage to California and soon after wrote his mother, sending for him."

The galley mate nodded, looking pleased. But his hands still hovered in the air, ready to grab at me. I tried to make sure I continued to breathe so that when my moment arose I'd have the wind to run.

"I thought I'd like some company in my hellish pursuits," said the professor.

"'Tisn't hard work to book passage as a galley mate. And the way the professor described San Francisco, I couldn't wait to come," said the boy. "No one knows anyone's name."

"The lawlessness that reigns out here!" the professor added. "Thousands of anonymous men, drunk out of their minds, unaware of what a professor and a boy could be doing to the sluts around them. It's a brilliant place for us to work! And with a volunteer police corps that couldn't give a damn!"

"Aw, they're hilarious!" said the galley mate.

"So, at present time, this boy and I have a rather symbiotic relationship. As the blood curdles, he leaves and I enter," explained the professor. "I do so like to look upon the mayhem he inflicts, and record it for all posterity with my ink."

"He's right good with those inks. Have you seen the ones of the whores with their throats open wider than their mouths?" the galley mate asked.

"She's seen only the watered-down version in the newspaper," said the professor.

They laughed. "You should get him to show you his sketchbook!" said the galley mate.

"Oh, she's already too nosy!" said the professor. "Had to go to the police with every little thought she had. Had to talk to the rag merchant about her theories. I knew it wouldn't be long until you pieced it all together, Nora. That's why I brought you here. I wasn't about to hang like that German fool you got killed!"

Wild, daft laughter from both males came again. I halfway listened but, shaking like a spent horse, took two steps toward the front door. The galley mate took them with me, like a mirror reflection.

One more. He took it as well.

Then I ran in a burst of speed that was not enough, for he grasped me around the waist and spun me around. I flailed my arms and knocked over a fancy stained-glass floor lamp, which crashed and sprinkled shards all over my feet. I trod on the flames as I danced with my hunter and smelled the hot leather of my boots burning.

I used all my weight to knock against him, and together we careened into the small table that held the opium appurtenances and burst it all onto the floor.

Long wood splinters worked into my flanks, but I barely felt them. The professor clapped. "Ugly table," he hooted. "Its demise is a blessing."

The galley mate and I scrambled up together, clinging like drowning swimmers.

"She seems to be getting the best of you," said the professor.

I twisted in his arms and used my knee to knock bottles of wine off a side table. Again, glass everywhere. I wondered now if neighbors might hear the scuffle and help me. I screamed and immediately a meaty arm thrust into my mouth, janking my jaw beyond its expanse and bloodying my lip. I gagged.

As he swooped me around, I plucked up a shard of glass and held it in my hand like an arrowhead. With all my strength, I drove it in his calf. He screamed and crumpled forward into the pile of glass.

Jumping up, I gathered my skirts and leaped over his body. It was the highest in the air I'd ever been of my own power, and my head grazed the little chandelier and set it to jangling. I joined my voice to the sparkle of sound and screamed clear crystal, jets of light in my eyes.

I landed and saw my salvation.

A clear route to the door. I could make it! My hand outstretched before me, the doorknob the perfect size to nestle in my palm...

I was almost there, feeling the brisk air of the San Francisco evening, my ragged breathing, and the sharp inhale of water off the bay. My feet propelling me ever faster, ever faster—

A knock on the head sent me to the floor again, punished by the heaviness of my own corporeal body. The galley mate had thrown the fireplace shovel at me.

An instant later, he was straddling me.

I looked into his eyes. There was white all around the pupils; nowhere did they touch the lids. I began to quiver under his grip like an apple the boys shake to bring down from the tree.

Despite the eyes, the rest of the face was blameless. He had the soft skin and long eyelashes of a child, and lips that spake no evil. I inhaled, waiting.

He pulled out the knife and ran it along my hairline, starting at the ear and moving up above my brow. Tracing the outline of my face.

"So pretty," he said, and there was a reverence in his young voice.

"Please let me go," I said. I don't know how I said it; my will was stronger than my own lips and tongue.

"After all this?" asked the boy.

The professor came over and pinched my cheek so hard I wondered if his thumbnail had plundered clean through the skin.

"Time to accept it, Nora," he said, hissing in my face. "You're breathing your last breaths."

"The beautiful thing is when I open up your throat," the boy said, "it just *opens*. It's like you accept it, and your skin does, and you open wider than what I cut. Wider!"

He didn't blink. Long moments and his eyes simply penetrated. I saw the man now inside the boy.

"It's the most amazing thing I've ever seen. And then the blood just spurts and gushes and it's like a dance of sorts. A dance that's always going on under the skin and we never see it," he said.

"That isn't beautiful," I whispered. "That's an abomination."

He dragged the knife over my lips and down to my throat. "See? In a moment, you'll be lifting your chin for me. Like a dog that gave up."

"I can attest to this," the professor said and laughed cruelly. "I have sometimes watched from the window as Thomas works, so as not to interfere. And this phenomenon he mentions is a remarkable thing to observe."

I choked out a sob and bent my chin down, trapping the knife in the folds of my skin. I wouldn't do what he said; never would I ask for the knife.

The boy laughed and looked over at the professor. It was the expression of a son asking a father to come help him play with his toys. "I never saw that before."

Speaking with my chin buried so deeply into my throat that my voice barely carried, I asked, "But why do you want this?"

"This?" he asked.

"To kill women like this."

The galley mate cocked his head and appeared to consider. I moved my hand so that it touched his, holding the knife. "I visited a…what's the term, professor?"

"Phrenologist."

"I went to see one of those once, to learn if it was the bumps on my head making me wrong. But he thought I was 'of a calm persuasion.' It's not like my mother slaughtered a hog when she was waiting for me to be born or anything. There seems to be no true reason."

"Mysterious," agreed the professor. "A flaw in our very making. The creator's—"

And then the professor bleated and I heard a *whoosh* as the galley mate's weight left me.

There was another man there all of a sudden, and he had kicked the galley mate into the corner with his thick boot, and was now hurling himself onto the professor with a hardy blood cry.

It was Abe.

I saw two teeth fly from the professor's mouth with a gorge of blood. He fell down backward onto the glassed sofa and groaned as the shards punctured his skin. He tried to rise, gingerly.

Abe then fetched the galley mate from the corner where he still lay crumpled, and punched him in the chin. The bones in his jaw reshaped. He howled and fell, clutching his face.

"It's that fucking dullard she likes," yelled the professor, and saliva and blood spewed where his teeth were missing. "How'd he get in?"

"Broke a window," said Abe as he walked across the room to deliver another punch to the professor, who tried to duck it and won it on his ear.

I had the wits to rise up and shinny my hand around for the knife that the galley mate had dropped. He was still holding his jaw and screaming. I got to my feet and began to totter over toward him, terrified at what I would have to do.

"No, Nora," yelled Abe. "Stay there!" He beat the professor like it was a schoolyard brawl. Bruises formed instantly, and the pulpy mess that was the professor staggered into and through Abe's quick fists.

The professor sank onto the floor and Abe returned again to bludgeon the galley mate with the raw dint of his fists. The galley mate screamed in agony from each blow, far worse to hear than the reserved grunts the professor had uttered.

"Fuck you, stop now, you've done all you ought," he shrieked at one point, and the tremoring of his yelp made me sob.

The clamor a soul makes when it fights for its size of shadow in this world is enough to make a mortal ear turn to iron. Abe tortured the child with the ceaseless onslaught of his blows, and the boy's thin body was like a sheet of tin hammered by a sledge.

I hovered nearby, trying to speak for him. Sure, he'd not have spoken for me, but these sounds—those of just a boy—were building my remorse.

Yet the look on the galley mate's face silenced me. There was no release for him now, even if Abe never touched him again. He was dead already, and only some remnant of his soul still lingered in the body, moving it and making it whimper, like the steam still seeps from the kettle after the water is poured out.

It was fitting for Abe to continue the task then, to send him clear to his halting death. Finally the blows stopped and all I could hear was Abe's rasp of breath.

Then the professor groaned.

"Ah, you fecking heap of devil's defecation!" I screamed. I rushed over to him and put the knife right to his heart, vertical-wise, as if I was planning on leaving a knife in the cutting board for another day.

His eyes fluttered open and he stared up at me. "Nora…"

"You better speak your regrets fast, you miserable bastard. I'm two breaths away from sinking this into your putrid, decomposed heart," I said.

"I didn't…want to," he said.

I dug the knife into him a little, not even as deep as a needle goes into fabric, and he rustled around. "So it was all that one's fault, is that right? This mere child persuaded you into this life of butchery," I said.

"…not to you," he said.

"I don't find that any sort of a compliment," I snarled into his face.

"…loved you," he said.

That was it.

I had no words for such a man as this.

I put my second hand on the knife handle and simply pushed. All my might went into that thrust. The knife slid into his heart, between two ribs that did their best to protect it. Blood foamed around my hands and he twisted a little, pinned by my knife like a butterfly in a collection. His face, as near as I could see in the bruises and steady streams of blood, grimaced and laxened.

My knuckles were aching with the pressure I was using, and finally I let go. The knife remained erect in his body.

I looked over at Abe, still standing over the galley mate with his feet braced for fighting. Then he wilted a bit and exhaled a monstrous sigh. Coming to my side, he knelt down next to me.

"Are you all right?" he whispered.

With his hands helping, I rose to standing and looked at the catastrophe around me. Blood was all over. Spattered on the sofa, the floor, the wall. Furniture was in pieces or sitting askew. Glass, everywhere flickering the reflected light and blood.

The smell of blood was worse than the bull and bear fight, for it was human blood this time. A sickly and hot odor that made me long to retch. I myself was bleeding and scorched with glass burns.

I couldn't believe the jumbled mass of glass and wood and carnage. This bore no resemblance to a parlor. And then there were the things I didn't want to acknowledge. Besides all that abject clutter, there were two bodies with their heads turned away from me.

"Is that one dead?" I asked.

"I think so," he answered. "I was only trying to get him to stop moving, but just like with you last night, I wasn't sure how much pressure."

I crumpled into his arms and let the first sob happen. Then the second, and before I knew it I was crying like them Irish ghosts that wail in the garden. Abe rocked me in his arms and periodically wiped the tears from my cheeks, though they kept coming. Each time we moved, we heard the grind of glass beneath us. I kept looking at the bodies and waiting for them to rise.

"Abe, I would have been killed if not for you," I said finally, in half-spurts between the crying. "How did you ever know to come here?"

"I read the letters."

"What?"

Oh, death's crooked sickle, how I let my head dangle back on its own thin stem to look at Abe more closely.

"The ones from the trunk."

"There was something in those letters?" I pulled at my own hair, outraged to think I'd invited this on myself by not reading carefully. I'd had the evidence all along!

"It weren't much, but I caught it," he said. He pulled a paper from his pocket and handed it to me.

Dear Thomas,

Please make sure the professor draws a likeness of you, and send it to me so I can have proof you've made the long journey safely. It will do a mother's heart good, especially since you know I will be fretting all this time. My youngest boy, and not even fifteen! It is hard work to send such a stripling across the water.

When you meet him in San Francisco, give him my heartfelt thanks for sponsoring you. I have long trusted and held affection for this man who is so dear to our family that I may nearly count him a member.

Be good and do as he asks.

Your loving and sad
Mother

"Oh Abe, how did I miss this? How did I read over this and not see it?"

"Maybe you just didn't read as slow as I did," he said.

But with a few last-minute tears falling on the paper and sullying the mother's words, I realized what the problem had been. I'd read the letters before I'd ever met the professor. And a professor that *draws*? It was such a specificity in a city of unknown persons that I had simply discarded it.

But Abe hadn't.

"Oh, Abe, if you ever wonder if you've got all the wits you need, this is *proof* here! This is proof golden and everlasting! You are smarter than me, smarter than the police that wouldn't even stoop to look at the evidence...You knew there was something there and that you'd find it."

I pressed my hand against his heart, holding the letter between the two fleshes. "And you did the smartest thing anyone can ever do, Abe: save someone's life."

"I ain't never done anything I'm ever so proud about as this," he allowed.

Now I lay my head against the letter and listened to the factorywork of that brave and bold heart. He was simple and true! He ached over words and pressed his head through an entire day's worth of reading, just to be certain there wasn't something that could help me.

"You are the most pure man I have ever met," I said. "You make all else look like half-men."

He pulled my head up and gave me a penetrating look, just he and I in the world. "Will you love me?" he asked.

"'Will' is a future word. I always have, Abe! Now and for as long as both our hearts keep pumping."

Chapter 30

I asked Abe to go pluck my mother's likeness out of the trunk for me, but otherwise we left the pieces for the police to find. We made our way straight to his quarters, a second-floor flat in a shack boardinghouse. He poured water into his basin and we repaired ourselves as best we could. He removed his bloodstained shirt and put on the boiled cotton one I had given him.

"This is the first time you've come to see me," he said. "I'm right glad to have such a welcome visitor."

We were sitting on his bed, a thin cot·reminiscent of cowyard furnishings. We still wore our clothes and were trying to make our way through the strangeness of being in his world rather than mine.

I looked around. Wasn't much to assign my eyes to look at, but I didn't care. I was grateful for each inhale and looked at Abe like he was cast of pure gold. If I labored at a mill like the girls of my childhood or pricked my fingers sewing like Mehitabel, what of it? This was the life I would happily shoulder.

"It's wonderful," I said. "It's perfect."

"Are you serious, Nora? No, you're teasing, of course."

"No, I'm not. This is grand."

"But it ain't got velvet and pretty fixings like you always said you wanted."

"I don't want that anymore," I said. "I'm finished with that. Give me a good man over a good house any day."

"Well, you'll get both."

"I will?"

He nodded vigorously.

"A house out on the beach, like we talked about?"

"No, here in town, with a pretty view. You can see all around, Nora. There won't be one thing you can't see."

"On a hill?"

"Yes, yes, that's right. Nob Hill."

"But did you think I'd live in it?"

"Once I showed it to you, I knew you'd want to live there. It's pretty, just like you. I saw the picture, the drawing, and the arky-teck said he'd make it just like the picture."

A house on a hill, designed by an architect? But right now he lived in a tacky wood chamber with knotholes leading into the rooms on either side.

"What's it look like?"

"It's big. It's got towers, and pointy...you know, rooms at the top..."

"Turrets?" My mouth had dropped open.

"That's what the arky-teck said. Yes! And a front door and a back door, and a porch, Nora, so you can sit there in a rocking chair and see all the city spread out afore you."

"How many floors?"

"Three."

"Three?"

"And a root cellar underneath. I guess that makes four."

"How on earth can you finance this, Abe? Please tell me you didn't trust anyone with one of those wretched loans where they own you, soul and tooth, until the end of your days."

"I just paid for it."

"With what?" I felt I was close to shrieking.

"With me gold. And Caleb's gold."

"I thought you gave up prospecting because there was nothing to find."

"Oh, we found a lot, Nora! Such a lot! I had enough and after Caleb died I didn't have no heart to keep running my pick into the hills or standing in the icy water to pan. I just wanted to leave. I buried him there and made a cross, you know, to mark it."

I clutched at his hands. "Oh, Abe. Oh, Abe. Oh, Abe."

"It's funny how folks is so happy about gold. They killed each other for it, Nora; I heard tell of that."

"I believe it," I said. "I know they do."

"But to me, what can I use it for? I only came out here 'cause of Caleb. He's the one that cared. So now I know you like money, I can give it to you, and let you spend it, Nora. In your house."

I sat there a while, feeling bad and wildly good at the same time. I knew what Abe wanted from me—not only the avowal of love, which I freely gave, but also the promise of my hand in marriage.

"And there's another thing," said Abe. "Even though we took care of those bad fellas, there's plenty more rough ones in San Francisco. So I built myself a little house on the same lot; just an outbuilding's all I need. That way I can keep an eye on you and see you're safe."

"So…" I stammered. "So…you would give me a house even if I don't marry you?"

"As long as you promise not to prostitute yourself no more. That's the bargain."

"But how will I live, Abe? A fine house is wonderful—incredible!—but how can I live?"

"I thought you understood," he said. "The gold."

"You are freely offering to share your wealth with me," I stated.

"I love you, Nora. Ain't nobody else to spend it on." He took in a deep breath like a horse trying to keep the saddle loose. "And you just said you love me. Maybe in time you'll want more from me."

I nodded and said quietly, "I may."

He pushed my hands away and leapt around the room like the shadow of a sputtering taper. I laughed to see it. It was pure joy set down in Abe's body. He'd put a Shaker to shame.

And while he moved through all his exultation and gladness, I sat there like a paving stone, revisiting all he'd said. *We found a lot. Such a lot!* Maybe he'd be taking care of me one way and I'd be taking care of him another.

And maybe I could ask Mehitabel to come live with me, and take care of her too. It would be wonderful to tell her she could cease the baking of the bread and the threading of the needle.

And we'd eat all the meringue and pudding that we wanted, and buy a fancy Oriental carpet for each room, and even the kitchen, and I'd have twenty dresses in every color, and even pay someone to invent more colors, so I could have more dresses! Gold, diamonds, rubies, emeralds! Gold! Did I not mention the gold?!

A pang hit me. Dark blood rushed into my heart. "Abe!"

He ceased his dance and sat next to me.

"Abe, did you use all your money to make the house?"

He shook his head and pointed to two steamer trunks, double the size of mine. I stood and went to one of them, and opened the hasp. Gold inside, gold. Gold. Feckin' serpent of Eden with its feckin' forked tongue and feckin' folds! I plunged my hands in and couldn't touch the bottom. I put my foot in, like into a bathtub, and wormed my leg until it touched. The ring and jangle of it! The heavy clanking sound of gold.

The coins, minted in this very city, spilled out onto the floor, displaced by my body. I dashed from the trunk and grabbed what clothing I saw to plug the holes to the other rooms. How careful had Abe been? There weren't even locks on the trunks!

"That ain't all, either," he said calmly. "I put a bunch in the bank. Not ever'body knows about banks, but I learnt it. Here, put the ring back on."

I dutifully slid it on, then asked, "How much in the bank?"

"Don't know. I got a book, though, that tells."

So now I had to celebrate the way that comes natural. I ripped off all my clothes for Abe, let him look long and hard. Emphasis on the aforementioned hard.

"How 'bout you?" I prompted. "Let me see what a rich man looks like."

There simply ain't no better sight than a handsome man and two trunks of gold. Leastways, not that I've seen. Maybe that view from the porch will surpass it, I don't know.

We put our bodies together and I don't have to tell you it was the best I'd ever felt. No sensation is akin to fucking in a room full of gold. This must be what the girls in the harem feel like, letting the sultan caress their curves with hands that *recently touched gold!*

Maybe I will go to hell, but I don't care. I arched my back and folded and curled with him. And turned and rose and fell and sunk. And sunk. Sunk under the weight of all that good man, that sweet and simple man, the weight of him and his tasty cock and his strong horse-guiding hands and his lovely smell and his, yes, sweet Jesus, his gold.

Chapter 31

P.S. His last name was McElhatten. And who knows if a Simms might exchange for that?

Acknowledgments

Thanks to two dear friends who read this manuscript several times: Tamim Ansary and Joe Quirk. Tamim, you have been there through many years, and Joe, thanks for advice on opening up the story for "Plot B." Other readers with excellent editorial insight were Ann Marie Thérèse Meyers, Barbara Roscoe, Anne McSilver, and Cindy McPherson. And of course huge gratitude to all the members of the San Francisco Writers Workshop. I'm so proud and happy to be a part of that community.

To my parents, Paul and Rosalie Mailman, thanks for making readers out of your daughters! I'm grateful to the librarians of the Kellogg-Hubbard Library, including my mother.

Research was conducted at the Oakland History Room of the Oakland Public Library, at the UC Berkeley library, and at the California Historical Society.

Thanks also to Debi Echlin, Alan Howard, Gary Turchin, Ted Weinstein, Claire Zion, Elsa Hurley, Naomi Schiff, Scott James, Melodie Bowsher, Kenneth G. Hecht, Jr., and every English instructor I ever had, especially Miss Ferris, who put me in a writing class in fourth grade and made me think I would someday be an author.

Last but not least, I want to thank the wonderful people of Heyday Books who made this possible: Gayle Wattawa, Malcolm Margolin, William E. Justice, Wendy Rockett, Lorraine Rath, and Lisa K. Manwill.

About the Author

Born in Vermont, Erika Mailman is a graduate of Colby College and the masters poetry program at the University of Arizona, Tucson. She now lives in Oakland, California, with her husband, Alan Howard. For the last seven years she has written a column on local history for the *Montclarion* newspaper, and she has published two nonfiction books on Oakland history. Her novel *Hexe* is forthcoming from Random House in fall of 2007.

HEYDAY INSTITUTE

Since its founding in 1974, Heyday Books has occupied a unique niche in the publishing world, specializing in books that foster an understanding of the history, literature, art, environment, social issues, and culture of California and the West. We are a 501(c)(3) nonprofit organization based in Berkeley, California, serving a wide range of people and audiences.

We are grateful for the generous funding we've received for our publications and programs during the past year from foundations and more than 300 individual donors. Major supporters include:

Anonymous; Anthony Andreas, Jr., Arroyo Fund; Barnes & Noble bookstores; Bay Tree Fund; S.D. Bechtel, Jr. Foundation; California Oak Foundation; Candelaria Fund; Columbia Foundation; Colusa Indian Community Council; Wallace Alexander Gerbode Foundation; Richard & Rhoda Goldman Fund; Evelyn & Walter Haas, Jr. Fund; Walter & Elise Haas Fund; Hopland Band of Pomo Indians; James Irvine Foundation; Guy Lampard & Suzanne Badenhoop; Jeff Lustig; George Frederick Jewett Foundation; LEF Foundation; David Mas Masumoto; Michael McCone; Gordon & Betty Moore Foundation; Morongo Band of Mission Indians; National Endowment for the Arts; National Park Service; Poets & Writers; Rim of the World Interpretive Association; River Rock Casino; Alan Rosenus; San Francisco Foundation; John-Austin Saviano/Moore Foundation; Sandy Cold Shapero; Ernest & June Siva; L.J. Skaggs and Mary C. Skaggs Foundation; Swinerton Family Fund; Susan Swig Watkins; and the Harold & Alma White Memorial Fund.

For more information about Heyday Institute, our publications and programs, please visit our website at www.heydaybooks.com.